Chesapeake
Mystery

***

On Farm Deadly

M·G·Lewis

Copyright © 2020 Michael Gene Lewis
All rights reserved.

ISBN-13: 9798606281343

Cover photo by author

This book is a work of fiction. Names, characters, places, and incidents are the product of the author's imagination or are used fictitiously. Any resemblance to actual events, locales, or persons, living or dead, is entirely coincidental.

Also by M.G. Lewis

Bergeron Mystery
Death on Daugherty Creek
Foreseeable Harm
Beauty in Ashes
Deep is the Chesapeake
Mr. Boghossian Loses a Tenant
The Nuptials of Ezmeralda Gutierrez
Keypunchers & Other Villains
Bornheimer's Demise
On Farm Deadly

Other
Rune's Riddle

Nesrady Clone Series
The Clone Who Loved to Bake Bread
The Clone Who Loved to Fight
The Clone Who Loved to Swim
The Clone Who Loved Voltaire

Tuesday
3:00 pm

Special Agent Corentin Georges Poirier of the Art Crime Team of the FBI had made an unprecedented request for two full weeks of leave; namely, the first two weeks of October.

And he had asked Jennifer for the same period. She had rolled her eyes, but it wasn't like he didn't have the vacation saved up.

But had Cory wanted to do something fun? Had they gone to Hawaii? Had they sampled sachertorte in an ancient Viennese cafe? Or gone to watch the awesome tides of the Bay of Fundy?

No.

For unexplained but apparently paramount reasons, Cory had dragooned him into a training course.

Beginning on the Friday before the two weeks of their vacation, they had gone to the gym, and Cory had drilled him in judo and boxing and other martial arts.

It wasn't like he was a complete novice since he'd been attending the dojo of Sensei Travis for a couple of years, but Cory had made the intimidating sensei seem like a cream puff.

And after that morning session of unarmed combat training, they had showered and gone to spend the afternoon at a gun range where they had donned safety glasses and ear muffs, and blasted away. Well, he had. Cory had just observed and criticized.

And they had repeated on Saturday, Sunday, and Monday.

Today was Tuesday, and he had learned the three safety rules: always point the pistol down range, no finger on the trigger, and make sure the pistol was unloaded, magazine and chamber.

At this point, his own name would fade from his aging synapses before those rules did.

But it was 3:00 pm, and he had already fired hundreds of bullets at the paper target.

Cory said, "You aren't concentrating, Bergeron."

"Am to!"

It was hard to concentrate when every muscle and joint in his body ached. He had been hurled, tossed, and pummeled to within an inch of his life.

He knew what wheat felt like after it had been threshed. But that wasn't the only thing weighing heavily upon him.

He unloaded the Glock. "Do we have to go?"

Cory said, "Yes. You promised, and Mother is expecting us."

He reloaded. He aimed at the target and put five rounds in paper man's heart and then four rounds into his head for good measure.

He looked over at Cory.

Cory shrugged.

Cory was the best thing that had ever happened to him so it was wrong to want to load a full mag into his Glock and shoot him repeatedly. Very wrong.

Cory smiled at him. "Somebody is getting cranky."

"Am not." He emptied the Glock at paper man; he hated paper man with a passion pure and fierce and true. "I'm beat. Can't we take a break?"

Cory hit the touchscreen to summon the target. He examined it and shrugged again.

"No shrugging, Poirier! Look at that grouping! I bet you can't do any better, Special Agent!"

Well, Cory could. He knew it, and Cory certainly knew it.

Cory said, "You're doing better." Cory was looking at the one measly bullet that had just clipped paper man's ear. "But you still lose focus at times, Gabe."

"Because I'm so tired my vision is blurry, and my arms are shaking." He was whining; even he could hear it. "Sorry. I'll do better next time, Sir. If next time is not today? Please? I'm starving too. It's after 3 pm, and I have to pack."

"We're only going for two days, Bergeron."

"To your mother's house! I have to be prepared for anything." Probably not black tie, but who knew?

"It's very relaxed, Gabe. It's a farm."

They might call it a "farm" but it was the "farm" of Cory's parents, Hubert and Laura Poirier, who were filthy rich and the scions of even richer, filthier progenitors. He could just imagine dinner.

Well, no, he couldn't which was part of the problem.

"How formal is dinner?" Cory smirked. "Right. So who else is coming?"

"Judd and Diane."

They were Cory's siblings, and he liked them. "Is that it? Not your grandmother?"

Cory shook his noble head, flinging his red locks hither and yon. Cory had let his hair grow out, and it crowned his head now like ocean waves reddened by the setting sun.

"I doubt it. She hasn't spoken to me for some time, Bergeron. Or to Mother either currently."

"And Hugh?"

"She hasn't allowed herself to be in the same zip code since he announced his retirement."

"Right."

He had spoken to Cory's maternal grandmother once...in Cory's condo...and she hadn't been pleased with her family's shameful lack of dedication to Holcomb Incorporated, the company founded by her father, the fabled Stephen Holcomb.

"Do you remember your great-grandfather?"

Cory shook his head. "Grand's father? No, Bergeron, he died long before I was born. But Mother says I look like him a bit."

"Are there pictures? An oil portrait? A marble bust?"

"I think so. Photos."

"Where are they?"

Cory turned to smile at him. "Why? What's going on inside that head?"

"Nothing. Just my totally natural, not-excessive curiosity."

"Mother has an album. Ask her about it tomorrow."

Tomorrow.

He didn't want to go to the Poirier "farm" which was probably closer to Versailles than to a farm with cows and pigs. He'd rather jump out of an airplane wearing a chute packed by murderous Cousin Nancy. Of course, Nancy was dead and sharing a vault with one of their ancestors. But still.

Cory said, "It will be okay. You might even enjoy yourself."

He snorted in derision, or he would have if Cory hadn't given up trying to look happy. This was his worried face.

"What's wrong, Cory?"

"Nothing. Fire another clip, Bergeron."

"Nope. I'm done." He put the unloaded Glock into the little basket, and he slumped to the floor.

"What are you doing?"

"I ache in places that have never ached before. I have carpal tunnel syndrome of the trigger finger."

Cory smiled. "You can't, Doofus."

"Then I have arthritis." He held up his right index finger. "Or rheumatism? Lumbago? Chilblains?"

"Get up, Bergeron. You're embarrassing me."

He rolled over and curled into a ball; the floor was hard, but he didn't care.

Cory tried to stand him up, but he was a boneless sack of meat, bruised, aching meat, and it was like grabbing a jellyfish.

"Get up!"

"Are we done?"

"Maybe."

"No, we are done! And why are we doing this?"

Cory looked tired too. And strained. "I want you to be ready."

"What?" He looked into the bottomless, blue eyes of Corentin Georges Poirier. "Ready for what?"

"I don't know."

"What the Hell, Poirier?"

But Cory was leaving the range with all deliberate speed.

He may have followed him, yapping at his heels like a rabid Chihuahua.

They drove to Cory's condo in silence. They rode the elevator in silence.

He followed Cory to the living room in silence.

Well, almost. "I say again: what the Hell, Cory?"

"I want you to be ready if you get into a situation...like you do. I want you to be able to defend yourself."

Which only sounded reasonable. "But there's more to this. You have something specific in mind, don't you?"

Cory glared at him. "No, I do not."

And Cory wouldn't say anything else on the subject. Cory had gone to bed in the master bedroom, and he had slept on the sofa. Which was stupid since there were two other bedrooms in the condo, but it was the principle of the thing.

He woke up at dawn with the rising sun blasting into his eyes.

He considered his options: he could freak out again trying to make Cory explain, he could walk out on Cory, or he could bide his time.

He made coffee and bided in the kitchen.

Cory came out of the master bedroom in his briefs. He had bed head, but there was nothing wrong with the rest of him; nothing at all. "Are you coming to the farm with me?"

Cory was worried about his family, and he had promised.

"I guess so."

"Good."

"But you have to tell me when I have to be ready...for whatever is coming, Cory! You know how I am with surprises."

Cory smiled. "I know, but there's nothing specific."

He didn't believe Cory for a second. "But if there were something...hypothetically...you'd tell me before the event?"

Cory shook his head and poured himself coffee. "There is no threat, hypothetical or otherwise, Bergeron. It's just that you keep getting drawn into shit, and I worry about you."

Which was nice. "Really? Are you sure that's all? You aren't training me for something specific? Maybe something you want me to do?"

Cory grabbed him and pulled him close until they were nose to nose. "There is nothing specific. I've been training you so you'll be ready the next time you decide to do something crazy even though I've told you not to, and you've promised me repeatedly that you wouldn't."

"That won't happen."

"Gabe."

"Really! I'm turning over a new leaf."

Cory was glaring at him, They were so close that he could feel the breeze when Cory blinked his eyes.

"Okay. I will do my very best not to let anything like that happen again, Cory."

Cory smiled and hugged him. He wanted to believe Cory. He really did. He was probably just being paranoid, but he wouldn't whine about the training any more.

He got dressed and finished packing. He wasn't going to obsess about this event that might require him to shoot a Glock 22 with deadly accuracy and fight like a Viking with an impacted wisdom tooth.

He needed to obsess about his stay chez Poirier in Loudoun County, deep in Virginia horse country.

At least, he wouldn't have to go to the gym or gun range.

But did this visit have anything to do with Cory's sudden fierce determination that Gabriel Bergeron should become a warrior?

Surely not?

Wednesday
1:00 pm

It was the second day of October, but the weatherpersons were enthusing about temperatures that might reach ninety. Lacking a hurricane or a blizzard, unseasonable temperatures were all they had to get hyper about.

Cory had two parking spaces in the garage beneath his condo. One was home to a large, silver Ford Explorer SUV, in which they were currently motoring. The other held a nondescript, gray Toyota Yaris; he wasn't sure why Cory had it unless it was for undercover work?

"We're going to be late, Cory." They were cruising along at a very sedate pace.

"No, we aren't."

They were to, and it was Cory's fault. Which was strange since Cory was never late. Unless Cory didn't want to be on time?

He didn't ask any questions.

Cory exited off the Dulles Highway onto Virginia Route 606. aka Old Ox Road, executing a great circle around Dulles Airport. After a few miles, he turned at the stoplight onto Route 50 heading west. Route 50 was still a divided highway at that point.

This highway, which boasted as many as eight lanes between Annapolis and DC, had shrunk to country road status by the time they neared the village of Aldie, and Cory negotiated a couple of traffic circles.

They crossed a stream called "Little River"; accurate but unoriginal. The bridge had stone parapets and was so narrow he doubted two trucks could pass without scraping granite. Cory didn't even slow down; he may have closed his eyes.

Brick walkways cut up the blacktop, and the speed limit dropped to twenty-five as they cruised through Aldie heading for Middleburg.

Middleburg had a Safeway and a collection of shops. A very narrow brick building with a overly grand front door was across from the Safeway.

Next door was the Middleburg United Methodist Church; a pretty brick building with a white, octagonal steeple.

Cory said, "Welcome to the 'Nation's Horse and Hunt Capital'."

"Hunt? As in fox hunting?"

Cory nodded.

"With the red jackets and the caps and the jodhpurs."

"Jodhpurs?"

"I read up." He had read Wikipedia articles on horse care, steeplechase, thoroughbreds, and such in preparation for this visit to the farm.

Cory smiled.

"Do you go fox hunting?" He wasn't sure how he felt about chasing a cute, little fox on horseback with a pack of hounds. Well, he was sure if the hunt ended with the hounds catching the cute, little fox and tearing it to pieces. He was very sure.

But Cory shook his head.

"How much riding do you do?"

"As much as I can, Gabe."

"Right. Excellent. Good clean fun in the bosom of nature. Do you race?"

"Point-to-point?"

He had no idea. "Sure?"

"A few times with friends...as a rank amateur...I'm not good enough."

"Did you want to be?"

Cory shook his head. "No. But Diane was really into it. For a while."

He was pretty sure that Cory really liked riding, and he

would have to encourage him to do it more.

He could entertain himself at the condo. Or go out. He needed to make some friends in DC. Or he could invite Neal. Or Baldacci. Or Billy? But Billy could be problematic.

Cory was looking at him. "What's going on inside that head this time?"

"Nothing. Well, quite a lot really. But mostly I am enjoying your company."

"Thanks for coming."

"To the Poirier Demesne? Delighted. So why are you worried about your family?"

"I'm not."

Liar, liar, pants on fire. "Is it about your father? His health?" Cory had never said anything, but Hugh's health was not perfect. "Or your mother?"

"They are both fine."

"Diane or Judd?"

Cory ignored him as they left Middleburg behind. They were just cresting a small hill when he got his first glimpse of the Blue Ridge Mountains in the distance; a bluish smudge on the horizon.

Cory turned north on a country road which rolled, pitched, and yawed through the verdant Virginia farmland.

The rolling fields on either side were lush and manicured and hemmed by rail fences. In other fields, huge round hay bales sat benignly awaiting whatever would come.

Little sections of woodland broke up the grasslands. They passed through one, deep and dark and forbidding after the bright sunshine.

Cory slowed and turned right onto a paved lane. Twin stone pillars topped with granite pineapple finials held a pair of noble gates, gleaming white. A brass escutcheon declared "Poirier."

He looked at Cory. "The Poirier Demesne?"

Cory smiled and roared up the lane.

Wednesday
2:00 pm

After passing through a mile of rolling fields and groves of trees, he could see the house in the distance. They were rocketing past another huge, grassy field. This one had an oval track complete with various barriers; some were wooden fences, some were hedge-like, a few had small ponds on one side.

Cory said, "Steeplechase track. It's 16 furlongs. Diane used it for training."

"Furlongs?"

"A furlong is two miles."

"Right. I knew that. Training for what?"

"At one time, she had this wild idea of riding in the Middleburg Spring Races."

He lacked data to judge how wild an idea that had been, and he didn't have time to ask as they approached the house.

It was a white, two story affair with a cellar made of massive stone blocks, and a steeply-pitched, blue slate roof. The long central mass had two stubby, single-story wings. A porch with Doric columns ran the length of the first floor, and above it, a duplicate balcony. Wide windows with black shutters broke up the facade.

It had a garden and old trees in front, and walkways led to a fenced area to the side and to a lane that ran to what might be a very fancy barn in the distance.

Cory didn't stop in front but circled the building. He turned and drove through a roofed archway and pulled into a black-topped parking area in front of a garage. Five cars were already lined up.

Cory smiled at him. "We're here."

He tried smiling back as he got out and grabbed his suitcase. He was going to keep a positive attitude.

They walked toward the stairs under the roofed archway. "Is this what's called a porte cochere? Very nice."

Cory smiled. "It's home. Well, one of them."

He'd grown up in several homes too, but his were sequential and not simultaneous. And not nearly so grand.

They ascended the stairs and entered a foyer with a marble tile floor. Facing them, maple stairs led up to the second floor.

Cory turned left and stepped through an archway framed with more white, Doric columns. "Mother? Dad?"

He followed Cory into a living room. They could see the dining room next to windows which were flooding the area with light. Laura was standing beside the table with Judd and Diane, Cory's siblings, beside her.

Two doors led off from the formal living room; the one in front of them was open, and he could see a sofa and a wall-sized TV. The one on the left was closed.

Laura said, "You're late, Corentin. We finished ages ago."

She didn't look happy; well, she did, but it wasn't her real, happy face.

Cory hugged his mother and kissed her on the cheek. "Sorry. Traffic."

"Are you hungry?"

He smiled. "I'll get something later."

Laura had long, auburn hair and blue eyes, which were not as intense as Cory's, but she had cheekbones that models would commit heinous crimes to possess.

"And what about Gabriel?"

Cory and his mother looked at him. Cory said, "He's okay. I fed him this morning."

Laura thought that was hilarious, but she wasn't about to acknowledge it. "Don't be silly, Corentin. Mrs. Villeneuve will get you both something."

And then Cory's grandmother lunged out of the door on the

left. Well, not so much a lunge as a stately procession; like Ivan the Terrible marching into a Kremlin decorated with severed heads.

Josephine Loncke was probably seventy-five, but still ramrod straight. She had long hair which had been plaited into a sort of gray Viking helmet. Her face was uniformly wrinkled, and her tiny eyes were mud-colored. Her lips were bright red; either from lipstick or the blood of her latest kill.

She fixed her daughter with a terrible gaze. "That can wait, Laura. You're late, Corentin. We're waiting for you in the library."

Cory didn't seem surprised to see her.

"No, Grand. I'm sorry, but I'm not joining you."

Which was apparently inconceivable. She paused, but when Cory's head didn't explode from the psychic energy of her disapproval, she pointed at the family room.

"Come with me, Corentin."

Corentin didn't wanna, but the black hole gravity of his grandmother sucked him into the room.

He followed Cory to the door.

Josephine spotted him. "This is between me and my grandson, Young Man."

He smiled at her. "Cory?"

But Cory nodded and closed the door.

Laura was very unhappy, but the smile was a work of skillful artifice. Cory's brother, Judd, touched her arm ever so lightly. "It will be okay, Mother."

Diane said, "Cory's tough."

Laura didn't appear to agree.

He smiled at Diane as he stood there with his suitcase in his hand and Cory's beside him.

Diane said, "Why don't I get Gabe settled, Mother?"

Laura nodded.

Diane was ushering him back toward the stairs when the door opened, and Cory shot out like he had been launched off an aircraft carrier sans jet.

Josephine said, "I'm not finished, Corentin."

"But I am." Cory's face was ablaze. He had thought he'd seen Cory angry before, but he was mistaken.

Cory was out the front door. He dropped his suitcase. "Maybe, I'll get settled later, Diane."

As he headed after Cory, Josephine said, "Jordan! I want to speak to you."

Judd, aka Jordan, looked shocked and pissed and confused. He was dark and slender and looked nothing like Cory; neither did Diane.

Judd shook his head, but he went into the family room and closed the door.

Laura looked lost, but she had Diane, and he had to catch up to Cory before Cory exploded, and the Poirier estate was reduced to a smoking crater.

Cory was already down the stairs and crossing the garden before he cleared the porch. "Cory!"

Cory kept striding.

He jogged until he caught up and fell into step. They were heading toward a substantial structure that might be a barn.

One look at Cory convinced him that silence was golden...and safer...as Cory continued to ignore him.

The barn was made of the same brownish stone that formed the foundation of the main house. It also had a slate roof, but it had four dormer windows and three cupolas. The central cupola had a copper roof with a weather vane in the shape of a horse being led by his rider.

Cory continued to stomp ever onward.

He could see three small houses placed in a grove of trees on his right; fenced-in fields were on his left.

The sun was shining, and it was hot. He started to whistle. Cory didn't smack him so he whistled louder.

He wasn't sure of the tune? It was part "Swing Low Sweet Chariot" laced with snippets of "My Bonnie Lies Over the Ocean" with a little "Scotland the Brave" tossed in.

Cory was slowing and not stomping quite so hard.

They reached the barn, and Cory wheeled right.

"Isn't it just a lovely day?"

Cory ignored him.

"I love October. It's my favorite month, weather-wise. We

could have a picnic under those trees. I know I was fed this morning, but I'm getting peckish. Maybe if we asked Mrs. Villeneuve very nicely, she'll make sandwiches? I'm assuming she's the cook? From what Laura said."

Cory sighed.

"I really like your house. From the little I've seen of it. Is your father around? How many horses do you have? I'm assuming they're in this barn though it seems a shame to call it that. I've lived in much less fancy places. What kind of stone is that?"

Cory suddenly wheeled about, and they were heading back toward the house.

He got a better look at the fenced area closest to the house. "Wait. Is that a pool? Could we take a dip?"

"Shut up, Gabe."

"Sir! Yes, Sir! So you were deliberately late, because you knew your grandmother was here, and you didn't want to attend this meeting?" Cory went back to stoicism. "I don't blame you even though I know nothing about what's going on."

Cory was heading for their vehicle.

He stopped. "No, Corentin. Bad Corentin."

Cory spun around glaring at him. "I'm leaving."

"Nope."

Cory marched up to him until they were nose to nose. "I'm leaving, Bergeron."

"Nope."

"You can't stop me."

He locked his arms around Cory. "Shut up. Go talk to your mother. She's upset."

"Let go of me!"

"Nope."

"I'm upset too, Gabe."

"I know, but Laura feels like she's letting you down."

"What?"

"She thinks she should protect you from Josephine."

"She can't do that." Cory frowned at him. "Nobody can, and I can take care of myself."

"I know, but she's your mother, and she thinks she should

be able to stop her messing with you and your life."

Cory said, "You think so?"

"I'm sure of it. And something's wrong with Hugh? I think? And I believe that's part of the reason we're here. Of course, that's just a guess."

Cory sighed. "Get off me, Bergeron."

He released Cory, prepared to grapple with him again, but Cory took the path back toward the house.

A young guy in a dark suit had appeared and was sitting on Laura's porch talking on his phone. He said, "I tried, Gita, but he kicked me out. Just what do you suggest? He won't listen this time."

And then he realized he had an audience. He glared at them, but he wasn't scary. He was a slender reed; a slender reed with a smirky expression and fluffy, blond hair.

He said, "I have to go, Mrs. Shaw." And he pocketed his phone and stared off into the distance.

Cory went into the house. Laura was in the kitchen which was off the dining room.

Cory hugged her. "I'm fine, Mother. She didn't say anything she hasn't said before."

Laura said, "I'm sorry, Corentin."

He smiled at her. "Why? Not your fault."

Cory hugged Diane and then headed for Judd. It looked like Judd was going to stand there like a statue and not hug Cory back. Judd was trying to tamp down his unhappiness, but it kept flaring into view. Was he envious of Cory?

A portly woman was watching the Poirier drama with him. She had been blonde but her hair was easing into white. She had brown, kindly eyes and a mouth made for smiling.

Cory hugged her too. "How are you, Mrs. Villeneuve?"

She said, "I am well, Mr. Corentin." She had a slight French accent.

She patted Cory's face, and then she looked at the stranger in the room.

Cory took the hint. "This is Gabe...Gabriel Bergeron."

She smiled and hugged him too. "Welcome, Mr. Gabriel."

No one had ever called him Mr. Gabriel. He felt like he should strike a blow for *liberté, égalité, fraternité* and tell her it was just Gabe, but he smiled. "Thank you, Mrs. Villeneuve. Happy to be here."

She said, "Are you French?"

"My family is French-Canadian. A couple of generations removed."

She gave him a big smile. "*Moi, aussi!*"

He smiled and kept his mouth shut. He had studied French in college, but he was a decade rusty, and he'd never been fluent to begin with.

He may have cast an eye at all the food that was being packed away, but he didn't drool.

Cory said, "Can we make some sandwiches, Mrs. Villeneuve?"

She said, "Of course! I will do it for you."

So they got their picnic on green pastures.

When he had wolfed down his second sandwich, he looked at Cory. "You knew about this meeting that your grandmother had set up, didn't you?"

Cory nodded. "I could tell that something was up so I called Mrs. Villeneuve, and she told me that Grand and two other guests were coming."

"Right. So who is the blond dude on the porch?"

"No idea. Someone from the company."

He had wanted to do some digging into Holcomb, Inc. and the stock owned by the Poirier family, but he didn't think he should. If Cory wanted him to know about his finances, he would tell him.

And he didn't really want to know how rich Hugh and Laura were. Well, with the way the stock had dropped in the last week, how rich they had been.

Maybe Judd had sold his stock just in time? But why had that upset Hugh and Laura?

Mrs. Villeneuve had given them some cookies too. He popped one into his mouth; dates and chocolate chips. It wasn't sachertorte, but it was very good.

Cory said, "Thanks, Gabe."

He tried batting his eyes. "Whatever for, Mr. Corentin, Sir?"

Wednesday
5:00 pm

And after their picnic, Cory took him on a tour of the pastures and woodlands of the Poirier estate.

The three white cottages belonged to employees; Mrs. Villeneuve lived in one, the second was occupied by the housekeeper, Mrs. Foote, and the third housed Mrs. Prentice and her family. She was the farm manager.

Cory concluded the tour with an inspection of the barn. It was just as nice inside as out; he could move in and be perfectly comfortable.

Well, he'd need to move the horses out and give the place a thorough cleaning; a steam cleaning...and replace the floors.

A plump, gray cat rubbed against his leg and yowled speculatively at him.

"Sorry, but I have no food."

Green eyes looked him over and found him useless; a swishing tail bid him adieu

There were stalls for dozens of horses, but only five were occupied.

Cory said, "When I was a boy...when grandfather was alive...we had forty horses."

"Which grandfather?"

"Dad's father, Sébastien Poirier."

"Right." It was on the tip of his tongue to ask what had led to a thinning of the herd, but he held it in. "Well, these guys are beautiful."

And they were...in a horsey way. They had noble profiles and shiny coats.

Cory smiled and proceeded to introduce each one. "This is Loki, and that's Shadow Dancer."

Loki was brown with a black tail and a white spot on her forehead. Shadow Dancer was gray and white with a black tail and mane and white spots on her rump. She was beautiful.

And the two horses seemed to know Cory and nuzzled him.

Zephyr was a lighter brown than Loki and had three white feet. Rhythm was coal black and had his rump to the stall door. Possibly her rump?

Cory was moving on. "And this big fellow is Bucephalus."

Bucephalus was shiny black with a white star on his forehead and blue eyes; wild, blue eyes. And he was massive.

"Have you ever ridden him?"

Cory looked surprised. "Sure. Many times."

Bucephalus nuzzled Cory's hand looking for a treat.

"He won't bite you, Bergeron. None of them will."

"Right. Good to know." He kept his distance all the same, because they had very big teeth.

They walked back to the house. It appeared that Josephine's meeting was ending.

Diane and a big guy in a suit were talking in the dining room. The guy was standing very close, leaning over her. He moved even closer and took her arm, but she pulled free and went into the kitchen.

The guy might have followed her, but he saw them looking at him. He smiled and walked over.

He pumped Cory's hand, smiling harder. "Cory! So good to see you. How is the FBI business?"

Cory said, "It has its moments. How are you, Mr. Shaw?"

Craig Shaw was the current CEO of Holcomb, Inc.

Hugh had been the CEO until he had retired, but he was fighting to take back control of the family business for some reason.

Shaw was about forty with salt and pepper hair. He had happy brown eyes and a big smile. He was an inch or two taller than Cory and looked like a former rugby player whose efforts to stay in shape were paying dividends.

But he didn't actually look very bright. Which was probably unfair, but he didn't.

Cory said, "Do you know my sister?"

Shaw cranked up the megawatts on the smile dial. "Sure. Super gal."

Cory was contemplating punching Shaw in the face; all the signs were there.

He smiled and extended his hand to Shaw. "And I'm Gabriel Bergeron."

He thought that Shaw was going to ignore his outstretched hand, but he gripped his hand in a vise. He matched Shaw's grip. They smiled at each other.

Shaw let go first. "I know who you are, Gabe. An accountant in Philadelphia?"

"I am. It's very nice to meet you." Why did the Holcomb CEO know who he was?

The slender blond guy was at Shaw's side. "We need to go, Sir."

Shaw glanced around. "There you are, Erik. What's the rush, Pal?"

"You have an engagement with Mrs. Shaw."

Shaw contemplated that statement. "Okay?" He smiled at Cory. "Erik keeps me on my toes. Don't you, Erik?"

"I do my best, Sir." Erik managed to smile while looking like he would enjoy shoving a meat skewer through one of Shaw's brown eyes.

He held out his hand to Erik. "I'm Gabriel Bergeron."

Erik examined the appendage aimed at him for a second before grabbing the tips of his fingers. "Erik Varner, executive assistant."

Shaw smiled at everybody and at the Universe, which was lucky enough to have him in it, and departed with Erik trailing behind.

Cory said, "Is it me or is he just slimy?"

He said, "It's not you. He has to be smarter than he looks?"

Cory shook his head. "No, he doesn't. Come on. Dad should be in his office."

They crossed the formal living room and went through a door into a library. It had shelves to the ceiling and many a quaint and curious volume of unforgotten lore. It even had those rolling ladders to reach the top shelves.

It also had Josephine. She was sitting with two older men. They looked up at Cory, but he didn't even slow down. He went through the open door into an office with a grand desk.

Hugh was sitting behind it with his eyes closed. Cory's father was built like his son. He was probably sixty; his hair was gray but still thick and professionally tousled. He had little blue eyes and perfect teeth.

He looked healthy enough, but Cory was worried about him.

"Dad?"

Hugh's eyes popped open. He smiled and hugged his son. "I'm glad to see you, Cory."

"I'm glad to see you too, Dad. I'm sorry I was late."

He said, "That was all my fault, Hugh. I had a small emergency."

Hugh didn't like him as much as Laura did. He knew it, and Hugh knew that he knew.

"What kind of emergency would that be, Gabriel?"

"A work emergency. A client appeared to have misplaced a sizable deposit and was freaking out."

"Really? That was careless of him."

"Her. But she didn't really misplace it. She runs an art gallery...."

But Hugh had lost interest in his tale.

Cory said, "How are you, Dad?"

"Never better."

Which is all he would ever say in front of Gabe Bergeron.

Cory paused. He cared nothing, less than nothing about Holcomb, but he loved his father.

He jumped in again. "So how was the meeting, Hugh? I met Mr. Shaw; he's quite something, isn't he?"

Hugh gave him a look. "You could say that."

"Is his picture on the company prospectus? That smile alone would sell a few shares. If you ignore the vacant look in the eyes."

Hugh's glare softened a bit; there might have been a twinkle in his eyes.

And then Josephine darkened his office door. "Hubert, it's decided." She turned to glare at the older men. "No more delays. Do it today!"

They nodded.

She said, "I'm leaving Hubert."

He didn't need to take a poll to know that the general sentiment was "Good riddance."

Cory glared, needing only to paint his face blue to pass for an angry Celtic warrior, but Hugh managed to smile and take her arm to escort her from his home.

He and Cory followed.

The two older guys had resumed chatting. The younger got to his feet and blocked their exit. He was around sixty with a fluffy mane of white hair and brown eyes. His face was ruddy and wrinkle free except for laugh lines at the corners of his eyes.

He was stocky and might be five feet five on a good shoe day. He smiled at Cory.

"Do you remember me, Cory?"

Cory smiled. "Of course, Mr. Kennard. How are you, Sir?"

"Excellent. Still happy at the FBI?"

"Very much so, Sir."

Kennard said, "I told Josephine that you had made your choice years ago."

"I keep telling her the same thing...eventually she'll hear me."

Kennard gave Cory a big smile and a shoulder slap.

The other man, who looked twenty years older, said, "When did Josephine ever listen to something she didn't want to hear?"

Kennard smiled. "This lugubrious fellow is Childers."

Childers got to his feet slowly. He didn't offer his hand. His right eye seemed lower than his left, but his mouth drooped in the opposite direction. The flesh of his face and neck sagged, as did his shoulders, like he was in a deeper gravity well than the rest of them.

He also had a deathly pallor; comparing him to Kennard, it was Snow White to Rose Red. If they weren't storybook characters...and were male...and old...and not pretty.

Childers said, "She'll never agree, Kennard."

Kennard smiled and rocked on his feet. "She will. Circumstances will force even her."

Childers walked out of the library without another word.

Kennard smiled again and patted Cory's shoulder some more. "Have you thought about what we discussed, Cory?"

Cory smiled. "About selling my Holcomb stock? I'm not interested, Mr. Kennard."

"I see, but I could give you a price above market? Jordan was very happy with our arrangement."

"Thank you, but no."

Kennard nodded and departed as well.

"And who are they, Cory?"

"Board members. Allies of Grand, I think. At least, they were at one time."

It was none of his business, and he wasn't going to ask about the shares. He certainly couldn't ask how many shares Cory owned.

Cory was smiling at him. "What?"

Cory laughed. "Nothing."

Thursday
8:00 am

Cory was out of bed, standing by the open door that led onto the balcony. Cory was wearing nothing but a pair of skimpy, emerald-green briefs.

Which he'd bought for him. Which had been such a sound investment.

"Cory?"

"Yes?"

"Everything okay?"

Cory was staring out the door. "Define 'everything' for me, Gabe."

"Are you currently in robust, good health? Are you still employed by the FBI? Is your family currently snug and secure here chez Poirier?"

Cory smiled. "Yes."

"Excellent. Is there anything I can do to help you?"

Cory turned and jumped back into bed. Cory smiled. "Nope."

Cory said, "Why not?"

"Diane is on the other side of that wall. She has a door that leads out onto that self-same balcony."

"She does."

"And Judd is in the next room, and beyond him are your parents, Hubert and Laura."

"And?"

He hugged Cory and rested his head on Cory's hairless,

muscled chest; a chest worthy of Michelangelo and the finest marble. "Not happening, Corentin."

"Okay."

"So what's on the agenda for today?"

"For us?"

"Sure. And for all the inhabitants of Poirier Land?"

Cory said, "Well, the horses will be fed and groomed and possibly ridden."

"Human inhabitants. Specifically, your father and mother."

Cory frowned. "Shaw is coming back for another meeting."

"And Josephine?"

Cory smiled. "Grand is pissed with all of us and is disinheriting us as we lie here."

"Good. Let her keep her ill-gotten gain." Which was easy to say since he had never been in the last will and testament in the first place.

"So how did your great-grandfather get his start?"

"No idea."

He snuggled down under Laura's thousand thread count sheets. Everything was white or beige in the room. Well, the comforter was an aggressive taupe.

From what he'd seen, the whole house was like that. Not that it wasn't attractive in a passive-aggressive, casual way; every pillow, throw, magazine, and objet d'art having it's place.

But it wasn't cozy. He didn't think Laura kenned cozy.

They got dressed and descended to breakfast served on a porch that budded off the kitchen. It had been glassed in to form a solarium. Mrs. Villeneuve did everything but spoon feed Cory, who lapped up the attention all unaware.

Diane was smiling, but Judd was not amused.

Mrs. Villeneuve made excellent coffee so she was okay in his book. He sipped and smiled at the assembled Poirier family. "So I understand Mr. Shaw is returning?"

Laura frowned. The siblings snorted, but Hugh ignored him and got to his feet with his coffee cup in his hand.

Laura looked at him. "I have to make a call." And he crossed the kitchen bound for his office on the other side of the house.

Diane said, "Yes, he's coming back, Gabe. With Childers...he's on the board."

"I see. So how long has Shaw worked at Holcomb?"

Judd said, "Eight years."

"And I gather he's a piss-poor CEO?"

Laura said, "Language, Gabriel."

Which was kind of nice...that she was comfortable policing his language. "Sorry. He's less than ideal?"

Judd said, "He's erratic. He hired a new head for the chemical division, who is a disaster, but Shaw won't back down."

Diane said, "A disaster. How?"

Judd said, "Ms. Patterson isn't qualified or capable."

Diane said, "Why am I not surprised."

Cory looked up from his eggs and bacon. "How do you know so much, Judd?"

Judd said, "Because I talk to Dad."

Which was roughly equivalent to a knife fight breaking out in less refined families.

Cory blanched white like an octopus trying to blend into the linen tablecloth.

He wanted to defend Cory, but he scanned the faces around the table. It might be better to keep his mouth shut, but he'd never learn anything that way.

"So I saw you talking to Shaw yesterday, Diane?"

Diane said, "I couldn't avoid him."

"But you'd like to?"

"He's a pig." She flushed and wouldn't look at Laura or her brothers.

He decided that he really should shut up. Laura stared at Diane for a bit and then wrested the conversation away from Shaw and Holcomb and talked about the whole family vacationing in Costa Rica in January.

She smiled. "I thought we could all celebrate Christmas here this year."

Diane said, "That sounds like fun." And she wasn't being sarcastic.

Laura smiled at Judd. "Can you and Samantha come, Jordan?"

Judd/Jordan nodded. "I think so." Judd seemed like he was considering saying something else, but the moment past, and he went back to masticating his bran cereal.

Laura was looking at him. "Am I invited?"

"Of course, you are, Gabriel, but I know you always spend the holiday with your Aunt Florence?"

"I do. Without fail. Except for one year...." He looked at Cory. Cory didn't need to know about that year. "But I can visit her afterwards."

He smiled at Laura. What he would really like to do is get Aunt Flo invited and let her analyze the Poiriers, one and all.

Cory was looking at him. "What are you smiling about?"

"Me? Nothing. I have a smiling face."

Cory knew better.

Breakfast ended without further friction.

Diane made a call and then left the farm.

Thursday
10:00 am

Shaw arrived about an hour later, casually dressed in jeans and a pair of calf-high boots.

Shaw smiled and shook Hugh's hand. "I thought we might go riding after our chat, Hugh."

Hugh smiled back at Shaw. "Of course, Craig. That sounds like fun. And you haven't seen Bucephalus."

Shaw smiled. "Your stallion? No, I haven't."

And Hugh and Craig went into Hugh's office for a manly confab that probably included brandy and cigars.

He looked at Cory, but Cory wouldn't know what they were discussing. He needed to get Judd alone.

He smiled at Cory. "Fancy a walk, Mr. Corentin, Sir."

Cory punched him in the shoulder. Hard. But it was no more than he deserved. He contemplated trying to throw Cory across Laura's living room.

She said, "Corentin! Don't do that! Are you all right, Gabriel?"

Which hurt more than the punch; that she thought he was so fragile. "I'm fine. He barely grazed me, Laura."

But he escaped out the door before Cory could graze him hard enough to put him on the floor.

Cory followed. "I'm sorry about calling you Corentin, but everybody does it here?"

Cory smiled at him. "But you don't get to."

"Right. Understood."

Cory was upset but was doing his best to hide it. He showed him a lot more of the farm. It was still unseasonably warm and idyllic and bucolic.

When they finally got back to the house, Laura was sitting on the porch looking about as distraught as she got.

"Mother?"

She said, "Hubert and that Shaw went off riding. They've been gone a long time, Corentin."

Cory said, "We'll find them."

And they trotted around the farm some more, but there was no sign.

"Where are they?"

Cory said, "There are a lot of trails and fields, Gabe."

"So if they're just taking a leisurely ride around the demesne, then why is Laura worried?"

"He doesn't ride that much any more." Cory frowned. "I'm going to get a horse. I can cover more ground."

Cory looked at him. "Nope. I will continue on foot."

But he spotted a couple of riders crossing a distant field at full gallop. The closer one was whipping his horse. They were heading straight for a fence.

"What the Hell are they doing, Cory?"

But he figured it out before Cory could answer as the horses sailed over the fence, hardly breaking stride,. They raced onward crossing the field and swerved around a out building and suddenly heading in their direction.

He started to back away, but Cory wasn't moving. "Cory?"

He grabbed Cory's arm, but Cory wouldn't budge. The beating of the horses' hoofs was getting loud and a little ominous. He suddenly knew what infantry felt like when facing a cavalry charge.

The riders cleared another fence and another, and were still thudding toward them at breakneck speed. The rider on the left, Hugh, was slowing.

Shaw was still coming, but Cory wouldn't move. He didn't pull his Glock because he didn't have it, but this was how it had been when Cory had faced down that perp in the SUV last year;

standing rock-solid and firing at the driver as the vehicle came at him.

Until his partner, Matt Bornheimer, had tackled him and saved his life.

Which he was about to do to Cory, but Shaw swerved his horse at the last second and flashed past them. Smiling. Laughing. High as a kite on adrenaline.

He slowed and came trotting back.

Hugh was heading toward them at a walk.

Shaw said, "I won, Hugh."

Hugh smiled just as broadly as Shaw. "You did, Craig. I didn't know you rode so well."

Cory said, "That was reckless and stupid."

Craig dismounted, all limitless machismo. "Not reckless if you know what you're doing." He smiled some more at Cory. "You don't ride?"

Shaw was challenging Cory. He didn't know how well he rode, and he would hate for Cory to lose to this jerk.

"Cory?" Hugh was still in the saddle.

Cory turned away from Shaw and walked over to stand next to his father. He whispered, "Are you okay, Dad?"

Hugh nodded. "Fine."

But he didn't look fine at all. His face looked like a color photo that had been reduced to black and white, and the subject had been on a slab in the morgue at the time.

Cory looked from his father back to Shaw who was still in mid-gloat about his victory over a guy twenty years his senior. Shaw was looking at them.

Cory whispered. "Should I help Shaw on his way, Dad?"

Hugh nodded and smiled at Cory with lips that were pale but not blue. "Please."

He smiled. "Let me do that, Cory."

And he walked over to Shaw and patted him on the shoulder. "So how is the company doing, Mr. Shaw? I was thinking of investing, but I'm not sure that now is the right time."

Shaw said, "Just a small blip. The stock will go back up."

"Really? I've been looking into Holcomb, and I'm not so

sure. Are you staying on? As CEO?"

Shaw smiled. "Of course. You shouldn't listen to Hugh...."

"I wasn't, but I had a nice chat with Childers and Kennard, and they seem to think that there's a problem with the head of the chemical division. Her name is Patterson, I believe?"

Shaw wasn't smiling so much now. "Childers and Kennard shouldn't be talking out of school...."

Shaw had forgotten his name. "Bergeron. Of the Barnes Foundation, Mr. Shaw. We have assets of over a billion."

"What?"

He smiled. "A one followed by nine zeros. So there isn't a chance that Patterson will file a sexual harassment suit against you?"

Shaw flushed. "What?" He tied the horse to the fence. "What the Hell are you talking about? That's slander, Bergeron. Pamela and I are friends as well as coworkers...."

Shaw was backing away; his tanned face the color of candle wax now.

"No. You're her boss. But given the situation, you can't fire her, can you? I understand that the board isn't happy...."

"A bunch of old women!"

"Really? Childers and Kennard are old women? Isn't that kind of sexist, Craig?"

Shaw had balled up his fists. If he did throw a punch, he was pretty sure he could toss big Craig, which would be intensely satisfying.

But Shaw turned. "Shut up! I'm not talking to you. Stay away from me!"

As soon as Shaw was walking back toward the house, he spun around. Cory had helped Hugh off his horse and into the barn.

Hugh was sitting on a bench, being very still and breathing slowly.

He looked at Cory. "911?"

Hugh said, "I'm fine, Gabriel." He smiled. "You ran him off. How do you know all that? About the company?"

"I'm nosy. And I made up a bunch of it. And Aunt Flo doesn't have a billion."

Cory handed the reins of Hugh's horse to a hulking, blond guy. "Take care of them, Dolph."

Dolph grunted something and disappeared into the bowels of the barn with the two horses.

Cory said, "I could get my car, Dad?"

Hugh said, "No, I'm fine to walk."

Which was debatable, but Hugh was adamant.

They progressed along the lane and arrived in time to chance upon Childers in the garden, looking very like the serpent in it.

He was not alone; he and a beautiful, exotic woman were sitting knee to knee in a gazebo. She was smiling and talking and leaning close to Childers, who was avoiding her gaze.

He looked at Cory who shrugged.

Hugh said, "The lovely Gita. Gita Shaw."

"His wife? She could do better."

Hugh nodded. He was tiring out. "My office, Cory."

Cory guided his father away from the front steps and toward the single-story wing. Hugh was wobbly on the steps so he and Cory carried Hugh into his office.

Hugh said, "Put me down." Hugh sat carefully in his chair. "Cory, see if Shaw has left?"

After Cory went back outside, he said, "Do you need water? Or something else?" Hugh pointed at a cut glass decanter holding a brown liquid. "Really? Should you?"

Hugh nodded and took the decanter out of his hands. He sloshed a couple of inches into a glass and downed it.

He smiled. "Don't tell Laura. Or Cory."

"My lips are sealed. Well, probably. But sometimes things pop out. I don't drink alcohol myself, but I understand that in moderation it has...."

Hugh said, "I'm too tired for babbling, Gabriel."

"Right. Let me see what's happened to Cory."

He thought he should at least try to stop Cory from beating the crap out of Shaw. But Judd was hanging onto Cory's arm, and then Laura joined them in the garden.

Childers and Gita were still making whoopee in the gazebo.

Well, they were making something. He may have strolled over.

Childers took Gita's delicate, scarlet-nailed hand out of his lap and stood up.

She was wearing a long, teal dress with black and gold embroidery that began at the waist on each side of her body and swirled up to cup her breasts and coalesce across her shoulders. It made her look even more hourglassy than she was. And she had teal shoes too.

She said, "Please, Harold. Come to the house? I know we can come to an understanding."

Childers shook his gray head. "Not this time, Gita. He's finished." He smiled at her which was unfortunate, his teeth being yellow, and he walked toward the parking area.

He strolled over and sat down next to Gita, who might have hit the forty mark. She had luminous, black hair, parted in the middle and flowing half way down her back. Big brown eyes gazed at the world from beneath arched brows. Full lips and a generous nose didn't detract from her beauty.

Her teeth were startlingly white against brown skin. Her bosom poked out enough to be distracting; even for him. So he focused on her dangly earrings.

"Hello."

She eyed him and decided he was harmless. "Hello, yourself. Who are you?"

He held out his hand. "Gabe Bergeron."

She smiled. "Ah. The accountant. At Garst, Bauer & Hartmann." She smiled again. "Cory is very attractive."

"He is. So you and Shaw?"

She sighed. "I know."

She didn't specify what she knew. "How did you...meet him?"

"At university. It seemed like a good idea at the time."

"But in the cold light of day...."

She smiled and rose to her feet. "Good-bye, Mr. Bergeron."

And she swayed toward the parking area like a peacock in full plumage. Except she was female; very female.

He followed along at a respectable distance. Cory put a

hand on his shoulder. Laura and Judd joined them.

Shaw was pacing, but he spotted his wife and became a font of bonhomie once more.

"Gita! There you are. Did you talk to Childers?"

Erik Varner was in a black suit, standing beside a black, Lexus sedan, with a black look on his face.

Shaw was swaggering toward Gita; Erik tried to divert him, but Shaw threw a sweaty arm over Erik's shoulder and dragged him toward the lovely Gita.

She put up her hands. "No, Craig. We'll talk later. Please take me home, Erik." Craig kept advancing. "No! You're wet, Craig...and you smell."

Craig laughed. "That's the smell of a real man." He smiled at Cory and then released Erik, who stood there glaring.

Shaw hugged his wife and leaned over to whisper in her ear. She pushed at him, red nails digging into his chest, but he held her. She whispered something back.

He seemed to freeze up, and then he let her go. "Are you sure he won't, Gita?"

She nodded. Shaw looked around with a confused, scared look on his face. "But you said he would?"

She said something in a language not English. It didn't sound complimentary.

Shaw smiled at her. "I know I've been a bad boy when you bring out the Hindi."

He tried to kiss her, grabbing her wrists before she could slap him.

"Let go of me, Craig. I did warn you, Darling."

Craig's smile was fixed in place. "Sure, Babe. I know. But I'll drive you home, and we can talk."

"Erik can drive me...."

"No! I'm driving you. And you're going to figure this out."

And he half-dragged her to his car, which was a silver Porsche 911. He smiled and waved at all of them, and then rocketed out of the parking area, wheels spinning to get traction.

He shot through the porte cochere just as Childers was descending the steps. He didn't hit the old man, but it was a near thing.

Erik got into the sedan and followed at a reasonable speed.

Childers went to his own car still glaring after Shaw. "That man should never have been CEO." And he departed as well. There was the odor of brimstone or maybe it was just hot asphalt?

He looked at the Poiriers. "So he's officially out?"

Laura just smiled, but Judd nodded. She went back inside.

Cory said, "I'm going to stay on another day, Gabe, but I can take you back to DC?"

"Nope. I'm fine. Who would have guessed that life on a horse farm would be this exciting."

The Poirier brothers shook their heads.

Cory looked at Judd. "We should see how Dad is."

But Hugh was sitting in the family room with the TV tuned to a football game. Laura was sitting beside him on the sofa, holding his hand.

Diane had returned and was sitting on the other side of Hugh.

Hugh said, "I was just winded, Cory. Nothing to be concerned about." He smiled. "That was fun though I hate losing to Shaw."

Laura said, "He's fine, Corentin." She turned to Hugh. "I spoke to Mrs. Prentice today; Jack doesn't have long now."

Hugh nodded. "I'm sorry to hear that. And nothing can be done?"

Laura shook her head.

Cory walked out of the family room; he followed.

"He looks okay, Cory."

"But he isn't."

So Hugh wasn't okay, but he didn't seem to be in any immediate danger. He didn't think Cory had any idea what was really wrong with his father.

And he wasn't going to find out from Hugh and Laura. Which had to suck big time.

They had dinner, watched some boring TV, and at a sedate hour, he hugged Cory, and they went to bed.

Friday
1:00 am

He woke up freezing a few hours later. Cory had left the windows and the balcony door open. The temperature had dropped forty degrees, and the breeze was coming directly from Hudson Bay. And he was in his briefs.

He closed the door, but one of the windows was stuck.

"Cory?" He patted Cory; he was toasty warm as usual. It was like sharing a bed with a heater. Which could be very nice at times. "Cory."

Cory slept on. He went rummaging for something warm to put on. He found a pair of sweatpants and a t-shirt, but he was still cold.

He tried to close the window again; he saw a light flash on and off. He wasn't sure where it was located.

"Cory?" Totally inert.

He went onto the balcony and started shivering, but there was a bright flash of light from the barn and a noise. It was country quiet or he would never have heard it.

He kept watching. The barn area was illuminated by two lights on poles and a light over the main door. The ends of the barn were in darkness, but he thought he saw a shadow moving.

He kept watching. He heard a horse whinny or shriek or whatever sound horses make when they're scared and upset, following by banging and crashing.

That went on for a minute or two, and then a dark horse shape ran out of the side door of the barn and galloped away.

"Cory!"

"What? Gabe?"

"Get up! Something's going on at the barn."

"What?"

"No idea. Hurry up!"

Cory was a man of action and had reflexes like an uber-cheetah. When he was fully awake. Rouse him from a slumber and not so much.

He ran out of the bedroom and down the side stairs which led to the library. He shot through Hugh's office and out the door.

He was wearing sandals, and it was freezing. It was hard to run in sandals.

He was almost there when he saw a shape heading in the same direction.

"Hugh?"

Hugh turned. "Gabriel? What are you doing out here?"

"Something's going on at the barn."

"I'll take care of it. You should go back inside."

He didn't want to go back inside. So there. He kept trotting toward the barn and detected another shape running alongside him.

They were within the glow of the barn lights now. She was blonde and middle-aged, and she was fully dressed in jeans, a jacket, and boots which looked quite warm.

Hugh said, "Mrs. Prentice, what's going on?" His face was white from the cold; he was rubbing his hands.

She said, "I don't know, Sir. Dolph and I will check it out and let you know."

Dolph was the blond hulk who had taken care of the horses for Cory. He was looming behind her.

Hugh said, "I want to check on Bucephalus."

Her face was pale, but she smiled at Hugh. "I'm sure he's okay, Sir. The weather's turned; you shouldn't be out here without a coat. You'll catch your death."

"I'm fine, Mrs. Prentice."

They were heading toward the main door. "I saw something that looked like a horse run out of the side door."

They altered course and found the double side doors open

and swaying in the wind.

Hugh said, "What is going on?" He ran down the line of stalls to the one where Bucephalus resided and stopped.

Mrs. Prentice said, "What is it, Mr. Poirier?"

He joined her in looking around Hugh. There was no horse; that much was obvious.

But there was something on the stall floor. The light was bad, and he couldn't make it out.

And then his brain put the blobs of color and shadow together into a coherent whole.

"Shit!" He looked away. "Is he dead?"

Which was stupid. It was hard to go on living without a face. He took another glance. The blood had splattered the walls of the stall. But maybe there was a face under all that blood?

It wasn't likely. *Yet who would have thought the old man to have had so much blood in him?*"

He pulled out his phone and dialed 911.

He told the lady that he needed an ambulance, and the police should come too.

Hugh shook himself. "Where is Bucephalus?"

Which wasn't the most urgent matter, but Hugh was probably in shock. He turned away from the bloody stall and went outside calling for his horse.

Mrs. Prentice remained. She said, "Go help him, Dolph."

But Dolph was currently being very sick in the next stall.

Mrs. Prentice said, "Do that outside!"

He said, "All that blood, Momma."

"Well, go outside in the fresh air and help Mr. Poirier look for Bucephalus. He doesn't have a flashlight."

Dolph nodded.

Mrs. Prentice said, "I'm Hilda Prentice, farm manager."

"Gabe Bergeron."

She nodded. "Mr. Corentin's friend. Do you know who this poor soul is, Mr. Bergeron?"

The body was lying supine with the arms flung out. The right arm was closest to them. He knelt, being careful to touch nothing. "There's a ring."

Mrs. Prentice had a flashlight.

It was a signet ring and looked very like the one that Craig Shaw had been wearing earlier.

"I think it's Craig Shaw. The body size is right. And the ring looks like his."

Mrs. Prentice nodded. "I saw him with Mr. Poirier...riding like a fool." She shuddered. "Poor man."

Cory yelled, "Gabe!"

"In here!"

Cory was awake now. "Gabe? Bucephalus?"

"No idea. Gone when we got here. I called 911."

Cory patted his shoulder and looked at the body. He had his own flashlight.

"See the ring."

"Shit! Craig Shaw? What the Hell is he doing here?"

"Excellent question, Mr. Poirier."

Cory said, "Bucephalus did this?"

Mrs. Prentice said, "It looks like it, Sir."

"Where is he?"

She said, "Mr. Poirier and Dolph are looking for him."

Cory said, "Are you okay to stay with the body, Mrs. Prentice?"

She nodded. "Yes, Sir. I'll make sure no one touches anything."

"Thank you, Mrs. Prentice. Gabe, help me look for Dad."

"Sure." Mrs. Prentice handed him her flashlight. "Thanks."

And he and Cory ran out into the wild night looking for a man looking for a horse. Well, two men.

"Which way, Cory?"

"No idea." And then they saw a tiny circle of light bouncing in the distance.

They trotted in that direction, but he fell behind because of the whole improper footwear thing. He followed Cory into a grove of trees and promptly tripped and lost a sandal.

He found it. "Cory? Cory!"

No Cory. He went deeper into the grove of trees which were thrashing in the northerly gale; leaves and sticks were whirling around him.

He almost missed the van.

It was parked on a narrow, paved road that ran behind the barn. It was empty, but he flashed his light about in a circle.

And he spotted a lump. It was probably a rock. There were rocks poking out of the ground all over.

It was a very human shaped rock.

"Cory!"

He stepped closer. He should just go find Cory and let him deal with whatever this was. Cory was the FBI agent after all.

He aimed the flashlight at the body. The guy's eyes were open, but that wasn't a good thing. "Shit! Cory!"

He was scruffy looking and middle-aged and had a tattoo on his neck.

He also had a pistol with a silencer and a lot of red wetness on his chest and stomach.

"Damn it, Cory! Where are you?"

And then he remembered he had his phone. He called. He didn't hear Cory's phone ringing, but Cory answered.

"What?"

"I found another body."

Cory took a moment. "Say again?"

"I found another body. This one doesn't look horse related. But what do I know? But the holes in his chest look smallish and not hoof sized. Or like a bite mark. But again I'm not a horse person and...."

"Gabe."

"Yes, Cory?"

"Tell me where you are."

"Near the van."

"What freaking van, Bergeron?"

"The one parked on the road behind the barn."

"Okay. Stay where you are. Don't touch anything."

"Roger. Will do. Over and out."

He had to hold it together. He remembered he was cold. He'd be a withered, freeze-dried husk in another half hour or so.

He walked away from the body toward a tree. He would

shelter behind said tree until Cory found him.

And then he spotted what looked remarkably like another person-shaped lump.

"Shit! Shit! Shit!"

He aimed his flashlight. A slender, young guy with a blond beard and lots of teeth was lying beneath the tree. He also had a hole in his chest, but it appeared smaller and there was less of the red wetness.

He had a knife. And not just any knife either.

He called Cory again. He heard Cory's phone ring this time.

"I'm coming, Bergeron."

"I found another one."

Friday
6:00 am

The deputies and officers of the Loudoun County Sheriff's Office were suspicious of him.

He could hardly blame them for that, but they were also deeply unhappy about his lack of cooperation which wasn't fair since he was cooperating his little heart out.

He just didn't know anything even if he had found bodies strewn all over the Poirier estate.

Well, in the barn area.

He had answered the same questions over and over.

Which he could understand; a double homicide or possibly a triple homicide appeared to be a rare event in Loudoun County; a one off.

If Craig Shaw's death wasn't really a horsicide? An equinicide? If someone had tossed Craig under the flailing hooves of Bucephalus?

Which was a stupid name. Even if the horse supposedly bore a striking resemblance to Alexander the Great's horse.

He probably shouldn't have told the first deputy on the scene, a giant of a man, that the knife was a Fairbairn–Sykes fighting knife; a double-edged dagger first issued to British Commandos and the SAS during World War II.

And it really hadn't helped when he tried to explain that he knew about it only because Yuri Corzo, a Russian-Cuban spy, had tried to kill him with one some years ago. He hadn't told them about the Cabrera paintings; even he knew that it would just confuse them more.

He was exhausted and cold, and his mental processes were at a low ebb.

He was sitting in the farm office which was on a mezzanine level of the barn.

Detective Sanders, who seemed to be in charge of the investigation, said, "The major will want to talk to you. Hell, the sheriff will probably come."

He had already talked to a great many people. Their names and ranks had all melted into a sludge at the bottom of his brain.

The one constant was the detective. Sanders was looking from him to a photo of the Fairbairn–Sykes knife.

Sanders smiled at him. "Tell me again about the knife."

He was too tired. "Yuri Corzo. Spy. Cuba. Cabrera paintings."

"What Cabrera paintings?"

"Yuri wanted them. He didn't get them."

Sanders had about five years and a few inches on him. He looked remarkably fresh and was still wearing his suit jacket.

He had a round face with buzzed, blond hair except for a longer patch on the top of his head. His eyebrows were also blond and straggly. He had prominent ears but an average nose.

His mouth was always smiling even when the hazel eyes weren't.

Sanders pulled out photos of the two victims who still had faces.

"I'm sorry, Detective. If I knew anything, I'd tell you. Really. I don't know either of the guys. I barely know Craig Shaw. I met him two days ago. If it was Shaw? Was it Shaw?"

Sanders didn't want to answer, but he made a head motion that might be construed as a nod.

"So what happened to Shaw? Did Bucephalus trample him to death."

Sanders had a little twinkle in his eyes and some dimples that matched up to his smile as he said the name. "Bucephalus."

"It's a silly name, isn't it? Alexander the Great or not."

He knew they'd found the horse after half the deputies in

the county had scoured the fields for him. "Did he have blood on his hooves? And fetlocks? Is fetlock the right word?"

Sanders didn't answer. He made a note and looked up and smiled again. "You're staying here, Mr. Bergeron."

It wasn't a question. "Yes. We were supposed to go home on Saturday. What day is this? Friday? Right, Friday."

"You and Mr. Cory Poirier? And home is in DC?"

"Yes, 23rd Street, NW. Cory's condo. But I work in Philadelphia and have an apartment there. But I'm on a sort of vacation, so I don't have to go into the office on Monday."

He had already given the detective his address in Philly and told him all about Garst, Bauer & Hartmann. Well, not all; that would take days...weeks.

"And you and Mr. Cory Poirier are...together?"

"Two years, almost three."

"And he's FBI?" Sanders smiled; his voice had a dubious tone.

"He is. You can check. Danielle Elkins is his boss."

Sanders made another note and then looked at him.. It wasn't like Vonda's intimidating stare. The smile should have softened it, but somehow his was colder and more clinical.

"After the patrol deputies secured the scene, they called in the patrol supervisor. He went up to the house, and the only person there was Mrs. Poirier?"

"Laura. Right. And?"

"Where were the other son and the daughter?"

"Judd and Diane? I don't know."

Sanders leaned in close, put a hand on his shoulder, and upped the wattage on the smile. "Did you speak to them at any time after you left the house?"

"No. I talked to Hugh...and Mrs. Prentice...and her son. Dolph. Not that he said much. And Cory. But nobody else."

Sanders really wanted to know where Judd and Diane had been. He was curious himself.

Sanders leaned back. "And you didn't see anyone else, Gabe?"

"No one."

"What about Poirier...Cory? Was he in the room when you woke up?" Sanders was smiling at the desk like it had just told him a funny story.

"Sure. He was beside me in bed when I woke up."

Sanders flicked his eyes up to his face and down. "And he hadn't been outside?"

"No, Detective. It was freezing outside, and Cory was warm. And deeply asleep. After three years, I would know."

Sanders nodded. He was wearing a wedding band. "But you didn't go out together?"

"No. Cory wasn't waking up fast enough."

"Okay."

"Okay what? I can go?"

"For now. I'll have more questions."

Sanders gave him a card. It read "J. D. Sanders" along with phone numbers and the logo of the Loudoun County Sheriff's Office.

"Sure. Right."

He got to his feet. He was stiff, and his feet were dirty and scratched up. And cold; very, very cold.

He found the stairs down to the ground floor of the barn and wandered around looking for a door.

Hugh, Laura, Diane, Mrs. Prentice, and a guy he didn't know were huddled around Bucephalus' stall; his new stall.

The guy said, "He seems to be okay, but we'll keep an eye on him."

Bucephalus snorted and reared, looking crazier than ever, but Diane whispered to him and rubbed his face, and he calmed down.

Hugh said, "Thank you, Dr. Crain. I appreciate you coming out."

Crain was in his mid-fifties. "Of course, Mr. Poirier. After Hilda called, I knew it might be serious." He smiled at Mrs. Prentice and examined Bucephalus again. "But he seems to have come through the ordeal in good shape."

A lot better than Craig Shaw.

He wandered some more until he found a door.

He stepped out into the chill. The sun was shining. He walked slowly to the house and found Cory in the family room.

"He let you go?"

He may have glared at Cory. "You sound disappointed, Poirier."

Cory smiled. "No, Gabe. Just relieved."

Right.

"But you shouldn't have mentioned the knife."

Which was true.

"What time is it?"

"7:00 am."

"Right. Which way is the bed?"

Cory guided him up the stairs and into his room. He sat on the bed and tossed his sandals. He should wash his feet, but he thought he'd fall over if he tried to do that.

Cory said, "What's going through that brain? I hear the hamster wheels spinning."

"Do not! All my hamsters are exhausted....not that I have hamsters anyway. I was just wondering about the blood bath...the sequence of it? I mean who are the other two guys? And what was Shaw doing here? After midnight? They found his car, right?"

Cory looked tired too. "On the county road. He must have walked."

"But why?"

"No idea. Go to bed, Gabe."

"An excellent idea, Corentin. Don't hit me."

Cory smiled. "Never."

And then Cory slugged him, but he was too tired to register the blow; well, his arm hurt a bit, and there would be a bruise.

Cory was trying to be stoic and flinty-hard and fearless, but he was worried about Hugh and the family. Who wouldn't be?

But Hugh hadn't tossed Shaw to the horse or shot/stabbed a pair of strangers. Why would he?

He was pondering that when sleep took him.

Friday
3:00 pm

He woke up alone and totally confused as to when or where he was. He looked around the room. He saw a team photo with Cory in the middle.

Right. He was in Cory's room in the Poirier house. Not that it looked much like Cory, but he had moved out years ago.

He was still groggy. What time was it? After three. He was starving. He looked out the balcony door; a patrol car was parked at the barn.

His feet and legs were filthy and scratched up. He looked in the bureau mirror; he was scary. He needed to shave, shampoo, and stand in a hot shower for a long time. And even then.

He grabbed a change of clothes and peeped out Cory's door. The bathroom was diagonally across the hall. He didn't see or hear anyone.

He sauntered across. He had a bad taste in his mouth so he brushed his teeth first. He washed his face and shaved. He looked better but still like he was dead, and rigor was just passing off.

His eyes were a faded gray today; sometimes they were bluish. He needed a haircut. He flexed his muscles. His biceps weren't bad, but he would never have six-pack abdominals.

And he would never have Cory's muscles.

He didn't want to think about all the dead bodies, but images kept popping up in his head.

He got into the shower and cranked up the hot water.

There was a knock on the bathroom door.

He said, "Occupied."

He grabbed a towel just as a lady opened the door. She had a round, rosy face set upon a round body. Her hair was dark and trimmed into a round ball. She was wearing an apron and rubber gloves.

She said, "Oh!" She didn't look away. "I'm really sorry, Sir. I'm Mrs. Foote, the housekeeper? I didn't know anyone was in here."

He wrapped the towel about his loins. "I'm taking a shower."

She smiled. "I can see that, Sir. Would you be Mr. Bergeron?"

"I would." He gazed at her. "I'd like to finish my shower."

She giggled. "Of course, you would. Silly me. I'm running late cleaning this place...with all the deputies running in and out and asking fool questions...."

"Mrs. Foote?"

"Yes, Mr. Bergeron?"

"Could you step out? And close the door?"

She giggled some more. "Of course. Terribly sorry, Sir."

And she slowly withdrew after having memorized the contours of his body.

He finished his shower and got completely dressed before exiting the bathroom, but Mrs. Foote had vanished.

He descended the side stairs which were right outside Cory's room and headed for the voices coming from the kitchen.

The Poirier family was assembled in the solarium.

Cory said, "Join us, Gabe." He looked perfect; no dark circles under his Aegean eyes.

Hugh and Laura didn't look well. Laura smiled and started to get up. "You must be hungry, Gabriel?"

Diane said, "Please sit down, Mother. I'll get him something."

Judd and Cory smiled. Judd said, "Let me do that. We don't want to poison the poor man after the night he's had."

Diane glared at her brother. "I can make toast. Or cereal." She opened the refrigerator. "I could make a nice sandwich."

Judd hugged his sister. "You're tired too. You should sit down, Diane. I'll take care of Gabe."

He looked around. "So how is Bucephalus?"

Laura said, "I was so worried about him, Gabriel."

Diane said, "He's fine. He's a trooper."

Right. He was sort of a pet, and they loved him. A large pet with hooves of death. He would never be a horse person.

"I'm glad." Cory was looking at him. He may have raised an eyebrow.

Cory burrowed into his coffee cup to hide the smile.

"Is there more coffee by the way?"

Judd poured him a cup.

He sipped. "So Detective Sanders has gone?"

Cory said, "For the moment."

Laura said, "He isn't coming back, is he, Corentin?"

"I'm sure he is."

She was perplexed. "But we don't know those men...those poor men. Do we, Hubert?"

Hugh shook his head.

She said, "Could they have been thieves? And as for Shaw, well, he should never have scared Bucephalus. That was just a tragic accident."

He said, "Is there anything valuable in the barn?"

Diane said, "Bucephalus."

How much did a stallion go for? "He's a thoroughbred?"

There was a silence, nay a shocked gasp, and then they all glared at him. Well, Cory didn't; Cory looked embarrassed. Laura wasn't smiling for once.

Cory said, "Yes, he's a thoroughbred, Gabe."

He had the feeling that Laura would have been less offended if he'd suggested that her mother had spent her youth as a pole dancer at a Tijuana strip club rather than question the lineage of Bucephalus.

"I'm sorry. One horse looks very much like another to me."

Which didn't make things better. He was going to be ejected from the farm and banished for life.

Which might not be a bad thing.

"But why did Shaw come here? After midnight? To the barn?"

They all looked at the table. Even Cory. And then Hugh glared at him.

Judd gave him a ham sandwich. It wasn't bad, but it tasted funny. He didn't look inside, but he could see funny creamy stuff with funny dark bits oozing out; the funny stuff was probably meant to make it taste better?

He ate it anyway.

Laura was looking forlorn. Which he could totally understand. Hugh took her upstairs.

The sun broke through the clouds; the wind wasn't quite so fierce. Cory said, "Let's go for a ride."

He looked at Cory and snorted.

Cory laughed at him. "Judd? Diane?"

But they declined.

He said, "You go, Cory. I'll find something to do. TV. Or take a nap."

Cory said, "Are you sure you don't mind?"

"No, of course not. You love to ride. Go." He wanted to tell him not to ride Bucephalus, but that might be counter-productive.

"Okay. If you're sure."

Cory ran upstairs and came clumping down in boots and sauntered off toward the barn.

He looked at Diane. "He won't ride Bucephalus, will he?"

"No, I'm sure he won't." She was looking at him funny, but he wasn't sure why, and then she got up. "I think I'll join him after all."

"Good? I'm sure he'll like the company." Had he done something? He drank more coffee to wash away the lingering oily taste of the funny white stuff.

He looked across the table at Judd. "Don't mind me if you want to go riding, Judd?"

"No! I never liked riding that much. I'm not like Diane. Or Cory."

"Are you staying on?"

He nodded. "Until Sunday. I called Samantha."

"How is she?"

Judd said, "She's doing well for the most part...." And then he stopped.

"Is there a problem? I don't mean to be nosy." He said that with a perfectly straight face.

Judd smiled a fake smile worthy of Laura. "No problems, Gabe."

"Good. Glad to hear it. Want to watch some TV?"

And they went into the family room. Judd said he didn't care what they watched, but the TV came to life with a football game in progress.

Which Judd wanted to see.

He watched a good five minutes of it. "So, when did you realize something was wrong last night, Judd?"

Judd glanced at him. "When I saw all the cars and flashing lights."

"And then you went outside looking for Bucephalus?"

"No, I didn't know he was missing. Until Dad came back to get a coat."

He didn't think Judd was telling him the truth. Or not the whole truth. Where had he been when the officer had checked on the house? And where had Diane been?

They watched another five minutes of football in which nothing happened as far as he could tell. He sighed.

Judd said, "We can change the channel?"

"No. it's fine. So is your grandmother still furious with you?"

Judd looked at him; the gaze was short on the milk of human kindness. "What makes you think that she's angry with me?"

"Well, she called you into the family room for a confab."

"I remember, Bergeron."

"And I'm guessing it was to demand that you become CEO of Holcomb in lieu of Cory or your father." Judd stared at him. "Since Cory had refused her, and she's not keen on your father?"

Judd got up and walked out of the family room.

He sat and watched large men in tight pants ram their

helmeted heads together...for thirty seconds...and then Judd came back.

"What makes you think I turned her down?"

"I don't...."

Judd was a slender, vertical cauldron of fury. "Maybe I said yes, and maybe I'll be the best CEO the company has ever had!"

"Right. I'm sure you could be."

"Damn right."

"But is that what you want?

"What I want is of no importance."

He smiled his very best smile. "Don't let Josephine put words in your mouth, Judd. What you want is the only thing that matters...you and Samantha. Right?"

Judd nodded. "But I could do it."

He didn't think that CEO was an entry level position, but he wasn't going to say that. "Have you told Samantha yet?"

"You don't think I could. Nobody does."

"I'm sure you could learn to do it."

Judd said, "If Cory could do it, then I certainly could!"

And Judd exited again.

He turned off the TV and had a nice nap.

Saturday
11:00 am

Cory had gone off riding again. Which was fine. He wanted Cory to enjoy himself and not think about his parents.

It was the fifth day of October and a brisk fifty degrees. Autumn had finally found its autumnity, and he was glad he'd packed long-sleeved shirts and a jacket.

He hadn't seen Diane at all, and Judd had gone off with Hugh and Laura after breakfast; shopping or something. Laura had asked if he wanted to go along, but Hugh's frown had made it plain that he should say no.

So now he was wandering lonely as a cloud about the estate.

There were three cottages in a grove of trees southwest of the main house, just north of the barn area.

He had been told that the first one belonged to Mrs. Villeneuve. He knocked on her door.

She opened the door smiling, which seemed to be her default state. She smoothed her long, white-blonde hair; she was wearing a fluffy, black sweater over a deep-red dress.

"Mr. Gabriel! Come in, come in. How are you? After all the...unpleasantness?"

"Fine. Well, not too bad. Three bodies, Mrs. Villeneuve!"

"I know! *Incroyable! Quelle horreur!*"

"It was a shock."

She sat him at her butcher block kitchen table, poured a cup of coffee and sliced a wedge of chocolate cake. She was obviously a wonderful person; the salt of the earth.

"Of course. Mr. and Mrs. Poirier are shaken. It is obvious." She nodded to herself. "And the giant, black horse killed the poor Mr. Shaw?"

"It looks like it. He certainly stomped on him."

She shuddered appreciatively.

"Did Detective Sanders talk to you?"

"He did, but I could not help him."

"You didn't recognize the other two men?"

"Strangers, Mr. Gabriel. What were they doing here?"

He said, "I'm sure the detective will find out."

"Perhaps."

"You don't think so?"

She frowned. "Who can say?"

"Did you see those men arrive? Or maybe hear the van?"

She shook her head vigorously. "Nothing. Not last night."

He smiled. "But other nights?"

She shrugged. "There are things going on here...secret things, I think."

He smiled at her, "What kind of secret things?"

She looked out her window at the little cottages next to hers. "I shouldn't say, Mr. Gabriel."

"Please call me Gabriel or just Gabe, Mrs. Villeneuve."

"Then I am Madeleine."

"Good. So can't you give me a hint, Madeleine?"

She shook her head vigorously, but she looked at the cottages again.

He smiled. "So who lives in the closest cottage?"

"Mrs. Foote." She frowned. "But you should not go there, Gabriel."

"Why is that?"

"She likes handsome, young men. Too much."

So the bathroom invasion hadn't been accidental. "Right. And the far cottage? Mrs. Prentice?"

She nodded. "And that son, Dolph. And the poor husband, of course. He doesn't have long."

"And should I visit Mrs. Prentice?"

"She will tell you nothing, Gabriel. And don't eat any of her food. If she should offer. Which she won't."

She looked at him. "Mrs. Poirier told me that they were lunching in Middleburg today and not to bother with anything, but what will you and Mr. Corentin do for lunch?"

"We're going out too, Madeleine." It was an idea.

"But I could make you something, Gabriel?"

"Thanks, but we're good." He finished his cake. "Thank you, Madeleine. It's been a pleasure."

"For me too, Gabriel."

And she smiled him out of her cottage.

He gave Mrs. Foote's lair a wide berth and knocked on the door of the third cottage, which was the closest to the barn.

No one came to the door, and he was about to stroll away when he saw Mrs. Prentice walking toward him.

"Good morning, Mrs. Prentice."

Seen in the light of day, she had blonde hair just long enough to reach the collar of a gray, padded vest. A red and black, plaid work shirt covered her arms.

She had tiny, blue eyes, a square face, and a thin-lipped mouth. The mouth turned down at the corners; asymmetrically. The left hook was a lot deeper than the right.

She looked him over. "Good morning, Mr. Bergeron."

She didn't smile; he was willing to wager a handsome sum that she hadn't smiled in the last decade. If he wagered.

"How is Bucephalus?"

She said, "Better than I would have expected."

He smiled his best smile. It bounced off her Kevlar face, but he was undeterred. "Did you know either of the dead guys?"

"No, Sir." She stuck out her chin. "As I told, Detective Sanders."

"What about your son, Dolph?"

The chin went up an inch. She gave him the same icy, determined look she probably gave to injured horses that needed to be put down.

"Dolph answered the detective's questions."

And wasn't about to answer his.

As she opened her door, a beat up pick-up coughed and wheezed to a stop on the gravel lane that connected the cottages to the paved farm road.

A young guy slid out of the truck. He might be twenty, and he was mostly hair. He had his shaggy, brown locks crammed into a red baseball cap with a frayed brim; a bushy beard reached his chest. Shorn, he might weigh one thirty.

He smiled at Mrs. Prentice. "Dolph?"

She said, "He has work to do, Bennie, so you get back into your truck...."

But the door opened, and Dolph moved his mother out of the way with his bulk. He was blond with red cheeks like someone who worked outside. He was tall and broad, neither fat nor muscled; unformed like a lump of dough that was never going to rise.

He had her eyes and mouth, and yet looked nothing like her.

"Dolph! I need you here."

He shook his head and climbed into Bennie's truck. Bennie scurried to catch up. They took off.

The door to the cottage was still open, and a voice from inside said, "Hilda?"

She turned. "Coming, Jack."

"Where's Dolph?"

"Gone off."

"But I want to get into my chair, Hilda."

"Well, I can't lift you!"

"I'm sorry, Hilda."

The resignation convinced him. "Maybe I could help, Mrs. Prentice?"

She turned. "You?"

"I'm stronger than I look."

She shook her head, but Jack said, "Who is it, Hilda?"

She marched across the living room. He may have followed on cat's paws.

The space was more hospital room than bedroom. A man, who had been large, was lying in bed in a graying t-shirt and pajama bottoms; he was emaciated. The wheelchair was beside the bed.

Hilda turned to glare at him, but Jack was looking at her and didn't appear to see him. "Is he still here?"

He smiled. Jack had snow white hair and a gaunt, pallid face with sunken cheeks. He was old but not as old as he looked. "Yes, I'm here. I'm Gabriel Bergeron. I'm visiting with Cory...Corentin."

Jack smiled. "I don't see so well anymore, Sir. And how is Mr. Corentin? Still with the FBI?"

"He is. He loves it. Do you want to get into your chair? I think we can manage it?"

"That would be very kind, Mr. Bergeron." He smiled in Hilda's direction. "Wouldn't it, Hilda?"

Hilda would rather have had a leper with AIDS touch her husband. "Dolph will be back soon enough."

Jack said, "Did he go off with Turtle? Tell him to come see me if he comes back."

Hilda closed her eyes and took a breath.

He said, "He went with Bennie...with the beard."

Jack laughed. His eyes were the only part of him that still looked alive. "Boy is mostly fur. He was hairy by the time he turned eleven."

Jack tried to lever himself up, but he had no strength. Hilda grabbed his legs and swung them over the side of the bed and rolled the wheelchair closer.

She looked at him. "If you're going to help, Mr. Bergeron, now would be the time."

He put an arm around Jack and helped him get his torso vertical, and then he lifted and guided his body into the chair as Hilda handled the legs.

It wasn't that hard, but Hilda was on the petite side and moved stiffly.

Jack said, "Thank you...Mr. Bergeron...just have to get out of that bed...for a bit."

"You're welcome, Mr. Prentice."

Jack was tired out from the effort, but he tried to smile.

Hilda said, "Thank you, Mr. Bergeron. I can handle things from here."

Jack said, "Terrible thing...about those men...at the barn...."

Hilda gave Jack a look. "Don't worry yourself about that, Jack."

And he subsided and closed his eyes.

She herded this Bergeron guy to the door.

"I am grateful, Mr. Bergeron. He doesn't have long."

"I'm so sorry, Mrs. Prentice."

She nodded. "The doctor says he could go at any time. But now I have to get him some lunch, which he won't eat, and there's so much work to do."

And she helped him out the door and slammed it harder than was actually necessary.

Well, he could tell when he wasn't welcome. But he hadn't done anything? He resumed wandering.

Saturday Noon

The barn was directly ahead, but he wasn't sure he wanted to revisit the scene of the crime.

But then he saw Diane walking out the main door with Bucephalus plodding menacingly behind her.

Well, the horse was just walking, but still.

He waved. She looked exhausted; she frowned at him.

He smiled his very best smile. "Is it safe?" He pointed at the enormous horse.

She laughed. "You can come closer, Gabe. He's over the shock." She patted the giant animal. "Back to his old, sweet self."

Diane's powers of observation were sadly lacking. Bucephalus was in no way sweet.

But he did get a little closer. "Good." There was a van with "Crain Veterinary" on the side. "The vet came back."

Diane nodded as she walked Bucephalus down the lane.

And Dr. Crain popped out of the barn. "I'll be going now, Diane."

She smiled and yelled back to him. "Thanks for checking on him again. This is Gabe Bergeron."

Crain said, "Yes, I remember...terrible business."

He nodded as Diane and Bucephalus walked on. "Yes, it was. So any thoughts on how it could have happened?"

Dr. Crain shook his head. "I didn't know the man, but Mr. Poirier said he knew horses so I can't imagine."

"So Bucephalus isn't...." He didn't think he should refer to the horse as homicidal. "...flighty? Easily spooked? Likely to lash out?"

Dr. Crain checked that Diane was out of earshot. "What do you know about horses, Mr. Bergeron?"

"Nothing."

Crain smiled. He had an oval face with a salt and pepper beard buzzed like the hair on his head. Which was receding fast. He had black-rimmed glasses that were a little too large for his face, but he had a nice smile and kindly blue eyes.

"Any horse can be spooked, Mr. Bergeron."

"But is Bucephalus especially susceptible?"

Crain lost the smile. "Why are you asking?"

"Just curious."

"Are you with the FBI?"

He laughed. "No! They wouldn't let me within a city block of the building. Why?"

"Well, you're with Cory...and the questions...."

"You know Cory?"

"Of course. A fine horseman though not as good as his sister. I've cared for the Poirier horses for years."

Diane was heading back.

Crain said, "Well, I have to be going."

"Sure. So why was everyone so concerned about him?" He pointed at the giant animal bearing down on them.

"Horses are very delicate, Mr. Bergeron. I know they don't look it, but they are. And Bucephalus is very valuable as well as beloved."

"How valuable?"

Crain frowned.

"Can you take a guess, Doctor?"

"Well, if I had to guess...low six figures." He smiled. "But they would never sell him."

"Right." Which was very interesting.

And Dr. Crain got into his van and drove about fifty feet and stopped at the Prentice cottage. He got out and knocked on Hilda's door.

She let Dr. Crain in. She looked at the barn and gave him a

fresh glare. He smiled and waved at her. She made a feeble waving motion before she ducked back inside and slammed her door again.

He waited for Diane and followed her and Bucephalus into the barn.

He waited until the horse was in his new stall.

"So what do you think happened? With Shaw, I mean?"

She shook her head, not looking at him. "I have no idea. Shaw was comfortable with horses and sort of knowledgeable. Even if he'd gone into Ceph's stall, it should have been okay."

Ceph snorted; a large, blue eye was tracking the approach of this Bergeron guy.

He smiled at the horse. Which didn't seem to have any effect. "Right."

Diane said, "You've never ridden?"

"On a horse? No!"

She smiled. "I could teach you. You'd enjoy it."

It was amazing that she thought that. He suppressed a derisive snort. "Thanks, but no."

"You could ride with Cory?"

"As tempting as that is, I'll pass."

She smiled again. She was tall and robust in her boots and jeans and sweater. Her dark hair was parted in the middle; she had pulled it back into a ponytail. She was quite attractive if not classically pretty. She was certainly three dimensional.

"Did you go riding with Shaw?" She closed her eyes, and gripped the stall door as if she needed to steady herself. "Are you okay, Diane?"

"Fine." Bucephalus snorted and shook his head. "Easy, Ceph. It's okay."

Still not looking at him, she said, "Why would you think I went riding with him?"

"Well, he went riding with Hugh so I thought it wasn't impossible? Did he make a pass at you?"

She glared at him. He should learn to count to twenty before asking questions. "I'm sorry, Diane."

"No, you didn't do anything. Shaw was a womanizer, but that word is inadequate to define his level of sleaze."

Shit. "I'm sorry, Diane."

"No, I let him know how I felt about him. Maybe, I shouldn't have with the company situation, but I couldn't help it, Gabe."

"Of course, you couldn't."

They walked out of the barn. It was on the tip of his tongue to ask if she'd told Hugh, or maybe Judd or Cory, but that would imply that she couldn't take care of herself and needed a male family member to fight her battles.

But was someone like Shaw likely to take no for an answer? But it didn't make any sense coming to the barn after midnight; Diane wasn't going to be there.

And Shaw couldn't steal Bucephalus in a Porsche.

They were at the side of the barn close to where the two bodies had been. "Did Sanders show you pictures of the two guys?"

"He did, but I didn't recognize them."

She was staring at a tree that didn't look all that fascinating. "But you aren't sure now?"

She smiled at him. "I can understand what Cory says about you. The younger guy, the one with the scraggly beard? He seemed sort of familiar, but I can't place him."

"Well, maybe it will come to you. And what has Cory been saying about me?"

She laughed. "Nothing bad."

"Right. But what? Exactly?"

"Here he comes. You can ask him yourself."

She waved at Cory and then got into her car and drove off heading toward the county road.

Cory was riding up on a black stallion. Well, a black horse with an as yet unspecified undercarriage.

He looked very nice; Cory, not the horse.

"Gabe."

"Hi. So what have you been saying about me to Diane?"

"What?"

"Never mind. So how about you shower, and we get lunch? Somewhere off farm?"

Cory got down from the horse. "Sounds good. I have to take care of Rhythm, and then I'll shower."

"Sounds like a plan."

And Cory did the stuff he needed to do for Rhythm, and then they walked to the house.

"Where's everybody?"

"Judd and your parents went shopping. Diane drove off as you know."

"You talked to her?"

"Sure?"

Cory was looking at the floor. "Is she okay?"

He nodded. "She seems fine?"

Cory smiled at him. "Good. So the house is empty?" Cory smiled at him some more.

"Right. Maybe I need a shower too?"

Cory said, "A clean mind in a clean body."

He smiled as Cory guided him into the bathroom.

Cory stopped. "Just one thing."

"Which is?"

"Always lock the bathroom door." And he did so.

He helped Cory out of his sweaty things. "Because of Mrs. Foote?"

Cory laughed. "Sorry, if the warning comes a bit too late."

Saturday
1:00 pm

But they didn't get to go off farm for lunch.

They were barely clothed when Detective Sanders came knocking.

This was his first good look at the detective. His smiling face shone brightly with something that looked like puppy dog friendliness. He managed to radiate harmlessness.

He also had freckles on the backs of his hands.

Cory said, "My parents aren't here, Detective."

"And your sister?"

"Not here either."

Sanders nodded. He had traded his suit for khaki pants and a black polo shirt. He smiled. That's fine, Sir, but I do need to talk to them. When do you expect them back?"

"A few hours."

Sanders nodded. "I want to talk to you and Mr. Bergeron."

Cory said, "Of course. Fire away."

Sanders looked shy and deferential. "Alone is better, Mr. Poirier...sorry, Special Agent Poirier."

He was being ejected from the family room. "Roger that."

He went into the kitchen and rummaged around. He made another ham sandwich on crusty, French bread and made coffee. He ate his sandwich and looked for snacks.

There were apples and pears and something in the citrus family, but he couldn't find more of the cookies that Madeleine had given him. Or any baked goods.

He heard Sanders. "Gabe?"

He strolled through the dining room coffee cup in hand. "Here." Sanders beckoned him. "Want some coffee?"

But Sanders shook his head. "Thanks, but I'm good. I have just a few follow-up questions."

Cory's face was totally blank as they passed.

Which meant he was way upset. Shit.

He sat on the sofa as indicated. Sanders pulled a chair closer. He was as tall as Cory but tending toward stockiness.

"Could you go over for me again, Gabe?" He smiled diffidently like he'd forgotten everything he'd been told the previous night.

"What? Finding the bodies and everything?"

"That's right, Gabe."

So he did.

Sanders said, "You woke up because it was cold?"

"Freezing."

"And you heard noises and saw flashes of light? Can you describe them for me?"

He tried, but he wasn't even sure of the sequence now.

Sanders sighed.

"Sorry. So did Bucephalus kill Shaw? I mean it sure looked like he did?"

"The autopsy will tell us."

But "us" didn't include Gabriel Bergeron.

"Have you talked to Dr. Crain?"

Sanders smiled. His answer to almost any question was a smile.

"And Mrs. Villeneuve?"

Big smile. "Any reason I should speak to her, Gabe?"

"Not really. Just that her cottage is close to the barn. Well, so is Mrs. Foote's and the Prentice cottage. But it was very dark. So have you identified the two men?"

"That's ongoing."

Which meant no?

Sanders was gazing at him, all rapt attention. "What do you know about the relationship between Craig Shaw and Diane

Poirier?"

It was universally known that he wasn't quick, but a warning bell clanged inside his brain. This was what had upset Cory.

"He was a business associate of her father's."

Sanders' hazel eyes bored in. "And that's all?"

If Sanders was asking the question, he already knew the answer or suspected it. But it wasn't his place to confirm or deny.

He smiled at the detective. "Well, he's been here to the farm, but I don't know if they even spoke. This is my first time here, and I just met Shaw myself."

Sanders leaned in. "If you know something, you should tell me, Gabe. It's best to get everything out into the open from the get-go."

"Right. I couldn't agree more, but I don't know anything."

"Did you like Shaw?"

"Nope."

"Why not?"

"He was...expansive."

"Sorry?" Sanders smiled at his obtuseness, but his voice sharpened. "What does that mean, Gabe?"

"You sound like Vonda."

"Vonda?"

"Vonda Golczewski. She's a detective with the Philadelphia Police."

"And you know her? How?"

"We're sort of friends, but we weren't at first. The first time we met, I don't think she liked me...."

Sanders smiled as if that was unbelievable.

"And she wasn't sure I was telling her the truth about Roy and Dale smashing my knuckles with a bricklayer's hammer, but she came around after she got to know me better."

"Roy and Dale?"

"They were loan shark enforcers...from Chicago....and they had me confused with my half-brother Donnie. They're the largest men I've ever met."

Sanders stopped taking notes and held up his hand. "Stop

talking!"

He tried not to smile.

"What's funny?"

"Vonda has said the very same thing...many times."

Sanders had closed his eyes momentarily, trying to regroup, when his phone rang.

He shook his head, but he answered. "Hi?"

He listened smiling a real smile with dimples. "I can't."

He listened some more. "I have to go. You always say it will only take two seconds, but it never does."

He listened staring at Laura's rug. "Okay, I'll be there. Bye, Babe."

He raised his eyes, and his professional smile reformed. It was remarkable.

"Your wife?" A nod. "Cory talks to me like that when he's working on a case; especially when he's undercover."

Sanders was sorely tempted to ask about Cory's cases, but he resisted.

"Not that I think of myself as his wife. Or his husband...at this point in our relationship...."

Sanders smiled as he held up a hand again. "Why didn't you like Shaw? Was it because of Diane?"

"Nope."

"Sure about that, Gabe?"

"Yep."

Sanders said, "His harassment of Diane Poirier had nothing to do with how you felt about him?"

"Sorry?"

"Are you telling me you don't know about that?"

"No, Sir, I don't."

Sanders circled round and round like a smiling terrier, but there was nothing for him to dig out since he knew nothing about the harassment.

Well, he knew that Diane hated Shaw.

He and Cory watched Sanders stride across the field heading for Mrs. Villeneuve's house. Which was his fault, but if she'd seen something, she should tell the police.

Unless it incriminated Diane. Shit.

He looked at Cory. "What did he ask you?"

"Just went over it all again. To see if I remembered anything significant."

Cory was a big fibber, but he didn't say anything.

"If I tried to hug you, would you punch me?"

Cory glared at him. "Maybe yes, maybe no."

He hugged him anyway.

Saturday
4:00 pm

Hugh and Laura and Judd had come home.

And been interrogated. Neither they nor Sanders looked happy afterwards though the detective kept smiling.

Laura was now on the phone with her mother; not that he was eaves-dropping or anything.

"Yes, Mother. Two men besides Shaw. No, I don't know who they were."

And Josephine had apparently asked for a complete accounting of the men and their deaths before letting Laura go.

Sanders waited in his car for Diane to return. And he spent more time with her than with anyone else. She came out of the family room close to tears.

Cory was considering assaulting a Loudoun County detective so he made sure to stand between them until Sanders finally left.

Laura said, "Such a long day. I think I'll lie down until dinner. Hugh?"

He patted her hand. "I have some calls to make. I'll be up soon."

And he headed for his office as she went upstairs.

Cory was looking at him. "What?"

Cory smiled. "There's a soccer game on TV."

"There's always a soccer game on TV. The sun never sets on soccer. Wait. You want me to watch this soccer game?"

"I want to talk to Diane. Do you mind?"

"Nope."

And Cory went upstairs and found Diane. He watched them walk down the lane heading south toward that stupid barn.

He understood. Cory wanted the full story on this harassment. And Cory didn't quite trust him not to let something slip to Sanders. He totally understood.

He turned on the soccer game. Well, there were three. He wasn't sure which one he was supposed to watch, but he went with the Bundesliga.

Judd came in and flopped down beside him. "Bundesliga? Really, Gabe?"

"I like the Bundesliga, Poirier. Is that a problem?"

Judd held up his hands. "Excuse me!"

They watched, but he couldn't focus. He was too pissed with Cory.

Judd said, "I know where Mrs. Villeneuve hides the cookies."

He smiled at Judd. "Lead on."

They were homemade, and they were divine. They went back to soccer.

Judd was leaning forward as the red team was close to the yellow team's goal. "Samantha's pregnant."

"What?"

"With child. Sperm has found ovum. Conception has occurred."

"Congratulations?" Judd was smiling like an idiot. "That's great! How many months?"

"Four."

He slipped to the door and scanned the horizon from library to foyer to dining room before turning. "And have you told your mother?"

Judd shook his head.

"Well, I can sort of guess why, but you do know that this will not go well for you when she eventually finds out?"

"I am aware."

"Right. So Cory doesn't know either?"

"No. Just you. I had to tell somebody."

"And you aren't afraid that 'somebody' will let it slip?"

"No. Your babbling is deceptive."

"I don't babble, but forget that. Am I to tell Cory?"

"Not yet."

"Why? I don't know, Judd. I guess I can do it, but I don't feel right...." But Judd was smiling at him. "Bastard."

Judd said, "Gabe?"

"Yes?"

"I'm going home tomorrow after lunch."

"Right?"

"Could you let it slip to Mother after I'm gone?"

"Absolutely not, Poirier."

Judd's phone chimed. He looked at it. "I have to take this, Gabe. Hi. What's up?"

A distant whispering.

"No, I can't. I told you." More whispering but louder. "It's not my fault. No, I wouldn't say that it all went to Hell."

The whisperer was pissed. "Look, he was supposed to be reliable. I'm hanging up now."

But he didn't. He looked over at that Bergeron guy with the acute hearing and departed for the outdoors.

He watched Judd walk back and forth in the mild October breeze.

Cory and Diane came downstairs and went to talk to Hugh in his office; Hugh slammed the door in his face. Well, he shut it, but the intent was clear.

And when the chat ended, Hugh and Diane went upstairs, and Cory was pretending that all was well. He dropped onto the sofa next to him. "What's the score, Bergeron?"

"No clue."

Cory tried smiling, but his tense, need-to-kick-somebody's-ass face couldn't relax enough to pull it off. It was his baby sister who was in jeopardy after all.

He just hugged Cory and didn't ask a single question.

At a moment of high drama, or as high as drama ever got with soccer, he said, "Samantha's pregnant. Judd hasn't told your mother, and you can't either."

71

So Cory was looking at him when a truly amazing goal was scored. Cory punched him in the arm.

Which was unnecessary since he got to watch the goal on the replay.

Dinner began as a somber, sober, silent affair.

The stiffness of the upper lips in the room was positively British; the British in the World War II films like "A Bridge Too Far" or "The Dam Busters."

He said, "Baldacci is getting married."

Cory was the only one who had any idea who Baldacci was. "He's a coworker of Gabe's."

Laura struggled womanfully to be polite. "That's nice, Gabriel. Who is he marrying?"

"Carla Wong. I give it two months tops."

Laura said, "You're joking, aren't you, Gabriel?"

"Not a jot. She'll suck him dry. Baldacci will be a dusty, moldering husk before the spring rains. Mark my words."

Cory said, "Have I met Carla?"

"You wouldn't ask that question if you had, Corentin. Poor Baldacci."

Diane was almost smiling. "She can't be that bad, Gabe."

"Bad? She isn't bad, per se, but she has been likened to lichen...on a granite boulder...."

Cory said, "By you."

"Yes, but never in her hearing. In her presence, I tell her she's 'remarkable' which she is, but it really doesn't commit me pro or con."

Cory said, "I have met her! She's pretty."

"She is. I might even go so far as to call her alluring. But Baldacci has always been the ravisher and now he is the ravishee. He will not long survive. And I can't imagine what will happen when he takes Carla home to meet his Italian mother. The mind boggles."

And he kept up a near constant patter about Baldacci and Carla, besmirching their reputations shamelessly, for most of the meal.

"And I'm very much afraid, he's going to ask me to be his

best man."

Cory looked at him. "Gabe."

"Well, he might. Baldacci and I are cubicle neighbors, and that bond runs deep."

After dinner, Cory and Judd and Diane watched golf with Hugh. He drew the line at golf.

He wandered around the house and found Laura talking to Mrs. Villeneuve. They smiled at him.

Laura said, "Will you and Cory be here for lunch tomorrow, Gabriel?"

"We will."

Laura said, "Then we'll be eight for lunch, Mrs. Villeneuve." Laura looked at him. "May I speak to you, Gabriel?" He nodded taken unawares. "Come upstairs with me."

He followed Laura to the master suite; besides a bedroom and a sumptuous bath, there was a sitting room with comfy chairs.

"This is nice."

She smiled. "My sanctuary. Thank you, Gabriel, for telling the story about Mr. Baldacci and Miss Wong. You saved dinner."

"Of course. No problem at all."

There was a display of hats; at least, he thought they were hats. He didn't want to stare, but he couldn't seem to pull his eyes away.

One was tan with a vast, floppy brim with a bilious green butterfly the size of a Cessna lashed on and a matching green band.

A black and white hat had fake lemons and red asters encircling the crown.

Another was a shiny, black umbrella with an enormous velvet bow festooned with black, white, and magenta feathers.

Laura smiled. "Do you like my hats?"

He smiled. There was no way that Laura Loncke Poirier had ever worn these in public?

She said, "These are my favorites from the Spring Races."

"The Spring Races?"

"The Middleburg Spring Races, Gabriel. The steeplechase races...they're held every year. Hubert and I have attended for more years than I care to admit."

But that didn't explain the gruesome headgear?

"There's a contest for the most elaborate, the most glamorous...the most outrageous hat. I won three years ago."

"Congratulations."

"Sit down, Gabriel."

He sat and smiled. And waited.

Laura said, "I know that everyone is upset about how that man treated Diane."

"Shaw?"

She nodded unwilling to say the name.

"They think I don't know, but I do. And they won't tell me, Gabriel, but is Diane in some kind of trouble?"

Shit. "No, I don't think so. Sanders might think Shaw was here to see Diane, but that's on him. I'm sure Diane didn't ask him to come here."

Laura looked scandalized. "Of course, she didn't. He was an awful man, Gabriel. In every way."

"Yes, he was." Or that was the received opinion. Which he didn't doubt so far.

"So Diane will be all right?"

"I think so, but Sanders may come back."

"But why? It was an accident."

But was it? Sanders seemed more focused on Shaw than the other two dead guys whose deaths were definitely not accidental.

Did that mean that he still hadn't identified them? And consequentially had no clue as to what had gone down?

"I don't know if that's true, Laura."

"Corentin says he can't do anything to make Sanders stay away. He says it would only make things worse if he tried to intervene."

"It would."

"But you can."

"Me? Intervene? But how would I do that?"

She smiled. "I'm sure you'll find a way. Promise me you'll help Diane?"

"I'll do whatever I can. Of course, I will."

"Thank you, Gabriel." She frowned. "There is one other

thing."

He couldn't imagine.

"My mother may come to lunch tomorrow. Can you look after Corentin?"

"Sure. Absolutely. Why is she coming?"

Laura shook her head. "Why does she do anything lately? Something to do with Holcomb. I hate the company, Gabriel. I wish it would go bankrupt and vanish from the face of the Earth, but I could never tell Hubert."

He should ask why not, but he was tired, and he was already hip deep in Poirier family problems.

But he had a thought. "Laura?"

She looked at him with eyes that were like Cory's but paler and also far more opaque. "Yes?"

"Do you have a picture of your grandfather, Stephen?"

"Of course, Gabriel. But why?"

"Does Cory look like him?"

She smiled. "Very much."

She walked to a small bookcase and pulled out a leather bound album. "Jordan keeps promising to digitize this for me."

She was turning pages. "Here. This is the best one of him."

Stephen hadn't been as athletic as Cory and didn't have the shoulders or chest, but the faces were very like. Stephen's jawline had been a bit more delicate, but he had been handsome.

The photo had originally been black and white, but it had been colorized? The red of Stephen's hair was suspect, and all the colors had a cartoonish quality.

"His hair was red?" She nodded. "And when was this taken, Laura?"

"1946."

Stephen was sitting in a chair staring at the camera sans smile. He didn't look exactly sad but resigned? Or was he just projecting?

He didn't know.

But the little girl who was sitting in his lap was delighted. She was around three...four?

"Is that your mother?"

Laura smiled. "What did you expect? Horns?"

"Well, not exactly horns...." Horns, fangs, and a forked tail. "She looks very happy."

"She loved her daddy very much."

"Where is your grandmother?"

Laura closed the album. "She wasn't around when the photo was taken."

Right. He thought he should depart.

Laura said, "Please do whatever you can for Diane."

And he went downstairs. He sat beside Cory and watched golf which was more than any man should have to suffer even for true love.

Sunday Noon

Childers and Kennard had come to lunch, but Josephine was a no show. So far. He had his fingers crossed. And kept checking his thumbs for the pricking due to evil this way coming.

Childers, Kennard, and Hugh were heading for Hugh's office.

Childers said, "We have to do something, Poirier. The stock plunged when Shaw's death was reported. Did you see the Friday's closing share price? And it will only be worse on Monday."

Hugh said, "Things will stabilize, Childers."

"Not if you're seen as just an interim figure; a caretaker."

Hugh smiled. "I hope to be more than that."

Kennard said, "But how is your health?"

And then Hugh closed the office door, and he and Cory and Judd and Laura couldn't eavesdrop any longer. Which was disappointing.

Diane had already left for her apartment in DC. She had been teaching history at George Washington for the last year.

Judd hugged his mother. "I'm going, Mother. Samantha is having a few friends over tonight, and I have to help."

Laura smiled. "You mean cook everything."

Judd smiled back. "But I like cooking."

"I know you do. How are the new pants? Do they fit properly? I could have them altered?"

She was tugging at Judd's waistband and checking the fit across his butt. "They're perfect, Mother, and thank you for helping me get them. Tell Dad...well, I don't know what to say. Tell him to forget about Holcomb."

She was still smiling. "He'd never do that, Jordan."

"I know."

Judd hugged Laura again and then gave Cory a glancing pat on the shoulder.

He followed Judd out to his car. "Bye, Gabe."

"Bye. Don't let Josephine talk you into anything."

Judd's head was set upon a long, slender neck in keeping with the rest of his appendages. His dark hair was mounded up on the top of his head but trimmed close on the sides and neck.

And he had dark eyes that could look almost black in a certain light, but when he smiled, as he did now, he looked a little like Cory.

"That's why I'm running away, Gabe."

"Good."

"Is there something else?"

"No. Except have a safe trip. And tell your mother that she will shortly become a grandmother. You should do that soon."

Judd laughed and got into his car, a Chevy Impala, which didn't look up to the journey back to Philadelphia.

He went back inside. Cory was watching TV. It was stock car racing which was worse than golf; much worse.

He sat beside him.

Cory said, "I want to stay until Dad's meeting is finished."

"And what are you going to say to him?"

Cory shook his head. "No idea. He's so stubborn."

He smiled to himself and watched the cars go round and round the track.

The cars were still circling when they heard a voice.

"Laura? Hubert? Are Childers and Kennard here?"

He hugged Cory. "Stay here."

Cory smiled at him. "You expect me to hide from her?"

"I would if I were you. I've got this."

Cory smiled, but he didn't stir from the sofa.

He bounced into the living room and shut the family room door behind him.

Josephine's jacket was scarlet; her dress was white; her heart was black.

"Hello, Mrs. Loncke."

She gazed at him. "I don't want to talk to you, Young Man."

"How will I live with the disappointment." Which he probably shouldn't have said.

"How dare you! Impudent nothing. You're less than nothing...."

Footsteps could be heard pounding down the stairs. Laura popped into the living room behind her mother.

"Mother! I didn't think you were coming."

Josephine spun. "Sorry to disappoint you. I hope I'm still welcome in my daughter's house?"

"Please don't say things like that, Mother. You know that I love you."

Josephine regarded her daughter. "I think you do, Laura." She looked at him. "But why did you let that into your house?"

Laura said, "Because Cory loves him."

Josephine raised her chin and sniffed. "Is that all? Love doesn't last, Laura."

Laura didn't appear able to speak.

Josephine said, "Don't upset yourself. I didn't mean that I don't love you. I do. I gave birth to you after all."

She appeared to think that was an extraordinary act.

Hugh had entered the living room with Childers and Kennard behind him. He said, "It's all right, Laura. I'll talk to your mother."

Josephine looked at him. "You don't look well, Hubert. We need someone young and vital to become CEO."

Childers said, "And you have someone in mind?"

"Jordan."

Childers sniffed himself. "I thought Corentin was the anointed one?"

"Sarcasm is as unattractive in the very old as it is in the very young."

Childers said, "I'm younger than you!"

She waved that aside. "Where is Jordan?"

Laura hesitated so he said, "He left. He had to go home to be with Samantha."

She glared at him. "I'm not speaking to you."

Hugh said, "Jordan has gone. He's not interested in being CEO, Josephine."

She shook her head in amazement. "Why does no one in my family understand sacrifice?"

Childers said, "We need to find someone with experience, Josephine."

Kennard smirked. "Someone like you?"

Josephine said, "Jordan will assume the position of CEO."

Childers laughed. "I'd be much better than some librarian."

Josephine closed with Childers until they were rheumy eye to rheumy eye. "Jordan has Holcomb blood in his veins, and he is infinitely better than you."

Childers said, "You liked me well enough once upon a time. You crossed an ocean to be with me."

This sounded like the beginning of a very, unsavory fairy tale.

Hugh said, "In my office."

Josephine marched past Hugh with Childers behind her.

Kennard was smiling, almost dancing on his stubby legs. "Childers should never have laughed at her grandson."

"You want to be CEO?"

Kennard looked at him as jolly as a hundred St. Nicks. "Only if the stockholders find me worthy."

And Kennard laughed and laughed and did a samba into Hugh's office. He didn't appear to regret Shaw's passing all that much. Had Sanders questioned him? And Childers for that matter?

And what about Josephine? For Cory and Laura's sake, he hoped that Sanders didn't get around to her.

He didn't have long to wait before the meeting broke up, and Josephine departed. Childers and Kennard were right behind her.

He knocked on the family room door. "It's safe to come out. The danger has passed, Corentin."

Cory looked at him. "You will never tell anyone that I hid

from my grandmother."

"Absolutely not!" Unless fodder for amusement was in short supply.

Cory went into Hugh's office. He waited some more. And then Cory came out shaking his head.

Cory hugged his mother. He may have hugged Laura too since she looked like she needed it, and Josephine certainly hadn't done it.

They ran for the SUV and set sail for calmer seas and Cory's condo.

Monday
5:00 am

He was wide awake at a ridiculous hour. Cory was still in slumber land. They had discussed this vacation, such as it was, and agreed that maybe they should go back to work and try again when things were calmer.

He didn't need to be at Union Station until 7:00 am to catch the Acela Express to Philadelphia. He would get into the 30th Street Station by 8:30 am and not be too late for work.

Jennifer Garst Boltukaev was his boss and eventual suzerain of Garst, Bauer & Hartmann, the semi-reputable accounting firm which had the great good fortune to employ him.

His current schedule had him spending Monday through Thursday in Philly, working with rare dedication, and spending his nights in his apartment on Arch Street. Alone, all, all alone.

But on Thursday, he got to take the train back to DC and spend his three-day weekend with Cory.

That is, if Special Agent Corentin Poirier wasn't flying across the country to track down art thieves with his partner, the indomitable Matt Bornheimer.

Cory's eyes were closed, but he said, "I can hear the wheels turning in your head."

"No, you can't. We've discussed this before. All my internal parts mesh silently. I'm getting up."

Cory said, "Are you okay?"

"Sure. Wait. You mean after finding the dead bodies and being in the eye of Hurricane Josephine? Well, no, the eye is calm, and your grandmother is never that."

"Gabe."

"I'm okay. I really wish I hadn't seen Shaw. Really. It was a lot worse than Nemec...visually. But otherwise. What are you doing today?"

"Hoover Building."

"Roger that. Cory?"

"Yes, Gabriel Henri?"

"If there's anything I can do...?"

Cory looked at him. "Like what?"

"Excellent question. But if you think of something, I am but a phone call away. Or a pithy text message."

And he had gotten dressed, eaten a toaster pastry, downed half a pot of coffee, and Cory had dropped him at the station.

He got out of the taxi on South 16th Street in a cold, pouring rain and ran for the door of the Mahr Building.

Keller was on duty at the security station. Keller nodded, looking even more frail than usual. He also looked hungover.

"Good weekend?"

Keller grunted and put his heart into ignoring him.

"Mine was terrible too."

He took the elevator to the eleventh floor.

Dana looked up. Her eyes were circled in black, and the rest of her makeup was thick enough to provide an adequate sunscreen on Mercury. "Are you supposed to be here?"

"Of course. I work here."

She went back to her fashion magazine without a word. Everybody was grumpy today.

His desk was covered with mail; he could just imagine his email inbox. He turned on his computer anyway. He sighed and went to the breakroom and made coffee.

He went back to his desk. Where were Baldacci and Carla? And Jennifer? And Neal?"

He strolled over to fellow accountant Chatterjee's cubicle. "So where is everybody?"

Chatterjee had so far resisted his charms; not that he was trying to seduce the guy. He just wanted to make conversation now and again.

Chatterjee was very dark and looked very young. Large brown eyes examined him. "I don't know."

He had oodles of black hair; wavy and shiny and nice. "Baldacci?"

Chatterjee was focused on his display. "Just late, I think."

And he stood there, but the conversational well was dry. He went back to his cubicle and got to work on his inbox.

"Take one week off and come back to a mountain of junk." Nobody was paying any attention to him. "It's hardly worth it."

And then Baldacci and Carla came in.

"Greetings, fellow cubicle dwellers!"

They glared at him. He was sorry he'd come back, and he was done being cheerful.

"So is the wedding still on?"

Carla had been patting her very black hair which always looked like she had styled it by sticking her finger into an electrical socket. She smoothed her charcoal suit over her ample bosom and adjusted her ruby cravat before favoring him with a glare.

"And why wouldn't it be?"

He smiled. "No reason. I'm sure Baldacci can't wait to marry you." Which was actually true and only sounded snarky.

Baldacci was his height but stockier and getting more so. The hair remaining on his egg-shaped head was as thick and black as his beard. He had brown eyes which were usually mischievous and not quite so murderous as now.

"What's that supposed to mean, Bergeron!"

"Nothing. It's just I've been gone a week, and a lot could have happened?"

Baldacci said, "Nothing happened. Carla and I are very happy."

"I'm glad to hear it. Just this past Saturday, I was telling Cory's parents how lucky you were to be marrying Carla."

Baldacci said, "Cory's parents?"

"Yep. Chez Poirier...on the estate...amid the horses and rolling fields of clover or maybe just grass...in Loudoun County, Virginia."

Carla, focusing on the important bit, said, "What did you say about me, Bergeron?"

"Only good things, Carla."

She was looking at him coldly. "What did you say exactly?"

"I said you were remarkable, and I stand by that. Where's Jennifer?"

Baldacci said, "Meeting with Bauer."

Carla gave him one last soul-searing scan and got to work.

He sighed. That had been fun, but he went back to his four hundred and twenty-three emails.

At some point, Jennifer had entered and taken possession of her office. She was working away.

He thought he should explain his presence; not that she seemed interested.

She was wearing her navy suit which molded nicely to her fullback shoulders. Her long, brown hair was all shiny and bright, but she had taken to mangling her eyebrows again.

After the birth of her second son, she was looking very matronly; not that such a comment would ever pass his lips.

She looked up. "What?"

"I'm back."

She snorted. "And I forgot to order a cake."

Which was just cold. "I was supposed to be on vacation this week."

"So?"

"So I decided to cancel the rest of my vacation, but I don't want to talk about it."

"Good."

"Good? That's it?"

She looked up. "Does the reason affect the firm?"

"I don't see how."

"Good."

And she went back to work.

He stomped back to his cubicle and deleted every last email. So there. He should take an early lunch, but it was only nine-thirty.

He sat and stewed. He got more coffee and hunted for cookies, but the breakroom was bare. He might have to buy his own.

He went back to his cubicle and tried to retrieve the deleted emails. He found out they weren't really deleted after all, and was both sad and relieved about that for a while.

Baldacci said, "Stop sighing, Bergeron."

Carla said, "Or else."

He looked at them. Chatterjee was silent but smiling. He hated them all.

He worked on his emails.

Client Marge had some kind of problem which she failed utterly to explain. She was going to prison one of these days.

He should call her or go see her; he was short his quota of second-hand smoke for the month.

A mighty voice roared, "Bergeron!"

He leaped from his chair and landed in a cat-like crouch.

Jennifer was pointing at him with the phone in her hand.

He straightened his tie and strolled over to her office.

"Shut the door."

"What?"

She stared at him, waving the phone at him like the hammer of Thor.

"You got a phone call? Telemarketers? I'm so sorry, Jennifer. That call blocking registry doesn't work, does it?"

"Shut up, Bergeron."

"Yes, Jennifer."

"The call was from the Loudoun County Sheriff's Office. I've been talking to a detective named Sanders for the last half hour."

"Really? I can't imagine why he called. What did you tell him?"

"He asked me about you. About your character."

"I see."

"What did you do? This time?"

"Nothing."

"He didn't want to tell me what it was about but he finally

admitted it was a homicide investigation."

"Right. And what did you tell him?"

"He asked about Yuri Corzo and the Cabrera paintings, and I told him that you weren't a criminal and had helped the police many times."

He frowned. "Anything else?"

She nodded. "I told him about Nemec and Garth Adams."

Shit. "Right. And what did he say?"

"I don't think he believed me."

"Good."

"Good?"

"Well, I don't want him to think that murders happen wherever I happened to be. He might get suspicious, Jennifer."

She shook her head. "So what happened, Bergeron? Who got murdered?"

"I may have found three bodies."

Jennifer took a deep breath. "Tell me the whole story."

And he did. Well, part of it. Not about Diane.

"So you go to a horse farm in Virginia and just happen to find three bodies."

"Yes. The vacation hadn't been going that well before, but that was a significant downturn."

"But Cory was there with you?"

"Most of the time."

Jennifer was looking worried. "Enough of the time to give you an alibi?"

"Sure. Nothing to worry about." He wasn't sure that Sanders wasn't suspicious of Cory too.

She shook her head and rolled her eyes. "Have you called Max Nagy yet?"

"I don't need a lawyer, Jennifer. Really."

She didn't believe that for a second. "Go back to work. You could have warned me, Gabe."

"Right. I should have. Sorry, but it will be okay."

And then he and Jennifer saw Vonda walk up to Dana.

Jennifer closed her eyes. "You'd better go talk to the detective, Gabe."

"Right."

He gave Vonda his best smile. "Hi, Vonda."

She glared at him. "I just had a phone call, Bergeron."

"Detective Sanders?" She nodded. "He's been a busy boy. Let's go into the conference room."

Baldacci and Carla and all the cubicle dwellers were watching them like prairie dogs mesmerized by a circling eagle.

She took off her rain coat and draped it on a chair.

Detective Vonda Golczewski of the Philadelphia Police Department was just as slender as when they'd first met years earlier. Her black hair was pulled back into a tight bun. She was wearing a dark brown suit, lighter than her large eyes but darker than her cocoa skin. She had accessorized with an emerald green scarf

"Nice scarf."

"Sit down, Bergeron."

"Yes, Vonda. I didn't do anything."

"That's how the craziness always starts, Bergeron! Every time. Tell me about it."

So he did.

"Is that it? What aren't you telling me?"

"That's totally it, Vonda." Except for Diane and Shaw's behavior toward her.

"A triple homicide. Are you involved in investigating this mess?"

"Nope. Cory wouldn't like it."

She looked at him. "How is Poirier coping? The sheriff's office isn't telling him anything?"

"Not a word."

She nodded. "They can't. He's part of it."

"I know. What did Sanders tell you?"

She shook her head. "No way, Bergeron. If it was my case, maybe, but it's not."

"Of course, Vonda. But did he say why he's focused on Shaw's death? Which might have been accidental?"

Vonda frowned at him. "I'll tell you one thing. He said Shaw was murdered."

"What about the other two guys?"

"He didn't say, Bergeron."

"Thanks, Vonda."

She got to her feet. "Try to stay out of this."

"I will. Really."

"If you need anything, call me. I may not be able to help you, but you can ask. I did vouch for you, Bergeron. I told the detective you'd been helpful in the past."

"Thanks again, Vonda, but Sanders will solve the case all by himself, and I won't get involved."

Vonda smiled at him like he had told her he was seeing purple unicorns, and she walked out of the office.

He went back to his cubicle. He spun around and looked at Baldacci and Carla. "I don't want to talk about it."

Baldacci said, "Not again, Bergeron?"

Carla was smiling. "Think how boring this office would be if we had somebody normal sitting in that cubicle."

"Hey! I am normal. Mostly. I don't want to talk about this." Baldacci smiled at him. "No, Harry, I mean it!"

"Just tell us who and where, Gabe? Please?"

Carla said, "Come on, Bergeron. You never know when you might need friends to bail you out."

Which was a good point. "I guess."

Carla and Baldacci rolled their chairs over like killer robots going in for the slaughter. "Cory wanted to go his parents' farm...to check on his father who may or may not be unwell...."

Baldacci said, "And he got shot dead in a hale of bullets?"

Carla smacked Baldacci on the back of the head. "Gabe wouldn't be here. Don't interrupt, Harry."

He glared at Baldacci. "Cory's fine, and his father is fine...well, he wasn't shot! So we went to the Poirier farm in Loudoun County, Virginia. And I was being a perfect house guest...."

Baldacci said, "Get to the blood and guts, Bergeron!"

"And I woke up in the middle of the night and sensed that something was wrong at the barn, which is too fancy to be called a barn...being made of stone with a slate roof...."

They were glaring at him. He may have smiled at them. "And I found three bodies when I got there."

Baldacci just shook his head.

Carla said, "Who were they?"

"One was Craig Shaw, CEO of Holcomb, Inc."

Baldacci was looking confused. Carla said, "Cory's father was CEO there before he retired. And the other two bodies?"

He shrugged.

Baldacci said, "So how did they die?

"One was shot, one was stabbed with a Fairbairn–Sykes commando knife, and Shaw was trampled by a giant horse. And we don't know who the other two guys were. Well, I don't, and I don't think the Sheriff's Office does either."

Carla said, "And they don't suspect you?"

Baldacci said, "Yet?"

"No! They do not! And now I'm going back to work."

And he did.

Until lunch.

The rain had paused, but it was still damp and chilly and windy, but Baldacci followed him down the street to CoffeeXtra. He waited until they had ordered.

"What, Baldacci?"

"I have something to ask you. Not about whatever you've gotten yourself into this time."

"Really? What?"

"It's about the wedding."

He had rehearsed what he wanted to say if Baldacci asked him to be his best man. He was shaking his head.

"I'd like you to be a groomsman."

"Oh. Okay. I can do that. Wait. Who's going to be your best man?"

"My brother, Tommy." Baldacci smiled. "You thought I was going to ask you?"

"No. Certainly not. Why would you?"

"Sorry, Gabe, but I want a real bachelor party." Baldacci grinned at him. "I don't want to think what you'd put together."

Which was true. He had no idea where you hired an exotic

dancer. Or what booze to get. And he was unsure about food?

"Okay. Sure I'll be a groomsman, Harry. When is the wedding?"

"February 12th is the day...Carla's family picked it out...something to do with the Chinese calendar."

"What year is it?"

"2020, Bergeron."

He smiled and patted Baldacci's cheek. "No. The year in the Chinese calendar?"

"No idea."

"Maybe you should find out? Score some cultural sensitivity points with the parents. And maybe Carla?"

"Right. Can do. So you think you'll be out of jail by then, Gabe?"

"Not funny, Baldacci. And probably."

Baldacci said, "Are you okay?"

"Sure. Sort of. I'm worried about Cory who's worried about his family."

Baldacci said, "Anything I can do?"

"Nope, but thanks."

He finished his banana bread. It was time to return to the salt mines.

But Martin, the head barista, was waving at him. One of Martin's girlfriends was sitting on a stool gazing lovingly at him. This one was Selena? But it could be Astrid? He wasn't going to devote perfectly good brain cells to distinguishing them.

Martin himself was tiny. He had black hair, waxed and spiked, brown eyes, a wide nose, and an even wider mouth, which seemed to bisect his face when he smiled.

Said smile made him look as intelligent and capable as pond scum; less because pond scum was capable of photosynthesis.

But Martin wasn't smiling now.

"What?"

"Billy needs to see you." Martin winked at Selena/Astrid. "Pronto."

They giggled, and he sailed past them without a word, but

Martin actually hopped over the bar and chased him.

He turned. "What is so urgent, Martin?"

"You have no sense of humor at all."

"Do to. Tell me."

Billy Stanko was his client and the owner of CoffeeXtra; well, half owner along with his mother, the mysterious Penelope.

Martin said, "Billy really needs to talk to you. So call him."

"Okay." He started walking again. "Wait. He has my numbers, and he knows where I work...and live."

"But he thought you were in Virginia, and he wanted to talk to you in person."

He came to a full stop. "How did he know I was in Virginia?"

Martin spread his hands. "He didn't say."

"So tell him I'm back?"

"He's off the grid."

Martin was fidgety. He wasn't sure why? "Is he in some kind of trouble?"

"Nope." Martin smiled.

He had no idea. "Could you give me a hint, Martin?"

"It's some math thing...he needs to focus. No distractions."

"Okay. Right. That's the off the grid part. And you don't know what he wants to tell me?" Martin shook his head. "Then I'm going back to work."

Martin scrunched up his face. "Penelope."

Which was a name to conjure with. "What about her?"

He had never met Billy Stanko's mother, but they had conversed on the phone. She had forsworn her married name and wouldn't tell him what her current one was.

She didn't like him.

He didn't like her either. She was probably harmless, but he was just a tad frightened by the voice.

Martin said, "Have you seen her? Or talked to her?"

"No! And I haven't done anything to Billy."

Martin nodded. "I know."

He looked at Baldacci who was enjoying himself. "I didn't...lead him on, Martin."

A nod and a face-splitting smile.

"And it wasn't my fault that Peter Hahn tried to kill him."

Another nod.

He sighed. "Do you have a number for Penelope?" Martin laughed at the sheer absurdity of the question. "Why is that funny?"

Martin said, "You'd have to know her."

Which pray God would never happen.

"So I know Billy wants to talk to me. Is that it?"

Another nod, but Martin had lost focus. A voluptuous woman in a red dress was walking his way.

Baldacci appeared similarly distracted, but he grabbed his arm and dragged him away.

He should have given Billy's account to Carla and let her deal with Penelope. It still wasn't too late.

He settled at his desk, and went back to work. He made it until almost 2:00 pm before Cory called.

"Gabe, I'm going back to the farm."

"What's up?"

"Mother called me. She wasn't making a lot of sense, but I think they took Diane into the sheriff's office in Leesburg for questioning."

"Shit, Cory."

"Yeah. But Diane has a lawyer. So I'm leaving now for home."

"Right. Want me to come too?"

"You don't have to."

"Right. I have to tell Jennifer, and I'm on my way."

Monday
5:00 pm

He had retrieved his very yellow, Jeep Wrangler Rubicon from the parking garage on Arch Street and motored to DC.

He hadn't hit the Capital Beltway at an auspicious hour, but he had soldiered through, and eventually had found himself on the Dulles Toll Road.

And now he was turning, at long last, into the Poirier's lane. He parked next to Cory's SUV and got out.

The sun was breaking through the clouds as it set, and it was warmer than Philly.

A red, Ford pickup pulled in behind him.

Diane got out looking exhausted and shaken. He walked over and hugged her. "Are you okay?"

She nodded. "I'm fine."

Which was a brave but utter and complete falsehood.

A large, bearded man had gotten out of the pickup. He was standing very close to Diane and staring at him.

Diane smiled. "This is Finn Beck, my fiancé."

He held out his hand. "Gabe Bergeron."

Finn processed and then smiled and shook. He had large, rough hands. "Happy to meet you, Gabe." He laughed. "Diane's told me some stories about you."

"Good stories? Believable stories?"

Finn was a bit larger than Cory but not so defined. He had brown hair clipped short, brown eyes, and a brown beard. He was wearing a red and gray plaid shirt, worn jeans, and boots. He was very jovial along with a definite lumberjack aura; Paul Bunyan meets the Jolly Green Giant.

It was mild enough that he had rolled up his sleeves to reveal powerful arms. The tattoo covering his right forearm read "USMC" in block letters filled in with stars and stripes. His left had "Semper Fi" in red and blue script. He was not unattractive.

Finn chuckled. "Both. And some not so believable. The best kind of stories."

He said, "It's the Cuban spy story, isn't it? The unbelievable one?"

Finn grinned. "Nope. Haven't even heard that one."

"Really? I can tell you all about it. Maybe later." He looked at Diane. "Was it awful?

"The interrogation? It wasn't pleasant, but I wouldn't answer any questions until Dad's lawyer got there. Sanders just smiled at me like he was my big brother and told me that it made me look guilty, but I knew better. And Cory had told me they might call me in and what they might ask. And he gave me the lawyer's number."

"What did Sanders ask?" Finn was glaring at him now. "I'm sorry, but did they tell you how they knew that Shaw was murdered?"

"He was hit on the back of the head with something. All the injuries from Bucephalus were on the front of the body."

"Did they say anything about the other two men?"

"Nothing. I asked about them, but they wouldn't say."

"He knew about Shaw harassing you?"

She nodded.

Finn said, "But he didn't know how bad it was."

"Why do you say that, Finn?"

"I left work as soon as Diane called, and as soon as he found out I was her fiancé, he questioned me too. But he didn't ask about some of the things Shaw did, and I didn't tell him."

Diane said, "It's over now, Finn."

He said, "How bad was it? The harassment?"

Diane said, "Bad."

Finn said, "He came by her apartment. The bastard even

showed up at the university. And he called her."

He looked at Finn. He didn't look like the kind of guy who would have put up with that; not for a second.

Diane shook her head. She didn't look happy with Finn. "I could cope with the calls and the emails, but I was upset when he came on campus." She looked ready to cry. "I should have called the police, but I knew Dad had to deal with the man until he was out as CEO."

Finn hugged her.

He said, "But it is over now, and the police will find out who really killed Shaw."

She said, "You think so, Gabe?"

"Yes. Absolutely." They weren't doing so well thus far.

Finn looked at the house and then at Diane. "Ready?"

Diane said, "Are you sure you're okay with me just saying you're a friend?"

"Sure. Your folks have enough on their plates right now."

Diane nodded.

He followed Diane and her large fiancé into the Poirier residence. Judd and Samantha were having a baby, and Diane was getting married, and neither had told Laura yet.

This was going to get ugly.

Laura and Hugh and Cory all hugged Diane while glancing at the large, bearish man standing in the foyer.

Diane said, "This is Finn Beck, a friend. He was kind enough to drive me here."

Laura might not be able to deal with the police, but potential suitors were in her wheelhouse. She smiled. "I'm Laura Poirier, and this is Hubert. So nice to meet you, Mr. Beck."

Finn gave her a big smile. "Nice to meet you too, Ma'am."

He shook her hand delicately.

Cory said, "And I'm Diane's brother, Cory."

They shook.

Finn said, "You're a FBI agent, Sir?" Finn was young, mid-twenties or a little older. "Pleasure to meet you, Sir."

Cory was looking from Diane to Finn and back.

Laura was laser-focused on the essentials. "What is it you

do, Mr. Beck?"

Diane rolled her eyes. Finn smiled. "I'm a ranger...I work for the National Park Service, Ma'am."

Laura smiled, but it wasn't her best work. Her analysis of the way Diane was holding onto Finn was not making her happy.

Hugh said, "Well, come in. We were just about to eat. Please join us, Mr. Beck."

Finn was shaking his head, but Laura grabbed the arm that Diane wasn't locked onto, and pulled him toward the dining room.

"Of course, you must join us. And thank you for driving Diane."

And they had dinner, and no one mentioned Sanders or Shaw or the other two dead men.

But Laura did find out a lot about Finn.

"So you work at the Shenandoah National Park?"

"Yes, Ma'am." Finn was just as happy as a koala bear in a bamboo forest.

She looked at Diane. "I never knew you were a camper, Diane."

Diane smiled at her mother. "I'm not." And she was not going to enlighten her mother.

Finn was glancing between them obviously totally at sea in Poirier waters.

Cory and Hugh were smiling to themselves, safely excluded from the titanic struggle between mother and daughter.

He smiled at Finn. "So how did you meet Diane?"

He thought he earned a gold star from Laura for that one.

Finn said, "My sister took her course on the Middle Ages."

"At George Washington University?"

Diane said, "Not my course. I'm just an assistant."

Finn smiled at Diane. "My sister thinks you're great."

And it was apparent that her brother shared her opinion.

Laura was more alive than he had ever seen her; the crackling of synapses was like bacon in a hot pan. "And you went to see your sister at the university and met Diane?"

"Yes, Ma'am. I was fetching Niamh and all her stuff at the end of term, and she introduced us." Finn smiled at Diane, utterly besotted.

Diane said, "Finn and Niamh are twins."

Laura calculated how long Diane and Finn had known each other. "Isn't that nice?"

Hugh was smiling at his wife. "Why don't we have coffee in the family room?"

Laura wanted to know everything about Finn, but she wasn't going to haul out the thumbscrews until she got Diane alone.

Cory, who knew his mother, smiled at Finn. "Do you like soccer?"

Finn scrunched up his face. "I'm more of a football guy."

"Australian rules football?"

Finn smiled. "That's wild."

"It is. There's a game on soon."

And Cory snatched Finn away from Diane.

Laura said, "Can you help me in the kitchen, Diane?"

He smiled and tagged after Cory and Finn and Hugh.

Australian rules football wasn't boring.

Tuesday
8:00 am

Diane and Finn had escaped from Laura's silken snares around ten. It was very probable that Finn was going to be staying with Diane at her place.

But Laura hadn't seemed upset. It appeared she was still forming an opinion of Mr. Beck; she had extracted his parent's names and occupations before Diane and Finn had fled.

Cory's bed was comfortable, but his eyes had popped open way too early. Cory wasn't beside him. He got dressed and went downstairs.

Cory was on the phone, sitting in the kitchen. Hugh was across the table leafing through a sheath of papers; they had finished breakfast.

Mrs. Villeneuve said, "Would you like coffee, Gabriel?"

"Yes, please. Thank you, Madeleine."

Hugh stood up. "I'm off, Mrs. Villeneuve. Mrs. Poirier said she didn't want breakfast, but maybe you could fix her a tray?"

"Of course, Mr. Poirier! She must eat!"

Hugh smiled and was off to play CEO games at Holcomb. He realized he had no idea where Holcomb was; well, the office part that was within commuting distance.

Cory was still on the phone. "What do you think, Matt?" Matt thought something that made Cory smile. "Really? Okay. I'll be in."

Cory hung up.

"Back to work?"

Cory said, "For a few hours. Can you hang here?"

"Sure." What was he supposed to do? "No problem."

He was going to be alone with Laura. It might not be so bad since she was focused on Diane and Finn at present.

Cory smiled at him. "Have fun."

He would have said bad words, but Madeleine was smiling at Cory.

He decided he could check up on his clients. This was officially the worst vacation ever...if it could even be called that.

He didn't bother calling Marge; she didn't function well before noon.

He called Ochoa Imports, hoping to talk to Mikhail, but he got his mother, Valentina, who wanted to talk about Mikhail's upcoming wedding.

He called Excelsior Tea and got Gary Armstrong. Which was unfortunate. Not that he didn't like Gary, but his brother Ned was a bit more anchored to reality. "Have Ned call me. Okay, Gary?"

"Sure, Gabe! I'm writing it down."

Ned would find some more Dead Sea Scrolls before he found this note that Gary was writing. He should visit them ASAP. He could get some tea for Aunt Flo and bathe in the beatific smiles of the brothers Armstrong.

He sighed and called CoffeeXtra.

A woman said, "Yes?"

He was very afraid that the voice belonged to Penelope X.

"Hi, is Billy there?"

"Who is this? Bergeron?"

"Yes. Is this Billy's mother?"

"Of course, it is. Why are you calling my son?"

"I'm his accountant." She sniffed. "Is he there?"

"Why are you asking?"

He was going to remain calm. "If he isn't, who's running the shop? Not Martin?"

"Martin is a lovely boy. I won't hear a word against him."

"Right. So may I speak to Martin then."

"He isn't here."

He was going to brave the rush hour traffic on the Capital Beltway and drive to Philly and shoot Penelope. It was long overdue.

"What is your last name? If you aren't Stanko any more?"

"Wouldn't you like to know."

And she hung up.

And he did say bad words, but Madeleine was out of earshot.

He poured another cup of coffee, but before he could sip there was a knocking on the door.

He opened it to find Detective Sanders gazing at him.

He managed to smile back at the detective. "Good morning, Detective?"

Sanders had a paper in his hand. "Morning, Gabe. I'm sorry but I need to speak to Mr. Poirier."

"He's gone to work."

"Mrs. Poirier then."

"Sure. Hold on." He left Sanders on the porch since it wasn't his house.

Laura was dressed but not prepared for dealing with police.

Sanders said, "I have a warrant to search the buildings and any vehicles, Mrs. Poirier."

Laura took the document and handed it to him. "What does it say, Gabriel?"

He read it through with Sanders standing in the doorway. "It says he can search the place, Laura."

Sanders turned and marched toward the barn; he had half a dozen deputies with him. Some were headed toward the garage.

Laura said, "I'm going to call Hubert."

"Let me call Cory first."

She nodded.

Cory picked up on the second ring. "Gabe?"

"Sanders is here with a warrant to search the premises and any and all vehicles. What should we do?"

"Did you see the warrant?"

"I read it."

"Then there's nothing you can do." Cory paused. "Except

watch him."

"For?"

"Try to find out what he's looking for. Which may give us a clue as to what happened to Shaw, and what Sanders is thinking."

"I can do that."

"I know you can." Cory was smiling; he could feel it.

"Okay. I will be the shorter, svelter shadow he never knew he had. Bye."

Laura said, "Is he coming home?"

"No, I don't think so."

She nodded and sat down at the kitchen table.

"Are you okay, Laura?"

"I'm fine, Gabriel."

"Okay. I'm going out to watch Sanders."

She nodded.

He jogged toward the barn which seemed to be a hive of activity. The sun was shining, and it was warming up nicely; another last taste of almost summer before winter bleak.

Most of the deputies were searching toolboxes in the barn and in the backs of the trucks parked behind the barn.

But two had metal detectors and were searching the area all around where the two bodies had been found.

Sanders was helping the guys rooting through tool boxes. "What are you looking for?"

Sanders was wearing 5.11 cargo pants and a black polo shirt embroidered with the LCSO badge and his name. He looked focused.

"Gabe." He smiled, but it required effort. "I'm sorry, but you can't be out here right now."

"Sure. I understand."

One of the deputies was heading for Sanders. He had a tire iron in a plastic evidence bag.

"Shaw was hit with a tire iron? To stun him so he could be dragged into the stall for Bucephalus to finish him off? Would the blow have been fatal?"

Sanders' hazel eyes raked over him, but he'd been stared at by killers and monsters and IRS agents. He gave Sanders his best smile. "I just want to help, Detective."

Sanders nodded. "I understand, but you can't. Now this deputy is going to escort you back to the house, and I'd really appreciate it if you stayed there."

He smiled at Sanders. "Of course, Detective."

The giant deputy wasn't as big as Roy but he was a fair match for blond Dale, and it appeared he was already mildly furious that he had to rummage through barn detritus.

The white name tag above his right chest pocket read, "Huska."

"Move it."

So he did. He walked swiftly back to the porch, but he didn't go inside. It was a free country, a country of laws, and he felt a fair case could be made that he was "in" the house.

Huska said, "If I go back, are you going to stay put?"

"Yes, Deputy. Promise. I won't step off the porch."

He grunted and lumbered down the lane.

Laura came out. "What are they looking for, Gabriel?"

"Tire irons." She shook her head. "It seems likely that Shaw was clobbered...."

She winced.

"...was rendered unconscious before he was...dragged into the stall...with Bucephalus."

She shut her eyes. "He really was murdered. How awful, Gabriel." She looked at him. "And it happened here. In our barn. He wasn't a nice man, Gabriel, but who could have done something like that?"

"I don't know. Do you have binoculars, Laura?"

"What? She was shaking.

"Is Mrs. Villeneuve around?"

She nodded.

He smiled at Laura. "Is it okay if I help you back inside?"

Tears were welling up in her eyes. He wrapped an arm around her and half carried her into the house and to the kitchen.

"Madeleine?"

"Yes, Gabriel?"

"Mrs. Poirier could use some tea...strong tea...with maybe

some fortification?"

Madeleine took one look. "Ah, Mrs. Poirier, should I call for the doctor?"

Laura shook her head. "I was just light-headed for a moment, Mrs. Villeneuve. Do you think you could call Hubert for me?"

"Of course, Madame!"

He said, "It will be all right, Laura. Sanders will leave soon."

"But he keeps coming back."

"I know, but try not to worry." Which was so easily said.

He left Laura in Madeleine's capable hands and searched the library and Hugh's office.

Hugh had a pair of powerful binoculars; Swiss with Hubble Telescope-grade lenses.

He took up his position on the porch and scanned the forces of the Loudoun County Sheriff's Office as best he could.

He called Cory. "I have the enemy in sight. Well, they aren't really the enemy, and I'm on the porch, where they banished me, but I have your father's binoculars so I could count their nose hairs. If I wanted to do something as gross as that."

Cory said, "Focus, Bergeron. Do you have anything to report?"

"Well, they seem very interested in tire irons. They bagged one."

"So Shaw was stunned by a blow to the head?"

"It appears so." Cory was silent for a second. "Cory?"

"Still here. I don't know what Sanders is hoping to find four days after the crime?"

"Blood, hairs, fingerprints?"

"He has to try. Now that the autopsy has given him some idea what to look for. But the killer could have taken the tire iron. Probably did."

"So Sanders isn't likely to find anything useful?"

"No. Have you talked to him?"

"Not so much."

"Try."

"Really? Okay, I'll do my best."

Cory said, "How is Mother?"

"Upset. Madeleine called your father for her."

"Why didn't she call him herself?"

"She was upset, Cory. But she's better now."

"Shit, Gabe. I'll get away as soon as I can. Tell her it will be okay."

"I did, but I'll tell her again. Bye, Cory."

Laura had dried her eyes and was looking better. "Cory is coming home."

She nodded. "I shouldn't have let myself go, Gabriel. It was weak. I can just imagine what Mother would say."

Madeleine was facing the range; she made a snorting sound worthy of Ezmeralda.

"And now I've disrupted Hubert's day and Corentin's. When they're so busy."

"It's okay. They should be here. Family first, right?"

Laura frowned and sipped her tea.

He went back to his post on the porch. Sanders was in the garage now. He spotted a deputy with another tire iron.

Huska, the Dale-sized deputy, was messing with his Jeep. He may have trotted over.

Huska was not pleased. He resembled a black bear with squadrons of honeybees circling his head.

"I know I promised to stay on the porch, but this is my Jeep. It was in Philadelphia the night that Shaw was clobbered. Honest."

"I'm still searching it."

"Right. Okay. I'm not sure I have a tire iron. I guess there's one in there, but I've never actually seen it."

Deputy Huska pulled it out and bagged it.

"Back to the porch."

"Okay."

He was sitting on the porch when they finished up, and the patrol vehicles started leaving.

But Sanders parked in front of the house and walked up to the porch.

The sun had a surprising amount of power for October, and Sanders was sweaty and dirty.

He grabbed a porch chair and positioned it so they were face to face. He rubbed the grit in his right eye with a semi-clean knuckle.

He smiled. "Dirty job." He patted the clump of hair on the top of his head shaking loose debris.

"Right."

Sanders said, "He was hit on the back of the head with a narrow, cylindrical object; steel with some rust. The blow wouldn't have been fatal."

"But Bucephalus was."

Sanders nodded.

"So premeditated or a crime of passion?"

Sanders shrugged. "What do you think, Gabe?"

"I don't...wait. You're asking my opinion?"

"Yes. I talked to Detective Golczewski."

"Right. Well, it could have been either. Unless he was lured here? Any interesting calls on Shaw's phone?"

Sanders smiled; there was a smear of something brown on his cheek, which he wanted to rub off, but he kept his hands to himself.

"So I'm guessing there weren't. May I ask about the other two men? Have they been identified?"

Sanders sat there, but there was a slight shaking of the head.

They sat in silence for a bit. Sanders rubbed his head again, rolled his shoulders back and stretched. "Any ideas, Gabe?"

He was pretty sure that Sanders hated asking him that, but it was hard to tell with all the smiling.

"Not yet."

Sanders grabbed the front of his shirt and hauled him close enough for him to check the health of the detective's retinas. "Not yet? What the Hell does that mean?"

"It means that I don't know anything now. It means that I could poke around? If that would be okay with you? And also okay with Cory. Which I doubt."

Sanders kept staring into his eyes. He wasn't sure what he was supposed to do? Not blink? He tried to look like a crusader for truth and justice. Or at least not like he was guilty of something.

Sanders let go of his shirt and nodded. He leaned back in the chair. "I hate this case, Gabe."

"It is a puzzler. So no luck with the fingerprints or dental records or DNA of either man? Isn't that weird?"

Sanders shook his head. "Yes and no."

He smiled. "If I answered you like that, you'd probably smack me.

Sanders gave him a real smile with dimples. "I wouldn't, Gabe."

"So what do you mean, Detective?"

"The kid had never gotten around to doing something to get himself into the system, and from his teeth, he'd never been to a dentist in his pitifully short life."

"And he was shot by the gun with the silencer?"

A half nod.

"And the older guy? He had a spiderweb tattoo on his neck. I don't remember much else."

Sanders nodded. "He doesn't show up in any database...for different reasons."

"Could you expand on that?"

Sanders just smiled.

"Right. Okay. What about the gun?"

"A Beretta."

He wasn't sure, but he strongly suspected that Detective Sanders was not being totally forthcoming.

"But he was stabbed by the dagger that the kid had?"

"Likely."

"So the kid brought a knife to a gun fight, but still managed to kill the gunslinger?"

Sanders said, "That's what it looks like."

"It doesn't make sense. Unless the kid surprised the gunslinger?"

Sanders got to his feet and leaned over him. "So?"

"I'll talk to Cory."

"And if he turns you loose on this?"

He smiled at Sanders. "What did Vonda tell you?"

Sanders considered. "I hate to doubt the word of a fellow officer, but nothing I believed."

"Not even a little bit?"

"Just enough that I sat here and wasted time talking to you, Gabe. After wasting time collecting a bunch of rusty tire irons."

"Should I call you if Cory says yes?"

"No."

"No?"

Sanders wrote a cellphone number on the back of one of his cards and handed it over. "Call me only if you find out something. Something useful, Gabe."

"Right. I can do that."

Sanders gripped his shoulder. "Two things: we never had this conversation and don't get yourself killed."

Tuesday
2:00 pm

Hugh had gotten home, and Laura had been her old self.

Cory had rolled in about an hour later and had talked to his mother and tried to reassure her, but she knew everything was still in flux, and her home had been indelibly stained by the actions of a rogue or rogues unknown.

And then Hugh had taken Laura upstairs, and Cory had been able to interrogate him.

"So?"

Cory said, "Sanders is desperate."

"Right. And?"

"The older guy was probably a professional. Which is why he and his gun are untraceable."

"A hit-man?"

"Or a thief."

"And he came to the barn to do what?" Cory shrugged. "But he got killed by a kid with a Fairbairn–Sykes commando knife?"

Cory smiled. "I know. I'm glad this isn't my case."

Cory had ignored the part about him investigating so he was going to let it go. He would go back to work tomorrow and forget everything. Well, he would try.

Cory said, "It's a beautiful day."

"It is."

"Want to go riding with me?"

"Nope."

"Okay. Then I'll see you later."

And Cory was striding toward the barn.

He had watched TV by himself for an hour. Laura and Hugh were still upstairs.

He had searched the kitchen again for sweet, calorie-dense confections in vain.

And then he went for a walk in the bright sun looking for Cory, who had ridden off into the sunset...well, it was just past 3:00 pm, and he wasn't sure which way was west.

Wait. The Blue Ridge Mountains were west so Cory had been trotting north; well, his trusty steed had been.

But it made sense to check the barn first in case Cory had returned.

He was skipping along barn-ward when he saw movement around Mrs. Foote's cottage. A sturdy, young guy was throwing a bulging duffel bag into the back of a pickup.

He may have altered course.

"Hi, there."

The guy was in faded jeans cinched with a wide leather belt with a brass belt buckle featuring a long-horned steer. His shirt was a blue plaid; he had rolled up his sleeves. His camouflage pattern cap had an American flag patch in black and white.

His hair was brown and wild and ran down the back of his neck; it was as scruffy as his beard. A patchy mustache grew in four clumps on his upper lip; a single clump sprouted below his mouth. Wary brown eyes looked out from a square face.

"Hi."

He held out his hand. "I'm Gabe Bergeron. I haven't seen you before?"

"I'm Jed."

Jed shook. His hand was callused. And Jed was dusty.

Then young Jed studied the ground like he was thinking about plowing Mrs. Foote's front yard before he retreated back inside her house.

He was undeterred.

It was a lovely day, and he could wait. He spotted the curtains moving, but nobody came out.

He smiled; it was to be a siege then. He should have brought victuals and possibly a trebuchet? Burning oil? No, he thought that was more a defensive weapon.

He could always knock on her door.

The curtains jerked again. He smiled and waved.

The door opened, and Jed shot out of the house as if launched by a trebuchet of his own. He got into the pickup and revved the engine of an elderly, baby-blue and white Chevy.

But Jed was not alone.

Another slender fellow tossed a couple of garbage bags into the back and was hurtling toward the passenger door.

He may have intercepted him.

He smiled his very best smile. "Hi, there. As I told your friend, I'm Gabe Bergeron." He stuck out his hand.

The guy said, "He's not my friend."

"No? Maybe you could cultivate him?"

"What?"

"Never mind. So I'm visiting the Poiriers. Are you friends of Mrs. Foote?"

This guy was wearing a gray t-shirt; his jeans had ragged cuffs and a few holes.

He was even less of a conversationalist than Jed. "No."

He was more slender than Jed, and his face was oval and covered in freckles. He had the same brown eyes, but his hair was almost black. His beard was even more wispy and would never fill in if he never touched a razor for the rest of his life.

He was just as dusty as Jed.

"Who are you?" He still had his hand aimed at Freckles.

Jed said, "Get in the damn truck, Del!"

Del sighed, but he did shake his hand. "Excuse me, Sir."

And Del eased past him and got in. Jed let the truck lurch into motion. He could see Del waving his hands through the rear window.

Jed eased off the gas, and the engine quieted to a gentle purr as the truck virtually coasted past the barn and onto the lane that led to the county road.

He considered. They could be brothers, but Del was the

handsomer of the two.

But had sturdy Jed and handsome Del just burgled Mrs. Foote's house?

He should find out. He had noted the tag number of Jed's truck just in case.

But then he saw the curtains jerk again. He waved, and Mrs. Foote was polite enough to wave back. She smiled happily enough and appeared unharmed.

So Jed and Del had been guests chez Foote? Or what? He could go knock on her door and ask subtle, devious, probing questions, but he didn't want to do that. He wasn't over the bathroom incident yet.

He would inquire of Cory. Or Madeleine. Perhaps these guys were the secret things that she had mentioned?

He returned to exploring the farm, the estate, the demesne. It was warm, but there was a breeze as he walked toward the mountains in the distance.

The pastures were lush and verdant except where they weren't; scabrous patches of rock broke through the thin, green skin of the earth

He saw a rider coming toward him, and he waved like he was semaphoring vital information to Napoleon at Austerlitz.

Cory drew up along side him. Cory was pretending to smile and not be frantic over the eminent destruction of his family. He needed cheering up.

The black horse was snorting and too close to him, and very sweaty. Cory was also very sweaty and a lot more attractive.

"Come riding with me, Gabe."

"Nope."

"Please? It will be fun."

Cory was laughing at him. Cory thought he was a wimp, a wuss, a weakling, and other pejoratives beginning with "w".

"I'm not getting on top of a thousand pound animal with a brain the size of a walnut."

"That's dinosaurs, Bergeron."

"And I don't ride them either."

"Come on. I'll saddle Gentle Betty for you."

"Right. Like I'm falling for that one!"

Cory was smiling. "What?"

"First, you've already told me the names of the horses. This is Rhythm."

Rhythm was intensely black, even blacker than Bucephalus, but built a lot lighter.

"And I know that there is no 'Gentle Betty.' And even if there were, it's like calling a gigantic man 'Tiny.' She's a monster, isn't she? How many notches does she have on her stall door?"

Cory shook his head. "You do know that I wouldn't let you get hurt for a joke?"

"Maybe yes. Maybe no. You like horses. You don't see the evil gleam in their eyes."

Cory stripped off his shirt and said something about evil, but his reasoning centers had lost control of his brain...momentarily...as her perused the ebb and flow of Cory's glistening muscles.

"Gabe!"

"What? Sorry." He scanned the horizon in every direction. "It's very private out here."

Cory was shaking his head.

"If you took off your jodhpurs and rode around a bit, no one would see. Except me."

Would Cory allow himself to be videoed? It might be best to ask for forgiveness rather than permission?

Cory said, "I am not riding around naked for you, Bergeron."

"No! Of course not. Just in your briefs? Or maybe I could fashion a loincloth of some sort...."

He wasn't sure about the construction of such a garment? Just a length of fabric maybe? Wrapped and knotted? Silk would be nice...black silk to match the horse and contrast with Cory's pale skin....

But Cory was already riding off leaving him in the middle of a green field. It was a long trek back to the house, but he knew the way.

And he had his fantasies.

Wednesday
8:00 am

The sun was barely above the horizon, and Cory had been on his phone and laptop for hours.

Something was up.

He sidled up to the special agent. "What's going on?"

Cory was excited. "Remember Jerry?"

"I can't say I do."

Cory said, "The Jerry who tried to run over me? The bastard who almost killed Matt?"

"Oh, you mean Jerry Nolastname." This might not be good; given that Cory was obsessed with bringing Jerry to justice...or shooting him in a dark alley. "You have a lead?"

"We do."

"And you're going off after him?"

"Maybe. Matt's coming out here. We'll talk about it."

Matt must have been almost to the farm, because he rolled in ten minutes later. They were still having a pow-wow in the family room. He hadn't been invited, but the door hadn't been closed either.

So he may have drifted by from time to time.

Matt Bornheimer had been Cory's partner for almost five years now. He was smiling at Cory with flawless teeth that were as white as alpine snow. He wasn't quite as tall or muscular as Cory, but he was impressive all the same.

He had buzz-cut brown hair, but his eyes were his salient, signature feature. They were gray and widely-spaced and made him look all-knowing. But also faintly insectoid; something in the preying mantis family.

He was drifting in the family room area, when Cory said, "Gabe!"

He poked his head in.

"Come in here."

"Okay. Are you going?"

Cory was trying to look serious; Matt wiped a wisp of a smile off his face.

Cory said, "We're still gathering intel."

And then Matt shifted his weight and made a reaching motion toward him. He locked onto Matt's arm, twisted, and threw him over his shoulder. He finished with an armbar. Only the look on Cory's face stopped him from wrenching Matt's elbow as he'd been programmed to do.

Cory's tossing and slamming of him had often begun with just such a casual, reaching motion, and he was hyper-vigilant.

Special Agent Bornheimer was looking at him, and the shock was passing off.

Shit. He was a dead man.

He scooted away as Matt picked himself up. They got to their feet.

Shit! He should run. He could at least try to save himself. "I'm really, really sorry...."

Matt lunged for him.

His feet didn't seem to be running. He twisted like a matador...an agile, brave one in very tight knee pants...and used Matt's momentum to toss him in a lovely arc that ended with Matt flat on his back. Again.

Hugh and Laura were in the doorway, but they were just staring. He focused on Cory. "Help?"

Matt shook himself and got to his feet; a lot slower this time. Cory was smiling. Which did nothing to lessen Matt's rising blood lust.

"I'm so sorry, Matt. Really. I just reacted, but I'll never do it again...."

But Matt was already heading for him.

He tried to sweep Matt's legs, but something went very wrong, and he was on the floor looking up at Special Agent Bornheimer, who appeared to be contemplating punching him in the face. He curled his body upward and locked his arms around Matt's neck and held on for dear life while trying to roll Matt. He feinted right and rolled left, and for one brief, shining moment, he was on top.

And then something happened, and he was well and truly pinned to the floor with Matt's weight crushing him.

He smiled his very best smile at Matt while looking desperately around the room for Cory.

And then, a strange thing happened; Matt smiled at him. Well, he also slapped his face a couple of times first. "Don't ever try that again, Bergeron."

"No, Sir. I never will. I don't know what came over me, Sir."

Cory was kneeling beside them. "Not bad, Bergeron."

He tried smiling at Cory, but it was hard since Matt's two hundred pounds were lodged on his chest, and suffocation was imminent.

"Tell me where you went wrong."

"I met you in the coffee aisle at the Food Mart in Princess Anne; you were wearing a very fetching blue bandanna and were posing as a solar panel installer."

Matt smiled some more; a snorting sound escaped from his perfect nose. Someone else was tittering in the background.

Cory said, "Focus, Bergeron."

"Can't. Dying."

Matt rolled off.

He closed his eyes and took a deep breath. "That was the nexus that led inevitably to this point in space-time."

Cory said, "Open your eyes! Get on your feet, Bergeron!" He did so. "What did you do wrong?"

"I panicked a little bit and didn't commit to the throw."

"Exactly. Now try it again."

But Matt was shaking his head. "No way, Poirier." Matt eased himself deliberately into a chair. "Let him toss you around."

He didn't want to toss or be tossed, but Cory was focused. Matt said, "So?"

Cory was glowering at them both.

Matt said, "Make up your mind, Cory. Go or stay. I'm okay with whatever you decide."

Cory sighed. "I know." And then his phone rang. "Poirier."

Laura said, "Are you all right, Gabriel?"

Hugh said, "You should be asking Matthew that, Dear."

Matt said, "I'm fine, Sir."

He said, "I'm okay, Laura. Cory's been training me for I know not what."

Hugh and Laura were smiling at him, but he wasn't sure what was funny?

Cory listened and said, "We're on our way, Danielle. I'll call you as soon as we know something."

The conversation continued.

Danielle Elkins was Cory's boss. He sighed; Cory was going off somewhere. He didn't want Cory to see how disappointed he was so he looked at Matt. "Sorry."

"Nope. My fault, Bergeron. Cory told me to try a move to see how you reacted." He smiled again bringing all of his perfect teeth to bear. "I'm the one who wasn't ready. You're quick...when your brain doesn't get in the way."

He thought that was a compliment?

Cory put his phone away.

Laura said, "You're going off somewhere, Corentin?"

He nodded. "But I'd like Gabe to stay here to keep an eye on things? If that's okay?"

Which was news to him.

Hugh said, "Of course, Corentin." Hugh was looking at him funny again. "What else have you taught him?"

"He's not bad with a Glock. Actually, he's pretty good."

Hugh smiled.

Laura said, "Will I be able to call you?"

"Of course, Mother. We won't be undercover."

She nodded and took Hugh's hand.

Cory and Matt ushered him out of the house to the parking

lot.

He looked at Cory. "So how long are you going to be gone?"

"I don't know, but I'll call you."

"Good. And you want me to stay here?"

Cory was just standing there, and Matt was chomping at the bit...which he had seen an actual horse actually do.

Cory nodded. "And I want you to do something else for me."

"Sure. Of course. What exactly?"

He tried to listen to Cory, but he was staying with Hugh and Laura. The three of them. Alone. Together in the same house. Well, Diane was around some of the time. But still.

"...and keep an eye on them."

"On Hugh and Laura? And I'll be watching out for what? Alien abduction?"

"Don't let the police or Grand bother them. Or Childers. And if Dad has a problem with his health, no matter how minor he says it is, let me know and don't let him go into the office."

Cory was serious. "Shit, Cory. How do I stop your father from going to work?"

"Call Diane. She'll know what to do."

"Right. Okay." He considered. "As for the police, I don't think you have to worry." He considered some more. "If Mrs. Loncke or Childers show up, I will stick to them like a cocklebur, like a barnacle, like epoxy paint. Until they are begging me to leave."

Cory smiled.

"Some people say I can be annoying."

Cory hugged him. "And there's one other thing."

Shit! "Do I want to know what that is?"

"I want you to dig into this mess."

"Sure. Absolutely! Which mess exactly?"

"Gabe."

"No, Cory, I'm serious. What are you asking me? Not to solve this case?"

Cory nodded, his red locks coruscating in the sunlight. "I

can't help my family. Sanders has frozen me out which I understand. And now Matt and I have to go. I thought you could just talk to people? But don't go full-Gabe! And don't do anything stupid."

"Right. Okay. Sure."

But he had never been asked to help before...not by somebody from law enforcement. Or by Cory. Suppose he couldn't help? Suppose the well was dry? Suppose he was about to be unmasked as the nosy, ineffectual amateur he was?

Cory said, "Stop obsessing, Bergeron."

"Yeah? Wait. Obsessing is my thing."

"Well, not this time. I'm not asking you to solve this; just dig into it. And maybe you'll turn up something that will help Sanders and end all this."

"And if I can't?"

"Then that'll be okay."

He looked from Cory to Matt and back to Cory. "And if I find something.... What if...I mean I don't think anyone in your family had anything...."

Cory said, "They didn't. Don't worry about that. Okay?"

He had a stabbing pain in the center of his brain. He was going to have a small cerebrovascular incident.

Matt said, "He's freezing up, Cory."

Cory clapped him on the back, dislodging his uvula. "He'll be okay."

And they sallied forth.

But would he be okay?

Shit. Cory wanted his family cleared of even the slightest suspicion, and he had no idea how to do that.

Wednesday
10:00 am

Hugh had gone to the family room and switched on the TV. Laura was talking on the phone to Diane. Cory and Matt would soon be in the air.

And he had been appointed chief detective and defender of hearth and home and family.

He walked slowly to the scene of the crime. The doors on the east side of the barn were open, and he heard voices.

The horses were in the first, five stalls on the right, just inside the door. The sliding stall doors were wood and steel, riding on a metal track attached to a beam that ran from the end of the barn to the center of the building.

The top half of each stall door was made of steel bars set to leave a gap in the middle, and the horses had their heads through those gaps, looking curious and making horse noises.

The floor was paved with bricks. He spotted Hilda and Dolph and walked toward them, avoiding the horses, especially Bucephalus, who snorted at him.

The light came from the open door and two banks of powerful lights hung from the ceiling.

Hilda Prentice said, "Hurry up, Dolph. Don't take all day with that."

Dolph ignored his mother.

"Dolph!"

He muttered something as he cleaned out the stall where Bucephalus had trampled Shaw.

He counted the stalls as he passed; twelve stalls on each side, which gave twenty-four on the east side of the barn with a mirror image twenty-four on the west.

Dolph said, "What for, Momma?"

"Because we're being paid to keep this farm in order."

"Not enough."

She said, "You're paid as much as you're worth."

He decided to interrupt the family time. "Hello, Mrs. Prentice."

She turned and just stared. Dolph glanced and went back to staring blankly at the floor of the stall.

"Lovely day, isn't it?"

"What do you want, Mr. Bergeron?"

"I'm just walking around, taking the air."

He stood outside the stall. The bloody straw and wood shavings had been swept out into the corridor; there were dark stains on the rubber mats.

She decided to ignore him. "Cart all this bedding away and get those mats out. They need to be scrubbed and left out to dry."

"Think I don't know that?"

She smiled at the son who towered over her. "I wonder what you do know at times, Dolph. I truly do."

Dolph looked at her. He had a square, flat face. His eyes were washed out; his brows and lashes almost invisible. The only color on his face came from the ruddy cheeks.

"I know enough to know we should go...."

"You don't know anything!"

Dolph didn't say anything more, but he went off and came back with a wheelbarrow and began shoveling up the bedding.

He said, "This is a very nice barn."

Hilda looked at him. "Seen many barns, have you?"

Dolph made a snorting noise.

"This is my first actually. Except for barns on TV or in the movies. So did Mr. Poirier build this barn."

"In a manner of speaking."

He smiled his best smile. "And what does that mean?"

"Mr. Sébastien Poirier built this barn."

"Right. Cory's grandfather. Do you remember him?" Which was probably like asking how old she was, but she wasn't a pleasant person.

"Of course, I remember Mr. Sébastien and Miss Hélène, his wife. They were real horse people, Mr. Bergeron."

"Cory told me he could remember when there were forty horses in this barn."

She nodded and smiled for the first time.

Dolph said, "Ancient history."

Her face fell, and she looked sad and beaten down for an instant. "Not ancient to me, Dolph."

"What happened?"

She flushed. "Things change, Mr. Bergeron."

"Mr. Poirier, Hugh, isn't a horse person?"

She glared at him. "He is, through and through. It's not him...."

He thought that Hilda might have a bit of a crush on her boss. She shook her head. Dolph had a particularly nasty smile on his pale, pancake face.

Hilda said, "I don't have time for prying questions, Mr. Bergeron. I have accounts to work on."

And she about-faced and marched toward the center of the barn. He may have followed.

The center section of the barn had a mezzanine around three sides of the two-story, central space. She climbed the stairs on the right to the office area that Sanders had used as a temporary headquarters. She sat at the desk and snapped on a light.

He went out the main door and wandered toward the three cottages.

He supposed Jack Prentice was in his bed and might like some company, but he was certain Hilda wouldn't be pleased.

He walked on intending to bypass Mrs. Foote's house, but she stuck her head out the door and waved at him.

She was smiling. "Hello, Mr. Bergeron. Having a stroll? It is a lovely day." She patted her spherical hair which reminded him a bit of Carla's, except that it was shorter.

"Yes, it is, Mrs. Foote."

"I saw you go into Mrs Prentice's house the other day." She was smiling and staring at him; he felt like he was naked even fully clothed.

"Right. I helped Mr. Prentice get into his wheelchair."

"Oh, that was nice of you. It's very sad. He's almost completely helpless, and it all falls on her. She can't lift poor Jack, but I'll bet someone as fit as you had no trouble at all."

He didn't know what to say. "But Dolph...."

"Him! I don't want to tattle, but he's not nice. The stories I could tell you."

"I don't really know him."

"No. Of course, you don't. He didn't help with his aunt either."

"I'm sorry?"

"Oh, you wouldn't know, but Hilda's sister, Dorothy, passed away...a little over two years ago now. Hilda had to take care of her too. She had her and Jack in that little house for months before the poor thing went." She whispered, "It was cancer."

"I'm sorry to hear that."

"And Hilda and Dorothy looked enough alike to be twins, but they weren't."

She smiled. "I just made some coffee. Would you like a cup?"

No force on earth could compel him to enter her cottage.

"That's very kind of you, but I have to get back to the house."

She smiled. "You're staying then?"

"For a while."

She smiled at him. "Mrs. Poirier is lucky to have your company now that Mr. Poirier is going back to work."

She couldn't be suggesting what he thought she was suggesting? He started walking away.

She followed. "It was nice talking to you, Mr. Bergeron. I'm always here...if you need to talk...or anything. I'm not as lucky as Hilda."

He stopped. He knew he shouldn't. "How is Hilda lucky?"

She smiled like a succubus from Hell; not that he knew

what succubi looked like. "She isn't as lonely as I am."

He couldn't help from shuddering violently. "Are you saying she has someone other than Jack?"

She laughed.

"I don't tattle, but I see things, Mr. Bergeron. Scandalous things. Of course, Hilda's had a hard life."

He shook himself again. "Did you see anything the night of the murders?"

She frowned and pouted. "I was gone! Isn't that just the way it is? Nothing ever happens...except for Hilda and her hanky-panky...for years on end, and I visit with Momma, and there are deputies and other gentlemen thick on the ground."

He walked as fast as he could. The house was too far away, and he was in the open. He broke into a jog and got back inside the house double quick.

Laura said, "What's wrong, Gabriel? You look like you're being chased?"

"No." But he peered out the window to confirm that. "She didn't chase me."

Laura smiled. "Mrs. Foote?"

He nodded.

She smiled some more. "Mrs. Foote is a sweet woman, but she does have her little quirks. Didn't Cory warn you, Gabriel?"

"Not in time."

"And I reminded him too. Sometimes, I don't think he listens to me." She frowned. "She keeps the house immaculate. I don't know how I would ever replace her."

So if it came down to a choice between Gabe Bergeron and the immaculate but libidinous Mrs. Foote, he knew who would get the heave-ho.

Wednesday
1:00 pm

He and Laura had lunched in the kitchen. Madeleine made sandwiches; he was pretty sure that the base ingredient had been chicken.

He had chewed as little as possible and swallowed, and he had kept a smile on his face

Laura said, "And what will you do this afternoon, Gabriel?"

"I can check up on my clients, but I'd like to talk to you first."

"Me?" She smiled; it was a good eighty percent real. "What about?"

"About the farm mostly. It belonged to Hubert's father?"

She nodded. "Yes, to Sébastien and Miss Hélène. She was a remarkable woman, Gabriel. Even my mother liked her. I think the property belonged to Hubert's grandfather, but it was Sébastien who expanded it. He built the barn and this house. He loved it here as much as Hubert does."

"Right. And he had forty horses at one time?"

"Yes, he did. Hubert and I had twenty for many years."

"But now there are only five?

The smile sincerity meter dropped into the single digits. "Things change, Gabriel."

"They do. 'This too shall pass away' and all that."

Laura adjusted her scarf which was an iridescent blue like a peacock feather. "I told Hubert we could get a few more horses...to replace the ones we've lost, but we haven't gotten around to it."

"How did you lose them?"

"Horses are very susceptible to illnesses, Gabriel."

"Yeah, somebody said they're delicate. So you had horses get sick and die?"

"We lost Chopin just this past January. To colic."

"I'm sorry to hear that."

She said, "Would you like to see a picture of him?"

He thought this was liked being asked to look at pictures of a friend's children; socially obligatory.

"Sure."

Madeleine smiled as Laura went to get the photo.

"What?"

More smiling. "How much do you like horses, Gabriel?"

Before he could select the correct answer, Laura returned with two, thick albums. They were organized chronologically, and she began with the five horses still trotting.

The life and adventures and romances of Bucephalus had been documented; exhaustively. Major porn stars had fewer extant photos of sexual encounters. There was one which might have captured him *in flagrante delicto*, but Laura turned the page too quickly to be sure...for which he was very grateful.

They worked their way through the other four and finally reached Chopin. He was gray and looked very handsome in a horsey way.

There were dates beneath the photos: Chopin had gone to pastures celestial in January.

She had no intention of stopping at Chopin. He dug deep and smiled manfully.

"And this is Onyx. Wasn't she a beauty?"

She was a black horse. "Yes, she was. Gorgeous." Madeleine was facing the sink, and her shoulders were aquiver with silent laughter.

But Onyx had also died in January; the year before Chopin.

Laura said, "Lately, it seems like we lose a horse whenever we vacation in Costa Rica."

"Really?"

Laura nodded and turned the page. "Mrs Prentice called us,

of course, and we almost flew home for Chopin, but Hubert talked to Dr. Crain."

"And he told you that there was nothing to be done?"

She nodded and turned the page. "And this is Fleet Fellow."

At least Fleet Fellow had died in July.

His whole life was a blur by the time she finished the first album.

Madeleine said, "Madame, you're going to be late for your appointment."

Laura looked at the time. "Oh! Thank you, Mrs. Villeneuve." She smiled at him, and it was totally genuine. "We'll have to save the rest for later, Gabriel."

"Sure! I look forward to it." He would pluck out his own eyes before he looked at one more horse picture.

Laura bustled off.

He turned and glared at Madeleine. "You couldn't have warned me?"

"Some lessons are best learned first hand."

"Did you have to look at the pictures?"

She nodded. "There was only the one album when I came here. You are not so lucky, Gabriel."

Which wasn't news to him.

Wednesday
9:00 pm

He had pretended to be working when Laura had gotten back. He had made up a totally bogus October 9th Federal Fiduciary Filing Deadline.

Laura had smiled.

He wasn't a hundred percent sure she'd bought it, but he didn't care. There was a limit to what he would suffer even for Cory.

Hugh had puttered about the farm in the morning, but after lunch he'd gone into his office and spent all afternoon on the phone. He may have eavesdropped enough to know that Hugh was talking about Holcomb business.

He had dithered a bit about telling Diane that Hugh might be thinking of going back to work. And then he'd called.

"Hi, Diane."

"Is something wrong, Gabe?"

"Nope, everything is hunky-dory, but Hugh might be thinking about going to work tomorrow, and Cory said to call you."

"I was afraid of that. Thanks, Gabe. I'll take care of it."

But she hadn't hung up.

"Diane?"

She had laughed. "Just wondering how you're making out?"

"Excellent. Never better."

She had laughed again.

And after dinner, Hugh and Laura had retired to the master

suite, leaving Bergeron on his own. Which was fine. He had watched TV and read a chapter in his new book.

He tossed the book. It was only 10:00 pm, and he was bored and not sleepy at all.

At home, either at Cory's condo or his apartment, he could have ordered pizza. Which he didn't need. He patted his stomach.

Or he could have called Neal. Or even Baldacci. Which he could still do.

He sighed. He walked out onto the balcony. It wasn't really cold, but not short-sleeve weather any longer.

He perused the night sky, searching for Orion, but he spotted the lights of a vehicle instead. He watched it drive past the cottages, pull around behind the barn, and disappear.

It was a van, but that was all he could tell.

He pulled a dark sweatshirt over his head. Cory had some stocking caps in his closet. He selected a black one and pulled it down over his ears.

He didn't have anything to blacken his face with. Well, Cory had shoe polish, but he wasn't sure that would come off? And how would he explain that to Laura and Hugh.

Of course, they might just shrug. But he skipped it. Blackface was problematic unless you were a commando.

He sallied forth with Mrs. Prentice's flashlight which he'd forgotten to return. He was almost to the barn when a thought occurred: maybe he should call for backup?

This could be the person or persons who had slaughtered three people. How likely was that? Maybe this was what Cory had expressly forbidden: going full-Gabe?

He was sure it wasn't, and the van was directly ahead parked next to a pickup with no tags. He went into super-stealth mode, but it was empty.

It was also Dr. Crain's van.

A house call at this hour? Maybe one of the horses was sick? But wouldn't Mrs. Prentice have informed Hugh and Laura?

He crept ever onward.

There was a back door to the barn. He teased it open, but he didn't see any one; partly because it was dark and partly because there was no one to be seen.

He did hear something.

Conversation? Laughter? He was under the mezzanine office level now, and giggling was coming from above him.

He slid one foot forward at a time clinging to the wall. The desk lamp was on and that pool of light was the only illumination in the whole building.

There was a couch beside the desk.

And Dr. Crain was on the couch. He was nude; well, he had a t-shirt and socks on.

It was fairly obvious what he was doing even without the grunting.

And then the good vet and his partner rolled, and she took the top position and proceeded to bounce up and down on him.

Mrs. Prentice was completely nude. Which wasn't a good look for her.

He shut his eyes and began to withdraw as quickly as possible. He was almost to the door, when he heard a horse snort.

And then another one took fright, and they all went into a frenzy like thousand pound toddlers. He had told Cory horses were evil

He dove for the door.

He couldn't go down the lane directly to the house; he'd be spotted even in his Ninja costume. He darted past the van and crossed the lane to gain access to the woods beyond.

He could simply head east and then north, keeping the lane in sight. There was no way he would get lost. Even in the dark, in the forest primeval.

And to his relief and amazement, he didn't!

He almost stopped to call Cory and report this singular event, but he had to get back inside the house.

He was walking past the garage when he tripped on something and almost brained himself.

He pulled himself together and limped through the semi-dark house hoping that Hugh and Laura were asleep or semi-deaf.

He got to Cory's room. He was bleeding. He had scraped his knee as well as his hands.

He sighed. He retraced his path, wiping up the blood smears. He went to the bathroom, washed the gravel out of his cuts and bound his wounds as best he could.

He went back to Cory's bedroom and pondered. He wanted to call Cory, but he didn't know anything really.

But he had his suspicions.

Thursday
8:00 am

He had gotten down to breakfast in time to see Hugh motoring down the lane.

"Where's he going, Laura?"

"To work."

He shook his head. Whatever Diane had done had been ineffective. "But I thought he wasn't....is he well enough for that?"

She smiled, but her lower lip might have quivered a bit. "He's fine, Gabriel. And he promised me he'd only work a half day."

Shit. He had failed in one of his primary duties, and Cory was going to be pissed. But he had done as instructed. He sighed.

Laura had vanished upstairs, but the horse album was still on the kitchen table. He decided to avoid that by going for another walk which he would rather have skipped.

The sky was gray, the wind was blustery, and he didn't want to run into Hilda if he could avoid it. Not that he thought she'd seen him. But still.

He wandered along the lane that led to the county road and freedom. He left the road heading south. The land got rougher with more stone outcroppings among the green.

He climbed to the top of a little rise and got a lovely view of the Blue Ridge Mountains. Below him, a sinuous stream flowed in a hollow between two knolls.

A proper hill rose before him if he could ford the stream, but it was too wide to jump even at the narrowest sections. He followed the stream and found a rickety bridge.

He wasn't sure he was still on Hugh's land? But he nipped across and started climbing the hill. The trees were thick, and the wind made a sighing sound as it buffeted their crowns.

He was high enough to see the barn and the house. He spotted a woman walk out of the barn. She got into a truck and drove along the lane behind the barn.

He climbed a little higher and watched her turn onto the county road and disappear.

He could see for miles. He found a log and sat and soaked it all in. He would have to bring Cory up here.

But he had probably hiked the whole place when he'd been a boy? And ridden over most of it. He thought Cory had said he'd lived in Richmond? This was the country home.

He was cold; it was all right while he was moving.

He descended the hill and recrossed the stream, heading for the barn. Dolph was sitting on a bench leaning against said barn being his usual, industrious self.

"Hi, there."

Dolph glared at him. He had blood-shot eyes and a bald spot on the back of his head. "I'm busy."

"I can see that."

Dolph got to his feet. He was hulking but slow moving. "You go away."

"I'm a guest of Mr. Poirier, and I'm just taking a stroll."

Dolph glared some more. "I know what you are." He smiled his nasty smile. "You and Corentin."

Cory's name sounded really bad coming out of Dolph's mouth. He thought he could throw Dolph if he had to.

"Where is Mrs. Prentice?"

"Gone to town."

"Where? Middleburg?"

He shook his head but didn't elaborate. He sat on the bench again.

"So what do you think happened? With Mr. Shaw and the other two guys who got killed?"

Dolph shook his head again, but after a minute or so, he

rubbed his eyes. "Don't know. No reason for them to be here. Momma can't figure it out."

"Your mother is a smart woman."

"Yeah. I guess."

"Detective Sanders still hasn't identified the two men."

Dolph smiled. "That so? Maybe he won't never."

"Would that be a good thing, Dolph?"

Dolph focused on him. "What?"

"You don't want them to be identified for some reason?"

Dolph got to his feet again with his cheeks flaming and started toward him.

"Nothing to me! And nothing to Momma either. You get away from me or you'll be sorry. Nosy bastard."

He backed away from Dolph, stopping when he stopped. He let Dolph turn back.

"So who is Turtle?"

He was ready to run, but Dolph had long legs which made up for the paunch and doughy muscles. For a while.

He led him down the lane sprinting toward the house. Dolph tried to keep up, but he was lagging farther behind.

He slowed down to a jog so Dolph didn't give up. "Is Turtle a friend of yours?"

Dolph said, "You...shut...up!"

He led Dolph past the house and into Diane's steeplechase field; Dolph made it half way across before he couldn't put one foot in front of the other.

And then he collapsed and lay on his back.

He wasn't so easily fooled, but Dolph was gasping for breath. Hugh and Laura would be very cross if he killed their employee; even unintentionally.

"Dolph? Are you okay?"

Dolph couldn't speak as his chest pumped like a bellows, but he gave him the finger. He hadn't run in a long time.

"Right. So Turtle came here to see you?"

Dolph shook his head from side to side in pure, hypoxic fury. "No!"

"No? Okay. I'm going back to the house."

"Go!"

"Will you be okay?"

Dolph rolled over and tried to get on his hands and knees. He fell flat at the first attempt and grunted as the air was forced out of his body.

But he tried again and made it.

"Okay. I'm going now."

Dolph gave him a silent, murderous look.

He was sitting on the porch as Dolph trudged slowly back to the barn. He thought about waving, but Dolph probably had a gun somewhere, and he couldn't outrun bullets.

He pondered calling Detective Sanders, but he didn't actually know anything; not even Turtle's real name.

He sighed. That had been fun, but now he had to go inside and look at horse pictures.

But they had lunch first in the solarium and spotted Hugh's car coming up the lane.

Laura said, "Something's wrong."

He followed her to the porte cochere. Erik Varner was driving Hugh's car, and Hugh was slumped in the passenger seat.

Laura opened the door. "Hubert! What's wrong?"

Hugh shook his head weakly. "I'm okay, Laura."

Erik, the executive assistant, said, "He collapsed in his office, Mrs. Poirier, but he wouldn't let me call anyone."

Erik and his dark suit were both looking a little rumpled.

"He ordered me to bring him home."

Laura said, "Hubert? I'm going to call the doctor."

"No! Don't do that, Laura. I just need to sit down for a while."

Hugh twisted in his seat and threw out first one leg and then the other. When they were firmly on the ground, he tried to stand, but fell back. "Damn it all to Hell."

He said, "Let me help you, Hugh."

"No!"

Erik said, "Let me do it, Sir." He smirked. "I'm not sure Bergeron is up to it."

Hugh said, "I don't need any help."

Laura said, "Hubert! Let Gabriel help you or I will call for an ambulance and paramedics no matter what you say!"

Hugh looked at her and nodded.

He wrapped an arm around Hugh and got him out of the car, and Hugh managed to get to the steps, but that exhausted him.

Erik took his other side and together they carried Hugh up the steps and into the foyer.

Hugh said, "The family room."

And they carried him and got him into a chair. Laura knelt beside him. "Are you sure...."

"No doctors! Please, Laura. Just let me sit here and get my breath back. "

"Tea?"

He smiled at her. "Coffee. Irish coffee...more Irish than coffee, Dear." She nodded and headed for the kitchen.

Hugh said, "Thank you, Erik. Thank you both. If I could be alone now...."

He followed Erik out the door. They descended the steps side by side. Erik looked over at him and smirked.

Erik said, "Maybe you aren't the wimp I thought you were, Bergeron."

He smirked back. "Thanks, and neither are you. I was shocked that you made it up the steps."

Erik laughed. "I'm stronger than you are."

"I doubt that." Erik was slender but obviously wiry. "I've been training hard lately."

Erik said, "So have I. All my life."

"To be ready for what?"

Erik said, "For whatever comes. I'll park the car."

"I can do it. Wait. How will you get back? I could take you?"

"No thanks. My assistant is on her way."

He was handsome in a sort of delicate way; it would be easy to underestimate Erik Varner.

"So you were Shaw's executive assistant, and now you're Hugh's?"

The little smile faded away. "I don't know. I should be, but I doubt it. I know about every action Shaw took, and every decision and every blunder he's made since he became CEO."

"And they won't value that? Hugh won't?"

Erik smiled. "Executives value ability in subordinates, but sometimes it isn't the most important thing."

"What is?"

"Loyalty."

"Oh. So Hugh had his own executive assistant, and he'll want him or her back?"

Erik shrugged.

"And what happens to you?"

"They'll offer me something. Probably."

"That isn't right."

Erik smirked again, or maybe that was just his smile? "Don't worry about me, Bergeron."

"Right. So how is Gita?"

Erik looked at him. "How would I know?"

"I thought you were close?"

"You thought wrong. I had to put up with her, because she was Shaw's wife. That's all."

"Right. So has Sanders talked to you?"

"He's interrogated me several times. Not that I could help him. So Shaw was murdered?"

"What did Sanders say?"

Erik smiled. "Almost nothing. Which is the only professional thing about the smiling bastard. Has he talked to you?"

"Also several times."

"And he talked to your boyfriend?" More smirking.

"Of course, he talked to Cory. So why do you think Shaw's death wasn't an accident?"

Erik shook his head. "Do I look stupid? From the questions Sanders asked."

"Right. So any idea who killed Shaw?"

Erik looked down the lane. "No idea. A few dozen husbands might spring to mind if I cared enough to think about it."

"So he was a philanderer?"

Erik turned to stare at him; his eyes were a washed out blue. "That's much too nice a word for him. Why don't you ask Poirier's daughter?"

"Diane? What are you saying?"

"Nothing. It's just...if anyone wanted him dead...."

"It wasn't Diane."

"Sure about that?"

"Yes." And he was. Mostly. He was less certain about Finn. Erik was still smiling.

"What about Gita? Maybe she'd had enough of him?"

Erik said, "You'd have to ask her yourself. But maybe Shaw was just collateral damage? I heard they found two other bodies." Erik looked jazzed. "I heard it was a blood bath over there."

Erik was looking at the barn.

"How do you know about the other guys or that the murders took place at the barn?"

"Hugh told me."

"Why would he do that?"

"Ask him." Erik stepped closer to him. "Did you see the bodies?" He nodded. "I bet you got all faint, didn't you?"

"No."

"Lose your lunch?"

"No."

Erik took another step closer and poked him in the chest. "Really? I don't believe you."

He poked Erik back. "I've seen worse." He could still see Garth and Iona lying on the floor of the stock room.

"You've never been in combat, Bergeron. You haven't seen shit. You're just a bookkeeper."

"And neither have you." Which was a guess. "You're just a glorified secretary, Erik." Which Erik didn't like at all. "I found two bodies...people I liked...they had been shot and bled out."

Erik stared and him and then shook his head. "No, I don't believe that. But I almost fell for it, Bergeron."

He shrugged. He didn't care if Erik believed him or not.

Erik said, "So you saw the bodies? And Sanders talked to you and to the FBI agent? Who does he suspect? Gita? Poirier's daughter? Maybe Kennard?"

"He wouldn't share that with me or with Cory."

"He didn't tell the FBI agent anything?" He shook his head. "Not even who the two guys were?"

"No, and why are you so interested?"

Erik smirked at him again. "I don't believe you."

And Erik shoved him and tried to pin him against Hugh's car, but he pushed him away and set himself.

Erik came back. They glared at each other nose to nose. If the guy wanted to get physical, he'd be more than happy to plant Erik face-first into Hugh's lawn. A mouthful of grass would take the smirk off his face. He had tossed Bornheimer; Erik was a thistle seed by comparison.

He smiled and waited to see if Erik had the balls to take a shot.

They stood there glaring at each other until Erik's phone rang. The ringtone sounded like sitar music.

He smirked some more at Erik. "Going to get that?"

Erik glared at him, but the phone kept on. Finally, it stopped, and he thought they were going to get into it, but the phone started up again.

"Shit!" Erik stepped back and grabbed his phone. "Hello?"

And then he walked off mumbling.

A car was zipping up the lane toward them; Erik spotted it and put his phone away.

Erik said, "My ride is here."

"Why are you so curious about the murders?"

Erik watched the car approaching. "Just curious. Knowledge is always useful. Knowledge can be traded for more tangible things. Especially in a corporation in turmoil."

Erik stood there waiting for the blue Mini Cooper to pull in. "Are you investigating this, Bergeron?"

"No. I'm only a bookkeeper. Remember?"

Erik smirked one last time before getting into the car. "Maybe, we can find out just how tough you are another time?"

"I look forward to it, Varner."

Erik got into the car and was whisked out of harm's way.

He could have taken him easy.
   Probably.

Friday
9:00 am

After Erik Varner had departed, he had called Cory to tell him about Hugh's collapse at the office, but he'd had to leave a voicemail.

Hugh had gotten his strength back quickly after getting home and had seemed only tired. Of course, he wasn't a doctor, and there could have been subtle warning flags he had missed.

And he had no idea what had caused the collapse. Of course, he might have a better idea if he slipped into Hugh's bathroom and scanned the pill bottles that might be there?

But he wasn't going to do that.

He had called Diane however and given her a full report. She had asked him to call her again in the morning if Hugh tried to leave for work.

Cory had called back, and he had told him everything and that he'd updated Diane. Cory hadn't blamed him. Which was good.

And it was now almost 9:00 am, and Hugh wasn't dressed for the office. Which was very good.

Hugh and Laura had broken their fast in the solarium, and now they and Madeleine were having a discussion.

In French.

Which he should have been able to follow a little bit; theoretically. Since he had studied the language for two whole years.

He had no idea. But he smiled a lot which might be wildly

inappropriate.

He thought Laura knew how at sea he was because she handed him Hugh's tablet computer.

Written French and spoken French were hardly the same language. Well, they were exactly the same language, but they required different skill sets.

Hugh had read an article in a French-language newspaper.

It was about *le conquistador Hernán Cortés* and his arrival at Tenochtitlan. Well, it was concerning the five hundredth anniversary of that event; *un demi-millénaire.*

He tried to read about *la conquête de l'empire aztèque*, and was moderately pleased with his comprehension.

But Hugh was looking at him, and there was definitely some smirkiness in his smile as he said, "Gabriel, Hernán Cortés: *un héros ou un génocidaire?*"

He spotted the line in the article or he might not have understood. "*Un génocidaire, peut-être?*"

And then the conversation left him so deeply in the dust that he felt like a Joad in the *Grapes of Wrath*. He thought that Hugh was arguing for a more favorable assessment of old *Hernán*, and Laura and Madeleine were scandalized.

He sipped his coffee until there was a lull in the fireworks of French and said, "We don't have a word for that in English."

Hugh was observing him critically

Laura said, "*Un génocidaire?*"

"Right. I don't think 'genocidist' is a word."

Hugh led them to the library where they consulted all of the available physical dictionaries before Hugh consulted the Internet.

"No. It isn't."

He said, "It should be."

Laura said, "It should."

She and Madeleine returned to the kitchen. He was about to follow, but Hugh said, "Gabriel?"

"Yes?"

"I'm sorry if I was brusque yesterday."

"That's okay. You weren't feeling well."

"No. But I'm much better now."

"I'm glad to hear it." He looked at Hugh. "What do you think of Erik Varner?"

Hugh smiled. "He won't be working for me...after a transition period."

"Right. Because he was Shaw's man?"

"But he wasn't."

Which meant what? "So did you tell him about the murders? About the two men who were killed? The details?"

Hugh scanned him, analyzing. "Why are you asking?"

"He just seemed to know a lot of details."

Hugh said, "Are you looking into this...mess, Gabriel? I wish you wouldn't do that. I know you're curious, but you could hurt the family...hurt Cory. Unintentionally."

"I would never do that, Hugh." He didn't want to give the guy something else to worry about. "And I'm not investigating. I wouldn't know where to begin, but about Erik?"

Hugh closed his eyes. "I think he asked about Shaw on the way home. I really don't remember too clearly what I said. If anything. I was exhausted, and I was embarrassed about...being unwell at the office."

"Sure. Of course. So are you going to retire again? For good?"

"No, Gabriel, I'm not."

"Why not? I know it's none of my business...."

"No, it isn't." Hugh was looking out the window. "It's too important to me to give up."

"The company? But Laura wouldn't mind. She hates the company and would be happy if you retired."

Hugh's face tightened up as if he'd been bobbing for apples in a vat of Botox. "I think I know better what my wife wants than you do."

Shit. "Of course. I'm sorry, Hugh. I didn't mean to upset you."

Hugh summoned an awful smile with sheer willpower. "I'm not upset, Gabriel."

There was no way he could ask if Hugh was going back to work any time soon; Monday, for instance.

He smiled and wandered away and did his best not to upset Hugh for the rest of the morning.

It was almost lunch time before Cory called again

"Greetings, Special Agent. Your father still seems to be fine. He is even now strolling back from the barn with your mother."

"Did he say anything about this collapse at the office?"

"To me? No, he did not."

"But he looks okay now?"

"I would be hitting 911 if he didn't...no matter what he said. Or Laura would. And I don't know what this 'collapse' looked like. That was Erik Varner's description. They're on the porch now. Do you want to talk to him?"

"It wouldn't do any good. Did you call Diane?"

"Twice. And she has a plan of action though she didn't explain."

Cory laughed. "Then I won't either. Thanks for being there, Gabe."

"Of course. Any idea about when you're coming home?"

"If Dad needs me, I can be there in a few hours."

He wasn't sure what to say? If he said Hugh was fine and something bad happened, then Cory might never truly forgive him. "He looks okay, Cory. More than that...."

"Understood. I'll call back later."

"Roger that. How are you? Making progress in the Jerry tracking?"

"We think so. I have to go, Gabe."

And he was gone.

Hugh seemed to be in good spirits, but then Childers arrived after lunch. He marched in and fixed Hugh with a glare. "We need to talk, Poirier."

Hugh smiled. "And I can guess about what. Come into my office, Childers."

Hugh shut the door and short of just barging in, there was nothing he could do. Laura went upstairs to her sanctuary.

He paced from the family room to the kitchen ready to call the paramedics if need be.

After a half hour, Childers stormed out. "Where is Laura?"
"Upstairs."
"Get her!"
He gave Childers his best smile. "Excuse me?"
"Go upstairs and get her!"
Childers was too old and decrepit to punch or toss around, and he was suppressing some violent urges with difficulty when Laura came downstairs on her own.

She smiled at Childers too. If anything, her smile was scarier. "What is it, Harold?"

"I must talk to you. Now!" Hugh had come out of his office; Childers glanced at him. "Alone, Laura."

Laura shook her head. "No, Harold. I'll talk to you but only with Hubert present. But you will stop yelling, Harold, or I'll ask Gabriel to throw you out of my house. You wouldn't mind doing that, would you, Gabriel?"

"Not in the least. Would you like him to bounce just the once? Or I could try for a double?"

Childers snorted in derision, but he spun around and headed back into the office. Laura followed and shut the door.

He should have bugged the damn office. He was pacing when he heard another car pull into the driveway.

He was peering out when a vigorous knock rattled the door. He opened it, and Kennard tried to push past him.

He'd had a stressful morning, and Kennard was a lot younger and fitter than Childers. He may have swept Kennard's leg and sent him sprawling to the foyer floor.

Kennard was amazed. "Who do you think you are?"
"Cerberus."
"What? Never mind." He scrambled to his feet. "Get out of my way!"

"Try to get past me again, and I'll rip your arm off."

Which gave Kennard pause. He laughed, and then he stopped laughing. "You?"

"Little old me."

"But I have to see Hugh! I know Childers is here."

"He is."

"In the office?"

Kennard was thinking about rushing him when the door opened.

Laura said, "Could you really rip his arm off, Gabriel?"

He smiled at her. "A little hyperbole, Laura. But I could hyper-extend his elbow or mess up his shoulder, and he'd be weeks or month getting back the full use of his arm."

He looked at her hopefully, but she shook her head.

Kennard tried to keep an eye on him as he smiled at Laura. "I just came to talk to Hugh. And you, Laura. I apologize if I was a bit...forceful."

Laura said, "I see. I don't suppose it can be avoided. Let him pass, Gabriel."

With a sweep of his arm, he waved Kennard in.

Kennard followed Laura to the office. A minute later, Childers was ejected.

Childers glared at him and began to pace. He wanted to barge into the office again, but he continued to wear a rut in Laura's beautiful, living room rug. It was Persian; umber and muted red.

He stepped in front of Childers, who stopped and glared at him.

"So you want to be CEO?"

"That's none of your business!"

"No, it isn't. Did you murder Craig Shaw to get the job?"

Childers looked tired, like he'd been climbing a mountain for eighty years, and the peak kept getting higher, but he set his saggy face into a grimace. "I didn't kill him."

"Of course not. You aren't a barbarian. Did you hire someone to kill him? One of the lower classes?"

Childers snorted. "No, I did not. I don't know anyone, of any class, who would do such a thing. Why are you asking? For the FBI agent? For Josephine's anointed one?"

"You're really pissed about that, aren't you? Why? Did Josephine promise you the job?"

"She said...." But he stopped himself.

"What did she say? 'Rid me of this meddlesome CEO, and

the job is yours' or something like that?"

Childers smiled for the first time. "She wouldn't ask me."

"No? Then who would she ask?"

Childers' smile faded; the effort was too much for his facial muscles. "Do you really want an answer to that, Bergeron? Do you think Special Agent Poirier does?"

Shit. He was sure that Cory did not if his grandmother was involved in the death of Shaw.

"So you didn't lure Shaw here and smack him on the head?"

Childers shook his head. "This is tiresome. Go away."

"Do you know who murdered Shaw?" Childers ignored him. "Has Detective Sanders questioned you?"

"He had the impertinence to come to my home."

"Really? Isn't it awful when the 99 percent don't know their place?"

More ignoring.

"Right. So why did you want to talk to Laura?"

Childers said, "Because she has the largest block of stock after Josephine."

"Laura does? Or Laura and Hugh?"

Childers said, "Hugh doesn't own a single share."

So the fortune was Laura's and not Hugh's? "But he was CEO for a while, and he probably got a severance package. And aren't executives paid in cash and stock?"

Childers said, "He had stock. At one time."

"But he sold it?"

"Ask him." Childers managed another smile. "I'm sure he'd be delighted to discuss it with you."

Childers was a sarcastic, old bastard, and he was tired of talking to him.

He went to the kitchen and made coffee. He searched the pantry again: he needed to buy cookies and hide them in his room.

Cookies and toaster pastries. And he'd need to smuggle a toaster into Cory's room. And a coffee maker. If he was going to be here for much longer. And a microwave.

He heard voices.

Childers said, "You aren't going to be CEO, Kennard."

Kennard was bouncing on his feet, a squat coil of energy. "You're wrong about that as you are about everything else."

"We'll see."

Kennard was flushed and happy. "We will."

Childers exited looking more dyspeptic and moribund than when he'd entered, but Kennard's face fell after he was out the door.

"Things didn't go so well?"

Kennard said, "You know nothing about how these things work."

"You're right. So you want Laura's support to get Craig Shaw's job? And she won't give it to you?"

Kennard smiled and walked out the door, but he followed. "So did you murder Shaw?"

Kennard laughed. "No."

"Did you hire someone to kill him?"

"No. I've already talked to that detective at the office."

"Sanders? What did you tell him?"

"That there was no reason for me to do anything. Shaw was already finished; he just didn't realize it."

"Because he was stupid?"

Kennard got into his car. "He was. Incredibly stupid. But he had sailed through life getting whatever he wanted, and he couldn't conceive of the possibility of things not going his way."

"But if he was so dumb...."

Kennard gave a bark of laughter. "He was. It was remarkable really."

"Then how did he get to be CEO?"

"He had help."

"From?"

Kennard looked at him, eyes bright with joy. "Guess. It was someone very close to him."

"Gita?" The woman behind the man? Did women even do that any more?

Kennard snickered. He was in his way just as unpleasant as Childers.

"Yes. As long as he listened to her, he was golden. She

should have been CEO."

"Why wasn't she?"

Kennard shrugged and slammed the door of his silver Mercedes.

"But he stopped listening to her?"

Kennard ignored him and roared out of the parking area. He sped down the lane, wheels barely touching the blacktop.

Which meant what? Gita had Shaw bumped off so she could take his place?

He went back inside.

Laura and Hugh were in the kitchen drinking coffee. He poured himself another cup and sat with them, totally uninvited.

He smiled his best smile.

Laura smiled back. Hugh said, "Don't ask. Whatever it is, Gabriel."

"Okay. I was just wondering about Gita Shaw?"

Laura and Hugh looked at each other communicating telepathically. Laura said, "What about her, Gabriel?"

"Does she work at Holcomb?"

Hugh said, "No. Not any more."

"But she did?"

Hugh nodded. "For a couple of years, I think?"

"Kids?"

Laura shook her head. "No, Gabriel."

Right. He needed to go for a walk. Or a drive.

He said, "I'm going to the Safeway in Middleburg. Anybody need anything?"

They declined.

He ran up to Cory's room and got a jacket. On his way out the door, he heard a snippet of conversation.

Hugh said, "...going in Monday, Laura. I have to."

He sighed and departed in his yellow Jeep.

Friday
2:00 pm

He sped away from the farm.

He turned off the Middleburg main drag which was Route 50, and parked in the Safeway lot.

He grabbed chocolate chip cookies, sourdough pretzels, and a raspberry danish. He wanted ice cream, but he resisted its siren call. He added a jar of peanut butter and crackers to his cart.

He checked out and called Cory from his Jeep.

Who answered. "Gabe?"

"Everything is fine."

"But?"

"I'm pretty sure Hubert intends going back to work on Monday."

"Call Diane and tell her."

"Will do." He couldn't ask Cory about his parents' finances. Well he could, but he wasn't going to. "I miss you."

"I'll be home soon."

And he was gone. Cory had no idea how to end a phone conversation. But he was perfect otherwise.

He ate a cookie; well, five cookies.

He pondered and made a decision. He called Detective Sanders. "Gabe?"

"Yes."

"You have something for me?" He sounded profoundly doubtful.

"Maybe."

Sanders's sigh whistled from his cellphone to the cell tower and probably through a satellite in geosynchronous orbit before bouncing down to him. "Imagine that you're talking to someone with a temper and access to an arsenal and not a happy, gentle guy like me."

"Right."

And he told him about the supposedly dead horses and about Turtle.

Sanders sighed again. "So you have no proof of any of this?"

"Nope. But Bucephalus was the only thing of value in the barn, and if somebody wanted to horse-nap him, then Hilda is a likely suspect."

Sanders said, "And one of the dead bodies belongs to Turtle who was a friend of Dolph's. Right. I follow all that. Why would she do that, Gabe? She's worked for the Poiriers for years."

"No idea. For the cash? May I make a suggestion?" Sanders grunted. "Check Mrs. Prentice's bank accounts for last January and the January before that."

"For large cash deposits? I would have thought of that, Gabe Buddy."

"Sorry! Of course you would."

"But how in the Hell do I get a warrant?"

"Right." That was a puzzler. Sanders was silent for a long time. "Detective?"

"Still here. I'll see what I can do. Anything else?"

"Nope. Wait! Mrs. Prentice and Dr. Crain are having a torrid love affair." Sanders made a choked sound that segued into rolling-on-the-floor laughing.

"What's funny? Anyway, I caught them...in the barn. Not that I'm a peeping Tom or anything like that, Detective. But I'm sure he helped her. He confirmed that the horses had died to Hugh. So you might want to check his bank accounts too, If you can finagle that warrant thing?"

"That it?"

"Yes."

"Thanks, Gabe."

And Sanders was gone. He was glad he'd told him even if it was all just a tissue of supposition.

There was something else, but he couldn't pin it down. He ate one more cookie, but his brain wouldn't be forced.

He called Diane.

"I'm pretty sure your father intends going back to work on Monday."

Diane said, "I was afraid of that."

"So you'll come and talk to him?"

She laughed. "Actually I've arranged for something much more effective."

"Which is? Blow up the bridges between the farm and Holcomb?"

"You'll see."

"You aren't going to tell me?"

But she just giggled and hung up. Which was cruel and very unlike her.

But he had roughly fifty thousand calories worth of junk food so he'd endure.

Friday
8:00 pm

He was in Cory's room when he spotted the flashing lights of a sheriff's cars. He put on sturdy shoes this time, grabbed a jacket, and ran down the back stairs.

Hugh was coming down the other stairs. "What is it, Gabriel?"

"No idea. I'll find out."

And he ran full tilt for Hilda's cottage which seemed to be the epicenter of police activity.

He got close before a voice roared at him. "Whoa!"

He whoa-ed as a flashlight blinded him. He put a hand up and tried using his fingers as a light filter. It was the very large Deputy Huska.

"Hi, Deputy Huska. Is Detective Sanders here? What's going on? Could you point the flashlight away?"

Huska said, "You stay put, Bergeron."

He remembered. "Yes, Sir. I won't move. Can you tell Detective Sanders I'd like to speak to him?"

"If he wants to talk to you, he'll find you."

Huska was thinking about telling him to get back to the house, but the arrival of Hugh and Laura distracted him.

He may have slipped a little closer. Hilda's front door was open, and light was spilling out. He could hear voices.

Dolph said, "It weren't him!"

A shape was moving behind him. He spun without shrieking. He expected it to be Huska, but it was Mrs. Foote.

She was smiling. "What's going on, Gabriel?"

He was not on a first name basis with Mrs. Foote; mostly because he didn't want to be, but also because he didn't know her first name.

"I don't know." Huska was staring his way. "But I bet Deputy Huska could tell you."

She smiled a smile that would strike terror into the hearts of virgins everywhere. "I see him."

"Yep. How could you miss him? Look at the size of the man!"

He wasn't going to feel bad about siccing Mrs. Foote on Huska; he needed to find out what was going on.

Two deputies came out of Hilda's cottage urging Hilda and Dolph along. They shoved Dolph into a patrol car.

Hilda said, I can't leave Jack alone. I can't!"

Sanders popped out of the door. "We'll get someone...."

But Mrs. Foote executed a beautiful fake and got past Deputy Huska. "I can stay with him, Hilda."

Hilda didn't want to accept help from Mrs. Foote, but she was bound for jail, for prison, for the deepest, darkest dungeon of Loudoun County.

"Thank you, Celia."

Mrs. Foote, Celia, said, "Don't worry, Hilda. I'll take good care of him...until you come back?"

Sanders ignored the question in her voice. Hilda was put into another vehicle, and she and Dolph were driven away.

Mrs. Foote was standing at the door to Hilda's cottage. "I have to go in to see to Jack."

Sanders shook his head.

Jack was in his wheelchair and had somehow rolled himself to the door. "Where did you take, Hilda? I need her...please tell me where you're taking her?"

Sanders knelt beside Jack's wheelchair and smiled at him. "Don't upset yourself, Mr. Prentice."

"Who are you, Sir? I can't see your face."

"I'm Detective Sanders, Mr. Prentice, and Mrs. Foote here is going to take care of you." He spotted Deputy Huska. "Help her move Mr. Prentice and whatever he needs to her house, Deputy."

Jack said, "But this is my house." He started crying. "I don't want...to leave."

Sanders knelt beside the wheelchair again. "I'm sorry, Mr. Prentice, but we have to search your house. Mrs. Foote will take good care of you, and we'll have you back in your own house as soon as we can. I promise."

Jack said, "Did you...arrest her?"

"We took her in for questioning, Sir."

Jack nodded.

Laura walked past Huska and the other deputies. She smiled at Sanders. "I'll help Mrs. Foote, Detective." She gently touched Jack's shoulder. "Jack, it's Mrs. Poirier. Don't upset yourself. Mr. Poirier and I will see that Hilda's back soon. Now, it's too cold for you to be out here."

She pointed a delicate but imperious finger at Sanders. "I need a blanket, Detective."

And Sanders said, "Yes, Ma'am."

Laura draped it over Jack's skeletal shoulders, and she and Mrs. Foote wheeled him away with Deputy Huska in the rear.

Sanders looked at another deputy. "Nobody goes into this house until CID has checked every square inch."

Hugh marched over to Sanders. "What is going on, Detective? And why have you taken Mrs. Prentice?"

Sanders didn't want to answer.

Hugh said, "I don't want to call the Sheriff, Detective."

"No, Sir. We identified one of the murdered men, Sir."

"And who was it?"

"Seth Yates, aka Turtle. An associate of Dolph Prentice's."

"And you think Dolph had something to do with his death?"

"I don't know, Sir, but I do know that he and Mrs. Prentice lied to me when they said they didn't know the victim. He's been in their house several times."

Hugh nodded. "I see."

"Yes, Sir."

"Thank you, Detective. I'll arrange for them to have

representation."

"Yes, Sir."

And Hugh walked toward Mrs. Foote's cottage.

Sanders was looking at him sans smile, but he walked over anyway. "How did you identify Turtle?"

Sanders walked toward his car. "His grandmother filed a missing person's report this afternoon...not long after you called."

"Right. I see."

Deputy Huska was glancing their way.

Sanders hurried to get into his car, but he cracked the window. "Thanks for your help, Gabe."

"So you can check Hilda's bank account now?"

Sanders nodded and rolled up the window. And motored away. Which was a bit brusque. But understandable.

Laura and Hugh came out of Celia's house and walked away.

Deputy Huska waited until they were gone before he strolled back to Celia's and was admitted.

Saturday 10:00 am

Saturday dawned bright and calm or he imagined it did since it was like that when he woke up after nine.

He resisted the urge to call Sanders since it would be fruitless and probably result in getting his feelings hurt.

He got dressed. He downed a bowl of cereal with whole milk chock full of fiber and vitamins and protein and didn't feel so bad about the bag of cookies he'd eaten.

Hugh and Laura had already had breakfast.

Laura came into the kitchen. "Are you all right, Gabriel?"

"You mean breakfast-wise? Sure. Tip top. How are you? I'm sorry about Mrs. Prentice."

She didn't even try for a smile.

Hugh said, "Did you have something to do with getting her arrested?"

"No! Absolutely not. She lied to the police about not knowing Seth Yates." His grand theory of her horse thievery had nothing to do with it. So far.

"Why would she do that, Hugh?"

"I don't know."

Laura dredged up a brilliant smile. "I don't want to hear about that from either of you. I'll think about that tomorrow."

He heard the faint strains of the theme music from *Gone with the Wind* playing in the background.

"We have to go, Hubert. There's so much to do when we get back."

He looked quizzical.

Laura said, We'll be back by noon or so, Gabriel. Diane and Jordan are coming this afternoon."

"Great! Any occasion?"

"They always watch the rugby finals with Hubert." She smiled and patted her husband's face.

This smile said that it was silly, but she wouldn't gainsay them a bit of happiness.

They seemed a little overdressed for a drive. Laura was wearing a spiffy, gray wool suit; the tailored slacks fit her perfectly as did the blazer. She was wearing a black blouse and silver and turquoise jewelry.

Hugh was in a gray suit too with a gorgeous, burgundy tie made from silk spun by the very best silkworms. His shoes weren't bad either.

They looked as elegant as the One Percent were wont to do. Not that he begrudged them their wealth. Not really.

He had gone for another walk in a different direction and had found another babbling brook before the wind made him turn around. He was almost back to the barn and was pondering where he could get a pizza for lunch when he spotted an antique pickup truck struggling up the lane.

Clouds of smoke were issuing from its rear end. He had been told by his mechanic Stan that this meant it was burning oil. Which was a bad thing.

The truck rattled as far as Hilda's cottage and died.

An elderly lady got out and marched to Hilda's door. She began to bang on said door and yell.

He may have altered course.

"Hello? Mrs. Prentice isn't here."

She wheeled around. She had her hand shoved inside a purse deep enough to hold many things.

He stopped in his tracks and gave her his very best smile.

"Who are you?"

"I'm Gabriel Bergeron. And you are?"

She didn't appear ready to identify herself. "Where's Hilda? Gone off? Then where's that Dolph?"

"He's with her." And both of them were still in jail which he wasn't sure he should share?

"You're lying for them!"

"No, Ma'am! I wouldn't do that."

She was probably eighty. She was about Aunt Flo's size but bent over with a dowager's hump. She had gray hair hacked off, a large nose, and saggy jowls.

The large nose had a large mole. Bags of skin sagged over eyes of no particular color.

She was rocking on her feet.

Hilda had a couple of aluminum lawn chairs leaning against the side of the house. He grabbed one. "Would you like to sit down?"

She glared at him and rocked some more before she nodded.

He opened the chair and set it behind her. "Do you want me to help you, Ma'am?"

"No! I can do it."

She tottered a bit, but she managed to seat herself. She sighed and took a deep breath. "Pitiful."

"What's pitiful?"

She glared at him. "Me!"

And then she just sat there. Her feet and ankles had swollen out of her rundown shoes.

He opened the other chair, but the webbing was rotten, so he stood smiling at the little, old lady like an idiot. Her purse was more of a canvas tote bag and appeared heavy. She pulled it into her lap and wrapped her arms around it.

"Stop smiling!"

"Yes, Ma'am! Sorry. I do it when I'm nervous."

She regarded him. "What are you nervous about?"

"Well, I'm just wondering what you have in your purse thing?"

She smiled. "You aren't Dolph Prentice so you don't have to worry your pretty head about that."

It was nice to be called pretty though he would prefer handsome, but still.

"Maybe if you tell me who you are? And why you're here? I can help?"

She went back to glaring at him. "Just a real helpful fellow, aren't you?"

Which didn't sound like a good thing coming from her.

"I try to be. So I'm Gabriel Bergeron...."

"You said already."

"Yes, I did, and I'm an accountant."

"Work for them?" She pointed toward the house.

"For Hugh and Laura? No. I'm a...friend of their son, Cory Poirier, and I'm visiting."

He thought caution was called for so he wasn't going to tell her he was Cory's boyfriend, because there was a lump in her tote bag that looked very gun shaped.

"Don't know them." She smiled. "Never been invited to take tea at the big house."

"No? But you know Hilda and Dolph?"

"I know Hilda to speak to. Her and Jack. How's he doing? He still here?"

"I don't think he's doing very well." He should be in Mrs. Foote's house.

She nodded and frowned. "Spect I shouldn't have banged on the door. Scared him."

"But you're upset, and you thought you had to."

"I did! I need to speak to Dolph Prentice!"

"About what?"

She studied him some more. "Are you sure he's not here?"

"Yes, Ma'am."

"What was your name? Gabriel?"

"Yes, Ma'am. You look tired."

"I am. I used to be able to run. I could outrun any boy in the county." She shook her head. "And now I can barely walk from the truck to the door."

He sat on the ground next to her.

She pointed at the big house. "They home?"

"No. They're gone to."

"And this Cory fellow?"

"No, he's out of town."

She shook her head. "I don't know what I'm doing."

"Looking for Dolph?"

She glared at him. "I know that! I'm not senile. I just don't know what to do with him if I catch him."

"Why do you want to catch him?"

She started crying. "Because of Seth."

Which made everything crystal clear. "Seth who?"

"Seth Yates. My grandson."

Did she know Seth was dead? "Did something happen to Seth, Mrs. Yates?"

She nodded crying harder. "He's gone. I knew something was wrong."

"I'm very sorry to hear that. Did Dolph have something to do with whatever happened to your Seth?"

She pulled out a big-ass revolver. "This is my daddy's Colt 45, and Dolph Prentice is going to tell me what happened to my Seth, or I'm going to put six holes in his worthless carcass. May do it anyway."

He sat very, very still. "And Seth's nickname was 'Turtle,' Mrs. Yates?"

She nodded. "They called him that. I never did. He wasn't slow."

"No, I'm sure he wasn't. And he went missing?"

She nodded. "I talked to a deputy."

"And to Detective Sanders?"

She nodded and pulled out a gray handkerchief to wipe her eyes. "He didn't tell me nothing, but the deputy said Seth's body was found here." She twisted her head. "By the barn?"

"It was. Do you know why Seth would come here?"

"Something to do with Dolph!" She shook her head. "Seth just turned twenty-two...I made him a cake."

"I'm very sorry, Mrs. Yates."

"And I couldn't watch him all the time, but I should have known he was up to something." She glared at him and fondled her daddy's Colt.

"He told me he was going off with Bennie and Bennie's

brother, Randall. Randall's a few years older and not so...scatterbrained as my Seth and Bennie. I thought he'd be all right. I watched him ride off on his bike."

"He didn't have a car?" She shook her head. "What kind of bike?"

"An old red thing; more rust than metal. But I got him a new chrome headlight for it. He rode that thing all hours of the night.

"Where did he tell you they were going?"

"Fishing. On the gulf coast...Mississippi or Alabama...Seth wasn't too clear, but I thought that was just Seth being Seth. But after I didn't hear a thing, and he didn't answer his cellphone or get back to me, I called Randall, and he told me there was no fishing trip, but he promised to find Bennie."

The tears were rolling down her cheeks again. "And then Randall came to see me dragging Bennie. And Bennie claimed he didn't know nothing about Seth even after Randall shook him hard enough to rattle his teeth."

"And then you went to the police."

"I did. To the sheriff's office in Round Hill."

"And they figured it out."

She nodded. "I gave them a picture of Seth, and I could see it in their eyes. They knew right off."

She stopped talking and seemed to sag in the chair. Her eyes closed.

"Mrs. Yates?" She blinked at him. "Let's get you to the house."

He managed to get her into her rusty truck, and it managed to cover the few hundred yards belching black fumes.

He wanted to get her into the kitchen, but she shook her head. "Can't climb those steps. Can't."

"Right." He got her seated on a garden bench. The sun was shining, and, out of the wind, it wasn't really cold. But he wasn't eighty years old either.

He took off his jacket and put it around her shoulders. "I'll be right back, Mrs. Yates."

He ran up the steps and into the kitchen. Madeleine had the

day off, and she had already left the farm.

He made a cup of strong tea and spooned in the sugar. He grabbed a decanter of something golden-brown from Hugh's office.

He ran back to Mrs. Yates. Her eyes were open. Which was a good thing in this case.

He handed her the cup of tea. "Would you like to add some of this to your tea?"

She looked from him to the decanter. "I'm a Christian woman, Gabriel."

"Right. But this is medicinal."

She snorted, but she took the decanter and sniffed. She smiled at him. "Maybe just a drop."

He hadn't left enough room in the tea cup.

She sipped her tea and smiled at him. "Who would believe it?"

He sat on the bench beside her. "What's that?"

"I'm having tea at the Poirier place."

"You are." And drinking Hugh's brandy or whatever it was. "Are you feeling better?"

She nodded. "I am." She closed her eyes. "I had to identify the body, Gabriel."

"I'm so sorry. But what was your grandson doing here, Mrs. Yates?"

"Something that Dolph got him into. That evil bastard bullied my Seth into something and got him killed."

He didn't know what to say.

She was looking at him. "Tell me this, Gabriel, did he suffer?"

Shit. "No, Ma'am. He was shot." He put a hand over his heart. "It would have been like being punched in the chest and then nothing." Or that was his best guess and didn't sound so bad whether it was accurate or not.

She patted her tote bag. "I'm going to kill Dolph Prentice."

"I know you want to. I understand, but don't you want to know all the facts first?"

She shook her head, but she said, "What facts?"

And he told her all about Shaw and the other man.

"A hit-man? Like in the movies? That don't sound right."

"I know. And where would Dolph get an untraceable Beretta with a silencer and a commando knife?"

"He's a thief."

"Probably, but would he be bright enough to try to stage a murder to look like an accident with a horse?"

She shook her head. "No. Dolph's a stupid bully. He needs to be told to come in out of the rain." She looked up. "That mother of his. Maybe she did all this?"

"But we don't know that. And you should be sure before you shoot Dolph...or Hilda. If they need shooting."

She tried a smile. "What do you want me to do?"

"Go home. I'm going to talk to Detective Sanders. He'll get to the bottom of this. I'm sure of it, Mrs. Yates."

And she let herself be helped into her truck.

"Are you okay to drive?"

She nodded. "I'll manage. You talk to that Sanders and then come see me."

"I will."

She drove off. He got in his Jeep and followed her to see that she made it. She didn't live that far, which made sense since Turtle/Seth had biked it.

He watched her navigate the steps and the porch, which were in the process of detaching from the body of the house. The main roof ridge was sagging, and the shingles were shot.

But she got inside safely, and then he called Sanders and got his voicemail, but it was Saturday. "Hi, Detective. Mrs. Yates came to the farm looking for Dolph Prentice. She blames him for getting Seth into something. Of course, Dolph wasn't around, and I got her calmed down and back to her house."

He should just hang up. "So did you check Hilda's bank accounts? And what about the alibis of Harold Childers and Richard Kennard? They're both on the board of Holcomb, and they both really want to be CEO."

He didn't imagine he'd hear back.

He got back to the farm in time to see a deputy bring Hilda and Dolph back. Hilda marched over to Mrs. Foote's house with

Dolph trailing behind her.

Sanders hadn't been able to hold them? So he hadn't found the bank account? Or there wasn't one, and Gabriel Bergeron was just wrong about the whole mess? Shit.

Maybe, but he didn't believe it.

He was brooding when Laura and Hugh got back, but they were in high spirits.

Laura went into the kitchen and began to prepare food.

He followed Hugh to his office. If Hugh noticed the level in his decanter had dropped, he didn't mention it.

"Mrs. Prentice and Dolph are back. Sanders didn't hold them. Or they made bail?"

Hugh said, "Don't tell Laura." Hugh was staring at him.

"Okay."

Hugh went out the office door and walked over to Hilda's house and was granted admittance.

He went into the kitchen to help Laura.

Hugh came back and joined them in the kitchen.

Laura said, "You went to Mrs. Prentice's house, Hugh, so she must be back. How is she? And Jack?"

Hugh shook his head. "Upset, of course. Jack is okay. Do you want to hear?" She nodded. "She said she lied to the deputies because she was afraid Dolph would get into trouble."

He said, "But she made it worse by lying to them."

Hugh gave him a look. "As I told her, Gabriel." He looked at Laura. "She thought we were selling the farm."

"What? Why, Hubert? We would never sell the farm."

"I told her that. She seemed shocked and then relieved. She was sure...after we sold most of the horses two years ago."

Laura shoved a tray into the oven. "I'm glad you reassured her, Hubert. But we aren't going to talk about that any more."

"No, Dear. We won't."

Laura nodded and smiled. "Then help me. They'll be here soon."

Saturday
5:00 pm

Judd and Samantha had arrived first; Samantha wasn't showing yet or at least not in her flowing, amber dress.

Diane and Finn were next. He was so happy for the company that he hugged them all.

He was almost eager to watch rugby.

It appeared that this ritual included special game day foodstuffs which Hugh and Laura prepared.

Laura said, "It's just an assortment of finger food, Gabriel."

And Tiffany's was just a jewelry store.

One tray had a bowl of something orange surrounded by salami, waffle fries, peppers, radishes, carrots, cucumbers, and what looked like peanuts in the shell. And crackers.

He wanted to smell the orange stuff, but Laura was watching him. "The dip is pimento cheese with some spices."

"Right. Are those peanuts?"

"Yes, Gabriel. Boiled peanuts."

He could eat the crackers and the waffle fries and maybe try a peanut.

The next tray had hard boiled eggs sliced lengthwise and filled with colorful things. There was a bowl of tan glop next to them, as well as a plate of what might be small tomatoes filled with something white.

And there was something that had been harvested from the fertile fields of Chernobyl and then encased in bacon instead of lead.

He pointed. "Laura?"

She smiled, but it wasn't a nice smile. "Pickled okra."

He was pretty sure he didn't blanch. He did note that there was cheddar cheese. And a tray with shrimp and corn.

The main feast item was a mound of chicken wings, but they were a suspect reddish orange.

He slipped beside Diane and said, "What are the chicken wings coated with?"

And then he noticed that she looked as tense as a French nobleman passing a sign that said, "Guillotine: this way."

"What's wrong?"

"Nothing, Gabe."

Which was so not true. She and Finn were both on edge, and Judd and Samantha were too, but not quite as much.

Diane said, "It's a pepper jelly glaze."

He crossed the wings off his list. He had been wise to buy that jar of peanut butter.

He looked at Laura. There was no way she didn't know that something was up, but she was all Zen garden on the surface.

There was a choice of wine, beer, and diet cola. He and Samantha took the diet cola.

The game was being played in Japan for no obvious reason. England wore all white, and South Africa, the green tops and white shorts.

And there were lots of head bands worn low to cover ears, and some ears were taped up. But no padding, no helmets, and lots of tackling and piling on.

The game was underway before he sat down. It appeared that England ruled in the hearts of the Poirier clan.

South Africa kicked off, and two big players on England's team tossed a smaller teammate high into the air to try and snag the ball, but he missed.

And there was lots of running and tackling and wrestling until the referees stopped it for some reason.

And then they had a scrum in which a bunch of guys from each team locked horns and tried to push each other around. He thought the ball was involved in some way? But it was very confusing.

And then there was another penalty kick, but he wasn't sure how the penalty had been incurred since the ball could be tossed or kicked in any direction?

But the kicker was a very handsome, young man with noble cheekbones and a perfectly shaped head; his body wasn't bad either.

And then England had the ball. They were just a few yards from South Africa's goal line. One English player after another tried to smash his way across the line only to be stopped and smothered under a pile of enormous South Africans.

But the ball popped out of the sweaty man pile to another English player who tried again. This happened over and over with England trying desperately to score.

Judd and Hugh and Finn were screaming for England.

But it was all in vain though another mysterious penalty was called, allowing England to score a field goal.

There was some talk of a yellow card?

The major difference between rugby and football seemed to be that when the ball carrier went down, play didn't stop; not at all.

The carrier might be tackled and buried under a ton of beefy men who wrestled for the ball, but somehow the ball would often pop out of the pile to a member of the carrier's team, and play would go on.

It looked exhausting. And brutal. It was basically gang warfare in shorts and knee socks.

He watched a few more minutes and bailed. He liberated some waffle fries and went up to Cory's room.

He called but got his voicemail, but Cory called back in a few minutes.

"Your father is fine. He's watching rugby."

Cory said, "The world cup finals? Is that this weekend?"

"It is. And your mother made snacks."

Cory laughed. "Which you haven't tried. You could expand your horizons, Bergeron."

He finished spreading peanut butter on a dozen crackers. "My horizons are vast and limitless, Corentin."

"Did she make the okra with the bacon?"

"She did."

Cory said, "I want you to try it. For me."

"I don't know, Cory."

"Gabe."

"Maybe. So the reason I called." And he explained all about Hilda and Dolph and Turtle and Mrs. Yates.

"And he let them go?"

"He did. Couldn't he have charged them with obstruction?"

"He could. He still might. If he can't figure out what they're up to. You really think Mrs. Prentice sold two of our horses?"

"At least two." Cory didn't say anything. "So you think I'm off base?"

"I don't know. She's worked for us for years."

"Right. So where are you? I've been so distracted, I haven't even asked."

"Denver."

"Right. So about Monday? Jennifer is going to expect me back at Garst, Bauer & Hartmann?"

"Go."

"Are you sure? I could stay." He had his fingers crossed.

"No. Diane has the situation in hand, and I'll be home on Tuesday."

"Really? Excellent. Okay, I'll let you go."

"Bye."

He ate his peanut butter crackers and went downstairs. He looked at the trays in the kitchen. He was hoping that all the okra would be gone, but not so.

He sniffed it. It was wrapped in bacon. How bad could it be? He took a bite.

He chewed.

He swallowed.

Okra would never pass his lips again.

And he might rule out all foods beginning with an "O." But then he remembered Oreos.

He went back to the family room where the game was over. Hugh was looking grim.

"What's wrong?"

Hugh said, "England lost."

Which was a bad thing so he tried looking shocked and disappointed. But the real main event was about to begin. He was pretty sure he'd seen Judd and Diane doing rock, paper, scissors in the living room.

Judd was looking at Samantha, and she was smiling at him. She was tall and slender with a narrow oval face; her eyes were as dark as Judd's. Her black hair was parted at the side, falling to partially eclipse her left eye; every strand was trimmed to the same length, ending just above her narrow shoulders.

She squeezed his hand.

Judd said, "Samantha and I have something to tell you all."

So Judd had lost and had to go first.

Laura was smiling, but she'd be smiling as she watched a tsunami wave come up the beach to take her.

Hugh said, "Yes, Jordan?"

Judd smiled and took Samantha's hand. "Samantha is expecting."

There was riotous jubilation; Poirier style. After the subdued smiles and handshakes, Judd said, "And we're getting married."

More jubilation. Laura semi-hugged Samantha. The family room was awash in emotion, almost as unfettered as what you'd experience in the rare book room of your more boisterous library.

There was fifteen minutes of baby talk; well, talk about babies, past, present, and to come.

It all seemed to be going splendidly. He waited for the Diane-Finn shoe to drop.

Diane looked at Finn who nodded. He had obviously dressed for the occasion; his sports coat looked suspiciously new.

Finn was getting to his feet. "Mr. and Mrs. Poirier, Diane and I have been dating for six months now."

Laura's face was a mirror wherein men might read dark things. Hugh didn't realize what was coming yet.

Finn planted his size twelve feet. "And we're very much in love. And I would like your permission to marry Diane."

Finn was smiling.

Diane was focused on her mother. Hugh looked from Finn to Laura and back.

Laura was still motionless, face blank.

Diane stood up. "This is the man I'm going to marry." And she kissed Finn on the mouth with every indication of passion.

Judd stood up and shook Finn's hand as soon as Diane broke her lip-lock. "Congratulations!" He hugged Diane as did Samantha.

The pebble of panic that had jammed Laura's internal mechanism suddenly popped out, and she lurched into action. "When were you thinking of getting married, Diane?"

"In a few months."

Laura warped her lips into the scariest smile he had ever seen. "In the spring? Or June?"

Obviously the first battle would be a delaying action. Time to assess Finn and his family back ten generations, and if he proved unworthy, which was entirely possible, time to talk sense into Diane.

Diane smiled back at her mother. "Or we might just elope?"

Which was so cruel it violated half a dozen Geneva conventions and the Constitution.

Sunday 2:00 pm

Laura had not stroked out though it had been a near thing. Everyone had stayed over, and breakfast had been cordial.

Finn and Diane had left after Diane had endured a little chat with her mother.

Judd and Samantha had gone next with talk of a baby shower in their ears.

He wanted to go home too, but he still didn't see anything that would stop Hugh from going into work on the morrow.

And he had promised Cory.

He could sabotage Hugh's car? He didn't want to do too much damage; maybe he could take out the battery? He would probably need a wrench. Was there any danger that he might electrocute himself? Or fry the car's electronics? Some research was called for.

Laura and Hugh were looking at him.

Laura said, "Are you all right, Gabriel?"

"Me? Fit as a fiddle. Tip-top. Never better."

Hugh shook his head at the idiot his son had gotten involved with. "We're going for a little drive."

Laura and Hugh took a lot of drives.

He sighed and paced. He made coffee and drank it. He was about to call Diane and demand info when there came a rapping on the back door.

He opened it all unawares.

Two ladies were looking at him. The taller one said, "Our

bags are in the car."

And they pushed past him without so much as a by-your-leave. So two mad women had gone off their meds and escaped from a not-so-secure facility?

The taller one called out with a mighty roar, "Hughie? Laura? Come out, come out, wherever you are."

But they knew that Hugh and Laura lived here. And they were calling Hugh, "Hughie."

"Have to be family."

The shorter one turned. "Of course, we're family. I am Élisabeth Mayfield, and this is my sister Anne-Sophie Bine.

Élisabeth was younger than her sister though they both had short, gray hair; Élisabeth's was styled while Anne-Sophie's looked hacked off. They shared the same chin and shape of the face, and they had little blue eyes just like Hugh's but not his perfect teeth.

Anne-Sophie, who was the taller, louder one, glared at him. "We're Hughie's sisters, not that it's any business of yours."

Anne-Sophie was wrinkled like a relief map of the Himalayas; Élisabeth was more like the wheat fields of Kansas.

Élisabeth shook her head at her sister. "But who are you? Not Mrs. Villeneuve's nephew?"

"No, Ma'am. I'm Gabriel Bergeron. I'm Cory's...."

Élisabeth smiled. "You're Cory's paramour." She clapped her hands together. "I was hoping we'd get to meet you. Spin around for me."

"What?"

Anne-Sophie said, "Turn!"

He didn't want to, but he did it.

Élisabeth said, "Very handsome."

Anne-Sophie shrugged. "Cory could do better."

He was going to smack Anne-Sophie's upturned nose, and dare Cory to object.

Anne-Sophie said, "Our luggage is still in the car, Young Man."

Élisabeth said, "Yes, be a dear, Gabriel. Where are Hughie and Laura?"

Anne-Sophie said, "And Cory? Are you here alone?"

She thought he was stealing the silver. He didn't even like silver. "Hubert and Laura are taking a drive. Corentin is working...in Denver...but he'll be back on Tuesday."

Élisabeth said, "And how is Hughie?"

"Nobody will say, but my best guess is not tip-top."

Élisabeth said, "They are very secretive, aren't they?"

Anne-Sophie said, "Well, he isn't...."

He smiled at Anne-Sophie. "Family? One of us? Trustworthy?" Anne-Sophie just frowned at him. "Did you tell Hubert and Laura that you were coming?"

Élisabeth smiled. "Not exactly."

Anne-Sophie said, "Diane called us."

"I know. I called Diane on instructions from Cory. So you know that Hugh plans on going back to work on Monday?"

Anne-Sophie said, "That's why we're here...to stop that foolishness."

He gave them both his very best smile because he would soon be free to go home.

Hugh and Laura had no doubt recognized the car when they pulled in. So when they entered and were greeted by Élisabeth and Anne-Sophie, it was all hugs and kisses; literally. And manufactured smiles by the gross.

Hugh became more boyish, more French; Laura became the Ice Queen. And not your tepid water ice but methane ice or nitrogen ice...whichever was colder?

Élisabeth and Anne-Sophie looked okay. There was nothing wrong with their dresses or their sturdy, sensible shoes, but next to Laura they looked frumpy. They knew it, and Laura knew it.

They circled like scorpions. Well, they were seated in the family room; Laura on one sofa, the Poirier sisters on another. And they were smiling, but there was all kinds of metaphorical circling and stinger waving. The acrid stench of venom filled the air.

Hugh was sitting there. He had to be aware of the tension, but he had a layer of scar tissue from previous battles?

So they chatted.

Hugh tossed the grenade of Judd's impending fatherhood, which blunted his sisters' impending assault.

And then Laura brought up the suitability of Finn. She and Anne-Sophie swore a blood oath to derail the marriage.

Élisabeth said, "But if she loves him...."

She was roundly jeered, but she just looked amused.

So, all things considered, the sweetness and light lasted longer than he would have predicted.

Anne-Sophie said, "We need to talk, Hughie." And she stalked toward Hugh's office like Sasquatch.

Hugh may have sighed, but he followed after Élisabeth took his arm.

He and Laura were not invited. He thought Laura was as glad as he was.

He smiled at Laura.

She said, "Do you know why they're here, Gabriel?"

"Maybe."

"You called Diane?"

"Per instructions. Yes, Ma'am."

"I don't want Hubert to go to the office tomorrow."

"Right. No one does, but have you told him that?"

Laura shook her head. "I couldn't. He's very proud, Gabriel. He hates weakness."

He thought that Hugh believed that Laura was the one who hated weakness, but he didn't say anything. They waited as the volume of the frank discussion increased until Hugh burst out of his office and was out the door before Laura could say a word.

Élisabeth and Anne-Sophie came back to the family room. They glared at Laura until she excused herself.

Anne-Sophie said, "It's all her fault! Her and that ogre of a mother."

Which was the pot calling the pot black.

Élisabeth said, "But the company isn't doing well, Anne-Sophie. Really. The stock has lost half its value."

Anne-Sophie looked at her sister. "I hope you don't own any shares?"

"Me? Of course not."

Which was a fib he thought.

He smiled at Élisabeth; he debated putting his hand into the air, but she called on him. "Yes, Gabriel?"

"So Hugh thinks he's doing this for Laura?"

Anne-Sophie snorted. "Of course! He'd do anything for her! Even kill himself. But does she care?"

He said, "She hates the company. And she's not too fond of her mother."

Anne-Sophie said, "I don't believe it!"

Élisabeth said, "Did she say that, Gabriel?"

He nodded. "She did. She said she wished it would go bankrupt and vanish from the face of the Earth."

Élisabeth looked at Anne-Sophie. They smiled identical smiles. They waited for Hughie and Laura to return.

Élisabeth took Laura into the kitchen while Anne-Sophie dragged Hughie back into his office by the scruff of his neck.

And after a brief period, Élisabeth led Laura from the kitchen to the office.

And everyone emerged smiling. No one said anything, of course, but Hugh settled into his chair in the family room and found a football game, while his wife and sisters jointly began to prepare dinner.

He may have sat beside Hugh. It wasn't his place to butt in so he called Cory.

Who answered on the second ring. "Hi, Cory."

Hugh was looking at him.

Cory said, "Gabe?"

"I just had the pleasure of meeting your Aunt Élisabeth and your Aunt Anne-Sophie."

Hugh was staring at him.

"And they and your parents have had a wonderful exchange of views. Would you like to speak to your father?"

Cory said, "Is he right there?"

"He is." He handed Hugh the phone. "Cory would like to say hi."

And he walked out of the family room and then ran up the stairs taking them three at a time. He grabbed his packed bag and was back to the family room before Hugh hung up.

Hugh said, "Yes, Cory. I'm not going back until I feel better.

Certainly not tomorrow. Maybe never. Now that I know that Laura doesn't want me to, it makes the decision easier."

Hugh nodded. "Yes, Cory, no matter what Josephine says or does."

Hugh handed him his phone back.

"Cory?"

"I'm so relieved, Gabe."

"Of course. And?"

"And he told me he's not dying."

"Also good to know. So I don't need to call Jennifer?"

Cory laughed. "No, Gabe. You can go home and back to work. Has it been so bad?"

"No. Not at all, Cory. Bye."

Hugh was smiling at him. "I hope you enjoyed your visit, Gabriel."

"It was remarkable. Thanks for having me."

He was invited to stay for dinner, but he politely declined and sped home to Philly as fast as the laws of Virginia, Maryland, and Pennsylvania would allow.

Or a skosh faster.

Monday
8:00 am

He was delighted to see South 16th Street; more delighted than he would have imagined possible.

Even if it was raining and easterly gales were making umbrellas useless. Again.

He was not made for the S*turm und Drang* of the Poirier household.

He smiled at Dana ignoring her dourness. He patted his desk and wiped a spot of dust from his computer.

He went into Jennifer's office. "I'm back!"

For one heady moment, he considered hugging her, but good sense convinced him otherwise. That, and the fearsome look she gave him.

"What? I didn't do anything."

She sniffed and rolled her eyes. "Not everything is about you, Bergeron."

Which was obviously true. But still.

"Is there anything I can do to help?"

"No!"

"Is the firm on the verge of bankruptcy?"

"No!"

"Could this be an Andy problem?"

She pointed at the door. "I don't want to talk about him or hear his name! Now go away before I do something I'll regret. Eventually."

Andy Boltukaev was the love of Jennifer's life, or so he had believed. It appeared that Andy had sinned in some fashion.

He smiled at her trying to look supportive, but she rose from her desk filled with fell purpose.

He may have run back to his cubicle.

He got to work, and by exceptional diligence, he had cleared up most of the backlog by lunch time.

He reread a cryptic email from Marge of the Montgomery Gallery. It was almost time to call her. It was best to deal with Marge within a two hour period beginning at noon; after she had risen from her slumbers and before she was totally soused.

Marge bought and sold art; mostly paintings. She had a certain preference for cash transactions. He had warned her the last time, and if she was trying to hide income again, he was going to toss her to the IRS.

He decided he should visit her in person even with the rain.

Her gallery was on the second floor of a moderately rundown building on Walnut Street.

He tried the door, but it was locked. Which was unusual. He called all of her numbers; nothing.

He considered throwing a rock through her window, but he went to lunch at CoffeeXtra instead.

Martin knew his standing order. "So? Has Billy showed up?"

Martin said, "Nope."

He eyed Martin. "Are you doing the deposits?"

Martin smiled at him. He may have looked concerned.

"I know how to make a deposit, Gabe."

He was deeply dubious, but it was Billy's business after all.

"How long has he been gone?"

"A week and change."

Billy was going to return to the hollow shell of a business; not that he thought Martin was dishonest or even dumb.

"What about ordering?"

Martin smiled.

He washed his hands metaphorically and put Martin, Billy, and CoffeeXtra from his mind. He ate his banana bread.

He went back to GB&H and worked like a demon.

Well, until break time. He was sipping his coffee thinking about nothing at all when he saw Dana waving a silver-nailed hand at him.

The breakroom lacked a back door or even a window. Not that a window on the eleventh floor would have been very useful as an escape route.

He peeked out the door.

Billy was standing there, dripping on the carpet. Billy tried smiling at him, but his native despondency doomed the attempt.

He squared his shoulders and marched boldly to the conference room. Billy followed.

Billy, aka Vilim Stanko, was tall, thin, with a preternaturally hairy body. This wasn't apparent because he was wearing a gorgeous, navy pinstripe suit; the hairy body part.

He hadn't discovered where Billy got the money for the suits he wore; certainly not from the profits from CoffeeXtra.

Of course, Billy was Dr. Vilim Stanko, a mathematician, but how well could pondering geometric structures and differentiable manifolds pay?

He took a seat at the conference table; Billy joined him.

Billy focused the sad, brown eyes on him, but he didn't say anything as he shed his raincoat.

"Billy?

"Yeah, Dude?"

"Why are you here?"

Billy considered that; apparently looking at it from every angle in a ten dimensional space.

He got to his feet.

Billy finally said, "Mom wants to see you."

Shit. Well, it wasn't like he hadn't expected it at some point. "Okay? So she knows that I'm not leading you on? And Peter Hahn almost burying you alive was not my fault?"

"Sure, Gabe. I told her."

"And she accepted that?"

Billy nodded.

"So what's the problem, Vilim?"

Billy said, "Mom might ask you to do something."

"Right? Something to do with accounting and CoffeeXtra?" He knew that wasn't it, but he had his fingers crossed.

"No, Dude."

"So what is she going to ask me?"

Billy shook his head. "Don't know."

"You must know something?"

Billy stood up, but he blocked the door before he could run out.

Billy hugged him.

"Let go of me, Vilim."

"Just say no."

"To Penelope?"

Billy nodded with his arms still locked around him.

"No matter what she asks. No matter how...harmless it sounds, Dude!"

"Okay. I will refuse." Which is what he would have done anyway.

Billy released him and departed from GB&H at his best possible speed.

Friday
7:00 am

He had worked a full week. There had been no sightings of Penelope, but he had avoided CoffeeXtra.

He had taken the train to DC after work yesterday, and now he was in Cory's bed in Cory's condo. He still thought of it as Cory's, but he was careful not to refer to it as such to Cory. They had never discussed it. And he still had his apartment.

Cory was in the living room; he could hear him on the phone probably talking to Matt Bornheimer.

He went into the master bath and splashed water on his face after using the facilities. He studied his reflection. He didn't spot any gray hairs. He sucked in his belly and held it until he grew faint; rock-hard abs were overrated.

He wandered out of the master bedroom and took a left into the kitchen. He waved at Cory in the living room. He was already suited up and ready to take on evil-doers.

He poured a cup of coffee and searched for a pastry in vain. He dropped a muffin into the toaster and joined Cory.

Cory said, "I'm leaving now, Matt. Danielle will okay it."

Matt said something causing a frown to wrinkle the countenance of Special Agent Poirier.

"If you think we should?"

Danielle Elkins was the boss of Cory, Matt, and other agents too.

Cory hung up.

"What's wrong?"

"I want to fly back to Denver."

"And Matt doesn't want to go?"

"Not that. He thinks that Danielle's going to shoot it down."

"You can talk her into it." The toaster popped up.

Cory smiled. "Maybe yes, maybe no."

He retrieved his muffin and buttered it. "So you stay here this weekend with me."

Cory smiled again. "When you put it like that. I'll call you."

"Roger that. Go get 'em, Special Agent."

But Cory was already out the door.

He sat on the sofa and ate his muffin. Was it wrong to hope that Danielle grounded Cory? He didn't think so. Jerry Nolastname would still be stealing paintings on Monday.

He was in the shower when his phone rang, but it wasn't Cory.

"Hello?" Silence. But not a no-connection silence; a silence with presence. "Hello? Okay, I'm hanging up now."

Detective Sanders said, "Where are you?"

"DC. And where are you?"

"Leesburg."

"Glad we got that straightened out. Anything else I can do for you, Detective."

More silence.

"So how is the case going?"

Sanders said, "I'm calling you."

"That well? I'm sorry to hear that. Really, I am. If I had any ideas, I'd tell you."

"Nothing?"

"Not currently."

"Prentice sold those horses. Dr. Crain doesn't have a poker face, Gabe. So I know it, but I can't prove shit."

"You can't find the money?"

Sanders said, "No. We've searched her house and the farm, everywhere I can think of. Unless she buried it like pirate gold, I don't know."

"Right. Any accounts for Dolph, Jack, or Dr. Crain?"

"Checked all of them."

"The Cayman Islands?"

Sanders said, "If you aren't going to help, just say so."

"Wait! She had a sister. Dorothy something?"

Sanders sighed. "Dorothy Smullen, Died two years ago. I checked for bank accounts in her name too."

"Well, then I'm flummoxed, Detective, but I'll think about it."

Sanders said, "Thanks."

But he didn't mean it. He finished his shower. And ate a second breakfast like a Hobbit.

He was staring at the blank TV screen faintly aware that his brain was just as blank.

But there was something? So Turtle had ridden his bike to the farm. And the hit-man, who might not be a hit-man but was certainly a crook of some kind, had driven the van.

And Shaw had motored to his death in his Porsche.

So the hit-man had killed Shaw and Turtle, and Turtle had killed the hit-man? Or someone else had come to the farm?

If he ruled out Hugh, Laura, Judd, Diane, and especially Cory, then someone had come in another vehicle. Which might have left tracks? But Sanders would have found those?

But where was Turtle's bike?

He screwed his courage to the sticking place and called Sanders back.

"What?"

"Did you find tracks of another vehicle? Anywhere near the barn?"

"No."

"Okay. Did you find Turtle's bike?"

Sanders sighed. His sigh was like razor wire. "Why?"

"Well, his grandmother said he left her house on it so it should have been at the farm...near his body probably. I mean I was thinking that maybe he and the hit-man had come in the van, but I don't think so. And if somebody tried to hide it, there might be fingerprints; the killer's prints."

Silence. Between the sighing and the silence, it was very hard to have a conversation with Detective Sanders. "Hello?"

"I'll check."

"You didn't see it?"

"No."

"Okay. It's red and rusty but has a new chrome headlamp. Will you call me back if you locate it? Detective?"

"Yes, Gabe."

And he was gone.

He was considering eating a third breakfast when his phone rang, but it was only Cory.

He tried not to sound disappointed. "Hi, Cory. What's up?"

"We're flying to Denver."

"Good. I hope you catch him."

"We have a real lead this time, Gabe."

"Great. Does this mean going undercover?"

"Only briefly."

"So you'll call me whenever you can?"

Cory said, "Of course. I'm sorry about the weekend, Gabe."

"No, don't be. You'll make it up to me."

"I will."

And he was gone.

He looked out the window. It was a lovely autumn day, and he was in the center of a city rich with culture, high and low.

He was reclining on the sofa watching a episode of "CSI" when his phone rang again.

He took a deep breath. "Yes, Detective?"

"Deputy Huska saw it."

"Where?"

"Under Mrs. Foote's house. He didn't know that Turtle had ridden it to the farm. He thought it was junk."

"So you're going to get it?"

"On my way now. It may not be anything, but thanks."

And he did mean it that time.

He turned off the TV and considered. Cory had left in the Ford Explorer, but his gray Yaris was at the ready.

He grabbed the keys and was heading out of DC scant minutes later. He could call Laura and Hugh, but he was going to drop in.

He arrived as a Loudoun County Sheriff's car was leaving. He thought the deputy driving was Huska the Huge.

He knocked on Laura's door but got no answer. There was an unmarked car parked in front of Mrs. Foote's house.

He strolled over and knocked on her door.

Detective Sanders opened the door. He shook his head and shut the door again.

Which was just rude.

He saw Mrs. Prentice standing in her yard watching. She went back inside slamming her door.

A lesser man might have been put off, but he leaned against Sanders' car and waited.

And in the fullness of time, Sanders emerged with Mrs. Foote right behind him.

Her round, rosy face was red. She was wearing a black skirt with a purple sweater a couple of sizes too small. "I never put that bike under my house, Detective. I don't know how it got there. Which is what I told Deputy Huska."

She flipped from indignation back to her natural bonhomie. She smiled at Sanders and got very close to him. "You can believe me. I would never lie to an officer of the law."

Sanders tried smiling at her. "Thank you for volunteering your fingerprints, Mrs. Foote. I may be back with more questions."

She tried to keep smiling, but it was hard.

Sanders got into his car. He knocked on the passenger door; Sanders counted to ten before he unlocked it.

He slid inside. "Thanks, Detective. So you found the bike? Under her house? Do you know if it was Turtle's? This is a nice car, by the way. It still has that new car smell." Someone had sprung for the leather seats upgrade.

Sanders said, "It matches the description given by Mrs. Yates."

"And?" There was more; he knew it.

Sanders said, "We found some license plates in the saddlebag. They were stolen...from a neighbor of Turtle's...the neighbor couldn't say when they went missing."

"Right. To put on the truck and the horse carrier in back of the barn. To transport mighty Bucephalus."

Sanders smiled. "I'd say that's likely, Gabe."

"And?"

"And a road map of Ohio." Sanders looked at him. "With a route marked in red."

"Wither?"

Sanders smiled but shook his head decisively. "Okay. So Turtle was going to drive Bucephalus to a location in Ohio, and you are even now endeavoring to find out what or who is at that location?"

Sanders smiled.

"Just so. Okay. Good. So what is your first name?"

Sanders looked at him again. "You are one weird dude."

"Sticks and stones will break my bones."

"My friends have been known to call me J.D. or John."

"Well, John. This all sounds promising."

John shook his head, but he smiled. "Out."

"Right." He got out of the car. "So I can await events?"

John smiled a happy smile with dimples and drove off.

Mrs. Foote popped out of her house. "Gabriel? What's going on?" She laughed. "I thought that nice Deputy Huska was going to arrest me! My heart was just throbbing in my breast. It still is."

He jumped back before she offered to let him feel the throb. "I'm sorry, Mrs. Foote."

"This is about the murders? Did the murderer put that old bike underneath my house. He was right under my bedroom, Gabriel!" Her cheeks were beet-red; her eyes sparkled. "This is all so exciting."

He may have frowned at her.

"And terrible! Just awful! About those poor men!"

She walked around her house and pointed at a gap in the foundation. "It was in there."

A piece of plywood had covered the gap; probably an access point to get to the plumbing?

"In the crawlspace?"

She nodded. "I never knew it was there until Deputy Huska

found it."

"So did you see what was in the saddlebag, Mrs. Foote?"

She nodded. "License plates and a map. And a piece of cake wrapped in plastic; it looked like chocolate layer cake." She glanced at Hilda's house. "And she was watching just like she is now."

Hilda's curtain jiggled.

"I imagine she's curious too. But you didn't see who put the bike under there?"

"No, Gabriel. I would have told Chuck."

"Who's Chuck?"

The blush intensified until her cheeks were radiating in the infrared. "I mean Deputy Huska."

He wasn't going to worry about Chuck who was big enough to take care of himself.

"Thanks, Mrs. Foote."

She smiled at him. "Call me Celia."

That was never going to happen.

He smiled and fled to Laura's porch. It was almost noon. He was glad he'd eaten two breakfasts since he had no idea when Hugh and Laura would return.

Friday Noon

He was pacing on Laura's porch when he spotted Jed's baby-blue pickup swing around the barn and stop in front of Mrs. Foote's cottage.

Jed and Del climbed out and were granted admittance.

He should have found out who these guys were a week ago.

He knocked on Mrs. Foote's door.

No one answered. "Mrs. Foote? It's Gabe Bergeron. May I speak to you? It won't take a second. Please?"

The door opened. Mrs. Foote smiled at him.

"May I come in?"

She said, "I'm kinda busy right now, Gabe. Could you come back in an hour or so? I'm baking a pie, and you can have a slice. I know how much you love your sweets."

"You do? How?"

"From Madeleine, Gabe. And from the cookies and stuff in Mr. Corentin's room."

She had been in Cory's room. Well, she had to clean it, but his stash had been in a drawer. Along with his and Cory's clothes...and their underwear.

He might have to buy new underwear. After he did an inventory. But she just cranked up the smile as she slowly closed the door.

"Who are Jed and Del, Mrs. Foote?"

She looked at him, utterly bereft of an answer. And then the tears flowed out of her eyes and down her ruddy cheeks.

Shit.

"I'm sorry, Mrs. Foote! Really."

And then Jed opened the door wider and gave him a push. He stumbled back but didn't fall on his ass. He could see a table loaded with food, and Del with a fork in his hand.

Jed said, "You go on now!"

Jed continued to glare at him, but Del popped out of the house heading for him. Del's face was white, his freckles in sharp relief. Handsome Del was going to punch him.

He set himself, but Jed grabbed Del. "Del! Let him go. He ain't worth it."

Mrs. Foote said, "Del, Honey, you cool down now. Gabe is not a bad person, and we can talk...."

Del said, "After I hit him til he can't stand up, Aunt Celia."

He tried not to smile in triumph; he felt sure that Del would not take kindly to smiling.

"Del is your nephew?"

Solid Jed was still holding Del, but it was a strain.

Celia cupped Del's face in her hands. "It's all right, Del. I'm fine."

She was smiling at Del. He quit trying to break free.

"But he made you cry, Aunt Celia?"

"No. It's just having that detective questioning me and finding the bike underneath my house. And worrying about Mr. Poirier selling the farm. And Momma not doing so well. And just everything, Del. You can't go around losing your temper like this."

"I know."

Jed put an arm around Del's neck. "Yeah, cool off, Cuz."

Celia said, "Jed and Del are my nephews, Gabe. My brothers' kids." She nodded. "Why don't you come in?"

He looked at Del. "Is that okay with you, Del?"

Del nodded too. "Course. It's Aunt Celia's house."

Jed said, "'Cept it isn't."

He said, "But Hugh and Laura would never sell the farm."

Celia looked at him.

"I heard them say it, Mrs. Foote. After Hugh talked to Mrs. Prentice."

"Is that true, Gabe? And please call me Celia."

Jed said, "So the Prentice woman doesn't know what she's talking about?" He shook his head. "I told you, Aunt Celia."

"I know. I should have just come out and asked Mrs. Poirier direct."

Del said, "So you aren't going to lose your house?"

She hugged Del. "No, Honey. I guess not."

The atmosphere of the little house was almost solid with the aroma of good food; the warm, heavenly scent of an apple pie baking predominating.

Celia smiled at him. "Sit down, Gabe, and I'll make some coffee?" She opened the oven. "The pie isn't ready yet."

He wouldn't mind a slice of pie, but he still had questions. Jed was looking at him.

Celia said, "Boys, do you think you could take a look at my car? It's making that funny noise again."

Del said, "Sure, Aunt Celia. Come on, Jed."

And Del went out; Jed followed, but he smiled at Celia.

She blushed again. "It's not what you're thinking, Mr. Jedidiah Foote."

He held up his hands, but he was still smiling.

"That boy has a low opinion of me."

He said, "I'm sure he doesn't."

She laughed. "Well, he should. What do you want to know?"

"What's going on with Jed and Del?"

"Nothing at all. They visit...from time to time."

"I talked to Madeleine."

"She should mind her own business. Promise me you won't say anything to Mr. Poirier?"

"As long as it has nothing to do with the murders."

She went white; her face was hard-wired to her emotions. "Of course not! You think that Jed and Del had something to do with that? Well, I can tell you that they didn't! They're both good boys, and they weren't even here that night."

"But they are living here?"

"Some nights, Gabe. But not that night! It might look

suspicious, me not telling anybody, but I'm not sure how Mr. Poirier would feel about them staying here. It's his house after all, and I live here rent free."

"I don't think he'd mind, Celia."

"Maybe not. I hope not, because I can't tell them no. I'm afraid what might happen to them."

"Don't they have a home? Or jobs?"

"They work hard...when they can find work, Gabe. And they were living at my brother Harold's place. You see Del's father, Ralph, passed away two years ago, and Jed took Del in."

She sipped her coffee and sighed. "Harold got hooked on pain pills, Gabe. He spent every penny he had and borrowed against his place. And when the drugs finally killed him, he owed so much that Jed and Del lost the farm."

"I'm sorry to hear that."

"And they been living where they could. With buddies. With me. With one or the other of Del's girlfriends. I just want to keep an eye on them. I won't have them going down the same path as Harold." She was crying again. "I couldn't help Harold, but I will not lose these boys."

"I understand." He finished his coffee and got up to leave.

"Stay for a slice of pie, Gabe?"

"Thank you, but I want to see if Hugh and Laura are back."

She nodded.

And he walked out. He wasn't sure just how bad off financially she was, but she didn't need another mouth to feed.

The hood of her car was up, and Del's shapely butt was hanging out. Jed was holding a flashlight and a wrench.

Jed said, "Here. Take the flashlight, Del."

Del's voice came from the innards of Celia's car. "Where you going? Can't work and hold the light, Jed!"

"I'll be right back."

And Jed started walking and waved him away from the car. Jed made sure they were out of earshot. "We had nothing to do with the murders, Bergeron."

"I'm glad to hear that. Celia says you weren't here that night?"

Jed smiled. "We weren't. And we have an alibi. We were shooting pool in a bar outside of Leesburg when this Shaw and the others were killed."

"Right. And Detective Sanders can verify that?"

Jed nodded. "Sure. Plenty of people saw us at Red's Bar. If he has to." Jed stared at him. "And Poirier really isn't selling the farm?"

"No. He and Laura love this place. As do their children. You don't have to worry."

"Glad to hear it. Okay. Then I better get back before Del gets pissed."

"Is he a good mechanic?"

Jed smiled. "Give him any kind of machine, and he can take it apart and put it back together. Better than it was."

"And you?"

"Me? No, I can do small stuff but not like Del."

"So what kind of work do you do?"

"Anything to do with a farm. With horses especially."

He smiled at Jed. "You like horses?"

Jed said, "Course. Being born here and all."

And Jed walked back to Del and Celia's car.

Friday
5:00 pm

He was cold. And bored.

He could be in the middle of the Sahara as far as signs of life were concerned. Well, a chilly, oddly verdant Sahara.

He had seen a vulture circling, but not another animate thing after Jed and Del had left.

Except for Dolph.

Dolph had rolled up to his mother's house at 1:30 pm. He had stayed inside for thirty-odd minutes, and then he had tossed a few garbage bags of stuff into the back of his pickup and roared off, ignoring Hilda beating on the side of the truck.

He had called John, but John hadn't picked up, and he had left a message. He had then called the Sheriffs Office and asked for Deputy Huska. He had been told Deputy Huska was unavailable so he had left a message for him too.

He didn't really know that Dolph was running.

He sat on Laura's porch some more.

After Hilda had gone back inside her house, he hadn't seen anything, and the sun was westering low.

Shit. He was really cold. And he might be sitting in a rocker on a porch for nothing.

He called Cory, but it went straight to voicemail.

He pondered. Cory had commanded him not to go "full-Gabe" but had failed to define that mocking term.

For instance, would it be "full-Gabe" to knock on Hilda's door and ask a few innocent questions? He didn't think it would.

He knocked.

No response.

He knocked again, and Hilda opened the door. Her cheeks had caved in, and her mouth was bent in a downward curve. Her eyes were red from tears, shed and dried. She tried to stick out her chin at him.

"What do you want?"

"I'm sorry to bother you, but I saw Dolph leave?"

"He's gone."

"Is he coming back?"

She shrugged and turned around. She was looking out the window and wasn't really paying attention to him.

She walked into Jack's bedroom. He stood in the doorway. Jack was motionless; a blanket was pulled up to his chin and his face was pale.

"Is he okay?"

"He's fine. But I have to give him his shot."

She got a syringe and a vial from the nightstand drawer and filled the syringe. Jack made a faint grunt as she stuck the needle in.

"Stop. What is that?"

He took a step, but she pulled a pistol from under Jack's blanket. "You stay away from him!"

"But you don't have to do that, Hilda!"

"If you get any closer, I'll shoot you dead. I don't much want to, but I will."

And she was totally, deadly serious. She finished injecting the stuff into Jack and then leaned over and kissed him.

He said, "We can call an ambulance. It's not too late."

She shook her head. "No. He's already gone. He's free and maybe in a better place. At least, I hope so." She shook her head. "And I'm so tired of tending to the dying...first my sister and now Jack...."

He took a step back.

She looked at him. "Where do you think you're going?"

"I'm intruding."

She laughed and pointed the gun at his face. "You sit down!

On the floor. Now. And you don't move and don't make me shoot you. I need to think."

He stayed motionless for a few minutes as she sat next to the body of her husband. She got up and looked out. She shook her head.

It was almost dark out, and he could see flashing lights playing against the curtains now.

She sat down again. "This is your fault. Isn't it?"

"No!"

"Tell me the truth."

"I wanted to help Cory's parents."

"By finding out what happened?" She nodded. "I can see that."

He felt a draft as if someone had opened the outside door. "You stole the horses, didn't you?"

"I did. Oh, Dolph and Rusty helped, but it was my idea."

"Rusty is Dr. Crain?"

She nodded. "I hated to do it, but I was sure that Mr. Poirier was going to sell the farm and throw us out. And where would we go then, me and Jack? I had to do something, and it seemed like it wouldn't be too hard."

"So you found a buyer for Onyx?"

"Found two."

"So you tried it again with Chopin."

She nodded. "And Mr. Poirier didn't suspect a thing. I knew his health had declined, and I expected to be told that I didn't have a job any day. I could see it coming."

"And what did you do with the cash?"

"I bought a farm in Ohio...a little place near Lima...with most of it. I put it in my sister Dorothy's name. I kept all of her ID after she died. We looked so much alike, you see. I expect Detective Sanders knows all about that? Don't you, Detective? I know you're out there."

Sanders peeped around the door with his gun drawn. He saw the gun in her hand, but it wasn't pointed at anyone.

"Put that down! Do it now!"

She smiled. "Or you'll shoot me? Go ahead. I don't care."

"Put it on the floor! I won't tell you again."

She nodded and complied.

"Now kick it over here."

She did that too.

He grabbed the gun. "Now put your hands behind your head and stand up."

She laughed again. "I can't do that. With my back."

She grabbed the bed post and pulled herself erect.

"Now turn around."

Sanders cuffed her and then looked at him. "What the Hell are you doing here, Gabe?"

"Asking questions. How is Jack?"

Hilda said, "He's gone. I couldn't leave him with nobody to take care of him."

Sanders tried to find a pulse, but there was none.

Hilda said, "It was supposed to be simple. We would load Bucephalus into a carrier, and Turtle would drive him to Ohio and take care of him until the buyer paid up. And Dolph and I would be here the whole time doing our work, and nobody would suspect a thing."

"But I knew it was over when you pulled that bike out. And then the map! I felt like I was falling...like you do in a nightmare...but I was wide awake.

Sanders said, "Why did you kill Turtle?"

She looked shocked. "We didn't kill nobody, Detective! I don't know who did that." She started crying. "Turtle was a good boy, and I hated to get him involved, but we had to have a driver, and Turtle needed the money for something. He wouldn't say what."

"So you have no idea who killed Turtle or the other men?"

He looked at her. "Maybe Dolph did it?"

She shook her head. "I wouldn't put it past him, but he was with me the whole night. We were waiting for Turtle, but he never showed up."

"And then in the morning, I found his bike leaning against the house, and I told Dolph to get rid of it." She shook her head. "And the best he could think to do was put it under Celia's house?

And he left the map in the saddlebag! I swear that boy was switched in the hospital, and my rightful son is making some other mother proud."

Sanders said, "Where is Dolph?"

"Running. I begged him to help me get Jack into the car, but he ran off. I was going to try for Ohio, but he left us here." She looked at Sanders. "I hope you catch him."

"We will."

Friday
6:00 pm

Hugh and Laura had come home, and he had tried to tell them what had happened, but he wasn't making much sense.

He sat in the family room and let the dancing pixels and whispering voices offer what anodyne they could.

After a while, he heard Detective Sanders' voice talking to Hugh and Laura. And then Sanders was sitting beside him.

"Is Jack really dead?"

Sanders nodded. "She gave him a massive dose of horse tranquilizer...that's what the doc thinks."

"Shit. It's my fault."

Laura said, "No, it's not, Gabriel. Jack was dying. Mrs. Prentice told us he had a seizure on Wednesday and hasn't really been conscious since then. It was only a matter of days...or hours."

"But she killed him. And I watched."

Sanders said, "She had a gun, Gabe."

He nodded. "But I liked Jack. I only met him the once, but I liked him."

Laura said, "We did too, Gabriel. He was a lovely, kind man and so good with the horses, but his passing isn't your fault."

"It sure feels like it is."

"Thanks, Gabe, for your help." Sanders smiled and rubbed the tump of hair on the top of his head. "If you have any ideas about Shaw or the third man...."

"No!" He shook his head. He tried to smile, but he wasn't a good fake smiler. "No. I'm done."

Sanders nodded and put an arm around his shoulder and gave him a tentative squeeze before he got to his feet.

"I have to go."

"Sure. I understand. And you have to catch Dolph."

Sanders said, "You think he killed them?"

He shrugged. "I don't know."

And Sanders left.

Laura sat beside him, but he couldn't think of a word to say.

She said, "Jack was dying, Gabriel, and this was quick. I hope someone will do that for me when my time comes. I can't bear the thought of being hooked up to a machine and having it inflate my chest and pump blood to my dead brain."

She shuddered. He would have hugged her, but if he did, he was afraid he might bawl like a child.

"And Hilda should have come to us and asked about the farm."

Which was true.

She said, "Hugh would have told her the truth, and even if things had gotten so bad that we needed to sell, he would never have just evicted her and Jack."

Noblesse oblige.

Laura said, "Are you hungry, Gabriel?"

He shook his head. Hugh shoved a cup of coffee in his hand. He sipped, but it was only about half coffee. He shook his head. "Thanks, Hugh, but no."

Hugh said, "Stay here tonight, Gabriel."

"No. Thank you so much, Hugh. Thank you too, Laura, but I want to go home."

Laura said, "Are you sure?"

"Yes."

He felt as if he'd run for miles and miles. He thought he could make it to Cory's condo, which wasn't home but would do for tonight even if Cory wasn't there.

Tomorrow, he would go to his apartment on Arch Street. He could go see Aunt Flo? But he didn't want her to see him like this. It would upset her.

Saturday
6:00 pm

He was still in Cory's condo.

The thought of taking the train to Philly was just too much. He had ordered pizza, but he hadn't taken a bite. The box was on the sofa next to him, and the smell was making him feel a little sick.

He heard the lock click.

His first thought was that Laura had come to check up on the condo and possibly on him.

His second thought was that he was in his underwear.

His third thought was she had seen plenty of guys in their underwear: Hugh and Judd and Cory sprang to mind.

But still.

Cory didn't go in for throw pillows. He may have grabbed the cushion out of the closest armchair as a modesty shield.

Cory smiled. "What the Hell are you doing?"

"Nothing! I thought it was your mother."

"And?"

He glared at Cory. "Okay, the next time we visit Aunt Flo, let's see you march down to the kitchen in your briefs."

Cory laughed. "Point taken. So put the cushion back, Bergeron."

He did, and he flopped back onto the sofa. Cory sat beside him. There was a fly fishing show on the TV.

Cory looked at him quizzically. "What are you watching?"

"No idea. So change the channel, Poirier."

He did. He found a college football game.

Cory looked at the pizza. "Help yourself."

And Cory grabbed a slice and munched away, but he still couldn't eat.

Cory was in one of his FBI suits which were beautiful but somber as befitted an agent of the law. The tie was black with delicate red stripes.

"So you're back sooner than I expected?"

Cory swallowed. "Mother called."

"Right."

More college football happened; athletic young men did fierce, semi-civilized battle for territory and possession of a ball.

A strange, oddly-shaped ball at that.

Cory said, "Do you want to talk about it?"

"Nope."

Cory watched the rest of the game. It was nice to have Cory beside him; he was getting hungry.

He ate a slice as Cory found another college football game

He groaned.

Cory ignored the groan. "My mother is concerned about you."

"That's nice of her."

"It is. She called Danielle."

Danielle was Cory's boss. "Shit! Not my fault, Cory."

Cory turned his head and looked at him from six inches away. "No, it wasn't, and what happened at the farm wasn't either."

He looked at the screen, but he couldn't quite focus on the game. He put his half-eaten slice back into the box.

Cory said, "Did you shower today?"

He glared at Cory. "I beg your pardon."

Cory said, "I have hygiene standards, Bergeron. And you need a shave too. Get cleaned up. We're going out for dinner, and you're going to tell me what happened."

He shook his head. "That's a categorical no. To all of that."

Cory got to his feet and loomed over him. "I will carry you to the shower, Bergeron."

He would.

"All right. I'll take a shower, but you can't make me go out." He tried smiling at Cory. "Well, you could, but I could kick and scream and make a scene?"

"No, you won't."

He smiled again. "Okay. I'll take a shower, and we'll discuss the rest after."

He got in the shower and turned on the hot water. Cory's shower was in a corner and had two glass walls and two tile walls; the tile was a black, tan, and gray mosaic. It had a rain shower head plus a hand held shower and a comfy bench.

It looked like a giant aquarium; he had toyed with the idea of plugging the drain just to see how high it would fill up.

Cory put the lid down on the toilet and took a seat. "So Mrs. Prentice was stealing our horses? With the vet's help? And selling them to buy a farm in Ohio?"

"I don't want to talk about it."

"Just tell me that much."

"Well, yes. But she thought that Hugh was going to get rid of the farm and kick her and...her family out on the street...or onto the county road, in this case."

"Dad would never do that. He'd die first! Or rob a bank to keep the farm! And he wouldn't have just kicked her out!"

"Right. But she didn't know that."

Cory said, "She should have! He's always treated her well. Always, Gabe! For fifteen years. I think she just wanted the cash."

Which was possible?

Cory said, "She's telling Sanders she did it for Jack. He thinks it's just a story so the prosecutor will go easy on her."

"You think?" It sounded very Machiavellian, but Hilda wasn't overly-endowed with the warm fuzzies.

"I do."

"I don't know, Cory."

Cory stood up. "And how do you know she or that Dolph didn't kill all three guys? She was in the middle of stealing Bucephalus when Shaw showed up. Yates, her accomplice, gets shot in the free-for-all. She tries to cover up Shaw's death by tossing him in Bucephalus' stall, but you get there before she can dispose of the other bodies."

He shook his head. "But she didn't have any blood on her."

Cory said, "She changed her jacket."

"And why was Shaw there?"

Cory shook his head.

"And who was Third Guy?"

Cory said, "Her buyer?"

He stared at Cory, but he couldn't keep the images from popping up in his brain. "I watched her shoot the stuff into his vein, Cory."

He had to keep it together.

"And he was a nice guy, Cory."

He could feel the tears welling up. He was going to blubber in front of Cory, and he really didn't want to do that.

He tried to think of something else, but it was no use, the tears would not be dammed. He put his face into the shower and tried not to make a sound.

He wasn't entirely successful.

He felt Cory's arms wrap around him. "It's okay, Gabe."

It wasn't. "It's my fault, Cory." Cory was getting wet. "Jack would be alive if I had just stopped asking questions."

"You can't think about that. I know what it feels like. I've had innocent people get hurt in the course of an investigation before, and it sucks, but this is not your fault."

"But I'm not an FBI agent. It isn't my job; I'm just a nosy busybody."

He put his head on Cory's shoulder and hugged him. "Your hot water bill is going to be horrendous."

Cory laughed. "Let me worry about that. Gabe, I asked you to investigate so it's my fault, if it's anybody's."

He hugged Cory some more which was nice, but the shower was steaming up. He let go and looked at Cory.

"You're all wet."

"So are you, Bergeron."

"Yeah, but I'm in my skin which is impermeable and can be towel dried. And your tie is ruined! Get out, Cory."

Cory stepped out of the shower totally soaked.

"Take off your suit." He blew his nose. "Think it's ruined?"

Cory shrugged as he striped down to his skin too. He grabbed a towel and dried Cory's hair and chest.

Cory said, "Jack was dying, Gabe. I've shot guys, and guilty or not, it never feels good."

"No, I'm sure it doesn't." He looked at Cory. "So who hugged you when you felt bad about stuff that happened?"

"Nobody. But I've got you now."

""Right. You do. But you'll have to tell me if crap happens, Cory! You can't be all macho and stubborn and hide it from me."

Cory smiled. "You'll dig it out of me if I get stubborn."

"I will."

Cory said, "I talked to Sanders. He didn't say much, but I think he's being pressured to add the murder charges to the others against Hilda and Dolph."

"But he doesn't even know who Third Guy is?"

"True."

He shook his head. "I don't care, Cory. I'm done."

Cory nodded. "Shaw and the third guy are not your problem. And you never have to investigate anything again. If you don't want to?"

"I don't."

Cory hugged him again. "Okay."

Monday
10:00 am

He was so very tired. He hadn't gotten a lot of sleep since he'd watched Hilda calmly murder her helpless husband; three nights of dreams bad enough to make him jump out of bed.

Screaming.

And waking Cory.

He had come home to his little apartment last night, but it hadn't helped. Well, Cory had probably gotten some rest.

He shook his head and rubbed his eyes. But he was safe in his cubicle now, and all was right with the world.

Well, he still couldn't reach Marge which was beginning to worry him.

And Carla and Baldacci weren't speaking. Which was good for him since they wouldn't ask about the murders at the farm, and he wouldn't have to think about Shaw or Jack or anything.

He looked at Baldacci and Carla; the wall between them might not be physical but it was as real and fiercely guarded as the Berlin Wall had ever been.

And Chatterjee had gotten a phone call and then hurled his phone across the office. Which was different.

But then he had walked over to it and stomped on it. True, he was a slender fellow and might tip the scales at one thirty, but he put his heart and soul and boot into crushing that phone.

Chatterjee had taken to wearing combat boots that had to take half an hour to lace up and a sleeveless vest thing that had more than a whiff of flak-jacket. He still wore a tie, but it was hung loosely knotted around his neck like a scarf. Which was also different.

And Jennifer and Neal were no where to be found.

How long had he been gone? Not even a full week.

Wait. Neal was on vacation.

He sighed and called Marge again. Even Marge's voicemail wouldn't answer now. He didn't know if Marge had any family?

He wasn't sure where she lived; the only address he had was the gallery. It might be time to pay another visit, but if she didn't answer, he wasn't going inside.

He was definitely not going to find another body.

Dana walked by smiling.

This was perhaps the most disturbing thing of all.

He stood up. He had sworn off being nosy about crimes and murders, but that didn't include ignoring weird behavior by his co-workers.

"Dana? What's up with you?"

She lost the tickled-pink smile. "What?"

"All this smiling and traipsing about the office. It isn't natural, Dana, and I want to know what's going on."

She glared at him. "I don't know what you're talking about, Bergeron. And it's none of your business anyway."

"So there is something going on?"

She picked up a fashion magazine which she had already read cover to cover in Jennifer's absence.

"I'm busy, Bergeron."

"Please."

She swung around in her chair and ignored him.

He went back to his cubicle. Carla and Baldacci were laser focused on their computers, back to back. Neither had moved since getting in.

Probably because moving might involve coming face-to-face since they were only five feet apart. So they were having a not-pissing contest?

He looked over the partition wall. "Baldacci?"

He didn't even turn. "I'm busy, Bergeron."

"You are not. You've been staring at that same spreadsheet

for twenty minutes without hitting a key."

Baldacci punched in random numbers. "Happy now?"

He was not happy. Steps had to be taken.

He went into the breakroom and got two cups. He filled one with water. He returned and stood between Baldacci Land and the Wong Republic.

He said, "I'm really thirsty."

He poured water from one cup to the other and then back again.

Baldacci half spun around being careful not to look a the back of Carla's head. "Can't you do that somewhere else, Bergeron?"

"Sure. Aren't you thirsty, Harry?" He poured the water into the second cup again and held it out. "I love water, sparkling, flowing water. It's wonderful stuff."

Baldacci was going to break. He knew it, and Harry knew it. He glanced at the back of Carla's head. It had a grim set to it. She would die before she went to the Ladies Room. Or wet herself. She was probably wearing adult diapers in anticipation of just such a stand-off?

Harry stood up. He walked down the aisle away from Carla, moving swiftly toward the Men's Room.

He followed.

Baldacci was relieving his pent-up urges. He didn't turn. Which was good, given his current condition. "I hate you, Bergeron."

"No, you don't. We're buddies, pals, friends." Baldacci was still going. "You could damage your bladder holding it like that."

"As soon as I zip up, I'm going to punch you in the face."

"No, you won't. Remember I'm your groomsman."

Baldacci shook, zipped, and turned.

"The wedding's off."

"Ah. What did you do?"

Harry looked hurt. "It's not me. Why would you think it's me?"

He didn't say because he'd known him for years. "Okay. Sorry. What did she do?"

Baldacci looked furious. "She did Nemec! In his office! On that nasty carpet he had."

Which, of course, he knew since Carla had told him that Nemec, their former boss, had been the second best sexual partner she'd ever had. And also implied that poor Harry was well down in the rankings.

Baldacci was staring at him. "You knew?"

"No! Of course not! How would I know? It isn't like Carla would come out and tell me something like that. Did she tell you?"

"No! Dana told me, but she didn't deny it when I confronted her."

He shook his head. "You confronted Carla? Harry, why would you do that?"

Harry looked hurt and misunderstood. "Because it was Nemec, Gabe! That worm, that bottom feeder!"

"Right. How many sexual partners have you had?"

Harry looked confused. "In total?"

"Ballpark it for me, Baldacci. A hundred?" Harry looked offended. "Shit, Baldacci. Two hundred?"

He shrugged. "Hell, Gabe, I'm thirty-nine, and I got started when I was fourteen."

All of Baldacci's numbers were suspect.

"And women like me." He smiled his bad boy smile.

"I'm sure."

"They do!"

"I don't doubt it for a second. So do you think Carla isn't aware that you've had multiple partners?"

"She probably has some idea...."

"And would she be happy with all of your choices for bedmates?"

He shook his head. "No, I guess not."

"And I seem to recall that you thought it was hilarious that Nemec and Dana were doing it."

"But that's Dana! Shit, Gabe, I don't love Dana."

"No, you don't." He let Baldacci stand there for a few seconds. "Wash your hands."

"What?"

"Wash your hands, Baldacci."

Harry smiled at him. "Are you my mother?"

"No. If I were your mother, I wouldn't feed you. So go tell Carla that you're sorry, and that you're just so in love that you're crazy jealous...even about a dead guy."

Harry was shaking his head.

"Harry, you love her. Of all your countless conquests, have you ever been in love before?"

"Not really."

"Then you know what you have to do."

"But she said I wasn't as good as Nemec, Gabe! In bed!"

"She was just mad, and she wanted to hurt you."

Harry was still shaking his head. "Gabe?"

"What?" This was not going to be good.

"Can you talk to her for me?"

"No!"

"Come on, Gabe."

"Maybe. Wash your hands, and I will."

Carla was still in her cubicle. Baldacci sat down and smiled at him. He sighed and rolled across the aisle. "We need to talk."

She glared at him. "No."

"Come on. Just two minutes in the breakroom?"

"Go away."

"Carla, I had the worst vacation ever. And I come back to find everything is messed up at GB&H too. Please, just two minutes, and I promise never to bother you again."

She was staring at him. "Are you okay?"

"Sure. Not really." He would never forget Shaw in that stall or poor Jack being euthanized.

She followed him to the breakroom and shut the door. "Two minutes, Bergeron."

"First, Harry is very sorry he got jealous over Nemec."

"You should have heard him, Gabe! I was the Whore of Babylon or something."

"I'm sure Harry didn't think that." Mainly because Harry had never heard of the Whore of Babylon; he was doubtful he'd heard of the Book of Revelation. "He loves you. He told me so, and he'll beg your forgiveness if you let him."

She was shaking her head.

"Do you love him, Carla?"

"I guess."

"Then let him apologize?"

"I guess."

"But you have to do one thing."

The air in the breakroom darkened and thickened with a foul, sulfurous stench. She raised a single demonic eyebrow. "And what is that?"

"You have to tell him that he's way better in bed than Nemec. Way, way better. And you can never tell anyone otherwise as long as you both shall live."

She smiled. "Men."

"Right. Like women aren't insecure. So do we have a deal, Ms. Wong?"

She grabbed his tie. "Maybe. But first...."

What was happening?

She hopped up on the counter, used the tie to pull him in, and wrapped her legs around his waist. "First, we're going to do it. I've always had a yen for you."

His heart stopped.

It was just as well. He'd had a good run, and this was a fate worse than death; far worse.

And that was ignoring the fact that Baldacci was going to come through the door any second now and catch him *in flagrante* with Carla. Well, fully clothed but in a *flagrante* position.

He kept staring at the door.

Carla said, "What the Hell are you looking at?"

He squirmed out of her vise-like legs and leaped away. "I'm waiting for Baldacci to come through the door."

Carla laughed and laughed.

He ran back to his cubicle. Harry was looking at him.

"Did you talk to her, Gabe?"

He nodded.

"Is it okay?"

He nodded some more.

"Should I go talk to her?"

"Sure."

Baldacci got up. He smiled. "Thanks, Gabe. It's the Year of the Rat."

"What?"

"The Chinese year. It's better than it sounds."

Monday
1:00 pm

He went to lunch. He considered going home and not coming out ever again. He could have food delivered and shop online for everything else.

He pulled himself together. Carla was just messing with him. She and Baldacci weren't there when he got back, but they came in a little later, smiling at one another.

But Carla walked by Dana and said something. It was hard to tell given the layers of makeup, but he thought Dana blanched.

If Carla knew that Dana had told Baldacci about Nemec, then Dana was a dead woman walking.

Not his concern.

He didn't feel like it, but he called Marge again.

"Hello."

"Marge? Are you okay? I've been calling and calling. I thought you were dead or trapped in a car slowly sinking into a swamp...."

"Who the Hell is this?"

"Gabriel Bergeron, your accountant."

"Gabe? I'm fine. What do you want?"

"I got your email."

"Oh, that. I took care of that."

"What did you do, Marge?"

"Nothing to worry about. I have to go, Gabe. I have an artist coming in."

And she hung up. Well, at least her decaying corpse wasn't

stinking up the gallery.

He went to get coffee. Chatterjee and Baldacci were talking in the breakroom, but they shut up when he walked in and looked at him funny.

"What's up?"

They smiled at him. Well, Baldacci did.

He shook his head and went back to his desk. He didn't want the coffee. He wanted to go home and achieve catatonia. He tried to do some work instead.

It was almost 4:00 pm. He was more exhausted than he'd ever been, and when the big hand hit twelve, he was going home, and maybe he'd be able to sleep perchance not to dream.

He was clearing his desk when he sensed a presence behind him. He didn't even look. "What?"

But it was only Dana. "You have a new client coming in, Bergeron."

"Do not!"

Dana was in her winter wear; she had topped a long-sleeved, brown, ankle-length dress with an olive caftan and wrapped a fuzzy, black and brown scarf round and round her neck until her head was barely visible. She could still nod vigorously.

"I sent you an email Friday. And another email when she called and confirmed before lunch."

He was about to dispute that when Carla returned to her desk. Dana, wisely, slunk away like a tent with feet.

He checked and found the emails, but he couldn't do it. He looked at Baldacci who knew what he was thinking. "Nope. Full up."

And Carla already had twice as many clients as he did. Well, a lot more anyway. He spied Chatterjee who was slumped in his chair and doodling. He shook himself into a semi-alert state and strolled over and leaned against Chatterjee's desk.

"A new client is coming in."

Chatterjee glared at him with big, brown eyes with Bambi lashes. "So?"

"And I recommended you to take the account."

Chatterjee sat up. "You did?"

"Sure. I told her you were the man."

Chatterjee smiled at him. "You really recommended me?"

"Sure. I'm always singing your praises to potential clients." He had no recollection of ever saying a word about Chatterjee to anyone. Well, maybe he'd complained about him to Cory once. Or twice.

A suspicious look blossomed on Chatterjee's face as he raked the glossy, black locks out of his eyes. "Who is this?"

"A Dr. Svetlana Kutuzov."

"What's wrong with her, Bergeron?"

"Nothing." He had no idea, but there was surely something. "I'm not quite clear what kind of business she has, but that's all part of the adventure, isn't it? Breaking new ground in the fast-paced field of accounting."

"Carla warned me about you." Chatterjee was shaking his head. "Does she have a criminal record? Are the police looking for her?"

"Absolutely not! But I can see you're reluctant so maybe you should sit on the sidelines and let me handle this...if you're not up to it?"

Chatterjee glared at him. "I'm up to it."

He had no idea if Chatterjee was even a mediocre accountant, but he didn't care. Which made him feel a little bad.

"And I do need new clients."

"Well, excellent!"

And right on cue, the elevator dinged, and a solid, gray-haired lady stepped out. She scanned the room and seemed to lock onto them.

But she marched over to Dana. "I am Dr. Kutuzov. To see Mr. Bergeron."

She had a heavy Russian accent.

Dana was about to point him out when he grabbed Chatterjee and dragged him toward the good doctor.

He said, "Dr. Kutuzov? I'm Gabriel Bergeron." She was his height but had a good forty pounds on him. "But I'm afraid I won't be able to handle your account. Dana should have explained to you how swamped I am." Dana gave him a look meant to scorch his face and fricassee his lying tongue. "But Mr Chatterjee will be more than happy to assist you."

He smiled his best smile, but she gave him a look as warm and cheerful as the look on the face of Lenin's embalmed cadaver.

Chatterjee smiled at her too and held out his hand. "Welcome to Garst, Bauer & Hartmann, Dr. Kutuzov."

She had a paw twice the size of Chatterjee's, who winced when she pumped his hand. She was wearing a gray suit styled by the house of Khrushchev, which made her look as much like a monolithic block as old Nikita.

Chatterjee said, "Thank you for coming in, Dr. Kutuzov. Shall we go into the conference room?"

She hesitated for a second, staring at Chatterjee. "*Da!*"

Dr. Kutuzov fired off one final glare at that Gabriel Bergeron before marching into the conference room. Chatterjee clomped after her.

He had never seen Kutuzov before, but the name was familiar? He didn't care. She was going to be a problem client; he had a sixth sense, and she had set off all the alarms.

But she was Chatterjee's problem client. He may have smiled and chuckled silently.

Baldacci rolled over. "You stuck Chatterjee with your new client?"

"I didn't stick him with her! I asked if he wanted her, Baldacci, and he did."

"She came here the week you were off."

He looked at Baldacci. "To see me in particular?"

Baldacci looked confused. "I think so? But I could be wrong."

Which was likely.

"She talked to Dana for a second and then left."

He casually strolled over to Dana. "So this new client...if that's what she is...Baldacci said she's been in before?"

Dana glared at him. "So? I'm busy, Bergeron."

He snorted in derision which sounded a bit like a pig snuffling for truffles. "Did she ask for me by name? It could be important."

Dana doubted that, but she marshaled all of her available brain cells and cast her mind back. "I think so."

"Did she or didn't she?"

Dana put up her hands. "Don't freak, Bergeron. I don't remember."

He was working with idiots. With memory issues. He went back to his cubicle and glanced at this Kutuzov. She was staring at him in an implacable, Soviet way.

She said something to Chatterjee who sprang to his feet and exited the conference room. His boots were heavy enough to give him a strange, rolling gait.

Chatterjee was heading for him.

"What?"

Chatterjee glared. "She says she's changed her mind. I'm too young or something. She wants you or she's leaving."

"Well, I don't want her! And I'm young too!" Baldacci and Chatterjee smiled at that. "I am."

Chatterjee said, "She's waiting, Bergeron."

He was down a few clients; not that they had dumped him. It was just natural attrition due to the fact that the great majority of small business owners had no business owning businesses; small or otherwise.

He sighed. He arose. He marched.

And he smiled at Dr. Svetlana. "Mr. Chatterjee said you wanted to talk to me? I don't mind, of course, but Chatterjee is the rising star of the firm, and you'd be in extremely capable hands if you selected him...."

She pointed at a chair, "Sit."

He sat.

She was staring at him, dark eyes boring in. She had a square face with skin and lips the color of oatmeal; her hair looked pasted to her skull. "Tell me about you."

Like he was going to do that. "What kind of business do you have, Dr. Kutuzov?"

"A clinic. Very small. Select clientele. Very profitable."

Which didn't sound suspicious at all.

"Tell me about you, Gabriel."

"I'm a CPA, and I've worked here just over four years. Is this clinic in Philadelphia?"

She nodded. "*Da*. Are you married, Gabriel?"

"*Nyet*. Dr. Kutuzov."

She smiled for the first time. "You speak Russian?"

"A few words. But I know people who speak it. What kind of clinic do you have? Have you incorporated?"

"Who speaks Russian?"

Matt Bornheimer did, according to Cory. "I know a guy. But we seem to be getting off the track, Dr. Kutuzov. Are you looking for an accountant?"

And then he remembered that Valentina's first husband had been one Sergei Kutuzov. Which could be a coincidence?

She said, "*Da*! But I want to know you, Gabriel. First. You understand?"

He did not. He wasn't sure who she was, but she was not a potential client. He had some expertise in this area.

"Not really, Dr. Kutuzov, but if you'd like to fill out some forms and supply some financial information, we can move forward?"

"You don't want to be my accountant, Gabriel?"

He smiled his very best smile. "I'd like nothing better. It would be a dream come true."

She actually smiled at him. "Is sarcasm."

"Not a bit. I need clients. I love my clients; each and every one of them. But I don't think you're looking for an accountant, are you, Svetlana?"

"*Da*! I will fill out your forms, Gabriel. So we can move forward."

"Great!" Chatterjee had all the forms on the table. He was almost sure she was as bogus as her Russian accent, but just in case, it wouldn't hurt to be polite. "Would you like coffee and a pastry, Dr. Kutuzov?"

She nodded and bent to the task of filling out forms.

He slipped into the breakroom and grabbed coffee, but when he returned to the conference room, the good doctor had vanished.

She hadn't gone past the breakroom to get to the elevator. He looked at Baldacci. "Where did she go? Ladies Room?"

Baldacci shrugged, but Dana said, "The stairs, Bergeron."

He handed Baldacci the tray with the coffee and sprinted to the stairwell. He didn't hear footsteps. He waited, limbs and ears aquiver. Had she gone up? Or down? Had she had enough time to get to another floor and out of the stairwell? He didn't think so.

He waited. He had a pastry of unknown provenance in his left hand. He sat on the bottom stair and ate said pastry.

He wasn't very comfortable, but he was okay for a while longer. He was shifting to his left buttock when his keen hearing detected a noise above him.

It could be just the building creaking, but he was tired of sitting, and he ran up the stairs. He heard steps coming from above him so he zipped past the twelfth floor, which was also Garst, Bauer & Hartmann. He heard the stairwell door slam against the wall.

He sped up, but when he opened the stairwell door, he didn't see Svetlana in the hall. This was the thirteenth floor, which most tall buildings chose to skip over, but not the Mahr Building for some reason? But the floor seemed to be mostly vacant so maybe they had made a mistake and should renumber the floors?

He tried each door as he went down the hall. They were all locked. But it was getting late so that didn't mean anything?

He paced up and down the hall before he gave up. He was walking down the stairs when it occurred to him that the stairwell door should have been locked.

So Svetlana, or whatever her name was, had planned an escape route? And had picked the lock or obtained a key in advance? Who did that? To see an accountant?

He went back to his cubicle. Baldacci and Carla were packing up. They kissed and cuddled on the way to the elevator.

But Chatterjee was looking at him.

"What? I'm sorry, Chatterjee. I really am. I thought I was doing you a favor, but now I don't know? She probably wasn't even a real client. Or Russian. What is the Russian for 'con-artist' or 'scam' or 'bullshit' I wonder?"

Chatterjee shook his head. "I don't care about her. Or this job." And young Chatterjee heaved his boots into motion and departed.

It was none of his business. He locked his desk and departed as well.

Tuesday
1:00 pm

He had gotten a little more sleep.

He had only sat up in bed screaming as Hilda came at him with a hypodermic needle the size of a caulking gun just the one time.

He had gotten lunch at CoffeeXtra; no sign of Billy or even Martin. Who was running the place? He knocked on the office door, but no one answered, and it was locked.

He called Billy, and it went directly to voicemail.

"Call me. It's Gabe. Who's running this place? CoffeeXtra, I mean."

He walked back to the Mahr Building.

There had been no sign of the spurious Dr. Svetlana Kutuzov. The phone number she'd given Dana was no longer in service. He was willing to bet the address of this "clinic" was also bogus.

Which should worry him? But he was too down.

He would tell Cory on Thursday. He sank into his chair.

Baldacci had rolled his chair across the aisle, and he and Carla were snogging.

"Please stop doing that."

Carla glared at him, but then she shifted gears. "Are you okay, Gabe?"

"I'm fine." Baldacci was looking at him funny too. "Really. Sorry. Continue ravishing each other."

But he had ruined it, and they got to work. He was no fun.

He was a Grinch, a party pooper, and a general wet blanket. He was also feeling sorry for himself.

A voice said, "May I speak to you, Gabriel?"

Chatterjee was inches away from him. He closed his eyes and took a deep, cleansing breath. "Okay. Go ahead."

"In the breakroom."

He looked at Baldacci and Carla; Baldacci spread his hands, palms up, in the universal sign for having no idea.

"Okay."

Chatterjee led the way. He was mystified. He considered bolting for the elevator.

"I'm sorry that the doctor didn't work out, Chatterjee. As a client."

He waved that away. "Not your fault. She was weird."

"Okay?"

"I have a family problem, Gabriel."

"Nope. I can't help you."

Chatterjee smiled. He had a very nice smile. "How can you say no when you haven't heard what it is yet?"

"You want me to solve a mystery. Or something like that. I'm out of the detective business. Not that I was ever really in it. But things happened and I got caught up. But I'm going to work on never letting that happen again."

Chatterjee nodded. "I can see you're not yourself. We've all noticed it. Something bad happened over the weekend. I'm not asking what it was."

"Right. Thanks. I don't want to talk about it."

"No, of course not. But this is a very small mystery. My grandmother's cat has gone missing."

"Her cat?" He smiled and shook his head.

"I know. But I've searched everywhere around her neighborhood, and I haven't found anything. The stupid animal has just vanished."

"Cats wander off. Is this a male cat?" Why was he asking questions?

"It was, but that was taken care of years ago. It never left the house even when the door was open. My grandmother is driving me crazy. She thinks I'm not trying to find her cat."

"Are you?"

"Yes, Gabriel! I put up posters around the neighborhood with a picture. I offered a reward, and I walk up and down looking for it every afternoon."

"He's either dead...hit by a car...or killed by a dog...or he'll turn up. I don't see how I can help?"

Chatterjee nodded. "I know, but if you'd talk to my grandmother? Tell her I've hired you to find her precious fur ball, then she might stop harassing me."

He smiled at Chatterjee. "You want me to help you deceive your grandmother?"

"Absolutely."

"Is this why you've been yelling into your phone?"

Chatterjee shook his head. "I would never yell at Nani."

He smiled at Chatterjee.

"It was my mother. She calls and calls. She wants me to get married. She has a girl she wants me to meet."

"An arranged marriage?"

Chatterjee shook his head. "Not exactly. Just someone she thinks is suitable, but it's totally my choice."

"Of course. But you don't want to meet this girl?"

Chatterjee said, "I'm not ugly, Gabriel."

"No, you aren't. You have great hair and nice eyes...."

Chatterjee was glaring; the air between them was suddenly frigid, and a coating of hoarfrost was forming on his nose.

"The point is, Gabriel, that I don't need help finding a wife."

"No, I'm sure you don't. So that's why you stomped on your phone?"

But he shook his head. "That was...that was something else."

There were more layers to Chatterjee than an Uttar Pradeshi onion; not that he knew where the guy was from.

"So will you talk to my grandmother, Gabriel? Please?"

"I don't know, Chatterjee. I mean it's a big ask, and we aren't exactly friends. You never talk to me, and I don't even know your first name?"

"I know. Sorry. It's just all the stories that Carla and Baldacci tell about you. And well, Nemec hated you, and I didn't want to get drawn into that. And after he was gone, it would have been weird to suddenly start talking to you." Chatterjee smiled and held out his hand. "I'm Dhruva." He frowned again. "Please don't call me Dave."

He shook Dhruva's hand. "I wouldn't dream of it. Okay. But I'm not making any promises."

"But you'll think about it?"

"Sure. I guess so."

Dhruva said, "You can come for dinner. Are you free tomorrow night?"

"No! Give me a little longer than that."

Lunch sounded more doable than dinner. If Nani prepared traditional Indian dishes, he was sure he couldn't eat her food. Too spicy. Too exotic. Too everything.

Dhruva patted him on the shoulder and left the breakroom.

How much trouble could come from a pretend search for a missing cat?

He walked back to his cubicle. He glared at Carla and Baldacci, but they just snickered.

Carla said, "The mystery of the kidnapped kitty!"

Baldacci grinned. "The felonious feline?"

Carla shook her head. "That doesn't make any sense, Harry. The cat didn't steal anything."

Baldacci raised a finger. "The fugitive feline?"

"Better."

And they proceeded to giggle and guffaw at him. He glared at them and arose from his chair. He didn't trust Dhruva, and he was going home before some elderly Indian woman stepped out of the elevator.

The elevator dinged. He grabbed his coat; he could run down eleven floors easy. But it was Jennifer, and she was being escorted by her husband, Andy.

She waved at him smiling. Which was unsettling even on a normal day.

Which this wasn't. He turned off his computer and put his pens, his sticky notes, his pocket calculator, and his favorite ruler into the middle drawer and locked it.

He straightened Cory's picture and arose from his chair.

Jennifer said, "Gabe?"

He pretended not to hear her. If he dropped and crawled on the floor, he might make it to the elevator?

"Gabe? I need to speak to you."

He closed his eyes. He trudged to her office.

Her hair was burnished bright, her eyes sparkled, her complexion had a ruddy glow. She was smiling. It was deeply unnerving.

She was smiling mostly at Andy. It appeared that whatever Andy had done to rile his spouse had been forgiven. He was a short, densely muscled individual, with baby blue eyes and steel cheekbones with angles sharp enough to cleave Arctic ice.

"Gabe."

"Andy."

He wanted to ask how he was doing, but Andy was not chatty. It was best to ease into a conversation. He looked at Jennifer, but she was still smiling at Andy.

Andy picked her up and spun her around. She may have squealed in delight. And then they kissed.

Was he supposed to cover his eyes? Depart her office? But Andy put her down before it became truly awkward.

Andy nodded to him on the way out the door. "Gabe."

"Andy."

He was pleased with himself. He had asked zero questions. Jennifer closed the door. "Sit down, Gabe."

"Okay?"

"How are you doing?"

"Fine. Tip-top. I thought you were mad with Andy?"

She laughed. "I wasn't really."

She really had been; cobra mad, wolverine mad. "Good. What did he do?"

She shrugged. "He was being stubborn."

"About?"

"Gabe, I want to talk about you."

"Nothing to talk about. So what was Andy being stubborn about?"

"He's really busy, and he's been thinking of hiring some people and buying another van."

Andy Boltukaev's locksmithing business was apparently flourishing which should be a good thing. "That's sounds great?"

"It is, but he wouldn't let me help him."

"Ah, financially."

"Yes. Men can be so stubborn."

"Right. Okay, well I'm glad that's all straightened out...."

She fixed him with an awful glare. "Sit! Now tell me what happened, or I'll call your Aunt Flo or Cory. Or the Poiriers. Or that Detective Sanders."

"Don't do that. Please, Jennifer."

She pulled her chair next to his. "Then just tell me."

So he did.

Jennifer was staring at him. "That must have been awful...."

And she hugged him. He managed not to flinch.

"It was. And I keep thinking it was my fault...."

She eye-rolled him good. "Your fault! No! Absolutely not, Bergeron! And if I thought it was, I would tell you. You know that."

Which was nice to hear, but he wasn't so sure. It was just possible that Jennifer liked him enough to try to make him feel better.

"Thanks, Jennifer."

"For what. Get back to work, Bergeron. Have you done anything today? Anything at all? I heard you lost a new client yesterday? Even before she finished the paperwork?"

"Not my fault, Jennifer! Really! She was a pseudo-client."

Jennifer shook her head. "Why is it that only you have that kind of client, Bergeron?"

"No idea. Karma?"

"Not karma. I think you're a weirdness magnet."

"I deeply resent that, Jennifer."

She sat at her desk and switched on her computer. She

waved him away. "Back to work. And no sneaking out early."

"I never do that."

"Out!"

He went back to his desk and stared at the blank screen. He should pretend work. How did one search for a cat? He had no idea. Wait. Did this cat have one of those ID chips?

Baldacci rolled over. "What's up? What did Jennifer want?"

"Nothing much."

"Are you okay, Gabe?"

"I will be, Harry. Want to help me look for a lost cat?"

Baldacci smiled at him. "That's a hard pass, Gabe. But anything else you need, you know I'm here."

Without turning from her computer, Carla muttered, "Me too."

"Thanks, Guys."

He had worked very hard at looking busy and productive, and then he had gone home.

He stretched out on the sofa. A Beethoven sonata for piano and violin was playing.

He was listening to the "Adagio molto expressivo" section.

And as the piano danced *en pointe* and the violin sang an ancient lullaby, sad but sweet, he drifted off to sleep.

Friday
9:00 am

He opened his eyes. He was in bed, and Cory was slumbering beside him.

He smiled to himself.

The rest of his week at Garst, Bauer & Hartmann had been normal. He had cornered Marge and found out what she didn't want him to know.

Carla and Harry had redoubled their public displays of affection. He hadn't spied Chatterjee's grandmother; he had barely seen Chatterjee. And Jennifer had been extra nice to him.

Cory said, "Are you okay?"

He rolled over and hugged him. Cory always smelled so good. "I'm excellent. So you aren't going in today?"

"Nope."

"Really? Excellent squared...cubed."

Cory frowned. "I have to go to the farm. Sorry, Gabe."

Shit! Shit! Not the freaking farm! Not again! "That's okay, Cory." He smiled with gritted teeth. "Why? Is everything okay?"

"Yes, but Dad needs some help taking care of the horses."

"Right! With Hilda and Dolph gone. Sure, I understand."

"Only temporarily. They're looking for someone."

"Another farm manager?"

Cory shook his head. "No, not after Mrs. Prentice. Dad's going to handle the financial side; they just need somebody good with horses."

"Right."

Cory was looking at him. "Gabe."

"It's nothing. It's just that I know someone who may or may not be good with horses, but I sorta think he is."

"Who do you know who's good with horses, Bergeron?"

"I don't actually know him." Cory was going to punch him any second now. "Jedidiah Foote."

Cory just shook his head. "Any relation to Mrs. Foote?"

"Nephew. He needs a job. But I don't know if he's really suitable. I've only talked to him once really. He could be a serial killer, but Hugh could check him out?"

"When did you meet this guy?"

"A week ago. It was before Hilda....did what she did."

"And he's good with horses?"

"He says he is. And there's another nephew, Del, who's a mechanic, but he's a bit volatile."

Cory laughed at him. "So are these nephews anything like Mrs. Foote?"

He shrugged. "Don't know. I think Celia is just lonely."

Cory said, "That's one way of describing it. Okay, I'll mention them to Dad."

"Good."

Was he supposed to go with Cory? He wasn't sure he wanted to see the farm again. At least, not so soon. And he didn't want to help with the horses. The only tasks he could handle were poop shoveling and such like.

Cory was staring at him. "You don't have to go."

Which meant he did. "No, I'd be happy to help out."

"Gabe."

"All right. Maybe 'happy' is stretching the truth. How does 'willing' sound? Or 'not unalterably opposed'?"

"No, it's really okay. Diane and I can handle it."

"Okay. If you're sure?"

"Very."

So he stayed in bed as Cory got ready. The special agent showered and put on a pair of faded jeans and scruffy boots, and a long sleeved t-shirt. The jeans and shirt were tight and molded to his body.

He may have had a few cowboy-barn fantasies.

Cory's phone chimed. He looked at it and sighed. "I'm on my way, Mother."

But there was more. "Yes, I see." Cory was looking at him. "No. I'd rather not. Yes, I know you have his number, Mother."

He smiled at Cory and held out his hand for the phone. "Does Laura wish to speak to me?"

Cory nodded and gave up the phone. "Good morning, Laura. How are you today?"

"I'm fine, Gabriel, but we have a mess here."

He shut his eyes tight. "What kind of mess? Not more bodies?"

Silence.

Peals of laughter.

"Oh, Gabriel! No, Mrs. Prentice has left the farm accounts in a terrible state. I can't understand what her system was, but she seems to have stopped doing anything two months ago. It's so confusing."

"And you'd like me to take a look?" Cory was shaking his head and waving his hands. He smiled at Cory.

Laura said, "Could you, Gabriel? This will be simple for you."

"I'd be happy to, Laura. But if I'm going to work on my day off, I must have cookies. Sugar cookies, shortbread cookies, or chocolate chip cookies: the chewy ones. Failing that, any kind of cookie will do in a pinch."

Laura laughed. "I can manage that, Gabriel. Is Corentin still there?"

"He is."

Cory sat on the bed and talked as he jumped into the shower.

He was in jeans too, but he didn't have the boots. He needed cowboy boots. And maybe a Stetson hat and spurs. Not that he was going near the barn.

Diane was waiting for Cory as they pulled in, and they went off toward the barn. He mounted the steps to find Laura in the kitchen, which smelled divine. He inhaled a nose full of cookie aroma and smiled.

Laura was in jeans and boots too. She smiled at him. "The cookies will be ready soon, Gabriel. Diane and I brought everything from the barn and put it in Hugh's office."

"Right."

"Even the filing cabinet, but she hasn't filed in months."

"No problem. Most of my clients eschew filing."

She smiled. "'Eschew'?"

"Shun? Avoid? Think it's unmanly or unnatural or unconstitutional?"

"I know what it means."

They went to the office; Hugh was on the phone. Laura said, "Did you talk to her?"

Hugh said, "I tried. She isn't ready to listen yet. I'm trying to do what I can, but the company needs someone at the office full time."

Laura took Hugh's hand. "But not you. Cory and Diane are at the barn."

Hugh smiled. "I'm on my way."

And Laura showed him the records; such as they were. One bank account was overdrawn; the other two were nearly so.

She brought him a tray of cookies hot from the oven and a pot of coffee.

"Thanks. That's great."

"How does it look?"

"Too soon to tell. I have to burrow in."

"You don't need me?"

"No, I'm fine."

She nodded and tied a bandanna around her hair. And with her loins thus girded, she marched toward the barn.

He reconciled the bank accounts first. There were a number of checks written to cash. And nothing had been recorded in the accounting software for months.

Hilda had been winging it.

She had also been embezzling.

He munched a sugar cookie which was first rate and examined the previous years, checking the vendors. Hilda had set up half a dozen, new vendor accounts.

He felt sure the vendors didn't actually exist, and with a little investigation, he was able to confirm that.

Hilda had never thrown out a slip of paper so he was able to go back ten years.

At some point, Laura had brought him a sandwich and more coffee.

Cory said, "Time to eat, Gabe?"

"What?" He looked up at Cory. It was dark outside. "But I'm almost finished?"

"After dinner, Gabe."

"Okay. Mrs. Prentice is a bad bookkeeper and a worse employee, Cory, ."

"You can tell us all about it after dinner."

He had brought Hugh and Laura up to speed on the dire financial situation of the farm accounts. They had been shocked all over again at Hilda's perfidy, and that embezzling on a small scale had been going on for years.

He had finished what could be done until the vendors were contacted. He had a feeling that a number of them were close to cutting off deliveries to the Poirier farm.

But that was for Hugh and Laura to deal with.

He shut off the computer and headed for the family room. Hugh and Cory were dozing. A football game was unfolding unobserved.

He didn't know where Laura was, but Diane was in the kitchen. "Hi, there. Are the horses okay?"

She nodded. "They had to take care of them or we would have noticed that."

She was gripping the lip of the farm sink hard enough to make her forearm muscles pop. She was staring out the window into the night.

He should just walk back to the family room and mind his own business. "Is something wrong?"

"I don't know what to do."

"About what?"

"Finn."

He smiled, but she didn't. "Cold feet? Laura?"

"No, I love him, and Mother will come around."

Had she met her mother?

"But?"

"Please don't repeat this...even to Cory."

He liked Diane. "I won't volunteer whatever this is, but if he asks me, I can't lie to him."

"No. I know."

She sat down at the table in the solarium. The glass was black and reflective. He could imagine eyes staring at him hidden in the depth of the night.

"I have to know, Gabe."

"This is something about Finn?"

"I have to know if he had anything to do with Shaw's death. I don't believe he did, but before I marry him, I have to know if he's the man I think he is or...."

"Or there's another side to him?"

She nodded. "I told him about Shaw. About all the things he'd done to me. I shouldn't have, but I was upset, and he knew it."

"When was this?"

"Thursday morning. When I left the farm after breakfast."

And Shaw had been killed half a day later. "And what did Finn say?"

"That's what scares me. He just got quiet."

"Have you asked him about it, Diane?"

She laughed. "Asked my fiancé if he murdered the guy who was harassing me?"

"Right. That would be a difficult conversation."

She said, "He was a marine, Gabe, and he's had all kinds of training. He joined up when he was eighteen, and he served six years. He was deployed to Afghanistan. Twice."

"Right. But that doesn't mean that he laid a finger on Shaw, Diane."

"I know."

"And if he'd been going to do anything to Shaw, he wouldn't have done it here. He would have gone to Shaw's house or to the office. Or waylaid him somewhere."

"I know, but maybe he followed Shaw here?"

"Okay, but why would Shaw come here in the middle of the night? It doesn't make any sense."

"But he knew he was out as CEO. Maybe he came here to try to hurt Dad, hurt me. To get back at us."

"By doing what?"

"Hurting Bucephalus. He knew how much I love him, Gabe."

"So you think Shaw came here to hurt Bucephalus, and Finn followed him."

"And they fought, and Finn hit him too hard."

Which sounded plausible enough. "But would Shaw do something like that? If he was pissed, wouldn't he sue the company and Hugh?"

"He was a petty man, Gabe."

"But that doesn't explain about Turtle and Third Guy." Unless Finn was cleaning up. "But I'm sure that Sanders checked on Finn's alibi?"

"He doesn't have one."

"No?"

"I was talking about that night, and he just told me that he'd been in his apartment alone."

Which was certainly odd.

"I can see why you're concerned."

She looked at him. "I need to know for sure. Can you find out for me, Gabe?"

"No."

"Please, Gabe? I don't think I can marry him not knowing."

He shook his head. She didn't know what she was asking. If Shaw had come to the farm to maim the horse, then Hugh or Judd were more likely suspects than Finn. Or she was.

Or Hilda and Dolph had killed all three.

"Tell me you'll think about it, Gabe."

"I'll think about it." He didn't need to.

He was going home, and he would probably never come back to the farm again.

Saturday 10:00 am

He didn't really have anything left to do on the farm accounts, but Cory was at the barn. He was enjoying the work and didn't want to leave. .

Finn had showed up and pitched in. He appeared to know about horses or at least he wasn't afraid of them.

He ate another cookie and stared out at the barn. He had eaten all the sugar cookies and was working on the shortbread cookies now.

His phone trilled; Sanders.

He could just let it go to voicemail and then delete the message.

"Hi, Detective?"

"Where are you?"

"The Poirier farm, and where are you?" They'd had this conversation before.

"Not far. I'd appreciate it if you could meet me in Middleburg. At the Safeway."

"Why?"

"We arrested Dolph Prentice on Tuesday and Dr. Crain yesterday."

"Great."

"And I have something to tell you, Gabe."

And Sanders was gone. He ran up to the bedroom and grabbed Cory's keys off the dresser. He looked at himself in the mirror.

"You don't care what he has to tell you. You're not curious one little bit. You're going to call him back and tell him exactly that."

He pulled into the Safeway parking lot and looked around for Sanders, but he hadn't arrived.

The sun was shining, and it was sixty-five according to the dashboard of the SUV so he got out and strolled. The streets were tree-lined; the sidewalks were brick.

The shops looked expensive. He could purchase custom cabinets or a wedding gown. There were a few shops which were so exclusive that he couldn't figure out what they were selling.

There were two tack shops selling horse paraphernalia; price tags were not in evidence. Which was always a bad sign.

He randomly asked the price of a riding helmet thing which looked like something major league baseball batters wore to keep from getting beaned by the pitcher: five hundred.

And not five hundred pennies either.

But there was a book store which was nice. He had his face pressed to the glass reading titles when he sensed a presence.

Sanders said, "Thanks for coming, Gabe."

He was in jeans and a purple long-sleeved knit shirt; clingy enough to display muscular arms. But he looked tired, and the smile was strained.

"I'm glad you caught Dolph. And Dr. Crain, Detective."

Sanders said, "Me too. We can sit in my car."

They walked back toward the Safeway, but turned left onto a side street. Sanders got into a dark blue Chevy SUV.

There were kid's toys in the back and two car seats.

"I don't need to know anything, Detective."

Sanders said, "But there are a couple of things you should know, Gabe."

"Okay?"

"We never had this conversation." He was staring out the window.

"Okay? Sure."

"Crain admitted to lying to the Poiriers about both horses. He claimed that Hilda had a nursing home lined up for Jack, and that he was going to join her in Ohio as soon as he could."

"But I thought Jack was dying?"

Sanders nodded. "According to his doctor and the medical examiner, Jack didn't have long...a month...maybe longer. So that part was true."

"Okay? What part wasn't?"

"I checked with the nursing home; they had never heard of Hilda Prentice or Jack." Sanders turned to look at him. "I think she planned to kill Jack all along, but she didn't want to scare off Crain."

He just looked at Sanders.

"But Dr. Crain suspected. He got cagey when I confronted him about that. He swore she stole the tranquilizer out of his bag. But he wasn't going to admit that he had known about getting rid of Jack and be charged as an accomplice."

"But Jack was her husband?"

"She wanted the cash from the horse...Bucephalus." He still smiled at the name. "But she knew that the Poiriers would call us in, and she would be suspected. So she planned to kill Jack a few days after Bucephalus went missing and play the grieving widow to the hilt."

He looked at Sanders. "But you can't prove any of this?"

"No, but Jack was never going to see Ohio, Gabe. I'm sure of it."

"What about Dolph? What did he say?"

"Almost nothing. He's smarter than he looks. Or maybe dumber. I can't quite tell."

"But did he know about Hilda planning to kill his father?"

"Step-father. Not that it would probably make much difference to Dolph. Not a lot of family feeling. Or empathy there."

"No. Not a lot."

Sanders said, "I asked Hilda about the nursing home. She said that the folks at the home were mistaken. And then she said she didn't want anybody else taking care of her Jack. Before she clammed up."

"So is she insane?"

Sanders shrugged. "I'm no expert."

"Thanks for telling me all this...John."

He nodded. "I didn't want you feeling responsible for Jack's death."

"So you know about Turtle and Hilda and Dolph and the missing horses. What about Shaw and Third Guy?"

John smiled. "Not a freaking clue. Any ideas?"

John was looking at him. "I haven't been thinking about it...but no ideas."

"If you think of something, I'd appreciate a call."

"Of course." It was on the tip of his tongue to ask about Finn, but that would lead John back to Diane and the Poiriers.

John was staring at him with what could only be called piercing hazel eyes. He felt like a butterfly pinned alive to a board in a display case.

"Are you sure about that, Gabe?"

"Sure. Wait. What about Gita? It's always the wife, right?"

John sighed. "Gita Bhattacharya Shaw has an alibi. Almost too good."

"Do tell?

"She was at a charity auction; a hospital benefit. Several hundred people saw her until almost 11:00 pm. Shaw was supposed to have been there, but when he didn't show, acquaintances offered to drop her off at her condo in DC. She was there when Shaw was killed."

"Right. So she didn't worry when he didn't show up?"

Sanders shook his head. "She said that as far as she knew he was asleep at their house."

"I see. Okay."

John rolled his shoulders and then locked his hands and stretched, making his muscles pop.

"Here comes Christina."

A pretty young woman with long, auburn hair came out of a shop with a bag in hand and was strolling toward the car. She smiled at John. She had a long, oval face and eyes the same shade of hazel as John's.

"Right. Okay." He got out and walked around to the driver's side of the SUV. "Thanks for telling me, John."

John got out of the vehicle too. "Telling you what?"

"Right." They shook hands.

John opened the door for Christina and smiled at her. He got to see what the detective looked like when he was truly happy. John leaned toward her, and they kissed; briefly but with brio.

He smiled at Christina, but John didn't introduce him so he walked back to the Safeway parking lot.

He sat in the SUV for a while before driving back to the farm.

Saturday Noon

He got back in time for lunch. The Poiriers and Finn seemed happy in their simple labors far from the madding crowd.

He needed to think about Jack and his death before he decided anything, but Finn was here, and he wanted to help Diane.

He pretended to work on the farm books again so he wouldn't be drafted for barn labor, but they quit at 2:00 pm.

Finn was saying goodbye to Diane.

He followed Finn out to his pickup which had a gun rack with two rifles in the cab and a tool box large enough to store a body in the back.

"I'm a decent shot...with a Glock 22."

Finn smiled at him. "Now that surprises me."

"But I've never shot at a man so I'm sure that's very different." He wasn't going to ask Finn if he'd shot anybody or killed anybody.

"Yes, it is, Gabe."

"You were in Afghanistan?"

"Twice."

"Not a garden spot."

Finn leaned against his pickup in no hurry to leave. He stroked his beard. He was in a blue plaid shirt, jeans, and boots today.

"No. But I liked some of the people. They don't have an easy life. Never have."

He tried leaning against the truck too, but he felt funny. "So you're a ranger at Shenandoah National Park. That must be nice?"

"It has its moments." Finn looked at him. "So why are we chatting, Gabe? Not that I mind."

"I've never met a marine before. Though I have met a park ranger; Kurt Hobbs. He's at Janes Island State Park in Maryland. We're friends."

Finn was smiling at him; he was pretty sure Finn knew seven ways to kill him without leaving a mark or alternatively could twist him into a pretzel shape using just his massive, tattooed forearms.

"I have to go, Gabe, so if you could circle around to the point of this conversation?"

"No point. I'm famous for having no point. I can talk for hours. Nobody has told you the Cuban spy story?"

"No, and I really would like to hear it, but not today."

"So who do you think killed Craig Shaw?"

Finn smiled. "I don't know, but he deserves a medal." He had a sweet smile when he wasn't contemplating Shaw's violent death.

"But Diane told you all the things he'd been doing to her?"

The large, brown eyes locked onto him. "She did. And I feel shitty that I didn't tear him apart. Is that what you think, Gabe? That a real man would have?"

"No! I'm sorry, Finn. I'm not saying that at all. She asked you not to get into it, right?"

Finn nodded. "She was definite about that. She said she could fight her own battles, but if Shaw had lived another day, he and I would have had a meeting of the minds."

"Right."

"But I wouldn't have killed him. I could have made my point without using a tire iron. And before you ask, Sanders collected my tire iron."

"I'm sure. He took mine, and I still haven't gotten it back but I'm probably not going to need it."

"You never know, Gabe."

"Right. It was a bad situation. What I can't figure out is why Shaw came to the barn at midnight?"

Finn grabbed his jacket and lifted him so that just his tiptoes were touching the blacktop. "Diane had nothing to do with that."

"I know she didn't. I like Diane, and I believe she's a good person. Could you let go?" Finn held on. "These are nice tattoos. Did they hurt much? Not that pain would daunt you. I had a friend who had an eagle tattoo on his throat. Not that he was more manly than you are. Maybe I should stop talking now?"

Finn smiled and let go, and his feet touched down.

"I feel like I can't help her like I should, Gabe."

"I know what that feels like, but I think she'd say that you don't have to fix everything; just listen to her."

Finn smiled again. "She said exactly that, Gabe."

"So your path is clear, Finn. Is that short for 'Phineas' or 'Finnegan' or anything? And I would never hurt Diane or get her into trouble."

Finn smoothed his jacket which had bunched up under his arms, and got into his truck still smiling.

He rolled down the window. "Maybe Shaw was knocked out somewhere else and brought here, Gabe?"

Which was a thought. "Why? To incriminate the Poiriers? That's not impossible."

Finn nodded. "And Gabe, I was in my apartment all night, but I don't have anybody to confirm that."

"I understand. The only person with a rock solid alibi is the lovely Gita."

Finn laughed. "Shaw's wife? I haven't seen her, but she sounds like she's something else."

"She is. Even I can see that."

Finn said, "Gabe, please tell Laura that I didn't murder Shaw, and I'm not going to freak out or anything. I'm stable and well-adjusted even after two tours in Afghanistan."

"I'll tell her. Not that she'll ask. Or has asked."

Finn shook his head and drove off.

It wasn't fair to Laura to let Finn think that he was asking questions for her, but it was probably better in the long run than him thinking it was Diane who doubted him.

Finn was handsome and had a great smile, but he was sure there was another side to him. Most people didn't pick him up by the scruff of the neck; so to speak.

But he didn't believe he'd murdered Shaw.

Cory said, "Gabe."

He jumped; just a little. He was definitely getting better. Or possibly more vulnerable?

"Hi, Corentin. How is the farm?"

"You tell me how it is financially, but first explain to me what just happened between you and Finn."

"Sure. Okay. I may be changing my mind about investigating this mess."

Cory hugged him. "You don't have to, you know?"

"I know, and thank you for saying it. And meaning it. But I had a chat with John."

Cory shook his head. "Who the Hell is John?"

"John is Detective Sanders; J. D. Sanders. I have no idea what the 'D' stands for. He thinks Hilda was planning on killing Jack all along."

And he told Cory the whole story.

"So am I letting myself believe John's theory so I can stop feeling guilty about Jack?"

Cory said, "No."

"Well said, Special Agent."

"It makes sense, Gabe."

"Right. I think so too. Anyway, I asked Finn a few questions...he has no alibi by the way...and he took exception to some of them. Which I totally understand."

Cory was looking at him funny.

"What?"

"You let him grab you."

"I did. Oh, I should have tossed him high into the air?"

"No. But you could have defended yourself."

"I could. Well, I could have tried; he's rather large, and he's had training too. But when you tell me why I need to be on constant Ninja alert, I promise to body slam anybody who comes near me."

Cory just shook his head.

"And the farm is a financial basket case, Cory."

Saturday
3:00 pm

If he was going to investigate, then he needed to talk to Hugh.

He didn't want to because he and Hugh weren't buddies to begin with and asking for an alibi wasn't likely to improve the situation.

But it wasn't impossible that Hugh had done the deed. It was even likely if he'd known about Diane and Shaw. And if so, then the only thing he could do was to protect Cory from ever learning the truth. Or anyone else.

Hugh was in his office on the phone. He was backing out when Hugh waved him in, pointing at a chair.

Hugh hung up. He shook his head. "You were right, Gabriel."

"I was? Of course, I was. About what?"

"The vendors haven't been paid in two months; some of them longer than that. I can't believe it, Gabriel. That woman worked for us for years."

"I know. I've seen it before."

Hugh looked at him. "Some of your clients?"

"Yes. It's surprising...sometimes it's the last person you'd suspect. So what did they say? Your vendors?"

"They want to be paid! And I told them they would be."

Did Hugh and/or Laura have the cash to do that? There was no subtle way. "Is that going to be a problem?"

Hugh looked up and then smiled. "No, Gabriel. We aren't

destitute."

"No, of course, you aren't! I wasn't thinking that, Hugh! But sometimes it can take time to tap less liquid assets?"

Hugh smiled again. "No, we won't have to sell the house in Richmond, Gabriel."

"I'm glad to hear it. When do you live there? I never hear Cory mention you being there?"

Hugh said, "We don't use it that much now. I like it here...we like it here...though Laura has friends in Richmond."

Hugh was looking at him. "My sisters like you, Gabriel."

"Really? Good. I like them too. Élisabeth is a sweetie."

Hugh smiled. "Actually, Anne-Sophie likes you too. And she's not easy."

He was still smarting from her "Cory can do better" comment. "I am aware."

"You told them what Laura said about the company?"

"I'm sorry. I know it wasn't any business of mine, but they were putting the blame on Laura. Which wasn't right...."

Hugh held up a work-roughened hand. "I'm grateful that you spoke up. This time."

Hugh really smiled. He was looking healthier the more days he spent on the farm...as Holcomb receded into the past.

"Laura and I should have talked, but we both thought we knew what the other wanted." He shook his head.

"I understand."

Hugh said, "You'll never have that problem. You don't let Cory get away with keeping secrets."

"Thanks. I guess?"

Hugh laughed.

He should just ask Hugh, but they were getting along so well.

Hugh said, "I was amazed at your judo skills, Gabriel."

"Right. I'm not so bad. I've been going to a dojo for a couple of years, and Cory's been training me too."

"Matthew was impressed."

"I just reacted."

"With grace and power."

Which was very nice to hear.

Hugh said, "You shouldn't doubt yourself, Gabriel."

"Right."

"When we first met you...when Cory was ill, and you were taking care of him in that seedy apartment, I couldn't imagine what Cory saw in you."

He waited for a "but" which didn't come.

Hugh smiled. "You were wearing a hat with ear flaps and seemed manic and unstable. And you kept waving that champagne bottle."

There had to be a "but" coming soon?

Hugh said, "And you snickered at Cory's full name."

He didn't recall any snickering, and Corentin was a funny name anyway!

"Laura liked you almost at once."

"She did? Why?"

"You protected Cory."

"He was sick."

Hugh nodded. "And you really protected him again from someone named Steele? I heard Cory and Matthew talking. You tackled this man? And both of you tumbled down a flight of stairs?"

"I did. He was...." He had been pointing a gun at Cory, but Cory didn't want his parents to know how dangerous his job could be. "He needed tackling."

"And when Cory blamed himself for Matthew's injuries, you talked to him."

"Of course, I did. He doesn't have to be a super man."

Hugh nodded. "No, he doesn't." Hugh stared at him. "And he listens to you."

"Sometimes. He can be very stubborn, but I wear him down."

"I'm sure you do." Hugh smiled with all of his perfect teeth. "So I've been hearing all these things about you...good things, brave things...but I've had a problem imagining you doing them, Gabriel."

He held his breath.

"But not any more. After having you here."

He smiled at Hugh.

"You're still very strange, but you're good for Cory. Even I can see that."

"Thank you, Hugh." He wasn't sure he liked the "strange" part, but he was happy about the rest.

"Now, Gabriel, what is it you want to ask me about Shaw's murder?"

Hugh was Cory's father and no dummy. "Nothing."

"Gabe."

He said it just like Cory did...when Cory wanted a real answer. "Well, when we ran into each other on the way to the barn, you had been outside for a while."

Hugh nodded. "I went for a walk."

It had been freezing; well, not ice-making freezing but not stroll weather either.

"Where?"

"Not to the barn, Gabriel. I walked along the lane almost to the county road. It was only the quarter moon so I stayed on the lane."

"But why go walking at that time of night?"

Hugh said, "I hadn't been feeling well, Gabriel. And I was worried about the company and about returning to a job I thought I was rid of. I just couldn't sleep. I was trying to wear myself out."

"And you heard a noise from the barn?"

"Yes, as I was walking back. And then we met." Hugh smiled at him. "Why were you wearing sandals?"

"They were the first shoes I could find."

"Of course, they were." He stopped smiling. "And Mrs. Prentice smiled at me and pretended nothing was wrong. She was hoping to find Bucephalus gone, wasn't she?"

"She was. I wonder what she would have done if we'd caught Turtle leading Bucephalus away?"

Hugh said, "I've wondered about that too."

"She probably had her gun, Hugh."

He nodded. "But she got a shock instead."

"So did everyone."

Hugh said, "I wonder if Shaw saw it coming?" He shrugged. "We'll never know. I didn't kill him, Gabriel, but I should have. Gabriel?"

"Yes?"

"Can you stop now?"

He meant the investigation.

"Dad?" Cory stuck his head into the office. "You wanted to pick up some supplies?"

"I do. Thanks, Cory."

But Hugh's phone rang. Hugh said, "Josephine? Yes, thank you for calling me back. No, as I've told you, I'm not going back. Not even temporarily. You need to get onboard with Kennard. Or we could start a search on the outside if you like? But Jordan isn't going to take the job."

Hugh smiled. "She hung up on me. I've called her a dozen times over the past few weeks...." Hugh smiled at them. "...since my sisters came for a visit."

He said, "And she won't listen?"

"Not yet, Gabriel. Now, we need to get going, Cory."

And they went off on a supply run.

So he might be getting to like Hugh a bit, but Hubert Paul-Émile Poirier had no alibi at all; not so much as a smidgen.

But still.

Saturday 4:00 pm

He had watched Cory and Hugh drive off in one of the farm trucks.

He was finishing off the last of the cookies while watching a *House* rerun when Judd arrived.

"Mother?"

She said, "I'm in the kitchen, Jordan."

He wandered into the kitchen behind Judd.

Laura said, "I'm glad you came. I found some more things for Samantha. I hope she'll like them?"

Judd smiled at his mother. "She'll love them."

Laura said, "Is she feeling all right, Jordan? How long is she going to work? I know it's the modern thing to work until the very last moment, but I don't think that's really a good idea in Samantha's case. She's always been delicate."

Judd kept smiling. "If the doctor even hints that she should stop working, I'll make sure that she does exactly that."

Laura hugged Judd, surprising both of them a bit. "You have to look after her, Jordan."

"I will. I promise."

"Good. I'll be right back."

And she headed for the stairs.

Judd shook his head. "This is not going to be easy, Gabe."

"Not for you, not for Laura, not for the pregnant lady either."

Judd laughed. "Right. This isn't all about me, is it?"

"Not so much. So Samantha is delicate?"

Judd shook his head. "She has the constitution of a tardigrade; I don't think she's had even a cold since we've been together."

"Tardigrade? Small, creepy-crawly thing that is immune to radiation and semi-immortal? As accurate as that might be, you should choose a different metaphor for your one-true love. So why does Laura think otherwise?"

"That would be because Samantha may have said she was sick...a few times...when Mother invited her to some function or other."

"Ah."

"Ah, indeed."

Laura came back with an armful of clothes which she draped across the dining room table.

"Some of these she can wear right away, and some are for when she's larger, Jordan. I have them sorted for her. I do hope she likes them. They might be a little bland for Samantha's taste?"

"They're perfect, and she really appreciates them."

"Good. And I have some vitamins. My friend Marlene raved about them. Her daughter, Cynthia, took them, and she's had five healthy babies. They do look a bit too much like Cynthia, but vitamins can only do so much."

Judd was smiling. He hugged his mother again, and started gathering up her offerings. "Thank you."

"Do you have to rush off, Jordan?"

"No. I can stay for a bit. How are you doing? With the farm? And everything?"

She took his hand and led Judd into the family room.

He took a walk. It was only a few days until Halloween, and it was bleak and forbidding, but not actually too cold.

He wondered if Cory had told Hugh about Mrs. Foote's nephews? Would they take over the house where Hilda and Jack and Dolph had lived?

He didn't believe in spirits haunting the site of their demise. If that were true, an ancient city like Rome would be Coliseum deep in vengeful ectoplasm.

He headed back to the house.

Judd was packing up his maroon Chevy Impala. It was rust pocked and had holey wheel wells.

Judd saw him looking at the holes. "It's a piece of junk."

"No! It's a fine exemplar of American automotive genius."

Judd smiled. "Okay. I have to get going, Gabe."

He stood there. He had never found out where Judd had been while Shaw was being battered to death, and if he was really going to investigate, then he needed to know.

"Gabe?"

"Right. So I was wondering about the night when Shaw was killed...and the other guys too."

Judd looked at him. "And?"

"I'm looking into alibis. Some people have them: Gita, for instance. And others don't; Finn springs to mind."

Judd laughed. "Are you asking me to account for my whereabouts, Mr. Bergeron?"

"No! Well, maybe. A little bit."

"A little bit? So you want a partial alibi? Did Cory put you up to this?"

"No." Judd didn't need to know.

It was almost five, and the parking area lights were buzzing and casting a bluish light over Judd's face.

Judd said, "Then Diane? Or Cory and Diane?"

He shook his head. "None of the above. So?"

"You really want to know where I was?"

"Yes, please."

Judd smiled. "Then get in the car."

"Okay. Where are we going?" He wasn't sure Judd's car would make it to the county road.

"Leesburg."

"Why?"

The car dome light was weak and yellow and made Judd's smile look a little bit frightening, but he got in anyway.

"You'll bring me back?"

"Sure." And Judd laughed.

The drive to Leesburg was uneventful in that they made it

without the Impala disintegrating.

Judd parked and walked into a shopping mall.

"Why are we here?"

"You'll see."

"And this has to do with your alibi?"

Judd smiled. His dark eyes looked very merry. He followed him anyway.

They walked and walked. Some stores had already started putting up Christmas decorations, but the shoppers didn't look as grim as they would when the season was truly upon them.

"Are we going shopping?"

"Nope."

He had been very patient. He stopped.

Judd smiled some more and checked his cellphone. "We can get coffee at the food court. It's just over there."

Which it was. They got coffee and sat at a table next to a marble planter filled with spiky greenery.

Judd said, "So I wasn't here when Shaw got it."

"No? Then why did you bring me here?"

"All in good time, Mr. Bergeron."

His cellphone rang. He smiled. "Hi, Samantha. Yes, I got the maternity clothes. And she sent you vitamins too. Yes, I know you do."

Judd listened.

"I'm at the mall in Leesburg. Yes, in a few minutes. Samantha, about the ultrasound....Mother might like to go with us."

Judd listened some more. "I know, but maybe you could call and invite her? It's her first grandchild. Please?"

Judd listened some more. "Okay. I'll see you tomorrow."

Judd put his phone away.

"So is she going to ask Laura?"

Judd said, "I hope so." He stood up. "Come with me, Gabe."

And he was led into a bi-level atrium with a glass roof, now black against the night sky. People were strolling through the atrium and along the mezzanine walkways.

Muted voices and the sound of footsteps echoed off the walls and the tile floor.

A grand piano stood forlorn at one end. Judd's course was taking them to it.

Judd deposited his briefcase and dropped his coat and scarf on top. He pulled out the bench. He sat and adjusted his derriere. He stretched his hands and rolled his shoulders. He positioned a foot ready to press a pedal.

"Judd, what are you doing?"

Judd smiled and began to play. It was something jazzy, and from what he could tell, Judd was an excellent pianist.

But he kept scanning the atrium for the first detachment of security, but they didn't show.

Judd smiled at him. "They're paying me to play, Gabe."

"Right! Oh. And you were playing here while Shaw was being murdered?"

"Nope." Judd smiled. "I was playing at Dulles Airport."

"Why?"

"Because they also paid me. They wanted classical. To soothe the savage travelers. And when I got back to the farm, the deputies were already there. And with the airport staff and the toll road, I have an alibi that satisfied Detective Sanders."

"Good. I'm glad to hear it. So can we go back to the farm now?"

"No, I'm being paid for three hours. You can wander if you like?"

"No. I'm good." It wouldn't really be polite to walk away.

And Judd played on. The shoppers ignored him for the most part, but a few stopped for a minute or two.

Judd switched to Broadway tunes, and more people paused and even smiled.

Judd played for an hour.

Without music.

He seemed to segue from one piece to another as the spirit moved him. It was remarkable...in the best sense.

Judd pulled out some sheet music and played something classical and then some contemporary music; contemporary enough that younger people started stopping.

There were into their third hour when Judd said, "Do you sing, Gabe?"

He may have been humming along.

"Nope. Well, I do, but not in front of people, and not here!"

"Why not? You'll never see these people again. What would you like to sing?"

He shook his head. "You don't have the music."

Judd smiled. "Just sing it, and I'll pick it up."

He looked around him. Nobody was actually paying any attention to them. He shook his head again.

"Come on, Gabe. I told you my alibi."

Which was true. But still.

Judd said, "Come sit beside me and sing it. Nobody will even hear you."

He sat. He looked at Judd. He smiled and looked a little like Cory. He sang the first verse of "Hasta Siempre, Comandante."

"Louder, Bergeron, I can barely hear you. This is in Spanish?"

"Of course. Can't you tell?" His accent wasn't that terrible; Ezmeralda would have told him.

He sang the chorus a little bit louder.

Judd smiled. "This is Cuban? About Che Guevara? I think I've heard it...somewhere."

Judd played a simple version of the verse, and he sang along. He may have gotten louder on the chorus.

Judd started playing a Latin rhythm under the melody.

He was belting out the second verse when he noticed a few people were looking at him. He stopped.

Judd played on. "Come on, Gabe!"

He checked to make sure that no one was recording his performance on a cellphone before plunging into the chorus.

More people had stopped to listen.

"You have to sing with me, Judd."

"I don't know the words, Gabe."

"I'll write out the words of the chorus for you."

And he did.

Judd played the verse. He sang very softly, but on the chorus, when Judd joined in, he sang with more gusto.

Judd had a much better voice.

On the second chorus, he thought Judd sang harmony. It sounded good anyway.

A couple were watching them and smiling. They looked Hispanic, but that didn't mean they knew the song or spoke Spanish.

But Judd smiled at them. "Sing!"

They had been waiting for an invitation.

The guy had a great tenor voice, and his accent sounded like Ezmeralda's. He sang the third verse. Which was good since Gabriel Bergeron didn't really remember all the words.

They all sang the chorus, but the lady did a wailing descant that made a tingle run up his spine.

The crowd kept growing. At the end, the ovation was thunderous. Well, enthusiastic.

And Judd launched into "Hasta Siempre, Comandante" again.

The couple took turns singing the verses, and everybody sang on the chorus; even the crowd.

Judd was smiling and looking happier than he'd ever seen him. He was moderately happy himself.

After it was over, the crowd dispersed, and Judd and the couple, who said they were Raúl and Alicia, congratulated themselves.

Raúl smiled at him. "And where did you learn the song, Mr. Bergeron?"

"From my great-aunt."

Alicia said, "And where did she learn it?"

"In Cuba, a half century ago. Or longer."

Raúl said, "And she still sings it?"

"She listens to it...in memory of her first husband."

Alicia smiled at Raúl, and they walked away.

Judd had finished packing away his sheet music. "Thanks, Gabe."

"For?"

"This has been the most fun I've had since I started doing these gigs." Judd was looking at him. "But we need to expand your repertoire."

"No, we do not. This was a one-off."

And they walked back to the car.

Judd was pulling out of the parking lot when he said, "Would I be crazy to quit my job at the library?"

"And do what exactly?"

"Play piano."

"At shopping malls and airports?"

Judd said, "I play at clubs and at receptions and parties. So I'd be totally insane?"

With a baby coming? "I can't say, Judd. You have to do...okay, yes, you'd be insane, and Laura would make sure that her first grandchild was born posthumously."

Judd laughed. Had he suggested this to Samantha?

They were almost to the farm when he glanced over at Judd. "So how are you and Cory?"

He couldn't see Judd's face clearly, but he didn't frown. He also didn't answer for a bit. "We're okay. Think I should apologize to him?"

"I don't think so. He's not so verbal. Maybe just hug him hard the next time you get a chance."

"I'll do that, Gabe. Mother has also talked to me."

"Right. So have you seen a photo of your great-grandfather, Stephen?'"

Judd glanced at him. "Probably. I don't remember. Why?"

"Get your mother to show you the photo she has. It may help explain why Grand glommed onto Cory first."

"Cory looks like him?"

"Very much. I'm betting it was the red hair that made her fixate on Cory."

"Really?" He shrugged.

He wondered if Judd and Diane realized how much they looked like Grand when she had been young and innocent; before she had gone over to the dark side?

Judd went into the family room. Cory and Hugh were watching sports. Judd sat beside Cory.

He went up to Cory's bedroom.

He looked at his cellphone. It was an hour earlier in Chicago.

He called Donnie.

"Hi, Donnie."

"Gabe? Hey, it's great to hear from you. What are you up to?"

"Me? Not much. Everything is peaceful."

He hadn't seen his half-brother since Donnie had escorted their nephew Caleb on his orientation visit to Temple University.

It had been two years since they'd spent any time together, which was way too long.

"What have you done, Bergeron?"

"Nothing!"

Donnie said, "When is the last time a cop interrogated you about a serious crime? Tell me the truth."

"It's been ages, Donnie."

"Not in Gabe time. In weeks. Or days?"

"Well, I wasn't interrogated...."

"When?"

"Today."

Donnie cackled and was obviously rolling on the floor wherever he was. He sobered. "Are you in jail?"

"No, I am not!"

"Have you been injured? Any casts or significant blood loss?"

"No, Donnie. I'm fine. Hey, I'd like us to get together over Christmas? I could come to Chicago? But I don't have to stay with anybody...I can stay at a hotel."

Donnie said, "You're staying with me. For as long as you want. Or until you get on my nerves."

"That sounds like a plan, Donnie."

Sunday
1:00 pm

He hadn't told Cory about his Chicago plans, but Christmas was months away. There had to be some way he could avoid a Poirier Christmas gracefully?

Donnie would be a lot more fun, and he wanted to catch up with his cousins and aunts and uncles.

He was in condo finishing a sandwich. Cory had gone off to do some sports thing with Matt Bornheimer; he thought they were playing rugby with some other FBI guys? Cory had invited him to tag along, but he had other plans. And he didn't want to see Cory getting tackled and crushed.

He thought he should talk to Gita Bhattacharya Shaw; even if she had a perfect alibi, she might know something.

So he motored to the Shaw residence which was a stately pile, entirely CEO-worthy.

But there was a "For Sale" sign so discreet that it didn't actually say that the property was on the market. There was a phone number and an agent's name with "Realtor" in microscopic type beneath it.

He still knocked.

And he may have circled the house and peeped in the windows. There were a few pieces of furniture, but Gita was not in residence.

He went back to the Yaris and motored away before some security guys or the police inquired as to his intentions.

He found a coffee shop miles away. He needed to talk to

Gita. He wasn't sure John would give him Gita's address in the city so he called Vonda.

Detective Vonda Golczewski of the Philadelphia Police said, "Are you bleeding or in danger of being killed?"

"Nope."

"Then call me tomorrow."

"But this is child's play for an officer of your caliber."

"No."

"I just need to know the address of a condo in DC; the residence of one Gita Bhattacharya Shaw. Or possibly Craig Shaw."

"Hold on." There was a voice rumbling in the background. "Let me put you on speaker, Bergeron. Okay. Shaw?"

Where was she? And who else was listening? He couldn't get sidetracked.

"Gita Shaw is the wife of Victim Numero Uno. But I don't actually know that good ole Craig is the central character in this triple homicide. Perhaps someone wanted Turtle or Third Guy dead, and Shaw of the One Percent was but collateral damage?"

Vonda said, "Turtle and Third Guy?"

"Ah, Turtle is the nickname of Seth Yates who was only trying to make a dishonest dollar by helping to steal a horse, and Third Guy remains an enigma."

"A horse thief? Really, Bergeron?"

"Yes, and the horse, Bucephalus, is worth six figures."

Vonda laughed. "You're making this up."

"Nope. Which part? The name? Or the value? Both are accurate, and horse thievery is apparently quite common even in these horseless carriage days."

"Someone tried to steal a horse named Bucephalus and got killed for it?"

"Yes. Maybe not 'for it' but 'in the process of it' might be more accurate in a causality sense."

Vonda laughed again and was joined by a bass chuckling.

"Vonda?"

"Yes, Bergeron?"

"Who's with you?"

She snorted. "That's need to know."

"Then where are you?"

"Also need to know."

"Don't be like that, Vonda. Is it your husband? I know you told me his name, and it's right on the tip of my tongue...."

She snorted like a rhino with hay fever. "No, I did not."

But a male voice suitable for the part of Jehovah in any Bible film said, "I'm David, her husband."

"The father of Sylvie?"

David said, "So my dear wife assures me." This was followed with a hearty laugh so deep and rich that it severely strained the woofer in his phone. If phones had woofers?

Vonda said, "Now you've done it, David."

"You said he's harmless, Vonda?"

"He is. Mostly. But he's like the puppy that followed you home. A puppy that needs constant attention and can't stop yipping. Day after day; yip, yip, yip."

"I do not yip." He didn't. "It's nice to speak to you, David. How is Sylvie? She's about two years old now?"

Vonda said, "Not another word, David."

"I just need an address, Vonda, and I will speak to Mrs. Shaw in my normal baritone voice."

"I'll see what I can do."

"Thank you, Vonda. So that will be this afternoon, Vonda?"

"Good bye, Bergeron."

And she and David were gone. David sounded very impressive which was only right; Vonda deserved someone with gravitas.

He sat and drank his coffee. This shop lacked ambiance and banana bread, and the baristas were unremarkable.

He was motoring back to DC when Vonda called and gave him the addresses.

"Thank you, Vonda."

"You're welcome. But don't call me on the weekend ever again. And don't try to meet David."

"I promise, but would it be so bad if I met David?"

"Yes!"

And she was gone.

As it turned out, Gita's address was not far from Cory's condo so he had wasted a drive into the wilds of Virginia.

The condo had security, and the security lady called Gita's apartment. He wondered if Gita would see him?

"Tell her I just have a few questions." The security lady was looking at him funny. "Won't take long at all."

Gita granted him an audience, and he rode the elevator skyward.

She opened the door. She was wearing a little number in a vibrant green; gold embroidery highlighted the neckline and the cuffs and the hemline which ended at the knees. An under-skirt in a matching green but with lots of gold embroidered moons reached the floor.

He felt like he'd arrived at a formal ball in cut-offs and a tank top; a dirty tank top.

She smiled at him. "Mr. Bergeron?"

"Thanks for seeing me, Mrs. Shaw."

She shook her head and set her dangly earrings to dancing. "Don't call me that. I'm Gita. And I can't give you long, I'm expecting someone very soon."

"Sure. Okay. I'm Gabriel. Or Gabe. I'm sorry about your husband?"

She smiled. "Thank you. Come and sit. Tea?"

Her living room was sapphire blue; well, the chairs and sofa were. The walls were covered with a blue silk with writhing branches and tawny, fantastical animals dancing across them.

But the gold chandeliers were a bit over the top.

"I like your condo."

"Thank you." She poured him a cup of tea. They sat on the sapphire sofa and sipped and smiled like civilized people.

"So I see the house is for sale?"

She stopped smiling. "You're very industrious. Did you want to speak to me so desperately, Gabriel?"

"Not desperately. I just thought you might be able to help."

"With what exactly?"

"I'm curious about his death."

"Craig's? But why?"

"Mostly because it happened on the Poirier farm. Not that it isn't terrible that he was killed."

"Yes, terrible." She stopped smiling. "I had to identify the body for that detective."

"Sanders. I'm sorry. I know that was awful."

She looked at him. "You found him...in a stall in that barn?"

"I did. He didn't suffer, Gita. He was unconscious when...it happened."

She nodded. "Thank you, Gabriel." She tried to smile. "But I'm afraid I can't help you. I don't know who killed him."

"Or the other men?"

"No. Absolutely not. Have the police discovered anything about them?"

"Yes and no."

She smiled then and patted his hand. "And what does that mean, Gabriel?"

"One of the men was Seth Yates, a friend or dogsbody of Dolph Prentice."

"I don't know who that is?"

He explained about Dolph, Hilda, and Bucephalus and poor Seth.

She nodded. "And this horse is worth a lot of money?"

"A princely sum. Low six figures or so I'm told."

Gita smiled. "Indeed. And the other man?"

"Ah, still a mystery. Third Guy seems to have taken pains to make himself and his pistol untraceable. He had his fingerprints removed."

She smiled, but something happened behind those lovely eyes. "A criminal? Possibly, a hit-man, Gabriel? How fascinating."

"Isn't it? So what can you tell me about Craig?"

She looked at him. "Why?"

"It might help."

"Help whom? The Poiriers? The police?"

"Both. Maybe."

She sighed. "I didn't love Craig. I did at one point, but that ended after the first few women."

"And after the first hundred, I stopped caring what he did. I had a good life, and I had my friends and my lovers...not as many as Craig. I like to think I was more discriminating than he was."

"And Erik is one of your lovers."

She looked startled. "Erik Varner?" She smiled. "You can't be serious, Gabriel."

"Then he was just your agent...at Holcomb."

She smiled at him like he was a fluffy but stupid kitty who had finally figured out what the litter box was for. "Of course. How else could I keep Craig on track? I had to have daily updates, and even then Craig would veer off course at the slightest breeze. But Erik was very good at making Craig believe that the ideas he relayed from me were actually his."

"I'm surprised that Craig didn't want a female assistant?"

"Oh, he did! But that was just a disaster. He banged them...every one of them. And when he moved on, they got hurt and then vindictive. Very vindictive. But I can't say I blamed them. Eventually, even Craig could see that they were an irritant."

"So what changed?"

She smiled again. "The head of the new chemical division...the female head...had managed to make Craig believe she could do no wrong though the numbers told a different tale."

She slipped off her gold sandals and put her feet into his lap. She had rings on her toes.

He wasn't sure what he was supposed to do with her feet? Massage them? He decided to ignore them since they didn't smell footy.

"Childers told me it was over for Craig when we were at the Poirier farm. I was expecting it, of course, but Childers made it plain that the board felt Craig had gone too far."

"But Childers likes you?"

"Childers lusts after me with a Dionysian passion, but I had rebuffed him too many times, and he wouldn't help me. I suppose I could have had sex with him, but it would have been like having sex with a walking corpse...can you imagine? All that slack, sagging flesh?" She shuddered. "And Craig wouldn't do what I told him to do."

"Did he always?" It didn't sound very manly. "He couldn't have liked being directed?"

"Oh, he didn't, Darling! He would dig in his heels and pout and lash out, doing something incredibly stupid, and then I would have to fix it, but he would eventually listen to reason. And he would find a new toy, and we would go on."

She was flexing her supple feet in his lap. It wasn't exactly unpleasant, but he wanted her to stop it.

She was smiling. "But I think poor Craig was finding it harder to seduce the sort of woman he thought he was entitled to...and he might have been a teensy bit frightened, for the first time in his life."

"He had always gotten what he wanted?" She nodded. "And now he didn't know how to deal with the waning of vigor and success."

"Exactly. Did you find him attractive, Gabriel?"

He smiled his very best smile. "And then what happened?"

"Is that a yes?" She smiled. "I saw that the path forward led only downward, and I wasn't going to lose everything. I told him that I was divorcing him."

"And he didn't like that."

"No. I was a possession, but I had hired a very competent divorce lawyer. And I had tons of evidence of infidelity. Poor Craig."

"So when was this?"

"The afternoon of the day he died, Gabriel."

"And where was this?"

"At the house. I had already moved most of my things here, and I walked out. I don't know what he did after that."

"I thought he was supposed to attend a charity auction with you?"

She smiled. "He was, and I would have played the part of the affectionate wife if he'd appeared. But he didn't, and I imposed on friends to drop me off here."

Which gave her a lovely alibi.

"And you never saw or talked to him again?"

"No, Gabriel. Not after I left around 7:00 pm." She sat up

and patted his face. "Do you think I decided to have him killed? My mother would be appalled, Darling. So bourgeois; plebeian even."

He didn't believe that having Craig killed was beyond her, but she wasn't about to 'fess up.

She took her feet out of his lap and curled them under her. She scooted close to him accompanied by a cocoon of fragrance.

"But if anyone hired some person to kill Craig, then it would be that evil, old woman."

"Which evil, old woman?" But he knew.

"Josephine Loncke, Darling! She loathed Craig, and I think she's mental. There's nothing she wouldn't do to protect her daddy's precious company."

"Do you have any proof of that, Gita?"

"No, Darling. That's where you and your insatiable curiosity come in, isn't it?"

"Where would she find a hit-man?"

Gita shook her head. "I have no idea. But it should be possible to follow the money trail? Don't you think?"

"I suppose so. I'm sure Sanders is looking into everything." He looked at her. "Kennard said that you should have been CEO and not Shaw."

She looked taken aback. "Did he?"

"But you didn't want to?"

"I worked at Holcomb for two, long years, Gabriel, in middle management. It was so boring, Darling. Truly soul destroying."

"Not like the fast paced world of bookkeeping then."

She laughed what sounded like a genuine laugh. "Point taken. But I got the lay of the land, and I found one thing I did enjoy."

"Do tell?"

"Corporate politics. It was fascinating...my milieu. And Craig looked the part of a rising star. I decided that I could have fun by manipulating him and that stupid company."

And then she got a call. "Of course. Thank you."

He nodded and stood up. "Thank you, Gita."

"Of course, Gabriel."

She escorted him to the door having amused herself by batting him around like a cat toy.

He was crossing her threshold when the elevator door opened.

Kennard bounced out. He stopped and stared as his face transitioned through surprise, anger, and then back to jollity.

"Why am I always meeting you at doorways, Bergeron?"

"Just lucky I guess." He looked at Gita. "Your visitor?"

"An old friend, Gabriel." And she turned and walked back into her condo.

Kennard was wearing a pale gray suit with a black and silver tie and a beautiful, black overcoat. It looked very soft.

Kennard leaned closer; he had doused himself with cologne. "I'd be jealous if I caught any other 'man' coming out of Gita's condo."

Good ole Ricky meant to insult him. He smiled and didn't punch him in the face. "Jealous? Of the widow Shaw? And your coworker Craig not even in the ground. Bad form, Ricky. What would your mother say?"

Kennard sniffed. "It isn't like Gita is in mourning, Bergeron. And she invited me."

Which was probably true.

He got into the elevator. He hadn't learned much, and what he had learned was not good.

Suppose Gita was right? He couldn't investigate Cory's grandmother. Cory wouldn't thank him for uncovering Grand's murderous plot. And neither would Laura.

He should quit. Again. But permanently this time.

Thursday
5:00 pm

His week at GB&H had been blissfully uneventful.

It was Halloween and cold and blustery but clear. He had taken off work a little early and had rolled into Union Station to be picked up by Cory.

And they were on their way to the farm. Again.

He hadn't said a word to Cory about Grand possibly hiring a hit-man, and he wasn't going to.

Cory said, "You didn't have to come. I just want to check on Dad and make sure there's no backsliding."

"Not a problem. I love the farm and all the horses."

Cory laughed.

"Well, the farm could be nice. You don't think Hugh would consider going back as CEO again?"

It had been three weeks since his collapse, and maybe he was feeling better?

"No, but I want to make sure. Mother said that Childers and Kennard were coming for talks."

"But I thought it was settled? That Kennard was the man?"

"Not yet."

"Because?"

"Because Grand."

"Ah, still has her heels dug in, has she?"

Cory laughed again. "The board is dragging her kicking and screaming all the way."

"Right. You have a very interesting family, Cory."

"I do. But yours isn't a Norman Rockwell painting."

"Absolutely not." He looked at Cory. "So is Grand expected to attend this confab?"

"No."

Which was good if true. But on the other hand, if she showed, he might get a chance to talk to her about Shaw and Third Guy?

Cory said, "What?"

Cory was quite perceptive as well as being devilishly handsome. "I was just thinking about getting a Christmas tree for the condo."

"Gabe."

"I was! We might even cut one at the farm?"

"The only suitable trees were planted by my grandmother and are verboten."

"Right. Of course. Which grandmother? Hugh's mother?"

Cory nodded and turned into the Poirier's lane.

They arrived just as Childers and Kennard were stepping into Hugh's office, but Laura went with them this time.

He didn't think he was supposed to know that Laura owned a nice chunk of Holcomb stock, and Hugh owned zero. He smiled at Cory. "Want to visit with Bucephalus?"

Cory raised an eyebrow, but he nodded.

They walked to the barn. It was dark and getting colder by the second. He should have brought gloves, but he thought Cory secretly considered gloves to be the garments of wimps. He avoided wearing them unless snow was falling, and the land was a sheet of ice. And Cory was out of town.

But the barn was surprisingly warm.

And Jedidiah Foote was there. He appeared to be talking to Bucephalus who was regarding him benignly.

He smiled at Jed. "Jed, this is Cory Poirier."

Jed smiled and shook Cory's hand. "Pleased to meet you, Mr. Poirier."

Cory nodded. "You too, Jed. How is he doing?"

Jed smiled at Bucephalus like he was his first born child who had mastered Chinese and French at the age of four.

"He's great, Sir." Jed patted Bucephalus. "He's a big, handsome fellow."

He was probably imagining it, but Bucephalus flicked his head up and down as if in acknowledgment and even in agreement with the compliment?

And the horse seemed pleased to see Cory. Well, not indifferent anyway.

Cory went to check out Rhythm.

Jed said, "Thank you, Mr. Bergeron."

"Call me Gabe. And what are you thanking me for?"

"Mrs. Poirier said you recommended me?"

"Right. You're welcome. So you like the job so far?"

Jed just smiled.

"Good. And how is Del?"

"Found a job too."

Which was good.

When Cory finished greeting each horse, they walked back to the house. Hugh and Laura were in the kitchen, but Childers and Kennard hadn't departed.

Hugh said, "Checking up on me, Cory?"

"Yes."

Hugh smiled and hugged his son. "Not to worry."

Laura said, "Why don't we go upstairs, Hubert, and talk?"

Hugh nodded.

He and Cory remained in the kitchen as Mrs. Villeneuve, aka Madeleine, worked. She hugged them both. "Are you hungry, Mr. Corentin?"

Cory smiled at her.

She smiled back at Cory, but then looked at him. "And how are you, Gabriel?"

"Fine. Better." He shook his head; he still didn't want to talk about Jack.

She nodded. "*Triste. Pitoyable.*"

And she set about whipping up a snack before tackling the dishes from dinner.

And with Cory thus distracted, he wandered to Hugh's office where Childers and Kennard were seated staring at one another under the harsh ceiling light.

Childers looked at him. "What do you want?"

"Me? Just wanted to see if you'd like coffee? Or a light repast? I'm sure Mrs. Villeneuve can slap something together."

Kennard said, "Coffee would be excellent, Bergeron."

He smiled at Childers. "And you Mr. Childers, Sir?"

Childers glared and nodded and then glared some more.

He fetched coffee. Cory and Madeleine were chatting in French and paid him no mind.

He poured a cup for each titan of industry and sat down in an empty chair.

"So how's Holcomb these days?"

Kennard smiled at him. "The stock price is up, Bergeron. Which you probably know?"

"I am aware. And your coronation is to take place shortly?"

Childers shook his head. "Nothing has been decided, Kennard."

"But it has. Laura is going to come back in a few minutes and give me her support, and then it's over, Childers."

Childers was not so much seething as stewing in the bitter bile of crushed hopes. "She's being stupid."

Kennard was so happy that he was bouncing in his chair; his substantial ass could achieve levitation at any time.

"So Shaw is dead. Long live, Kennard."

Kennard looked at him. "I didn't kill him, Bergeron."

"Right."

"I didn't need to. He was finished, and I was getting what I wanted." He smiled at Childers. "Now, Harold here, wanted to be CEO and to have Gita."

Childers sneered at Kennard. "I certainly didn't kill him. And I don't want Gita."

"That isn't true, Harold, and you know it. But maybe you had him killed for Josephine?"

Childers shook his head. "Don't be stupid, Kennard."

He smiled at them. "You told him he was finished as CEO the evening that he was murdered. So were you two the last to see him alive?"

Childers said, "I expect stupidity from you. He was fine when we left."

Kennard laughed. "He was alive, but he wasn't fine. He was furious."

Childers said, "And Gita was with him."

"Where was this?"

Kennard said, "We went to his house. Gita begged us to come for dinner."

Childers smiled. "But we only went to tell him it was over and to ask for his resignation."

Kennard said, "He would have accepted the package in the end. He had no choice."

"Wait. A severance package?"

Childers nodded. "A very generous one...much more than I would have given him, but he wouldn't even discuss it. He swore he would never resign."

Kennard said, "He was just blowing off steam. He couldn't afford to be fired and kicked out with nothing."

He said, "Because?"

"Because he and Gita were drowning in debt."

Childers shook his head. "No, I knew him. He wouldn't have resigned. And Gita knew it too. She was furious. Her and that Varner creature."

"Erik was there?"

Kennard laughed. "At dinner and afterwards. He was still listening at the keyhole to them fighting when we left."

Childers said, "We had given Shaw until Monday to accept the offer, and Varner tried to tell me to give Shaw a week. As if he was even part of the discussion."

The lovely Gita had failed to mention her debt and the potential loss of the severance package.

"When was this?"

"Around 6:00 pm." Kennard smiled. "It's always the wife, Bergeron."

"Is that what you went to her condo to discuss last Sunday?"

Childers turned bleached bone pale. "I knew it."

Kennard said, "We didn't spend our time talking, Bergeron." And he cackled at Childers.

"Right. I'm sure. But she has an alibi."

Kennard shrugged.

Hugh and Laura came back into the office, and he was urged to leave more by osmotic pressure than verbal cues.

He and Cory waited around.

And Kennard emerged triumphant a few minutes later.

Cory was relieved as were Hugh and Laura.

Childers was bitter.

Josephine aka Grand was probably livid and sticking pins in Kennard dolls. And Hugh and Laura dolls. And Cory dolls.

He probably didn't rate a doll.

It was midnight before he and Cory got home.

Cory went directly to bed, but he pretended to read. Would Gita have had ole Craig conked on the head and watched her share of the golden parachute float away? Or would she have gone to work to convince him to take it?

Had she told Craig about the divorce?

It was a puzzlement.

Friday 10:00 am

Cory had gone to work.

He had been left to his own devices. He had called Vonda again and gotten Erik Varner's address.

She had told him to be careful.

He would never have found Erik's house if not for GPS, and even then it wasn't easy. It was a townhouse hidden among a thousand others that looked almost identical; all of them lining streets that coiled and twisted like some Minoan maze.

Erik opened the door in a t-shirt and sweatpants; his arms were sinewy and more muscular than he would have thought. "What do you want?"

He smiled his best smile, but Erik looked tired and not too clean and very unwelcoming. "I wanted to talk to you about Shaw."

"Of course, you do. I don't know anything, Bergeron."

He peeped around Erik's lanky body. "Aren't you going to work?"

"I don't really have a job anymore."

"Fired?"

Erik smiled his bitchy, Mona Lisa smile. "Not yet."

"Maybe things are just disorganized right now, and they'll call you to come in when the dust settles?"

Erik shrugged. "They told me to come at 1:00 pm. Kennard's going to let me interview for my job...the job I've done for years."

"So that's good?"

He nodded. The wind was whipping around them, and Erik looked cold. "It's chilly out here."

Erik shook his head and walked away leaving the door opened.

"I just wanted to ask about Shaw's last day...his schedule and where he went."

He followed Erik into the living room which had nothing but a sofa and a TV. Erik dropped onto the sofa.

"I've told the police all that. Over and over."

"I know that he was at his house in the early evening, and Childers and Kennard came to give him the bad news."

Erik smiled. "The doofus was so shocked. It would have been funny if it hadn't been so shitty for me and Gita."

"But they offered him a severance package?"

"Which he threw back into their faces!"

"But Gita could have talked him around. As she'd done so many times before?"

Erik was looking at him like he was a new species of cockroach that had learned to speak.

"What do you know about what Gita did or didn't do?"

"Just what she and others have told me."

"You talked to her?"

"I went to her condo."

Erik was considering punching him. "Why don't you leave her alone, Bergeron. She doesn't need you harassing her. She's a widow."

But not a grieving one. He tried not to smile.

Erik said, "What?"

"Nothing. She didn't seem averse to having visitors."

"What the Hell? Was somebody else there?"

"Not while I was there."

Erik got in his face. "Is that the truth?"

"Yes."

Erik didn't believe him, but he didn't care. "So you don't think Gita could have talked Shaw down? Got him to accept the severance?"

Erik shook his head. "I don't know what she could have done." A smile crossed his face just for an instant. "But whatever she did wasn't going to help me, was it?"

"No. Not so much. Sorry."

"Keep your pity. Why don't you get the Hell out of here! I'm tired of talking to you, and I have to get dressed."

"Right. Just one thing. I can't figure out why he was at the Poirier farm?"

"Diane." Erik shut his eyes, but then he smiled his nasty smile.

"What about Diane? He was coming to see her? Why?"

Erik said, "Why do you think, Bergeron. You're really stupid at times."

He was not. Well, not really. "So you knew he was coming to the farm?"

"No! How the Hell would I know that? I wasn't his procurer."

He was pretty sure that Erik had done lots of things for Shaw.

"But Shaw let it be known that he was interested in Diane?" He nodded. "Why?"

Erik shook his head. "Sex."

"Right, but why her?"

"He wanted to hurt and embarrass her father."

"But she despised him?"

Erik laughed. "Didn't matter to him. In fact, it made it a challenge. But he was sure he'd have her like so many others."

"Do you mean force her to have sex? Rape?"

Erik considered. "Close to rape. He wasn't big on the niceties of consensual sex."

"How do you know that?"

"Because he told me about it! He had to brag to somebody, and he had nobody else but me."

"That's repugnant...but also kind of sad if you think about it."

Erik shrugged. "He didn't deserve to have any friends."

"So you left the house when?"

"I don't know! When Gita did. I drove her to her charity thing; she hates driving."

"And Craig didn't say anything about what he might do after that? Was he going to this charity event too?"

Erik shrugged and got to his feet.

"Why don't you get out of here."

"Okay. I'm going."

But he stopped to look at the only decoration he'd seen in the house. A wall display of pistols and medals in cases; military medals.

He looked at Erik. "These are nice."

The first medal was a star with an eagle holding lightning bolts; it was hanging from an orange and blue ribbon. A cross shaped medal was in the same case; the arms of the cross looked like airplane propellers.

Next was a golden medal with Arabic script hanging from a red, green, white, and black ribbon.

Erik said, "My mother saved all of my father's things. He was in Special Forces. That's from the Gulf War."

"I see. So he's not around?"

Erik shook his head. "No. He died when I was two. I don't remember him."

There was a heart shaped medal with what looked like a silhouette of George Washington on a purple field.

Erik said, "That's his purple heart. From Vietnam."

There was a coin type medal that featured a sheep with "British Forces Falkland Islands" across the top, and another one with a portrait of Queen Elizabeth.

He looked at Erik. "And these? I didn't think any Americans fought in the Falklands War?"

"He was Special Forces! He went everywhere, Bergeron."

Erik was glaring at him.

He said, "I never knew my father either. He was an architect."

Erik sneered at him. "Is that what your mother told you?"

"No, she died when I was ten; she never told me anything about him. Not even his name. I found out for myself later."

Erik's face went from ash colored to purest white as all the blood drained away. "Get out! I know about my father. He was a hero."

"I'm sorry. I didn't mean anything....."

"Get out!" And stay away from Gita!"

Friday
4:00 pm

He wasn't sure why he was doing this.

He parked the Yaris next to a silver Mercedes in front of the stately residence of Josephine Holcomb Loncke and got out.

Four massive, white columns rose three stories to support a Greek Revival pediment with a frieze. A balcony ran across the front of the house at the second level.

He walked up the brick walkway that ran between a pair of urns large enough for him to bathe in. Comfortably. In the summer.

He climbed the stairs and passed between the white columns and rapped upon the black door. Humbly.

The wind had picked up and was howling between the columns like the screams of tormented souls.

This was Grand's lair, the very heart of her web and sure to be gaily festooned with mummified bodies.

He could still run away? He might make it to Cory's Yaris before she released the Hounds of Hell.

And then the door opened.

A diminutive lady in a maid's uniform stared at him.

"Hello? I'm Gabriel Bergeron. I'd like to see Mrs. Loncke."

Which was both the truth and an utter falsehood.

The tiny, dark maid, who might be Chinese, stared some more. "Wait." And she shut the door in his face, slowly and gently.

He was being given a second chance to run. He should take it, but the black door opened too quickly.

A tall, gray-haired gentlemen in a black Mao jacket and

black pants took over the job of staring at him. He was also Chinese and wearing glasses with brass hinges and a brass nose piece with a trefoil design; the lenses were round and slightly tinted.

"I'm Gabriel Bergeron, and I'd like to see Mrs. Loncke."

"Do you have an appointment, Sir?"

Which he didn't. Which the guy knew.

"No. I was hoping she could spare me a few minutes?"

The majordomo smiled at such presumption. "Do you have a card, Sir?"

Which he actually did. He pulled one of his GB&H cards out of his wallet and held it in his hand and waited.

Majordomo said, "May I have it, Sir?"

"At other great houses, I'm offered a silver salver on which to deposit my card." He tried to look imperious, but he didn't think he pulled it off.

Majordomo smiled again; exactly as he had before. "I apologize, Sir, but our salver is currently being polished."

He placed his card in Majordomo's immaculate hand.

The door closed in his face again. He resigned himself to never seeing Grand. Which cheered him a bit.

And then Majordomo opened the door. "I'm very sorry, Sir, but Madame can't see you."

But he could see into the foyer, and he heard voices. One belonged to Grand and the other was also familiar.

"Is that Mr. Kennard? If you could tell him, I'm here?"

Majordomo wanted him gone, but Josephine aka Grand and Kennard appeared in the foyer.

She was wearing a black suit; the jacket buttoned from the left shoulder down. She had black stockings and shoes, but pearls made the ensemble a little less funereal.

Grand was looking down at Kennard; physically, spiritually, metaphorically. "I'd like you to go, Mr. Kennard."

Kennard was smiling and bouncing. "I know this isn't the outcome you hoped for, but I'm sure we can work together, Mrs. Loncke. We both want Holcomb to be successful."

Grand said, "It already is."

Kennard said, "But less so since Mr. Shaw has been CEO. I intend to remedy that."

Grand nodded. "I am glad he's gone." She cast around and locked onto Majordomo. "Smith, see Mr. Kennard out."

She turned to go.

He feinted left and, using Kennard as a blocker, went right. "Mrs. Loncke, may I speak to you for just a second? I have some news about Corentin which you might like to hear?"

A hand locked onto his shoulder; Smith aka Majordomo was about to toss him out.

She said, "About Corentin?" She waved at Smith. "Very well. Come with me, Young Man. Smith, you come to."

So they trooped across the foyer, down a hallway, and into a room that would be suitable as the office of any retired world leader or university president.

She sat in a high-backed chair behind a desk which had sprung from the destruction of a grove of walnut trees and stared at him.

And Smith was staring at him from the left. He smiled at her. "This is really a great house. I love what you've done with it. Really homey."

She got her glare on.

"Did your father build it?"

"He did."

He sat down in the nearest chair. "I was wondering if you know anything about the murder of Craig Shaw?"

She looked startled, and her glance shot over to Smith, standing silent and ramrod straight.

"Mrs. Loncke?"

"No! I don't know anything about his death." She waved a hand. "I don't believe it was murder. The stupid man knew nothing about horses and took liberties with Bucephalus."

He may have giggled slightly. "Liberties?"

She glared at him some more. "Horses are very sensitive...what is your name?"

"Gabriel Henri Bergeron of the Bergerons of Snow Hill." He didn't actually know what had been home turf for Andrew

281

Bergeron? Aunt Flo thought he'd mentioned something about Quebec? Of course, he was half Sullivan, so also Ireland.

She said, "Are you being impertinent?"

"Nope."

He glanced left. Smith was still smiling, but he wasn't reassured. "I'm just trying to find out what happened."

"Why is it any concern of yours...Young Man?"

"It isn't, except peripherally. Your daughter and your grandchildren would like to know what happened...for various reasons...and Cory...sorry, Corentin...asked me to find out. If I can."

"And why would he ask you? Of all people?"

Smith never made a sound, but he got her attention. "Yes?"

"The folder on your right, Madame."

She opened it and read slowly and carefully, flipping pages, and started smiling.

She looked at Smith. "This is fantasy, Smith. Surely?"

But Smith shook his head.

She closed the file. "I don't know anything about the circumstances of his death." She looked at Smith. "It's a mystery to us."

She nodded to herself. "But I'm not sorry he's dead. My mother would be appalled to hear me say something like that, but it's true."

Smith said, "He mentioned your grandson, Corentin."

She glared at him again. "Yes. What do you have to tell me about him?"

"Well, he's on the trail of an art thief who almost ran him down last year. He's really excited about putting this guy behind bars for the rest of his life."

"The guy stole a Courbet and other paintings from private collectors. I like some of his stuff...Courbet, that is...his self-portrait is wonderful. Do you know it?"

She shook her head.

"And Jordan and Samantha are having a baby in March. Diane is getting married to Finn Beck, a former marine and now a park ranger."

"Stop talking! I know all that." She looked at Smith who nodded.

"I'm sorry, Mrs. Loncke, but Corentin has no interest in the company."

"Is that your doing?"

"No. I would be happy to see him do anything he wanted to do, and I would help him as much as I could."

"You?"

"I'm a decent accountant, Mrs. Loncke."

Smith nodded ever so slightly.

"I saw a photo of your father. He was very handsome, and Corentin looks so much like him. I can see why you'd like him to become CEO, but was your father happy running the company?"

She looked startled. "Of course, he was!"

"Right. I'm sure he did a great job, but that isn't the same as being happy...fulfilled, is it?"

"I want you to leave my house. Now."

"Okay."

He got up and retraced his steps to the door.

Smith opened it. "Are you going to be a problem for Mrs. Loncke, Sir?"

"Nope."

Smith smiled the very same smile.

"No, I'm not because if I hurt her, I'd hurt Cory and his family, and I would never do that."

Smith nodded.

"Is your name really Smith?"

But the door shut with a solid, definitive thud.

Who the Hell was Smith? And why had Smith investigated one Gabriel Bergeron?

He wanted to ask Sanders, but if he did, he might focus scrutiny on Grand. Scrutiny which she and her minions could ill afford?

A voice said, "Bergeron?"

He may have executed a flawless grand jeté. He had been doing better, but Grand was unnerving, and Smith was just scary.

Kennard was leaning against one of the white columns and

laughing at him.

"What?"

"I'm sorry if I startled you."

He wasn't sorry.

"What do you want, Kennard?"

Kennard stopped laughing. The bouncy *joie de vivre* died, and he looked like a frightened middle-aged man. "Are you still looking into Shaw's death?"

"His murder. Yes?"

"Then you should take a hard look at Erik Varner."

"Did you interview him for the executive assistant job?"

Kennard nodded. "HR asked me to. I would never have selected him, and he knew it."

"And he didn't take it well?"

"He started off all right, but then I made the mistake of asking about the extra services he'd provided to Shaw, and he became rude. I'm not sure how Gita came up, but then he had the nerve to ask me if I was sleeping with her."

"To which you said, 'Hell yeah, Dude!'"

"Don't be stupid, Bergeron. I told him it was none of his business, and then he threatened me."

"He didn't believe your none-denial denial?"

Kennard shook his head.

"What did he say? Exactly?"

"He said he would cut out my heart. He said he had just the knife for the job, Bergeron!"

"And you called security?"

"And they escorted him out of the building."

"But now you're looking over your shoulder." Which he was, literally. "I'd call Detective Sanders for a tête-à-tête."

"You think so?"

He shrugged. "The threat might have just been jealous ranting. Or not. He was sleeping with her?"

Kennard laughed. "Of course. Everyone knew it, except for Shaw. Or if he knew, he didn't care."

And Kennard was heading for his Mercedes.

There was no way that Craig Shaw had known that his

subordinate, his lackey, was banging his wife and wouldn't have done something about it.

He turned and spotted Smith at the window; he had probably heard everything Kennard had said,

He waved, and Smith smiled.

He got away from Grand's house just as fast as the Yaris would take him.

Saturday 10:00 am

Cory ended a call. Cory was looking at him funny.
"What?"
"I have to leave."
"Right. The district? The country? The planet?"
Cory threw a book at him, and with his lightning reflexes, he almost caught it.
But it was a light book and hardly made a mark.
"Matt and I are flying to Denver. This afternoon."
"Jerry Nolastname?"
"Yes."
"Good. If you can't catch him, at least find out what his name is?"
"We'll try. What are you up to?"
"*Moi?*"
"*Tu.*"
He had told Cory about his chats with Kennard, Gita, and the lovely Erik.
"Nothing much."
"Gabe."
"Purely as a matter of idle curiosity, what do you know about Smith?"
"Smith?"
"Chinese fellow, possibly sixty-five or so. Smiles in a creepy fashion. Wears a Mao jacket. Possibly ironically."
"Grand's Smith? Shit, Gabe. When did you meet him? You

didn't go to Grand's?"

"I did."

"And she let you in?"

"I used guile and cunning."

Cory didn't scoff at all. Which was nice. "And you asked her if she had anything to do with Shaw's death?"

"No. I just asked what she knew about his death."

"And what did she say?"

"Denied all knowledge for herself and Smith."

Cory got very quiet.

"Cory?"

"Maybe you should stay away from Grand. And Smith."

"I intend to. I'm never going back there. But what about Smith?"

"Smith has worked for Grand for as long as I can remember. He's always been around."

"So would Laura know more about him?"

"Probably. Are you going to ask her?"

"Maybe. You trust me, right? I'm not going to do anything to get her arrested. Grand, I mean. Nobody would ever arrest your mother."

Cory nodded. "Just be careful. Don't do anything without running it by me first. Promise me, Gabe."

"I promise."

And he absolutely meant it.

Cory looked unsure, but he hugged him. "I will call you."

And Cory had left for the airport.

He was alone in the condo. It was a very nice condo, but he was bored. And he wanted to talk to Erik again.

But he didn't think that was a good idea. Best to let Erik cool off a bit longer before darkening his door.

He sighed and stretched out on the sofa.

And then his phone trilled.

"Hello?"

"Gabriel? It's Gita Bhattacharya. I need to speak to Cory Poirier at once."

"About?"

"About a matter of vital importance to him and his family!"

"Calm down, Gita. What matter?"

"No, he has to come here, Gabriel."

"To your condo?"

"Yes, and before 4:00 pm."

"I'll call him and get back to you."

"Please hurry, Gabriel."

He held the phone to his chest. His path was clear. He called Cory.

And got his voicemail.

He called Matt Bornheimer. Ditto.

He called Danielle Elkins, Cory's boss, but it was Saturday, and the person who took his call agreed, grudgingly, to pass on a message. Which she might get on Monday or on the Twelfth of Never.

He shook his head. He called Nadia Brunetti, Danielle's boss. He felt sure that Cory would not like this, but it didn't matter since he never got connected to anyone who would even take a message.

He was out of options and on his own. He was dialing Gita when inspiration struck like an electric eel goosing him in the butt.

He called Laura.

"Hi, Laura. It's Gabriel."

"Hello, Gabriel. What is it? You sound excited?"

"First, Cory is on a flight to Denver if you need him. On the trail of a purloiner of Courbet paintings."

"Yes? And what else, Gabriel?"

"Do you still have Danielle's home phone number?"

"Danielle Elkins? Of course. Hold on."

And she gave it to him.

"Should I ask why, Gabriel?"

"I need to talk to Cory as soon as possible to get his approval of a course of action."

Laura said, "Gabriel, I suspect you know he wouldn't approve."

"Do not. Anyway, thanks for the number."

He called Danielle's home number. Someone was probably

determining his location and assessing his threat level as the phone rang.

She didn't pick up, but there were lots of clicks, and he was pretty sure his call was being routed back to the Hoover Building.

He hung up before anyone official answered.

He sighed. He called Gita. "Cory is on his way."

"Thank you, Gabriel."

He jumped into the Yaris and made it to her condo in record time.

She didn't seem pleased to see him. "Gabriel? Where is Poirier?"

She was wearing a red sheath sporting green and saffron-yellow triangles and matching saffron, silky pants that bloused at the ankles.

"On his way. So what seems to be the problem?"

"I need to speak to Poirier!"

"And you will, but in the meantime you could tell me why you're so upset?"

He tried to look concerned and eager to please and competent.

She reassessed the situation. "You have to help me, Gabriel. You're so clever, and Cory would do anything for you." Her ruby lips curled into the smile that had never failed her in the first forty years of her life. "I can tell."

She took his hand and led him on her sofa.

"He absolutely would. I wear him like a ring. But how can we help, Gita? What really happened?"

She relaxed and put her feet into his lap again. "It's been a terrible few weeks, Gabriel."

"I'm sure. Is this something to do with Erik?"

She nodded. "I'm afraid of him. But also of Mrs. Loncke."

"Grand? Only prudent and sensible. What has she done?"

"She threatened me!"

"When was this?"

"Yesterday. She came to my door...with some Asian man...but I didn't let them in."

"And she said what?"

"That I should stop interfering in the running of Holcomb, or she would take steps to eliminate me!"

He looked at Gita. "Did she use the word 'eliminate'?"

"She did!" Gita smiled what was probably her best, seductive smile as she kneaded his groin like a cat making bread. "And I know she meant it, Gabriel!"

"How do you know?"

"Where is Poirier?"

"He's on his way."

She nodded not quite sure if she believed him. "I hope so, because I have to tell him that I have proof that she hired someone to murder Craig."

"Right. What kind of proof, Gita?"

"You don't believe me?"

"Maybe." He did. It was what he'd considered possible all along; it had become almost a certainty after meeting Smith. "But Cory will need more than just your word."

"Of course. And I can give him the evidence I uncovered. And perhaps he can help me with a little matter?"

"And what little matter would that be?"

"Erik." She checked the time on her cellphone.

"Right. He suspects about you and Kennard, and he's not happy with you."

"He has no claim on me!"

"He's your lover, and he's done things for you, hasn't he?"

She smiled. "I may have been foolish with Erik, but only once. And how would I know what he may have done?"

"Why don't you tell me what really happened after Childers and Kennard left your house?"

"Craig and I had a terrible row about the lovely severance package. He was being stupid and beastly, and I was so tired of him."

"Of course, you were. He was a jerk."

And her talk of divorce had been a total fiction.

She smiled. "And on the way to the charity auction, I may have vented to Erik about how awful he was being to me."

"And Erik asked for instructions?"

"No! Absolutely not, Darling. He said something vague about having a plan to take care of the problem."

"A plan that involved making the untimely death of Craig Shaw look like an accident?"

"I didn't let him explain this plan, Gabriel. I thought it was just talk; the kind of thing men like to do. Stupid men. But I told him not to do anything and that we would talk the next day. But I was a bit scared of Erik when he dropped me off."

She paused for dramatic effect.

"You have to believe me, Gabriel. I never knew what he was planning. I didn't want Craig dead."

"So you just sent ole Erik away with that cheery, little smile on his face?"

"You don't believe me?"

Never in a billion years. "Sure. Totally."

She looked hurt. "I'm telling the truth. I was upset and frustrated, Gabriel, but I never told him to do anything."

"But he didn't wait for instructions this time? The perfect tool went rogue?"

"Exactly! I knew you'd understand."

"Right. But why didn't you say something when you found out?"

She went for a frightened school-girl look. "But I only found out yesterday. He came here and told me, and I am very afraid of him, Gabriel."

Which was true.

"He killed three people, and he enjoyed it. You didn't see his face when he described the killings...it had been almost orgasmic for him. Truly."

He could believe that.

"The only thing he regretted was losing his silly knife. Cory needs to arrest him, but he shouldn't take any chances because Erik is insane and very dangerous." She looked at her cellphone again. "Is Poirier coming or not?"

"Not. He's on a plane to Denver."

She looked shocked. "You stupid, little man!"

She hopped off the sofa, found her shoes, and ran out of the living room. She came back seconds later with a coat and a suitcase.

She didn't even look at him as she headed out the door.

He followed her to the elevator as she punched the button savagely.

"Go away!"

"I will. As soon as I can."

She exited the elevator on the parking garage level and clip-clopped for her car as fast as her sandals would carry her.

He was wearing sensible running shoes.

Erik was leaning against her car. He was in camouflage gear head to toe; the winter version with a white background and shades of gray instead of green. He had the hood of his jacket pulled up.

Gita halted, reassessed, and smiled. "Erik, darling, you're early?"

Erik was glaring at both of them. "Why are you with him?"

"Oh, he's been asking more silly questions."

Erik grabbed her arm. "What did you tell him?"

"You're hurting me, Erik."

"What did you tell him about Shaw?"

She smiled and stroked his cheek. She pulled the hood down and ruffled his blond locks. "Nothing. I was telling him about Mrs. Loncke."

"Loncke. That crazy, old bitch? What about her?"

Gita went for a frightened demeanor again which wasn't hard since Erik was scary as Hell. "She threatened to have me eliminated, Erik. I was so frightened."

"Why would she threaten you?"

"She thought I was interfering with her precious company." Gita laughed.

"How would you do that with Shaw gone?" Erik processed and then blanched white. "Bitch. You and Kennard. I knew it. I was so stupid."

Gita managed to look affronted and wronged and hurt. "Kennard is nothing to me. I loathe the man."

Erik smiled. "Just like you loathed Shaw?"

"Don't be silly, Erik. I'm leaving with you."

Erik shook his head. "You told Bergeron that I killed Shaw. You made some kind of deal?"

She shook her head. "No! Why would I?" She looked frightened now and cornered, but then she smiled. "That Loncke creature hired a hit-man to get rid of Craig."

"What?"

This was all fascinating, but he didn't see it ending well. He took a step back.

"A hit-man, Erik."

"Who? The guy with the gun?"

"Yes, Darling, he was a hit-man."

"Mrs. Loncke hired him? I thought he was probably muscle hired by Shaw to take care of anybody who tried to interfere with his fun with Diane...like the big, bad FBI agent." He shook his head. "So he followed Shaw to the farm to kill him? Then who was the other guy? The young guy?"

Gita said, "He was a simple horse thief. The farm manager was stealing that horse with the silly name."

Erik said, "So I went to the farm and killed three men for nothing? The old woman's hit-man would have killed Shaw?"

"Yes, Darling. But who knew? Of course, I knew she was mental, but I never dreamed."

"How do you know, Gita? Or are you just making all this up?"

"Absolutely not, Darling Erik. She told me. She really is losing it."

He took another step back, but Erik pulled out a gun; the silencer made it look even more lethal. "You stay where you are." He looked at Gita. "You told Bergeron. You're trying to make some kind of deal. Like you always do. Aren't you?"

Gita dredged up a smile. "I would never betray you, Erik."

His smile was just as clown mask fake as hers. "Of course, you would. She told you that she had nothing to do with killing Shaw, didn't she?"

He didn't say anything. Erik was on the edge, and his trigger finger could squeeze off a round willy-nilly.

"She lied to you, Bergeron. She told me to get rid of Shaw. Putting him in with the horse was her idea. But I was happy to do it. I hated that bastard."

"That's a lie! I never did. I still loved Craig...even after he was so horrible to me."

Erik was shaking his head. "And what the Hell do I do now?"

He kept his mouth shut, but Gita said, "You should run, Erik. I have some cash; it's not much, but you can take it and be far away from here...."

Erik looked at the cash. "Is that all? How far do you think we can get on that."

She smiled. "I know, which is why I should stay here...to raise more cash. I'll send it to you, but you should go now, Erik."

"Shut up!" He pointed the pistol at her. "Pow! Pow!"

And then Erik aimed at him. "Pow! Pow!" He laughed.

Saturday
1:00 pm

But he hadn't shot them.

He had forced them over to a Land Rover parked next to Gita's car instead. It was a faded, military-green box with enormous, black knobby tires. It looked like something from a British army recruiting ad.

It had two side doors with a third in the back that had a spare tire slung on it. It also had slushy ice on the windshield and some on the top.

Erik said, "You're coming along, Bergeron."

The other option was probably being shot. "Okay. But why?"

Erik pointed the gun at his face. "Because you're going to come up with some cash."

He tried not to smile. "I have maybe a thousand in my account, Erik."

"But you're an accountant. You have clients, right? And access to their accounts? And you told Shaw about some Barnes Foundation? I need two hundred thousand, and you're going to get it for me."

"I can't do that!"

"Let's hope you can...for your sake. He looked over at Gita. "And you get to drive."

"No, I don't like driving in the city, Erik."

Erik smiled to himself, and then brought the end of the silencer close enough to her eye to ruffle her eyelashes. "You're driving."

She got in and buckled up.

Erik looked at him. "Try to run, and I'll shoot you, Bergeron."

"Where are we going?"

Erik poked the gun into his belly. "Some place nice and quiet where I can think. Now I'm getting in, and you're going to stand there and not move."

He wanted to run, but it was a deserted section of the garage, and there were no cars to hide behind. He stayed put as Erik climbed into the passenger side and slipped between the bucket seats.

The back seats were folded away, and Erik didn't bother setting them up; he knelt on the floor just behind the center console.

The back was filled with what looked like camping supplies; he saw a tent and blankets and a box filled with gray bags with "MRE" written on them.

Did he really think Gita would ever agree to go camping? And eat military field rations?

"Now get in, Bergeron."

He sat in the passenger seat.

Erik rested the silencer against his neck. "Now just do what I say, and nobody will get hurt. I promise."

Gita started the engine. She looked over at him; they didn't believe Erik for a second.

She pulled out of the parking garage. It was gray with a soupy overcast. Something was falling out of the sky. It wasn't rain or snow but a melange of sleet and freezing rain.

"What happened, Erik?"

"At the farm?" Erik leaned forward; they were inches apart. "It was a perfect plan, Bergeron."

"But it went wrong."

"No shit. But it wasn't my fault! I told Shaw that Diane wanted to meet him at the barn. He actually believed she'd come around, and he came like a lamb to the slaughter. Maybe I whacked him a little too hard, but he had this smirk on his face. And before I could drag him inside, this guy comes out of nowhere. He sees me dragging Shaw, and I saw the gun. I had to go for him."

Erik was smiling. "I'd never stabbed anybody before, but I knew just where to shove it in. The second time to the hilt. He got off a shot, but he missed, and I stabbed him again, and I could feel the life leave his body."

"And then?"

"I dragged Shaw into the stall. The stupid horse freaked, but he stomped Shaw good before he bolted. So I thought it was going to be okay, you know? I'd take the other guy's body and dump it somewhere, and nobody would know he'd been there."

"And Shaw's death would still look like an accident."

"Right! So I'm trying to pick up the body when this other guy walks up to me. He must have thought I was somebody else, because his eyes bugged out when he finally figured out I wasn't who he expected...and he saw the body."

"That was Seth Yates. He was expecting Dolph Prentice, the farm manager's son. And then he ran?'

"He started backing away. But I had the other guy's pistol, and I shot him. So I still think maybe I can stick with the plan except I have two bodies to dump, but then I hear voices and see lights coming to the barn. So I dropped the gun beside the first guy, and took the knife and put it into this Seth's hand. And smeared him with blood. And I ran for it."

"It should have worked." Erik stroked Gita's cheek. "The plan...Gita's plan."

They motored along streets that were amazingly empty for DC. Erik directed Gita south toward the Potomac and Virginia.

At every traffic light, he had to suppress the urge to open the door and run. He knew he wouldn't get far.

Unless Erik was a terrible shot.

But Erik could feel him tense up. "Try it, and I'll shoot you down, Bergeron. I've been going to the range twice a week for years, and you wouldn't get ten feet."

So he settled and kept his eyes open.

The sleet/freezing rain was coming down, and at every stoplight now, the Land Rover skidded when Gita braked.

She wasn't a good driver, and the icy streets were starting to panic her.

At the next stoplight, the Land Rover skidded almost into the intersection as the back end slewed around.

Erik said, "Don't slam on the brakes, Gita!"

She looked at him with tears in her eyes. "I can't do this, Erik. Let Gabriel drive? Please, Erik."

"No! You're doing this, or I'll shoot you both right here!"

He said, "Easy, Erik. Gita, look at me. Take your foot off the accelerator and down shift as you come up to the light. Don't hit the brake at all. And slow down."

"But they are honking at me, Gabriel!"

"Let them honk. If they want to drive faster in this mess, let them change lanes."

But then it occurred to him that an accident might be a good thing, and there was a car right on Gita's bumper. He wanted to tell her to jam on the brakes and force a collision, but Erik was breathing into his ear and poking the cold metal of the silencer into his neck.

She did better at the next light and then they were on the freeway. Which had a lot more traffic.

Shit. They were passing the Kennedy Center and would be out of the city soon.

They had driven through half of DC without seeing a single police officer, but a DC Metro police car was parked diagonally ahead, lights flashing.

An officer was directing traffic around a fender-bender as the sleet continued to fall, coating everything with a glistening layer of pure, transparent ice.

Erik was kneeling on the floor. He settled back and pulled the gun away from his neck,

"I have the gun right behind you, Bergeron. Make a move or a sound or do any freaking thing, and I'll fire through the seat, and you'll be dead, and that cop won't even know it's happening. Got it!"

"Yes."

But Gita was panicking as she tried to merge with the line

of cars going around the officer. She was crying and the defroster was barely keeping up with the sleet.

"I can't see, Erik!"

"You're doing fine! Just don't run into that car!"

But yelling into her ear was not what Gita needed as they rolled slowly onto the Theodore Roosevelt Bridge across the Potomac.

She turned too sharply, and the Land Rover started to skid.

Erik lunged for the wheel. "Stupid bitch! Where did you learn to drive!"

He punched Erik in the face.

Which he'd been wanting to do since they'd first met on Laura's porch.

And he grabbed the gun, but Erik was stronger than he looked, and they wrestled for it as Gita screamed.

Erik twisted his body and took sole possession of the gun, but he fell back onto the floor.

He managed to fire the pistol twice; one slug hit the dashboard and the other went through the windshield.

Gita, forgetting everything about driving on ice, slammed on the brakes. The Land Rover skidded into the rear of the car ahead of them.

Erik was flung forward, and he managed to punch him again as the pistol tracked toward him.

He opened the door and rolled out with Erik yelling and Gita shrieking.

He crawled on his hands and knees past the car which was on the Land Rover's bumper now.

The passenger side occupant, a frowzy woman with midnight black hair, gave him a deer-in-the-headlights look as he scooted past her window.

He kept going, not looking around, until he could get behind the car. Erik half fell out of the Land Rover and started firing at him.

The frowzy lady screamed as a bullet punched through her windshield; her bearded companion bailed out. He slipped on the ice and went down, but he got up and ran back off the bridge heading for the police, arms waving.

Erik aimed at the guy and missed. "Shit! Bergeron!"

Erik was aiming at him again, but he was running and ducking between the cars. And slipping and sliding.

And then Gita jumped out and ran. She had lost her sandals and was running barefoot; her saffron-yellow pants outrageously bright against the gray slush.

She looked back at Erik and screamed.

He yelled, "Gita!" She didn't stop, and he fired at her.

She went down.

Two police officers were running toward the melee. Erik fired at them, and they fired back.

Their guns weren't silenced and the crack of their weapons spooked Erik. He flopped onto the roadway and fired once more, and then he scrambled for the Land Rover.

He climbed in and roared off, but the roadway was slick, and he caromed from one side of the bridge to the other.

But Eric was getting away.

The police stopped running, and he slipped out from behind a pickup truck to join them.

Erik was coming up on a truck hauling an empty, flat-bed trailer. The red lights of the surrounding vehicles flashed on, but the trailer lights didn't.

Erik was still accelerating when he ran up onto the trailer and was launched over the guard rail in a perfect arc.

He and the two police officers ran to the trailer and looked over the side of the bridge.

The Land Rover was still floating.

The older officer turned and ran back toward his patrol car. "I'll call it in, Carl!"

He and the young officer, Carl, watched as the Land Rover sank out of sight."

Carl said, "I can't swim."

He shook his head. He could swim, after a fashion, but he wasn't jumping into the slate gray, frigid water for Erik. And he would probably pop up at any moment.

But they watched as the sleet continued to fall; he was

shivering, and his teeth were actually chattering.

He didn't want to think how cold the water must be.

Carl said, "He isn't coming up."

Carl was right.

Saturday
11:00 pm

A paramedic had looked him over and pronounced him unharmed. Which he was except for scrapes and bruises and being chilled to the bone.

He had watched as they loaded the frowzy lady and Gita into ambulances.

Frowzy was bleeding from the head, but she could still walk. And yell. She was not happy with her bearded companion who had abandoned her like a head of month old lettuce.

Gita's wound was in the center of her body. Nobody would tell him anything about her condition.

The DC Metro police had questioned him for hours, and he had told them everything.

Which might have been why they had looked at him funny? He wasn't sure that his narrative had possessed a cogent structure.

But it was now almost 11:00 pm, and he wanted to go home. He had managed to reach Cory and had told him that he was fine. Cory had said a lot of things, but most of it had sailed past him. He was very, very tired.

And he was still cold for some reason?

The door opened, and Sander's sunny face appeared. He closed his eyes and shook his head, but he detected the aroma of coffee.

He opened his eyes as Sanders sat down on the other side of the table and set a cup of steaming hot coffee in front of him.

"I could come to love you, John D. Sanders."

Sander's smile included the dimples and the hazel eyes. "You've had a rough night, Gabe."

"I have. Wait. How is Gita? And did they find Erik. Alive or dead? And the frowzy woman, though I don't know her. Still."

Sanders smiled some more. "The DC Metro police think you're insane."

"Why?"

"You don't know?"

He may have smiled at John, "You told them I'm not. Right?"

Sanders said, "Anyway, Gita is alive; she had surgery. We haven't found Erik Varner or his body. Divers in the morning. And the frowzy lady must be Mrs. Mahoney? She was treated and released."

"Good. Except for Erik. I guess I should have jumped in."

Sanders shook his head. "No."

"No?"

"Definitely not."

He still felt bad about not trying to help Erik, but he had no idea how deep the Potomac was at that spot; how deep he would have had to swim down. Into the cold blackness.

He shivered and drank very hot coffee. He was focusing a bit. Sanders was dressed up.

"So you look nice? And smell really good?"

Sanders smiled. "Date night, and Christina bought me some new cologne in Middleburg. But Gabe, tell me what happened. Start at the beginning and go right through to the end. Keep the detours to the barest minimum."

"Roger that."

And he did his best.

Sanders was looking at him with acute hazel eyes. "And that's it, Gabe?"

"Yes. That's it."

Which it wasn't. He had omitted everything about Grand hiring a hit-man, but he told himself that he had only Gita's word that Grand had done that.

And that she had proof.

"What did Gita say about Erik?"

Sanders said, "She confirmed your story. She was terrified of him after he killed three people. But she also told me about Mrs. Loncke."

"Did she? Gita's not a fan, but then I'm not either. Have you met her?"

He nodded. "And her butler."

"Smith? And what do you think of him?" He shouldn't ask, but he really wanted to know.

"He's a little hard to pin down."

"I'll bet."

Sanders smiled. "He's a citizen and appears to have been born in Hong Kong. When and how he came here is undefined, but he's been here since 1970 at least."

"Here, the U.S.?"

"Here, Virginia. In Loudoun County."

"Right." Which meant what?

Sanders leaned forward. "Gabe, you should tell me everything you know about Mrs. Loncke hiring the hit-man to murder Craig Shaw. If you don't, I can charge you with obstruction, and I don't want to do that."

He tried to remain perfectly still and not react.

"Gabe?"

"I'm sorry, but I don't have any evidence that even suggests that, Sanders. Truly."

"But you believe it?"

He shrugged. "Why do you believe it?"

Sanders smiled his jolliest smile. "I knew it the second I started talking to her. That woman is insane. And the butler!"

"I know!"

"And Gita confirmed it." Sanders was staring at him.

"But does she just suspect it like you, or does she have proof?"

Sanders said, "Did she tell you she had proof, Gabe?"

He shook his head; it was easier to lie with his body than with his words.

"But I will say that Mrs. Loncke does have a slight

obsession with her father's company."

Sanders laughed. "Slight? She'd wipe out half the planet to save that company."

He nodded. "A good third anyway."

Sanders said, "You know more than you're telling me, Gabe." Sanders left his chair and stood behind him, and even rubbed his shoulders. "You'll feel better if you tell me."

He felt his will to resist melting way; he wanted to tell Sanders everything. The good thing was that everything he knew was hearsay and supposition.

"I don't know anything."

There was nothing he could do if Gita really did have proof. Well, he could warn Cory and the family, and they could circle the wagons and fill those wagons with high-priced lawyers.

Sanders was leaning against him. "Sure about that, Gabe?"

"Yes, I am. I don't know what Gita knows or thinks she knows. You'll have to talk to her."

Sanders said, "I can't do that."

"Why not?"

Sanders leaned over and stared at him. "Because she died an hour ago. Blood clot after her surgery. Nothing they could do."

"I'm sorry to hear that. Not that she was a nice lady."

Sanders just stared at him. If there was any proof, he would find it.

"You're free to go, Bergeron."

"Really? That's good." He stood up and moved toward the door. He didn't think Sanders or any of the Metro police were going to offer him a ride to Cory's condo.

He didn't even know where he was? How late did the Metro system run?

He turned back to Sanders. "I know you want to wrap up this case, but you know that Erik killed Shaw. For Gita. Possibly on her instructions? Or not. And he killed Turtle and Third Guy. Would it be so bad if you can't prove why Third Guy was there?"

It would be bad because a crime had been solicited by a woman who thought wealth gave her the power of life and death. And she and Smith were going to get off without so much as a scolding. He wasn't happy about it either. He would have to talk to Cory.

Sanders was glaring and suddenly moved toward him. He may have doubled over to protect his stomach.

Sanders blinked. "Did you think I was going to punch you, Gabe?"

"No. Well, a little bit. I mean after Detective Oscuro, I'm gun shy...or fist shy, I guess...."

"Oscuro?" Sanders smiled, but the smile fluttered out like a candle in a draft. "No! Don't tell me. I've heard enough stories for one night."

Sanders was heading for the door.

"One thing, Detective."

"What?"

"Are you going to talk to Mrs. Yates? And tell her what happened to poor Turtle? But don't call him that. His name was Seth. And she loved him."

Sanders nodded. "Of course, Gabe. I'll take care of it."

And the detective walked past him and out the door.

He had to find his way to Cory's condo. No. To Gita's condo. To retrieve the Yaris.

And then, maybe tomorrow, he could call Diane and tell her that Finn was innocent and possibly fine husband material.

As far as he knew.

Wednesday 6:00 pm

His week at Garst, Bauer & Hartmann had been low stress so far.

But Cory was home and was coming to have a chat with him. Not that he didn't want to see Cory, because he did.

He had told Cory everything except the parts about Grand and her possible involvement in Shaw's death. Not that her hit-man had killed him, but the intent had been there. But she and Smith hadn't been arrested so far so Gita must not have had proof after all.

Or Sanders hadn't found it yet.

But he thought that Cory might not be happy with him about Erik and Gita and dodging bullets on the Theodore Roosevelt Bridge.

It was black outside the windows of his apartment on Arch Street. He closed the curtains.

He had stocked his refrigerator with all the stuff Cory liked; he had steaks ready to broil.

What was he going to tell him about Grand?

He jumped when the rap came on his steel door. He flung it open and smiled his very best smile at Cory.

Cory was blank.

"I'm sorry, but I tried really hard to reach you...."

Cory hugged him.

Which was good.

Cory kicked the door shut, and whispered in his ear, "Give

me one reason why I shouldn't hang you out those windows by your heels?"

"It's too cold, and I'm terrified of heights, and I did my very best to live up to my promise. I even called Brunetti."

Cory squeezed all the air out of his lungs. "Gabe."

He was going to pass out, but Cory stopped squeezing him. He took a breath. "I know, but after I couldn't get you or Matt or Danielle, I gave it a shot and called her. Not that I got anywhere near her, telephone-wise."

Cory stepped back. "So you did nothing wrong?"

There was only one correct answer. "I should have waited until I could reach you. I was totally wrong, and I'm very, very sorry."

"You should be!"

Cory sat on the sofa, and he joined him. "I really am sorry, but if I hadn't, Erik would have taken Gita camping."

Cory shook his head, but he smiled a little bit.

"No, I mean he would have taken her to some forest and buried her in a shallow grave, and we would never have found out what happened to Shaw and Turtle and Third Guy."

He could just forget about Grand, and he was going to do that. For Cory.

But Cory said, "But we don't have the complete picture, do we? There's still Third Guy."

He nodded.

Cory said, "So tell me what you suspect. About Grand."

So he did.

"And Gita said she had proof?"

"She did. That was her trump card, which she may or may not have actually had. Something to bargain with to make sure she wasn't charged as a conspirator when Erik went down for the murders."

He wasn't going to say anything else.

Cory was looking at him. "So do you think Grand did it? Or got Smith to arrange it?"

Gita had believed that.

He believed it. And so did Sanders. He looked at Cory.

Cory did too.

He hugged Cory. "It's over, and we'll never know."

"Thanks, Gabe."

"Sure. For what?"

Cory laughed.

"So how was your trip."

Cory was smiling like a cat with one paw on a saucer of cream and the other on a plump mouse.

"What? You didn't catch Jerry Nolastname?"

Cory kept smiling.

"You did! Tell me all about it, Special Agent."

"Gerald Allen Haas got cocky."

It was excellent that Cory had located his man, but what had he done to him after finding him? "And he finds himself behind bars as we speak?"

"He does. He and his partner and an art dealer from Santa Fe."

"That's great, Cory."

Cory said, "I didn't shoot him, Gabe, even when he gave me a perfect opportunity."

He hugged Cory. "That's also great. Wait. Did Matt shoot him?"

"Nobody shot anybody. Shots were exchanged, but we took him down without putting any holes in the smiling bastard."

Cory was also smiling.

"But you kicked his ass? At least?"

"Any ass-kicking was inflicted solely to subdue the perp."

"That's the best kind of ass-kicking."

"Matt agrees with you."

And they had a very nice evening at home, and it wasn't until he was leaving the next morning that Cory told him the whole family was invited to dine at Grand's house on Saturday.

And the whole family absolutely included Gabriel Bergeron. This time.

Saturday 6:00 pm

He was in the silver SUV with Cory. He was trying to suppress the urge to fling himself out the door every time Cory slowed down even a little.

"It's going to be fine, Gabe."

Right. Cory could say that. Josephine loved him; well, she considered him the one true scion of her father. And she did love Stephen Holcomb.

"She won't poison you."

Cory laughed. He had a very annoying laugh. Why had he never noticed it before?

"Relax, Bergeron."

"Nope. You trained me to be on my guard at all times."

Cory looked at him. "Do not toss my grandmother across the room."

"I won't. Unless she starts something first."

Cory glared at him.

Grand's lair was actually less than twenty miles north of the Poirier farm. Cory parked in front of the stately edifice.

"Do you hear that?"

"Hear what, Bergeron?"

"The sound of the flapping wings of a legion of flying monkeys?"

"No."

Cory got out as two more vehicles pulled up; Diane and Finn got out of his truck. Finn had brought his hunting rifles which might prove useful.

Cory was staring at him as Judd and Samantha got out of the Impala.

Where were Hugh and Laura? He wasn't going in without Laura. Not that he would ever use her as a human shield. Ever.

He stared at the giant urns and the white columns. He had promised himself that he would never go inside this house again.

Not that he was scared of Grand.

He was scared of Smith and what he might do for Grand, if she had a sudden whim that Bergeron had to go.

Cory was looking at him funny, but people often did that. "What?"

"You tell me, Bergeron. You froze up."

"Did not!"

Judd said, "Like a statue."

"Balderdash and poppycock."

Hugh and Laura pulled into the parking area. They were smiling. He had to admire their effortless sang-froid.

Hugh led the way and rapped upon the black door.

The tiny, Chinese maid didn't exactly bow to Hugh and Laura, but there was a definite head bob as she flung wide the door.

Where was Smith? He scanned the foyer to no avail, but Josephine Holcomb Loncke was marching toward them clad in silver and girded with diamonds.

Well, she had a nice brooch and a necklace lousy with what were obviously blood diamonds.

It was on the tip of his tongue to ask her where she got the brooch; Aunt Flo would like it. Not that he could afford one with diamonds. But maybe he could find one with cubic zirconia? Or Moissanite?

Cory gave him an elbow in the side. "What?"

"Gabe."

"I wasn't doing anything."

But everyone was looking at him; Josephine included. He smiled his third best smile; it was all he could muster.

They sat in a room that would not be out of place in your

ritzier funeral home. Well, the funeral home would have smelled like flowers instead of whatever was wafting around him.

But the place had a hundred rooms, and he didn't think the parlor was used that much. So he wasn't going to think badly of the tiny maid if she was solely responsible for cleaning this pile.

They chatted. About horses mostly. Josephine inquired about the health of Bucephalus after his upsetting experience stomping the life out of Shaw.

Grand congratulated Judd and Samantha, but she peered at Samantha like she'd never seen her before and wasn't too impressed.

Finn was introduced. Grand actually smiled at him and patted a beefy shoulder.

No mention was made of Holcomb, Inc.

So they were present to celebrate Diane's engagement to Finn and Judd and Samantha's baby with Grand? He wasn't sure why he had been included?

And then Smith entered.

A hush fell over the Poiriers and the hangers-on.

Smith actually said, "Dinner is served, Madam."

He almost choked stifling his laughter. Smith was still smiling, but he wasn't happy as his gaze raked over one Gabriel Bergeron.

They went in. And supped.

It was okay. He steered clear of the dishes he couldn't identify. He filled up on mashed potatoes. And there was a pie-like dessert. But he didn't touch anything that Grand didn't eat.

Just in case.

But everything was going swimmingly so far.

Smith herded them toward the parlor for brandy. He didn't want brandy so he lagged behind, and Grand came up behind him.

"Bergeron."

He closed his eyes; he had let down his guard and had been separated from the herd like the dumbest, weakest wildebeest, and the lioness was upon him.

Cory would be so disappointed in him. If he ever found out.

"Come with me."

He didn't wanna. He really didn't. But she opened a door and entered what was obviously the library.

She took a seat and waved at another one.

He was alone with Grand, but he didn't see any obvious weapons. He smiled his best smile. "I should be going. Cory has to get up early tomorrow morning and fly to St. Louis."

Which was a total lie.

"Sit down!"

He crossed the parquet floor and let his derriere hover over a wing backed chair.

A tall, turquoise ceramic pot on a matching ceramic stand was too near to him; it was the kind of thing he had been known to knock over. He should probably move it farther away.

Grand said, "That's a Minton."

"Right?"

"It's an antique and irreplaceable. My grandmother bought it at the factory in Stoke-upon-Trent."

He suppressed a giggle. "Stoke-upon-Trent?"

She fired up the glare to the ablative heat shield melting point. "In Staffordshire. England."

"Sure. I know it well. I had tea there." What else did one do in Staffordshire?

He studied it like he knew what he was looking at; a word from long ago popped into his head. "Majolica?"

Grand raised a dubious eyebrow. "Yes, a jardiniere."

"Sure. I knew that." Which was almost true.

Grand glared at him.

"Aunt Flo has nice things too. I'm not a barbarian."

He was however clumsy, but he sat very carefully trying not to obsess about the Minton jardiniere.

Grand was glaring at him. "Did you really do it?"

He shook his head. "Of course not!"

She smiled a mad smile. "Idiot. Did you solve Shaw's murder?"

"Oh, that. I helped."

"Idiot."

"Right. Thank you for dinner, but I must be going now."

"I'm grateful to you."

He took a moment to allow the foundations of his existence to cease rocking back and forth. "You are?"

"Of course. You exonerated Hugh. He's worthless, but he's a thousand times better than that Shaw person. And Diane too." She stared at him. "I didn't know how Shaw was behaving toward her. If I had, I would have shot him myself."

Which was totally believable.

She smiled again. "And you got rid of Gita."

"No, I didn't."

"You did. I don't know how you arranged it all, but you did, and I'm grateful for that too. She was trying to interfere with Holcomb again...with that popinjay, Kennard."

She smiled. She was going to offer him cyanide candy any second now.

"I suppose I could learn to accept you."

Like he was falling for that one. "You could?"

She nodded. "Corentin is very stubborn, and you have proved yourself useful. And Jordan's girlfriend is pregnant. He'll have to marry the trollop before the baby is born."

"Right." He backed toward the door.

She was staring out the window at the gathering dark. "Jordan isn't nearly as stubborn as his brother. He'll come round eventually. Corentin was always a willful child."

He just smiled at her. If Cory was willful, then he was just a chip off the old matrilineal block.

"But he looks so much like my father, Stephen. The same red hair, the jawline. I was sure he was born to take over the company."

"But he wouldn't."

"No. And Jordan wanted nothing to do with me, but I can bring him around. I know I can. And Kennard will do for now."

She closed her eyes and rubbed her forehead. "But I have to get rid of Shaw."

"But Mrs. Loncke, Craig Shaw is dead?"

"What? Of course, he is. I knew that."

Smith said, "Mrs. Loncke?

He kept very still and tried not to think about how close Smith had gotten to him without a sound.

"Yes?"

"Mrs. Poirier is asking for you."

"Laura?"

"Yes, Ma'am."

Josephine hitched up her silver gown and exited the library. He was about to follow when Smith shut the library door.

"She's failing a bit, Bergeron."

He nodded.

"I knew it, of course, but I owe her family everything."

He stood very still. "Do you?"

Smith smiled but every smile was as cold and lonely as the hydrogen atoms adrift in intergalactic space.

"Mr. Stephen got me and my mother out of China in 1949."

"Right. Wait. Was that the year that Mao took over?"

More smiling. "The Communist Party took over...led by Mao Zedong. I was only a baby, but my mother told me about it. Mr. Stephen had been doing business with my family for many years, and he agreed to help when my father asked."

"That was good of him."

Smith smiled.

"Your father didn't come with you?"

"No, he had a duty to his father and the rest of the family."

"So what happened to your father? And your family?"

Smith said, "They knew that the Kuomintang forces were going to lose the war after the Battle of Liaoshi in 1948, but they believed they could work with the communists...even join the Party if necessary."

"But that didn't work out?"

"It did. For many years, but then Mao launched the Cultural Revolution."

He had read about it a long time ago, but he was fuzzy. "The Red Guards? And that was bad for your family?"

Smith actually laughed. "Very. They were attacked. Verbally at first."

"I'm sorry."

Smith smiled. "Mr. Stephen tried to help. Again. He thought he could get them out of China."

"But he couldn't?"

Smith shook his head. "He went to Hong Kong in 1967, and he never returned."

"He just disappeared?"

"No. He was killed. The Hong Kong police told Miss Josephine that it was a street crime, but I never believed that. I should have gone with him." Smith closed his eyes. "I was seventeen...old enough to have gone with him."

So Smith felt a duty to Grand. "I understand, but maybe hiring someone to...resolve the Shaw problem was a bad idea?"

Smith nodded, looking old and sad now. "Yes, it was. I didn't fully realize...about Miss Josephine...but it won't be repeated. You have my word." There was a glimmer of a smile. "No one will be able to prove that Miss Josephine or I did anything, Bergeron."

He nodded. "Right. I believe you. What was the guy's name?"

Smith looked surprised for the first time. "What does that matter?" And then he smiled. "So very curious. He told me to call him "Bone." Not Mr. Bone, but just Bone."

"As in 'bad to the bone'?"

Smith shrugged.

"Thank you. So what is your real name?"

Smith's smile was a few lumens brighter. "I changed it. After Mr. Stephen died. After my family ceased to exist. I didn't know that they had been slaughtered, but I couldn't find any trace of them, and I had to assume it. And my former name was...inappropriate."

And Smith left the library. He followed, but Smith had disappeared, and he walked into the waiting arms of Laura.

Well, not exactly her arms. What did she know about her mother?

"How was Mother, Gabriel?"

"Just fine."

Laura smiled her Bodhisattva smile. "That's very kind of you, Gabriel."

"No, really! She even said she could learn to accept me...and that I was 'useful' so everything is hunky-dory on the Loncke-Bergeron front."

Laura smiled. "I'm so glad to hear that. Mother can be difficult, but she means well."

And she appeared completely sincere. So she had no idea?

Cory joined them. He smiled at Cory who smiled back.

Laura said, "I just spoke to Smith. He's retiring. I never thought he would. It won't be the same without him."

Cory said, "No, it won't, Mother."

"We'll have to find someone else to look after her. Someone who'll take a firm hand."

"How will Mrs. Loncke feel about that?"

Laura said, "I'm sure she'll see reason." More serene smiling. "Mother has been very upset lately, but now that Mr. Kennard is CEO, things should calm down."

He looked at Cory and raised an eyebrow.

Laura said, "You were in there for some time, Gabriel. Did she say anything else?"

"Oh, this and that. We talked about Minton majolica ware and Stoke-upon-Trent."

Laura smiled. "Gabriel."

"No, we did. Her grandmother went to Staffordshire."

Laura went off smiling.

He looked at Cory. "'The time has come to talk of many things: of shoes and ships and sealing wax....' and something else 'and kings'?"

Cory said, "Am I going to enjoy this talk?"

"Maybe yes, maybe no. But we need to warn Judd and Samantha to drop the portcullis, pull up the drawbridge, and stock the moat with piranha. Just in case."

Saturday 10:00 pm

He had told Cory everything on the drive back to the farm, and now they were sitting in the SUV outside the house.

Cory said, "So my grandmother's butler hired a hit-man named Bone to gun down the CEO of Holcomb, Inc.?"

"Just so, Corentin."

Cory shook his head. It was too dark to see his face. "I don't know how I feel about that, Gabe."

They sat there.

Cory said, "They entered into a criminal conspiracy."

"They did."

"Part of me, a big part, wants to throw both their asses in prison. But she's my grandmother."

"Smith said there is no proof, and I tend to think Smith knows what he's talking about."

Mostly because he'd surely done other stuff for Miss Josephine over the half century he'd worked for her.

Cory said, "What are you thinking?"

"Me? Nothing. Well, it's chilly in the car, and we could go inside?"

Cory jogged up the stairs and into the house. He stopped in the foyer and grabbed his arm.

Cory whispered, "You think Mother knows anything?"

"No. I'm sure she doesn't."

Cory nodded and headed for the family room. Hugh and Laura were sitting there; the TV was on but muted.

Cory said, "Gabe had a little talk with Smith."

Laura said, "With Smith?"

Hugh was looking very severe. "How did you manage that, Gabriel?"

"I think he wanted to explain to someone...." Hugh was glaring at him now. "About his family, and the debt he owed to Mr. Stephen."

Hugh relaxed.

Laura said, "What did he tell you, Gabriel?"

"About getting out of China."

Laura said, "I don't really know anything about that."

So he told her and Hugh everything Smith had said, except for the contract killer part.

Laura said, "That's all so sad. I knew he wasn't a happy person, but I never knew why. I knew his mother died, and Grandfather went away, and Smith came to live with us. I was eight, I think, and it's all jumbled in my memory."

"Smith said that Stephen went to China to rescue his family."

Laura shook her head. "I never knew that. I'm not sure that Mother did either? She has always said he was on a business trip to Hong Kong and was robbed and killed in the street."

"That's not what Smith thinks."

Laura nodded.

"So where was Stephen's wife?"

Laura said, "Grandmother Ciara died before I was born, Gabriel. And then Mother took over the running of Grandfather's household. She was very young."

"And she told me that when she got married, my father, Harold, moved into Grandfather's house too. But there was plenty of room."

So Laura had grown up in a household with Stephen and Josephine and Harold...and Smith. What had that been like?

And what had Harold been like? He had been either surpassing brave or monumentally dense to marry Josephine Loncke. Or both.

"When did your father pass away?" Laura smiled at him.

Hugh and Cory were smiling at him too.

"Sorry?" He wasn't sorry at all. "One last question, what is Smith's real name?"

Laura said, "I don't remember. It's been years, Gabriel."

They sat there all warm and snug for a bit, before she said, "I'm going upstairs. Hugh, are you coming?"

Hugh kissed her on the cheek. "In a few minutes."

She was almost out the door, when she said, "I don't remember the Chinese, but his name meant 'fortunate" or "lucky" or something like that."

And she continued on. When she was out of ear shot, Hugh said, "Did Smith admit it?"

He smiled. "I'm not sure I know what you mean, Hugh?"

"You know very well, Gabriel. Did he admit that he hired someone to kill Craig Shaw? On Josephine's orders?"

He looked at Cory who nodded. "He did. But he said it was a mistake, and he'd never do it again."

Hugh shook his head in amazement. "Oh, well, that's all right then, isn't it?"

Cory said, "How did you know, Dad?"

Hugh said, "I suspected her the second I knew that it was Shaw lying in that stall."

Cory said, "Does Mother know?"

"She has no idea. About any of it."

Cory said, "Is there more?"

But Hugh shook his head. "Not that I know of."

He and Cory exchanged a look.

Hugh said, "What are you going to do, Cory?"

Cory shook his head. "I don't know. Nothing?"

Hugh smiled at his son. "Nothing is good, Cory."

Cory looked at him. "Gabe?"

"I think Hugh is right."

Cory said, "But is Sanders going to give up?"

He shook his head. "I think he'll keep trying to find out who hired Bone."

Cory said, "But he'll get other cases and won't have much time to work on a cold case."

Which was probably true. But if Sanders did find proof, he wasn't sure he'd be sorry for Grand and Smith. And he wasn't sure that Cory would be either.

Hugh said, "In any case, her mind is going, Cory, and Laura and I will keep an eye on her from now on."

Which was an excellent idea. Just in case her mind wasn't as damaged as she'd have them believe.

Thursday
5:00 pm

He had put in a semi-grueling week at Garst, Bauer & Hartmann and was in a taxi pulling up at the 30th Street Amtrak Station to catch the Acela to DC.

The station was a massive classical structure; six gigantic Corinthian columns held up the porte cochere under which the taxi deposited him.

He was early so once inside he claimed a seat in the football-field-sized main concourse and stared up at the beautiful coffered ceiling and the massive pendant lights hanging from it.

The World War II memorial angel looked as dark and forbidding as ever; it was supposed to be the Angel Michael?

He was hungry, but he was too tired to get to his feet and walk the few steps into the food court.

He had his eyes closed when he felt a disturbance in the force; well, the vibration of someone sitting down close to him.

He pried open his eyes.

A blonde lady was staring at him. She looked sort of familiar? He tried smiling back, but she just stared. He turned away and made ready to depart post haste.

"I need to speak to you."

"What?" The voice was familiar too?

She shook her head. Her hair was parted in the middle and swept in graceful waves to her ears and to the collar of her turtleneck sweater. She had a square face and dark eyes and ruby lips. Her skirt and sweater strained to contain the voluptuous body she'd stuffed into them.

She could be in her thirties, but he was pretty sure she had already summited Mount Forty.

She sighed. "Sit still, Bergeron."

He got to his feet and took a step back. "Dr. Kutuzov?"

She was still as tall as he was, but she had miraculously shed forty pounds and gained an hourglass figure in a few weeks. And her hair wasn't gray.

"I knew that accent was fake. Who are you really? And what do you want with me?"

She smiled. "My name is Penelope Black. I was Penelope Stanko."

He shook himself as another row of tumblers clicked into place. "Billy's mother?"

Shit. His luck had finally run out, and he was face to face with the dread pirate Penelope.

Who had pretended to be a Russian doctor. What the Hell was going on?

And then Mr. Monroe stepped out of the shadows and stared down at him. Monroe smiled.

Well, it wasn't really a happy smile or a friendly smile. It was more of I've-got-you-now-my-pretty smile.

Monroe's hair was silver-gray. He was still lean, and his face was even more angular than before, but he was still verging on handsome anyway.

Little gray eyes regarded him coolly.

Monroe said, "Why don't we all sit down."

"I don't think so."

Monroe smiled some more. "Why don't I go first then?" And he did. He crossed long, elegant legs, adjusted the fall of his trouser leg, and patted the bench beside him. "It's okay, Gabe. No one is going to harm you. We need you."

Five months earlier, in June, Monroe had accosted him outside the Hoover Building and told him that he needed him for a job. Monroe hadn't identified himself except to say that he had been known to "liaise" with the FBI.

"Whatever it is, I'm not doing it."

Monroe said, "Again, Gabe, you haven't heard what it is."

Penelope said, "He can't do it. Look at him."

If sweet Penelope thought she was going to reverse psychology him, she was sadly mistaken. "No, I can't. Not a snowball's chance in Hell. And so I bid you both a pleasant evening."

He took a step toward the line that was forming for his train.

Monroe got in front of him. Monroe was very quick, lithe, supple. He gave Penelope a nasty look. "Thank you, Ms. Black. I'll take it from here."

Penelope was shaking her head. "I know I suggested him...."

Monroe was going to pull out an enormous pistol and shoot Penelope dead...or stab her with a Polonium filled syringe. He could see it coming. How was he going to explain to Billy how his mother had died? Not that she would be much of a loss.

But Penelope said something in what sounded like actual Russian, and Monroe said something back. He was pondering whether she and/or Monroe could really be Russian, when she kissed Monroe.

Well, it was mutual after Penelope got the ball rolling; very mutual. And then Penelope swayed toward the exit, never to be seen again. Hopefully.

Monroe wiped the lipstick off his mouth. Penelope had gotten Monroe excited, and Monroe was distracted. He should walk away before the blood flow to his brain was restored.

He said, "You have some on your teeth; lipstick I mean."

Monroe smiled and buffed his teeth with his tongue. It was sort of hot. He shook himself.

"Good-bye, Mr. Monroe."

"What do you know about your grandfather, Andrew Henri Bergeron?"

"What?"

"Your mother's father, Bergeron."

He wanted to toss Monroe across the concourse, which Monroe knew. Monroe smiled at him. "Not a good idea, Gabe."

"Says you. I don't know anything. He died when I was very young. I never even met him."

"And Florence Barnes hasn't told you anything about him?"

"Like what? No. Not really. What the Hell, Monroe? He's been dead for thirty years?"

"He has." Monroe was looking at him like Anubis weighing the hearts of the dead; a Nordic Anubis with a faceted face forged from steel and ice.

"I'm telling you the truth; I don't know anything."

Monroe smiled. "I believe you, Gabe. All I want you to do is stay at your great-aunt's bed-and-breakfast for a few days."

"Right. Wait. Aunt Flo doesn't have a bed-and-breakfast. She's talked about it, but she would have told me if she had actually started it."

Monroe got very close and whispered in his ear. "Maybe you should give her a call, Gabe."

"What does she have to do with this...whatever this is?"

Monroe smiled at him.

He grabbed Monroe by his expensive suit. He may have shaken him a little. "No shitty smiling! Is she in danger? You tell me right now."

Monroe wanted to hurt him. He could see it in the pale, gray, reptilian eyes, but there were too many people around. And a couple of uniformed officers with a police dog weren't that far away.

Monroe tried to pry his hands loose, but he had a good grip. He sighed and leaned in again. "No, Gabe. She isn't."

"Then why tell me to call her?"

Monroe whispered again. "Just to verify that I'm telling you the truth about her bed-and-breakfast."

He let go of Monroe's suit. "Okay, I'll call."

Monroe's cologne was making him sick. He took a step back. His phone rang long enough that he thought he was going to get Aunt Flo's answering machine.

"Hello?"

Not Aunt Flo. Possibly Annika or Ute? "Hello, this is Gabe Bergeron. May I speak to Mrs. Barnes?"

"*Ja!*"

He held on.

Aunt Flo said, "Gabriel?"

"Hi. So are you running an clandestine bed-and-breakfast, Mrs. Barnes?"

She giggle-cackled. "I was going to call you, Gabriel, but we've been so busy."

She sounded excited and happy.

"Sure. So you're open for business?"

"We are. Ezmeralda is doing the cooking. She insisted. Annika is handling the laundry and cleaning, and Ute is doing the bookings and advertising and customer relations. I'm just here for local color."

"Right. So you have people staying there now?"

"Our first guests are due tomorrow."

"I see. May I come to see you? Tomorrow morning?" He had to tell her about Monroe, and that would definitely be better in person. Was it possible she knew Monroe? Or Penelope?

"I think we're booked up." She laughed. "Of course, you may come! There will always be a room for you at Triple B."

"What?"

"The Barnes Bed-and-Breakfast."

"Good to know. So I'll see you tomorrow morning."

"I'm glad you're coming, Gabriel."

"Bye, Aunt Flo."

He shut off his phone and turned.

Monroe smiled at him. "Told you. So I'll be in touch when we need you at the B&B, Gabe. No firm date just yet."

"I'm not doing it, Monroe! No way! Not happening!"

Monroe said, "Keep your voice down. Your aunt is in no danger, Gabe...the B&B is just a convenient setting. Or may be."

The officers were looking at him, but he didn't care. "I won't do this. You can't make me, and I wouldn't let you involve Aunt Flo even if I was stupid enough to agree to this bullshit!"

Monroe didn't smile. He just turned and walked away, taking long, effortless strides.

"Monroe! Get back here!"

He tried to follow, but the officers intercepted him.

The shorter one said, "Is there a problem, Sir?"

"A problem! Yes, there's a problem! I have to stop him. Get out of my way!"

The taller officer was Vetter. Officer Vetter growled at him; his dog did too.

The shorter officer was Kepler. He said, "The tall gentleman?"

"He's no gentleman!" He had to calm down. Getting arrested wasn't going to do anybody any good.

Kepler said, "You have some kind of beef with him?"

"Yes!"

"Kepler smiled at him. "And what would that be?"

He shook his head. There was no way Officer Kepler was going to believe his story, and Monroe had disappeared anyway.

"It's nothing, Officer."

Kepler knew better; Vetter knew better. Even the dog wasn't buying it.

So Kepler asked for ID, and he and Vetter took turns asking questions that he couldn't answer. Primarily because he knew nothing about the bastard Monroe. But eventually, they got bored and let him go.

He called Cory and got his voicemail. "Something's come up, and I won't be at the condo tonight."

He ran out of the train station. He wasn't waiting for tomorrow. He was going to get his Jeep and drive to Aunt Flo's house just as fast as he could and warn her.

He just wasn't sure about what?